The Vampire Next Door

Ashlyn Chase

sourcebooks
casablanca

Published by Sourcebooks Casablanca, an imprint of Sourcebooks, Inc.
P.O. Box 4410, Naperville, Illinois 60567-4410
(630) 961-3900
FAX: (630) 961-2168
www.sourcebooks.com

Printed and bound in Canada
WC 10 9 8 7 6 5 4 3 2 1

To my husband, who wanted me to write a dirty dedication just for him. Okay, honey. Here it is!

Dirty, grimy, messy, soiled, spoiled, filthy, foul, gross, gory, muddy, marred, mired, polluted, ruined, smudged, sooty, spattered, tattered, weltered, unclean...

Oh, that's not what you meant? Okay, how about this? Slutty, skanky, trashy, tarnished, tainted, nasty, obscene... Why are you rolling your eyes?

And now the real dedication

This book contains a war between the witches. They're cousins from opposite sides of the Mason-Dixon line. Well, I'd like to dedicate this book to my wonderful cousins. Not only have I never fought with any of them, but they've always been there to support me when I needed family. I love every one of you!

Chapter 1

SLY FLORES OVERHEARD AN ARGUMENT EMANATING from a nearby alley. His inner vigilante vampire paid attention. Creeping closer, but using the long shadows to hide his presence, he watched and listened.

"You take that back!"

"Fuck you, I will not."

Sly crept closer to get a better look at the happy couple. The guy wore a leather coat and expensive sneakers. A hat created shadows that obscured his facial features.

A roar and then a scuffle ensued. Sly wasn't sure who threw the first punch, but it didn't matter. The woman was taking a brutal beating. He didn't care what she'd said or done... *nobody* deserved that.

She fell, and the man kicked her. Just as he was about to kick her a second time, Sly's fangs extended and he flew out from his hiding place. He grabbed the guy by his leather collar and lunged for the thick neck in front of him.

Instead of sinking his fangs into the brute's carotid artery, Sly encountered something rock hard and unyielding. He tried to pull back, but one of his fangs was caught. He tried to retract them, but something cold and hard hit his gums first.

The woman shrieked.

Sly shoved the guy with all his might. Something popped and fell to the ground, making a "ching" noise. The jerk stumbled several feet away before catching himself.

Searing pain hit Sly's gums like a hot poker used as a dental tool. *Shit! Fuck! Ow, dammit!* He'd never experienced this kind of pain—even the time he was caught in the sun. Fortunately, his friend Konrad had thrown his big coat over him just before he thought he might burst into flames.

As Sly held his jaw and hopped around, the couple recovered from their shock and took off. They charged down the alley to the main street.

Ordinarily, when he was hurt, his incredible healing powers took over and whatever was wounded would be on the mend by now. Why wasn't the pain stopping?

Sly stooped to pick up the item that had fallen. A thick neck-chain draped over his hand. It looked gold on the outside, but where the links joined, he saw something white glinting through.

Silver!

The enemy of every vampire he'd ever heard of. Dracula himself probably couldn't escape its blistering damage. Sly fell to the pavement, curled into a fetal position, and rolled back and forth.

Just my luck to get a rapper whose bling was a knockoff.

Morgaine opened her door the moment Sly knocked. She might have been standing there because she'd sensed someone coming to see her. Psychics were fun that way.

"Hi, Morgaine, uh…"

His throbbing fang distracted him so much that Sly

hadn't looked up to see her face yet. When he did, he was met with an intriguing surprise. The woman he thought would be dressed in black with long, black hair, and wearing heavy black eye makeup and red lipstick, almost looked like a different person. He had to blink and look again to be sure she was indeed the witch he was looking for.

She smiled. Her face seemed softer with glowing skin, pink lips, and golden hair falling around her shoulders. Her dress was a dark shade of purple. Maybe something called plum.

A few moments passed before he realized he hadn't finished his sentence and was staring at her.

"Sly? Is there something I can do for you?"

He recovered and said, "Uh, yeah. There ith. Can I come in?"

She tipped her head. "I invited you in years ago, didn't I?"

"Yeth. But if you'd rather not—"

"Don't be silly. Of course you can come in. I was just wondering if you thought vampires needed to be invited in again after a certain amount of time passed."

"Like an ecthperathion date? No. Even if there wath one, I'd knock and athk. I'm not rude, you know."

Her lips twitched in a smirk. He realized she'd noticed his lisp and she too was trying not to be rude.

"I know that. Please come in." She stepped aside.

He strolled in and admired her apartment. A far cry from his secret lair in the basement, hers was a bright and cozy place with a slipcovered couch, a rocking chair, and a trunk for a coffee table. Its only decoration was a glass dish holding some colorful rocks and crystals.

Lit candles graced the fireplace, making the lavender room glow. Wind chimes he'd heard during summer months hung silent in the window, which was closed against the chilly night air.

"You mutht like thith color." He indicated her dress and the walls.

"Yes, plum is my favorite shade of purple, and purple is my favorite color."

"Plum, huh? Ith pretty on you." He meant it.

He didn't often compliment people, not that he didn't appreciate a good-looking woman, but ever since his wife had died and left him a widower twenty-six years earlier, he'd had no interest in starting up a relationship with somebody else. It wouldn't be fair to let a woman think she'd be able to replace his late wife, so he avoided giving anyone the wrong idea. Morgaine had no such illusions though, so he felt safe telling her he'd noticed her attractive change.

"I had a makeover. Roz took me to a school for aspiring cosmetologists. It took them all evening to get the black dye out of my hair and recolor it to match my natural shade."

"Tho you're a natural blonde?"

"I guess so. My hair hasn't been natural for about thirteen years, but I don't notice a big difference at the roots now that it's growing out."

He wandered around the apartment, scanning the new-age books on her shelves and noticing how neat she kept the place. "You mutht have gotten into the goth thing a long time ago."

"Yeah, you could say I was the high-school weirdo."

He smiled. "We were all weird in high thchool."

She grinned back. "Have a seat. Can I get you some tea?"

"No, thanks. I came to athk you for thum magical help."

"You want me to heal your fang?"

"Yeth." He sat on the comfortable flowered sofa. "Did your thycic ability tell you what happened?"

"No, your lisp did." She giggled and sat next to him. *Man, she's pretty when she smiles.*

"Let me see." She scooted closer, and he opened his mouth.

Her gentle, warm fingers pushed his upper lip out of the way as she examined his mouth. Her own lips were slightly parted as she studied his injured fang thoroughly. Her breath was pleasant. Minty, as if she'd just brushed her teeth. He could lean in and capture those sweet pink lips in his and... *Whoa.* What was happening?

"Does it hurt?"

"Like a mutha. I have a metallic tasthte in my mouth too."

"I can see why you wouldn't be able to go to a dentist. It looks like the fang that isn't healing well won't retract, and I guess they're not able to work independently, so the other one won't retract either."

"Egthactly."

"It's not the fang that's broken—or if it was, it's healed."

"Yeth. The fang grew back, but the pain won't go away. I bit into a thick thilver necklath."

"Ohhh... You were poisoned. Okay, I'll have to make a healing poultice so I can apply it directly to your gum. It will draw out the silver poison in your system. I'll reinforce its power with a healing spell if you like."

"Thankth. Will I ever be the thame?"

"Of course you will. Unless you're talking about your pre-vampire days. That I can't heal."

He hung his head. "I know. I remember athking you that when I learned you were Wiccan. You thed there wath no thpell to cure vampirithm."

"I'm afraid not. I'm sorry." She rested her hand on his knee.

When he looked up, she had a soft, sad expression on her face. It wasn't pity—not exactly. *Empathy*. That's what it was. He knew she had a kind heart, but there was more to it than just that. She was a nurturer. Much like his daughter, Merry, the pediatric nurse. An innate healer.

"Pardon my curiothity, but... the makeover? Are you dating?"

Her face colored. "I—well, no. I wouldn't mind meeting someone, but it's just not in me to go out to bars or anything."

"Thumthing tellth me you wouldn't meet the right kind of guy there anyway. Have you tried the Internet?"

"Not yet." She hesitated as if there was more to say, but instead she placed her hands on her knees and pushed herself up to a standing position. "Well, I'll go whip up that poultice. You try to relax."

―᠊᠊ᜃ᠊᠊―

On the second floor, Merry extended her arms to allow for her expanding pregnant belly and embraced her best friend, Roz, while trying not to cry. Tears brimmed in her eyes anyway.

"I'm going to miss you like crazy. I wish you two could stay."

Roz and Konrad were engaged and moving to

Newton, where he was dean and she was a career counselor at the Newton Preparatory School for Boys.

Konrad stepped out of his apartment with a plastic milk crate full of books and smiled. "Newton isn't that far, Merry, and you're welcome any time. You can even take public transportation. The school is within walking distance."

"I know." She sighed. "But it won't be the same as having you right downstairs. Why are you taking stuff to Roz's apartment the night before you're leaving, by the way?"

Roz smiled up at him. "He doesn't want the movers to have to carry heavy things down an extra flight, so he's putting all the boxes and books in my apartment for tonight, and I'll sleep at his place. Isn't he thoughtful?"

Merry let go of her friend's hand. "Yup. He's always been that way. You got yourself a keeper, Roz."

Weird, soulful sounds drifted into the hallway from her right. "What the heck is that?"

Roz gravitated toward her fiancé and put her arm around his waist. "I think it's one of those nature CDs with whale calls."

Merry listened for a few moments. That was indeed what it sounded like. "I don't know our new superintendent very well. Is he the new-agey kind? Maybe he and one of the witches will hit it off."

Roz placed a fist on her hip. "What are you doing? Opening a matchmaker service?"

Merry laughed. "No. Like I said, I don't even know him. I guess I'm just so happy that I want everyone else to be happy too."

As soon as she said that, a door upstairs opened. They

all waited to see who'd be coming down the stairs. When Sly came into view, Merry's jaw dropped.

"Sly? Who were you... Oh, sorry. Never mind. It's none of my business."

Sly smiled briefly but didn't say anything. Merry noticed something a little odd about his face but couldn't put a finger on what was different.

As she was wondering about it, Morgaine leaned over the banister upstairs.

"Oh, Sly? I forgot to ask you to come back tomorrow..."

She had apparently noticed the others in the hallway because she hesitated a moment. "I—uh, I should check your—thing." She blushed. "I mean... You know what I mean. Make sure everything's okay."

He was looking up at her with a silly grin on his face. *That's* what was different. Before, he had seemed to be trying not to smile and show his fangs. But looking up at Morgaine, he didn't seem able to stop smiling, fangs and all.

"I'll be there."

Morgaine grinned, nodded briefly, and went back to her apartment. As soon as they heard her door shut, Sly said, "Hi, Merry," gave her a kiss on the cheek, and then winced.

"Are you okay?"

"I will be. Morgaine ith taking care of me. I had an accthident to my gumth."

Konrad chuckled. "I guess you can't see a dentist for obvious reasons."

"Yup. Thank goodneth for Morgaine. Theeth a magical healer. How are you feeling, Merry? Ith the baby letting you keep your food down?"

"Yes, thank goodness. No more morning sickness. Now I'm getting kicked every once in a while."

"Good! I'm thorry, I meant ith a good thing that the babyth healthy. I can't wait to be a grandfather."

She giggled. "I knew what you meant."

Sly turned to his good friends. "Konrad, Roth, good luck with the move tomorrow."

Roz shook his hand and said, "Thanks. We'll miss everyone, but you have an open invitation to our place in Newton."

"I'd come, but I know your pack friendth don't take kindly to vampireth."

Konrad set down the box he'd been holding. "A few of them are stuck in the old ways. But if you're uncomfortable, I'm sure we'll come back here to visit once in a while. We'll look you up when we do." He extended his hairy arm and they shook hands.

"Can I help you carry thumthing?"

"Almost done, buddy. I had about a hundred boxes of books, but you can help me carry down the couch if you want to."

"Thure."

As the guys retreated to Konrad's apartment, Merry grabbed Roz by the arm and pulled her to the other side of the hall.

She whispered, "What did you think of Sly's reaction to the new Morgaine? I thought I saw some chemistry there."

"I did too."

They waited while the guys carried the couch out of the apartment and down the stairs before continuing.

"I'll never get over how strong those two are," Merry

said. "They looked like they were carrying a two-by-four, not a whole couch."

Roz watched them. Then she turned back to her friend and said, "I sense you want to see someone else in the building hook up."

"I hadn't really thought about it until you said something, but Sly… He's been so lonely since my mother died and that was the day I was born—twenty-six years ago."

Roz shrugged. "Just get him to move into my old apartment and let it work its magic."

Merry snapped her fingers. "That's it! The love shack. When I lived there, I hooked up with Jason. Then you moved in and hooked up with Konrad. Now that you're moving out…"

"The love shack is available," Roz finished for her.

"But he doesn't have a job. How would he pay for it?"

"Does he have to? I mean, he's your father. Jason let his aunt and uncle stay in 2B rent-free for a while."

"You're right." Merry grinned and hugged Roz. "You're a genius. What will I ever do without you?"

"Oh, I'm sure you'll learn to be devious on your own one of these days. When you want something badly enough, you'll figure out how easily men can be manipulated."

"You mean like on *Desperate Housewives*?"

"Hell, no. Don't go to those extremes. Just cook his favorite meal and tell him how much you want this. Then if he says yes, give him a blow job."

Merry laughed. "It's that easy, huh?"

The guys exited Roz's apartment and ambled up the stairs.

"You haven't seen me carrying anything heavy yet,

have you?" Roz raised her eyebrows and Merry laughed, then sneezed.

"You know what? I think your moving is kicking up some dust—not that Konrad isn't a good housekeeper, but I might need my inhaler."

"Of course. And you're right about the dust. With all of Konrad's dusty old books, I wouldn't be surprised if your allergies flare up."

"I'd better go upstairs. I'll see you tomorrow before you go, right?"

"Absitively. Posiloutly."

Merry hugged her again. "Thanks for understanding. Besides, I can't wait to put this devious plan into action."

"Let me know how it goes."

"I might leave out the details of his thank-you, but I'll tell you the rest."

Chad had the advantage of being the only spirit to haunt the building. Well, in some instances it was an advantage, but on the other hand, it could be lonely. Fortunately, he had Morgaine. Some of the other residents knew he was there but rarely thought about him. *Out of sight, out of mind.* And he honestly thought some of them *were* out of their minds.

Not Morgaine though. The two of them had the kind of friendship in which they could rib each other, but they always knew the sharp jabs were said in jest. That seemed to be the only fun Morgaine ever had though.

He'd like to see her happy.

Chad's time had come and gone, and what did he have to show for it? Nothing. And no one.

But it wasn't too late for Morgaine. He had noticed the affection growing between Sly and the gifted witch he thought of as his friend. Ordinarily, he wouldn't match her up with a vampire, but she had limited her options by staying inside all the time. Hell, he wouldn't do something as girly as play matchmaker, but maybe if he just gave them a little push...

He forced his way through the door to her apartment and found her in the kitchen putting away the groceries her cousin Gwyneth had dropped off earlier.

Morgaine turned toward him and smiled. "Hi, Chad. What are you up to?"

"Not much. I just thought I'd drop by and see how you're doing."

"In other words, you're bored." She placed a head of lettuce in the crisper and returned to the bag on the counter.

"Are you saying I only visit you when I'm bored?"

"No. You're always bored."

Chad chuckled and situated himself on the other side of the tiny kitchen so she wouldn't have to pass through him and shiver.

"I'm not terribly bored right now. I actually thought I'd tell you something about Sly."

Her eyebrows raised and she turned toward him. "Sly? Is he okay?"

"Ah ha, I knew you liked him."

"Well, of course I like him. Why wouldn't I? He's a kind, decent per... uh, vampire."

"Yes, I know. His kindness and decency are even more impressive because he's a vampire. And I've noticed he likes you too."

"Oh." She turned back to her groceries. "Really?" The color in her pink cheeks was deepening.

"Oh, yeah. He's into you. But I'm worried about something."

"Like what?"

"I think both of you are so used to being alone, you've forgotten how to begin a new relationship."

She snorted. "That's ridiculous."

"Is it? How would you go about it?"

She shrugged and didn't answer him. She just opened a cabinet and tried to set a box of granola on the top shelf.

"I can't quite reach the top shelf, Chad. Can you give me a hand?"

"You're changing the subject."

She shifted uncomfortably. "Never mind. I'll stick it on the counter."

"You can stick it in your ear for all I care, just don't ignore the question."

She whirled on him and folded her arms. "I don't have to answer your stupid question."

Chad concentrated on the cereal box until it floated up to the top shelf and slid into place among the other boxes and cans up there. *"Okay, fine. Then think about why you don't want to answer it."*

"Because it's none of your business."

"Or because you can't. You have no idea how to approach an attractive man who's attracted to you."

She blew out a deep breath. "Okay, fine. I've thought about it. But our friendship is too important to me. What if it doesn't work out? I don't have that many friends."

"You can say that again. Now that Konrad and

Roz have moved out, you have exactly one cousin who you're fighting with half the time and a bored ghost. Your life sucks."

"Gee, thanks."

"I call 'em like I see 'em. And when I see you and Sly together, I notice the goofy grins on your faces. Think about it, Morgaine. If you snooze, you might lose. I've noticed Gwyneth seems to like him too."

"Well, then I better not get my hopes up. Any man will take the easy girl over the challenging one."

"I admit most of us are schmucks, but I don't think Sly's into superficial, dumb redheads. His eyes don't light up when he sees her like they do when he sees you."

"Whatever you do, never call Gwyneth dumb. She's super sensitive about it. Besides, she has a good mind. She just hasn't had the educational advantages a lot of people have had."

"You're changing the subject again."

"And with good reason. Not only is my life none of your business, but there's nothing you can do about it. He can't hear you."

"Yeah, but you can. And I might just decide to follow you around singing show tunes off-key until you go downstairs and make a move on him." He laughed maniacally.

"Chad, go away. You're pissing me off."

"Make me."

"Fine. I'll just ignore you."

"Aw, screw it. Go ahead and be lonely for the rest of your life. Maybe you can get a few cats or something."

"For Goddess's sake, Chad. Will you leave me alone?" Her tone had a chilly edge to it.

"OOOOOklahoma, where the wind—"

Morgaine clapped her hands over her ears and shouted, "Go away! I don't need your interference. If the opportunity presents itself, I'll do something about it, okay?"

"There now, was that so hard?"

Morgaine rolled her eyes toward the ceiling.

Chapter 2

"HONEY, CAN I ASK YOU SOMETHING?"

Jason sensed an anxious tone to Merry's question. He folded the newspaper he'd been reading and watched her in the kitchen. "Sure, darling. You can ask me anything."

"Well, first, before I ask that, can you sample this sauce? I'm making your favorite."

He jumped up from his chair. "Lasagna? For lunch?"

She grinned. "Yup."

He strolled behind the granite counter to where she was stirring her famous pasta sauce. Something was up. She didn't need him to taste the sauce. She definitely wanted something, and he suspected a bribe. Just the same...

She scooped some sauce into a spoon and held it out for him to taste. As always, the aromas themselves were making his mouth water. The tangy tomatoes and sweet cheeses mingled with the garlic and herbs she always added... mmm, perfection.

"That's fantastic. Now, what did you want to ask me?"

She set down the spoon and placed her arms around his neck. "You know how you let Dottie and Ralph live here rent-free for a while?"

"Yes... but that's because Ralph was the maintenance man. Now Jules is the super and getting free rent." *What's the little tease up to?*

She cozied up to him and her baby bump brushed his cock. He suspected that wasn't accidental, but he wasn't about to complain.

"Uh-huh. And you know my biological father, Sly, lives around here, but his place is really…" She seemed unsure of herself. Jason wasn't used to seeing her like this.

"Really what?"

"Substandard. Dark, dank, musty… He deserves better. After all, he's family, just like your aunt and uncle are."

Ah, here it comes. Jason had expected something like this. So, his sweet wife wanted her biological father to live closer to her. He had never found out exactly where the guy lived. At one point, Jason had thought Sly might be homeless, but he was too well dressed and groomed.

"So, I was wondering… Now that Roz and Konrad have moved out, and my old apartment is free… and it's so tiny. Really only big enough for one person…"

He could see her struggling. Should he help her out and say what he knew she wanted to hear? Or should he just let her squirm a while?

She was laying little kisses along his jaw and neck. Her lips were so soft and warm. *Yeah, I'll definitely let her convince me.*

As she continued her seduction, he glanced over her shoulder at his living and dining rooms in the open, airy penthouse. She had made his sterile place a home. The all-white walls were now a warm neutral tan shade. She had redecorated with more comfortable furniture, fitting his long legs. A beautiful painting of a falcon in flight stood proudly on the mantel over the fireplace. She'd given him the painting for his birthday.

"Well, what do you think? Can I invite Sly to be our next resident in 1B? That's not saying he'll accept, but I'd like to—"

Jason put a finger over her lips. "Shhh… You know I can deny you nothing. If you want Sly to move into 1B, go ahead and ask him."

She squealed and hugged him hard. "Oh, thank you, Jason. I just knew you wouldn't mind."

He chuckled. "I never said that, but if it's important to you, I can live with it."

She punctuated her thanks with kisses all over his face.

When he stopped laughing, he lowered his voice and said, "Now, can I ask you something?"

"Sure."

"Will that lasagna keep for about forty-five minutes?"

She smiled up at him coquettishly. "You know what I love about you?"

"What?"

"Everything."

Sly strolled over the hardwood floors, taking in the space that Merry wanted to give him rent-free. There were pros and cons to this arrangement. Large bay windows faced the street, and even though it was dark outside at the moment, sunlight would stream in during the day. The place was chilly with the heat turned off but still warmer than the basement.

His vampiric senses picked up a party going on in the nearby brainiac college's frat house across the street. Something he didn't notice in his basement. That could become annoying depending on how often geeks partied.

He had been on his way to Morgaine's apartment when Merry had stepped off the elevator next to the cellar door. She didn't seem to mind his presence in the upstairs hallways. In fact, she seemed pleased to see him there. He knew she wanted him in a *real* apartment, but he had little need of one.

"Think about it, okay? I feel just awful that my own father is stashed away in the basement when we have a perfectly good empty apartment for you."

"I appreciate that, Merry, but I don't have a job, so no way of paying rent."

"But that's just it. You don't have to pay rent. My husband owns the building, and professional athletes sure as hell don't need the money. I already asked him if it was all right, and he said yes."

"Oh, I'm sure he was real enthusiastic." Sly smirked.

"Actually, he said I can have anything I really want— and I really want this."

"Sounds like you've got him wrapped around your little finger."

She shrugged. "Is that so bad?"

His space behind the false wall in the basement was completely dark—like a tomb. This place would have to be darkened artificially with shades or blinds. He had no need for a kitchen since he was on an all-liquid diet. And as far as a place to store his stuff? He purposely hadn't accumulated much. He liked a Spartan lifestyle. All he owned fit in a cardboard box under his cot. Mostly photos and newspaper clippings. He had a change of clothes in case what he was wearing became dirty, but that rarely happened.

"Please?" She begged. "I've come to love my vampire

father. You've had such a raw deal in life... It's about time things started going well for you."

Aw, shit. His daughter loved him. That's all it took. He put an arm around her shoulder and kissed her hair. "It looks like you have us both wrapped, sweetheart."

Her expression brightened. "Then you'll take it?"

He sighed. "Possibly, but I have my pride, and I won't just allow myself to sponge off my daughter. That means I have to get a job."

Merry bit her lip. "I guess. There's no rush though. I'd rather you find something you enjoy doing. Don't just take a job to pay your rent. It's totally unnecessary."

"That's good, because it might take a while. I don't even know where to start looking. Most job interviews take place during the day."

"Maybe you can freelance—doing something you're good at."

"Like?"

Her face fell.

Yeah, she can't think of anything, either. "Look, I might take you up on your generous offer, but I don't want to commit to it just yet. This is something I hadn't considered until ten minutes ago, and I need a little time to adjust."

"Sure. How about if I look for you tomorrow night? Will you be around?"

He smiled. "I'm always around. Right now I'm going up to Morgaine's apartment, but unless she wants me to come up again tomorrow night, I'll be out front or in the basement."

"You and Morgaine are friends?" Merry asked in a hopeful tone.

"Yes. Why?"

"Oh, nothing," she said in a singsong way.

Sly looked at her crafty expression. "You're not trying to play matchmaker, are you?"

She put a look of innocent surprise on her face. "Me? Of course not!"

"Good, because I don't need 'help' in that direction."

She put on a fake pout. "But you've been alone for so long. I only want you to be—"

He held up his palm. "I didn't say I wasn't open to a relationship with her. I just said I didn't need any help."

Merry hugged him. "In that case, I'm glad. Go get her, tiger."

Morgaine opened her door, delighted to see Sly standing there.

"You look surprised to see me."

"Not really, it's just that I usually know when someone is coming to the door and somehow you snuck up on me. Come in." She grinned.

"Yeah, I'm told I'm good at sneaking up on people. I need to find something else I'm good at though."

"Really? Why?"

"Merry wants me to move into one of the vacant apartments."

"That's great! It's about time you joined the party."

"Don't tell Nathan there's a party or he'll move out."

They laughed and he smiled at her warmly. She and Sly understood each other. He seemed to be one of the few who "got" her. She pictured the two of them curled up on the love seat in front of a roaring fire.

Wouldn't it be nice to finally have that kind of soul-deep companionship?

"As nice as it sounds, that presents a problem," Sly was saying. "How am I going to pay for it since I'm unemployed and getting a job isn't easy—especially with my limitations?"

At that moment, the phone rang.

"I'll get it," Gwyneth called out from the kitchen and ran to the desk at the far end of the living room.

"Oh, I didn't realize your cousin was here."

Morgaine shrugged. "She just came over to borrow a couple of ingredients for a spell. Well, let's sit down so I can take a look at your gums. You sound a whole lot better today."

"Yes, the metallic taste from the silver is fading and I can retract my fangs again."

"I figured that since you've been saying your *s*'s." She chuckled. "You were kind of cute yethderday though."

He laughed. Sitting on the sofa, he patted the spot next to him.

Morgaine joined him and touched his chilly jaw. "Open wide." Getting used to a vampire always being cold could present a challenge, but that could easily be overcome with the *right* vampire.

"Ohhh… sugar. Y'all are makin' me so hot." Gwyneth had apparently taken a call on the phone sex line.

Damn! Why didn't she just take a message? What's Sly apt to think?

He raised his eyebrows and glanced in Gwyneth's direction, but with his mouth wide open, he couldn't say much.

I wonder how long I can keep his mouth open and

how quickly I can shut hers? Morgaine turned toward her cousin and hissed, "Gwyneth. Get off the phone."

Ignoring her, Gwyneth said, "I'm gittin' on my knees now. Open your zipper, darlin'."

"Oh, Christ, no." Morgaine slumped and felt her cheeks heat.

Gwyneth put her finger in her mouth and slurped around it.

Morgaine would have been fine with a black hole opening in the floor beneath her at that moment. But there was nothing she could do. She had to finish checking Sly's mouth, and it was too late to pretend the call was a wrong number. She'd just have to explain their business to Sly. His eyes were wide and fixed on Gwyneth. Morgaine doubted much of an explanation would be necessary.

As soon as she was satisfied that his gum was healing well, she leaned away and stammered. "I... um, I'm sorry about that. We, uh... We're—"

"Professional phone-sex providers?"

"Yeah."

Sly chuckled. Just then Gwyneth mumbled around her finger. "Is that good? You want more? Or do you want to fuck me now?"

Morgaine slapped her hands over her face and eyes. She could feel her cheeks burning up. She must be blushing furiously. "Oh. My. Goddess."

Sly sounded like he was stifling a laugh. The two of them sat stone still, listening while Gwyneth continued the phone call.

She was panting furiously. "Oh, yeah, baby. That's it. Oh, y'all feel so good way up inside me like that. Oh, oh! Are y'all close? Uh-huh. I'm comin' too, sugar. Right now. Aaaahhh, AAAAHHHHH, AAAAAAGGHHHHHHHHH!"

Sly and Morgaine collapsed in hysterical giggles.

"Oh, yeah… that was good, darlin'. Y'all call back soon, hear?" As soon as she hung up, she jammed her hands on her hips. "Did y'all have to laugh like that? I sure hope he didn't hear the cacklin'. That ain't good for business."

Sly straightened up and apologized, but Morgaine held her sides, doubled over, and laughed louder.

"What are y'all laughin' so hard about? I didn't have to take that call. I thought I was helpin' out. Maybe I shoulda let him go unsatisfied and lose us another customer?"

Morgaine waved away the giggles and calmed down enough to speak. "No, that's okay. I'm not sorry if Sly isn't."

"Me? Sorry? Hell no. That was quite entertaining."

Thank the Goddess he's so easygoing. Morgaine cleared her throat and composed herself. "Well, now that that's over, can I make anyone tea?"

"I'd love a cup of herbal tea," Gwyneth said.

Morgaine had hoped her cousin would say no and go back to her own apartment. She was, after all, just being polite by offering to brew three cups when all she wanted was tea for two.

"If you're making some anyway, I'll have a cup," Sly said.

"Sure thing." Morgaine laid a hand on his knee and proceeded to the kitchen where she filled the kettle and found the tea. Vampires warmed up from the inside out—that much she knew. You could tell when one had fed recently.

If that was the case, could a cup of tea warm his lips?

His bottom lip was full and inviting. The rest of him was pretty appealing too. Dark eyes and hair on the longish side. A fit body that would never change... She wondered what kissing him would be like.

As she was waiting for the water to boil, she overheard the conversation in the next room.

"I hear y'all need a job, Sly. I know they say crime don't pay, but I guess being a crime fighter don't pay much, neither."

"Hell, no. It doesn't pay at all. If I could handle daylight, I could enroll in a police academy, but I might as well think about flying to the moon."

"Now don't give up, sugar. The sun don't shine on the same dog's tail all the time."

"Huh?"

"Means y'all will have some good luck eventually. Where I'm from, people have to make their own way outta nothin' all the time. My momma sells her quilts once a year at the apple festival."

"Only once a year? And she makes enough money to live on?"

"Well, not entirely. My daddy has a business too, but it requires a couple of ingredients they have to buy. Momma's quilt money buys enough ingredients to keep Daddy in business for the whole year."

"So every year people know your mother will be there and show up to buy her quilts?"

"All the folks come down from the mountains with their wares, and rich city people show up and buy them. Beats the pants off of me as to why, but they do."

"It sounds like a good arrangement. I don't quilt, I'm afraid."

"No, and you're already livin' in the city, but there's somethin' else you could make and sell to folks here. The thing my daddy makes."

"Which is?"

"Moonshine!"

Morgaine heard the smile in Gwyneth's voice. She had to be kidding, right? Was her cousin actually suggesting Sly set up a still?

"My daddy makes the best moonshine, and people came from miles around to get some. He gets good money for it too. It's sort of illegal, but that's because of Prohibition. It used to be illegal then, because alcohol of any kind was illegal. They never changed the law though, because the government would lose out on all the tax money. It's cheap as wood chips to make."

"Wood chips?"

"Just an expression. Cheap as wood chips at a sawmill. You don't need wood chips to make moonshine. Just a still, cornmeal, sugar, and yeast. After you distill it, putting it through charcoal turns it into good, safe-drinkin' whiskey."

"Interesting. It sounds as if you know exactly how it's done."

Morgaine was torn. Should she interfere? She probably wouldn't have to. Sly would make some polite excuse not to get involved in something so illegal or simply change the subject. Any moment now...

"I used to help him. I remember exactly how it's done. You just put three pounds of sugar in a big bucket of hot water and stir it until all the sugar melts. Then stir in the yeast until that melts."

"You mean, dissolves?"

"Yes, that's the more proper way to say it. The heatin' up part comes later. That's where the still comes in."

Morgaine scratched her head... *any minute*.

"And do you know how to set up a still?"

"I sure do. If my memory needs refreshin' I could probably look it up on the Internet. The Internet can tell ya how to do anything."

Why was Sly still listening to Gwyneth's hogwash? Morgaine knew he was a gentleman and all, but— The kettle whistled. As soon as she'd moved it off the burner, she heard him say, "I could have people meet me after dark to buy it, I suppose."

"That's why I thought of it. They call it moonshine because people wait until the sheriff's in bed before they truck it out. A'course, our county sheriff was one of daddy's best customers."

Sly laughed.

Confused, Morgaine shook her head and poured the hot water into the teapot. She set everything on a tray to transport to the living room. Was he honestly considering that harebrained idea?

By the time Morgaine reached them, Gwyneth and Sly seemed to already be hatching a plan.

"If I vacate my spot behind the false wall in the basement, maybe that would be enough room for the still, and it can stay hidden. I don't want Merry to know about it."

"Why? She'd never report it to the authorities," Gwyneth said.

Morgaine poured a cup of tea and handed it to Sly, listening intently.

"I know she wouldn't, but I don't want to get her in trouble with her husband. The less she knows, the better."

"I understand. What do y'all mean about a false wall?"

"That's right. You've never seen my place, have you?"

"I've seen the laundry-room part of the basement. I know the other side's for storage. I never really thought about y'all hiding behind a wall. I just figured maybe you was holed up in the corner with a bunch of boxes blockin' the view of your coffin—or whatever."

He chuckled. "Nope. No coffin. And I built the wall as soon as I knew I'd be staying a while. Konrad took me in initially, but I couldn't take advantage of his hospitality long term. The old landlord never went down to the basement, plus it was almost completely dark, so for my purposes, it was ideal."

"Can I see it?" Gwyneth asked.

He sipped his tea. "Sure. I suppose you'll need to if you're going to figure out whether or not a still will fit in there."

Morgaine couldn't hold it in any longer. "Sly, are you seriously considering this?"

He shrugged. "Somehow I don't think my voice is sexy enough to get in on your business."

Gulp. Touché. There wasn't much she could say to counter that.

Chapter 3

"WELL, THIS IS IT," SLY SAID, AS HE SLID THE FALSE WALL out of its channel. "Home, musty home."

Morgaine and Gwyneth stared wide-eyed. Part of that may have been because Sly's area of the basement was so dark. He had purposely sabotaged the lighting fixture at the far end of the large room to further hide his lair.

At last, Morgaine said, "Amazing. How did you come up with that false wall?"

He smiled. "I used to be an engineer. Not bad considering what I had to work with. I scavenged the wood and used a hammer and chisel to take the part of the rocks I wanted. Then mortar and superglue, and voilà!"

Morgaine touched the stone face he had affixed to the double sheet of plywood. "It looks like a solid rock wall."

"And like it's been here since the day the place was built," Gwyneth added. "Y'all outdid yourself, Sly."

"Thanks. I was lucky the basement took a bit of a jog here. Otherwise I'd have had to make a much longer wall."

"It looks heavy, but y'all just picked it up like it was Styrofoam."

"That's vampiric strength for you."

Gwyneth sidled up next to him and stroked his bicep. "My, my. I had no idea you was *that* strong." She gazed at him like he had suddenly become a side of beef and she was starving. Maybe she was sex starved. How long ago had her old lover, Joe, moved out?

Morgaine cleared her throat. "I can see a potential problem or two here."

Sly transferred his full attention to her. "What kind of problems?"

"Well, ventilation for one."

Gwyneth said, "Oh, fiddlesticks. That's right. Y'all have any windows down here?"

"A couple." Sly moved a few boxes to clear a path and led them to one of two small basement windows along the side wall. Since it was dark outside and dark inside, they must not have noticed them. Piles of old furniture and boxes might have also obscured their view. "Is this big enough?"

"Does it open?" Morgaine asked.

"It's not supposed to, but it does. It used to be nailed shut, but I had to let Konrad in this way once when he got stuck outside buck naked."

Gwyneth laughed.

"I think I remember him telling me about that," Morgaine said. "He used to keep his clothes stashed behind the Dumpster before he shifted and went on his midnight runs. But he said they were stolen once."

"Twice. After that, he changed in his apartment, and either Nathan or I would let him out the door and back in again."

"Y'all shapeshifters and vampires might be strong as a team of horses, but you've got problems…" Gwyneth smirked.

He caught Morgaine sending her a sharp look. "It's okay for her to say that. It's true. I hate my limitations.

Hell, I missed out on raising my daughter because I'd never be able to drive her to soccer or band practice."

Gwyneth tipped her head. "I didn't know Merry was in soccer and band."

"She wasn't. I was just referring to all the things she might have wanted to do. Field hockey was her sport, and I think she took guitar lessons. Gave it up after her mother was killed by a stray bullet though."

"I thought y'all lost your wife from a vampire attack the night Merry was born."

"I did. I was referring to her other mother—the one who adopted her—Mrs. MacKenzie."

"The night you lost your wife… Is that when you were turned?" Morgaine asked softly.

"Yes." He hung his head, remembering that horrible night. "She was barely clinging to life, and the only way he'd help me get my pregnant wife to the hospital was if I allowed him to turn me."

"How awful!"

Gwyneth crossed her arms. "I wish I'd been there. I'd have kicked his bad ass into next week and left him there—then helped you myself."

"He'd taken us God knows where. I'd have been wandering around a deserted warehouse area carrying a dying pregnant woman."

"So what finally happened?" Morgaine asked. "Did he use his vampiric strength and speed to take her to the nearest emergency room?"

Sly frowned, remembering the fiend's face. "He laughed. He said now that I was a vampire, I could get her there myself and pointed in the general direction of the hospital. It turned out we were only a mile or so away. I got her there in time to save Merry, but Alice had lost too much blood and died on the operating table."

Morgaine touched his arm. "I'm so sorry, Sly. You didn't deserve that. None of you did."

"I know." He acknowledged her sympathy with a sad smile. "Thank you."

Her eyebrows knit and her lips thinned. "I'm with Gwyneth. If only I'd been there. I could have come up with some kind of spell to force him to help you, then punished the hell out of him after that. Screw the repercussions."

He chuckled. "It's a good thing you weren't there then. I understand using magic to harm another can backfire pretty badly."

"You're right. The negative energy turns on the sender three times. It's called the law of three."

"Sounds like a harsh law. Instead of an eye for an eye, it's an eye, arm, and leg for an eye."

"You got it. That's why I've drummed that law into my dear cousin's head."

"About a million times," Gwyneth added. "So what are all the things vampires can and can't do? Can you see yourselves in mirrors? Do you get burned by holy water and crosses? I know about the sun thing."

He laughed. "I'm not sure about one of those things. I can see my reflection and crosses don't bother me, but no one has tossed holy water in my face yet."

"Are there other vampires y'all can ask?"

Sly shrugged. "I don't know many vampires, but I've heard of one I'd very much like to meet someday."

"Who?" they both asked at once.

"His name is Mikhail. I don't know his last name. I think he's Russian originally, but I heard he was living in New York. He found some temporary cure for vampirism and managed to bottle it. It's in some kind of wine."

"Well, that's what y'all have to do then! Find him and ask him to give you some."

"He sells it, but I could never afford enough to make a difference. It costs a fortune. I guess most vampires who've been around a long time have managed to amass some wealth. If I never get cured, I need to find out how they do that. Something tells me they aren't just playing the stock market, and I refuse to do anything illegal." He looked at the space he was considering for the still. "Well, illegal enough to warrant a jail sentence rather than paying a fine."

Morgaine had been worrying her lip the whole time he was talking. Was something about this conversation bothering her?

"Morgaine, are you all right? You look concerned."

"I-I don't know if I should tell you this. I don't want to give you false hope. But I think I know the vampire you're talking about."

Sly almost swallowed his tongue when he gasped, "You do?"

"I *think* so. He made Baltimore his temporary home back when I lived there. I got to know him through the goth scene. His name was Mikhail, and he was very old. So old, he didn't have a real last name. Then he said he was moving to New York to buy and run some museum. I never saw him after that."

Sly was hanging on her every word. Did he dare hope he might find this elusive vampire and somehow learn his secret? Could Sly perhaps bottle his own cure? He gazed back at his open wall where he could hide the still during the day if he took Merry up on her generous offer.

"I wonder…" he began out loud.

Morgaine finished his thought with excitement in her voice. "Maybe if we can figure out how he does it, you can bottle your own cure?"

"Exactly."

"Great minds…" She smiled and winked.

First things first. He had to free up his lair for the still. Oh, but Morgaine said she saw another potential problem. What was that?

"Morgaine, I'll get back to your friend in a moment, but first, you said you saw a couple of problems with having the still down here. What was the other one?"

She grinned. "Forget it. We need a still!"

Merry was delighted when Sly told her he'd take the apartment. They didn't discuss rent or a security deposit. She just wanted to know what he needed to furnish his new place. Embarrassed to ask for anything at all, he'd insisted she squelch the urge to buy him anything new.

She offered him her old bed, now dismantled and in the basement. He agreed to accept it and asked to borrow some old blankets, if she had any, to curtain off the sun in his bedroom. She said all her old linens and towels were in a box labeled "Merry's linen closet," and he could have those too.

That's all he needed. Well, that and Sly needed the key to his new apartment, so he knocked on the door of apartment 2B, the super's place.

A salty smell assaulted his nose as Jules opened the door a few inches and peeked around it.

"Hi, I think Merry mentioned I'd be moving into 1B, downstairs. She said I should see you to pick up the key."

"Oh, yes. You must be Sylvestro Flores." He opened the door just a few inches wider so he could shake Sly's hand. "I'll be back in a minute with your key."

As soon as he was out of sight, Sly pushed the door open the rest of the way. He was still protective of his daughter's home and wondered what Jules Vernon might be trying to hide.

The floor plan looked the same as all the apartments on the B side of the building, but Jules's stuff was not what Sly had expected. Massive shelves surrounded the room, and on them dozens of large fish tanks held live fish. Not the pretty little tropical types found in most household aquariums—ugly saltwater fish. Sly recognized haddock, pollock, and blue fish. The most attractive were the herring and mackerel. At least they had iridescent stripes along their sides.

Seaweed floated on the water within most of the tanks, and nets hung from high hooks.

So that accounted for the smell, but what was that human-sized fish tank under the bay window about? Sly was glad to see the floor had been reinforced with long planks. They probably distributed the weight better. The only things in the tank were some sand and starfish at the bottom.

When Jules returned and saw Sly appraising his living room, he halted in mid-stride.

"Interesting decor you have," Sly said.

"Oh, uh… yeah! I'm an avid angler. Just love to fish

and hate the cold. I prefer the ocean, so ice fishing is out of the question. This keeps me happy in the chilly months."

Sly pointed to the human-sized tank by the front windows. "And what were you fishing for over there? Orcas?"

"Ha, ha... No. I just don't like the idea of fishing in those smaller tanks. Doesn't seem fair, you know? So I transfer them to the big one and give them a little freedom before they make their way to my dinner plate."

"I see." Sly folded his arms. "And you felt their five minutes of freedom was important enough to reinforce the floor?"

"Well, I can't let my tank come crashing down into your apartment, can I?" He let out a nervous chuckle, and Sly noticed Jules's teeth for the first time. They were pointed and quite sharp looking. Not exactly like fangs. They were much shorter and didn't look like they extended.

Something fishy was definitely going on here.

"You know my daughter owns the building, right?"

"Oh! Is Merry your daughter? I didn't know that."

"Yes, she is." Sly stepped a little closer and held the super's gaze. "We don't want anything bad to happen to Merry's home, do we?"

Jules raised his eyebrows and blinked. "Uh, no. Of course not."

He blinked? Sly's attempt to mesmerize the man hadn't worked—if he *was* a man. Sly was beginning to doubt it.

But Sly had his own secrets to hide, so he'd have to flush out the real identity of this "Jules Vernon" carefully—without putting him on the defensive. Besides, Jules seemed to have an excuse for everything. Sly would bide his time and try to catch him eventually in the act of—whatever.

———∞———

"Morgaine, why don't you just tell her how you feel?" Chad, the ghost, said.

Morgaine snorted, continued labeling her dried herbs, and tried to ignore the apparition that was making too much sense. "Oh, get a grave."

"Seriously. I know Gwyneth pretty well, considering we're roommates. She'll understand if you just give her a chance."

"You forget I lived with her for a long time before you did. She has to be the belle of every ball. You even called her that, remember?"

"So, what? Are you just going to step back and let her take over?"

"Look, I already got a makeover. What else are you telling me to do? Change my personality?"

"I think you're being oversensitive."

"About what?" Morgaine realized she had snapped at him, but he should mind his own damn business. Sure, he was probably bored out of his mind, but he could find other ways to amuse himself besides butting into her private life... like insulting people who couldn't hear him or listening in on the phone-sex line like he used to do.

"About your more extroverted cousin getting the attention you crave but refuse to risk rejection for."

She grabbed her mortar and pestle and another handful of herbs. "Oh, great," she muttered. "Now our spook thinks he has a degree in psychology." She took out some of her aggression and ground the sage force-fully. It didn't need to be turned into powder as if she wanted to cook with it. Courser herbs would do quite nicely for a spell, and she didn't plan to cook a turkey for another month.

Unfortunately, she couldn't think of a way to win the heart of a man with her cute, vivacious cousin around—unless she broke the Witches' Rede and resorted to manipulation. The rules made it quite clear that forcing the feelings and behavior of others would backfire on a witch big time. And would a night of false passion be worth it?

"I know what you're thinking."

"No, you don't."

"Oh, yeah? I'll bet you believe all men think with their little heads and you're not attractive enough to turn on a certain vampire."

The air rushed out of Morgaine's emotional balloon, and she sagged against the counter. "Okay, I guess you do know what I'm thinking."

"So, what are you gonna do about it?"

"What can I do? I can't turn my cousin into an ugly hag. I can't make Sly fall madly in love with me. Well, I could do those things, but that would be cheating."

"At the risk of sounding clichéd, all you need to do is be yourself."

"Thanks, Mom."

Carrying his one cardboard box tucked under his arm, Sly unlocked and opened the door to his apartment. He took one step and halted. This *was* his apartment, right?

He glanced back at the door and saw 1B proudly displayed in brass.

All he'd expected to find in his place was possibly Merry's bedroom set, but a worn leather couch, an old trunk, and an antique-looking chair were grouped around his fireplace. A braided rug covered the floor beneath the welcoming scene. Artwork, candles, vases, books... every comfort of home graced the walls and bookshelves.

As he stood in his living room, confused, he heard snickers coming from the back of the apartment.

"Surprise!" his friends yelled as they jumped into view.

Merry, Morgaine, Gwyneth, Konrad, and Roz stood there grinning and laughing.

Just then, Nathan strolled in behind him, carrying an old bird perch. At least that's what Sly thought it was. It looked like the tall metal T-bar that a parrot would sit on.

"Did I miss the big surprise?" Nathan asked.

Sly smiled. "Apparently."

"Good. I hate those things. Here." Nathan extended the item in his hand and set it on the floor next to him. "It's my old perch. You can use it for a coat rack—or something." Then he looked over toward the rest of the group. "Is there cake?"

Merry held up a bottle of champagne. "No, only this. Sly doesn't eat."

Nathan sighed. "Well, I'll be going then. Welcome to the neighborhood, Sly." He extended his free hand and Sly shook it.

"Jesus, man. I'll never get over how cold you are. Go drink a rat or something."

Gwyneth folded her arms. "Nathan Nourie, y'all git

back here. Not only was that uncalled for, but this here's a party and we're all celebratin'."

"I know. That's why I'm going." He left and closed the door behind him.

Gwyneth rolled her eyes. "I do declare, I don't know what's wrong with that boy. You'd think we was making him stand in front of a firin' squad."

"That's just the way he is, Gwyneth," Morgaine said. "I don't think we can change him."

"I suppose not. Ain't no point in beatin' a dead horse… 'course, it can't hurt none either."

Sly grinned and wandered closer to his friends. "I guess you gave me some of your old things?"

"Well," Roz answered, "Merry told us that *someone* was too proud to let her furnish the place with new stuff, so everything here is used."

"We figured y'all wouldn't mind a few little castoffs since it didn't cost us nothin'."

"Thank you." He scanned the cozy-looking living room, and a lump formed in his throat. "I'm truly touched."

He wandered over to the eclectic furniture grouping. His amplified sense of smell told him exactly who'd previously owned each piece.

The antique chair was from Roz. The couch was Merry's. He ran his hand over the back of it. The beat-up old brown leather only made it softer and more comfortable.

The trunk was Morgaine's, and a bookshelf held the scent of Konrad's wolf hair.

"We put a few items in the kitchen too," Gwyneth said.

He strolled past the dining area furnished with a tiny round table and two chairs, again with Merry's scent, and stepped into the galley kitchen.

Gwyneth opened the cabinets and showed off a five-gallon bucket and a couple of large copper pots. "These will come in handy later on when we set up the—"

Morgaine cleared her throat and sent her a quick head shake. "There's plenty of time for him to look around and see what's here."

Gwyneth looked over at Merry and must have realized she had almost spilled the beans about the still in front of the landlady.

"Of course. Silly me. What was I thinkin'?"

"And Sly," Merry added as she set the champagne on the counter, "if you need anything else, *please* ask. Okay?"

"I can only think of one thing I really need, and that's a way of darkening my bedroom during the day. Did you bring any blankets?"

"I didn't have to," Merry said. "Morgaine suggested room-darkening shades. It's the only thing I bought, Sly. I promise."

Sly looked over at Morgaine. She blushed slightly and dropped her gaze to the floor. Why was she embarrassed? She had thought of his needs and suggested the perfect way to meet them. He wanted to hug her, but not in front of an audience.

"I really can't thank you enough—everyone." Were those tears threatening to form in his eyes? No way was he going to let people see the big, scary vampire cry—especially gross, bloody tears. He grabbed the champagne bottle and said, "Did anyone happen to donate a corkscrew?"

Chapter 4

GWYNETH APPLIED HER BEST PERFUME, BRUSHED HER hair, and tiptoed downstairs to Sly's apartment, carrying her lit candelabra. She knew Sly wasn't using electricity in order to save money, and *he* might be able to see in the dark, but she couldn't. Besides, everyone looked good in candlelight. She wore a short, black skirt—a departure from her long, black, broomstick skirt. She hoped the black velour top that clung to her curves made her look as alluring as she felt.

Sly opened the door shortly after her first knock.

"Hey, Sly."

"Hi, Gwyneth, what a surprise."

"I hope y'all think it's a good surprise, and I didn't catch y'all with your pants down." She giggled and felt herself blush. "Well, hush my mouth, I didn't mean that quite how it sounded." *Or did I?*

Sly grinned and stepped aside. "Come in."

She sashayed in. "I know all y'all vampire folk have to be invited into someone's home, but is it the same the other way around?"

He shook his head but kept his smile and said, "Not that I've ever heard. Seems a little unfair, but… Please, have a seat."

Oh, good. It looks like my Southern charm, as Chad calls it, is workin'.

She settled herself on Sly's comfortable leather sofa

and hoped he'd sit next to her. No such luck. He took the rocking chair beside it. She set the candelabra on the table between them.

"Looks like y'all got a new chair. I don't remember it from the housewarmin' party."

"Merry said I could borrow it until the baby comes."

"Well, ain't that nice. Bless her heart."

"Yes, she's a special girl."

"She ain't such a girl anymore. She's a little older than I am, and I consider myself a grown woman." She arched her back just slightly, hoping her small chest would look larger.

"I guess you're right. So what brings you down here?"

"Well, two things. I need to give you a shopping list and directions to make the mash."

He took the piece of paper and skimmed the recipe. "Kill Me Quick?"

"That's what it's called. It's fast to make—it doesn't really kill ya."

He chuckled. "Well, since I'm already dead, I don't suppose I need to worry about that."

"Oh, speakin' of parties, I was figurin' on askin' you to attend a Halloween party with me."

He cocked his head. "I thought Wiccans had a different name for Halloween and considered it a solemn holiday."

Shoot. He knows about our traditions. Now what? "That's absolutely right, but Halloween looks like so much fun I thought maybe I'd participate this year. We could dress up in costumes."

"Hmmm… that's interesting. So who will be attending this party?"

She squirmed in her seat. "Well, I don't know yet. I thought I'd start with you and see how many folks could make it."

"Well, we know Nathan won't come. I doubt the superintendent will. How does Morgaine feel about abandoning her traditions in favor of a non-pagan holiday?"

"I'm not sure. I haven't mentioned it to her yet."

"Hey, Gwyneth," Chad interrupted. *"What the hell are you up to? You know Morgaine won't go to a costume party on Samhain."*

Gwyneth stuck a hand on her hip and looked toward the ceiling. "Chad, I don't recollect invitin' y'all to this conversation."

Sly looked at the ceiling too. "Chad's up there?"

"He's somewhere around. I can't see him. I can only hear him." She raised her voice slightly. "Y'all aren't welcome at the moment, Chad. Now, git. I'll talk to y'all later when I'm back in our apartment."

"Make me."

Gwyneth's posture deflated like a day-old balloon. "I guess we're stuck with him. He refuses to leave."

Sly shrugged. "I don't mind if he hangs out here for a little while. He must get awfully lonely, and you witches are the only ones he can talk to."

"Yeah," she mumbled absently. "He's powerful lonely. I just wish he'd go bother Morgaine for a while."

"She's asleep."

Gwyneth sighed. "Well, if he's stickin' around, I'll have to cut this short. So what do you say to my invitation?"

"I—uh, I don't know yet. Let me think about it and get back to you." He stood.

"Oh." She rose slowly, giving him a chance to

reconsider. Disappointment washed over her. Why was Sly less than enthusiastic about the "party"?

Maybe she should have been honest. He didn't know it would only be the two of them. She knew Nathan would have nothing to do with it, and she could count on Morgaine not cheapening the most sacred Wiccan holiday there is. She'd just "forget" to invite Jules or say she forgot accidentally on purpose because he's the super and doesn't like parties in the building. Sly doubted Jules would go anyway, so she could say she didn't want to put him in the awkward position of refusing.

"So, Samhain—I mean, Halloween—is only a couple of days away. Y'all won't forget to tell me soon, right?"

He smiled. "No, I won't forget."

As soon as he closed the door after her, she stuck out her lower lip. "Chad," she whispered, "I swear y'all ruin everything."

His voice followed her up the stairs. *"I didn't ruin anything, but you were about to."*

"What are you jabberin' about?"

"Your relationship with Morgaine. You know how competitive you two can be."

"I don't know what y'all are talkin' about."

"Yes, you do. I remember a couple of world-class fights between you two only a few months ago. It's a good thing Konrad was here to lift you off Morgaine and suspend you in midair by your macramé belt."

Gwyneth chuckled. "We was just scrappin'. Nobody got hurt."

"Well, he's not here now, and I can't very well keep you two from killing each other if you go at it again. Of

course, if one of you murdered the other one, I'd have some company, wouldn't I?"

"Probably not, since witches believe in reincarnation, but y'all don't have to worry, Chad. Nothin's gonna happen."

"Famous last words."

—⁓—

Morgaine had some appointments for readings the following day. This woman wanted a palm reading. Not the best for giving loads of information so she didn't do it often, but it was good to keep her skills sharp. She traced the heart line of her female client.

"Now this is a good, strong line. There are a couple of partial lines dropping down from it, which means you've had a couple of heartaches, but in general your love life is—"

A rap on her door interrupted her thoughts. *The energy is familiar—oh, it's Sly!* Now, how to get rid of this client so she could spend some quality time with him?

The woman leaned forward. "My love life is…"

"Oh." Morgaine patted the woman's hand. "It's just fine. You'll meet the man of your dreams soon, have two children, a house in the suburbs, and a minivan." She craned her neck to face the door and yelled, "Be right there."

The woman got the hint and pulled out her wallet. "How much do I owe you?"

"Fifty."

Her eyebrows raised. "Fifty bucks for a ten-minute palm reading?"

Morgaine sighed. "Okay, twenty. But you're only getting the discount because I hurried the end."

The woman seemed appeased, paid her bill, and opened the door just as Sly looked like he was about to leave.

Morgaine hurried over. "Sly, come on in."

"If you're busy, it can wait."

"No, it's fine."

The woman turned to Sly and whispered in his ear, "She's good, but her appointments are booked too close together. If she rushes you at the end, ask for a break in the price."

"Uh, thanks," Sly said. He watched her go.

"What was that about?" Morgaine asked.

Sly strolled into her apartment and waited for her to close the door. "Apparently you give discounts if you kick someone out before they're finished."

She felt her cheeks heat. "Uh, well. There was really nothing…"

He laughed. "Don't worry about it. I'm sure you had your reasons. I just hope it wasn't because I was outside your door."

She waved away his comment as if it was ridiculous. "Nah. I told her everything I had to say. Have a seat. Can I make you some tea?"

"No, I can't. The incense smell in here is kind of overwhelming."

"Oh! Sorry. It's all part of the atmosphere. I can run a fan and open—"

"No need. I just wanted to ask you one question and tell you something else."

Disappointed that he wasn't planning to stay long, she sank down on her sofa. "Okay. What did you want to ask and tell me?"

"First I'll tell you what I overheard. The super, Jules, is concerned with the increase in foot traffic. He knows you do readings from the apartment and seems concerned about the number of strangers coming and going."

"How did you hear that?"

"I think he was talking to Merry on the phone. I couldn't see him since I was downstairs in my apartment and he was upstairs in his."

"Yikes. You're vampiric hearing can pick up conversations right through the ceiling?"

"When it's relatively quiet elsewhere."

"I'm glad we have two floors between us. Especially when we're on the phone sex line."

Sly laughed. "That's when I'd give my right arm to live next door."

She had to giggle. Morgaine wished her psychic powers could tell her what Sly thought of her. He seemed to like her. Maybe he was interested, but he was too much of a gentleman to come right out and say so.

"There's something else I need to talk to you about."

"Sure," she said hopefully. "What is it?"

He seemed uncomfortable and hesitated a moment. "I'm not positive, and I'm going to be very embarrassed if I'm wrong, but it seems as if Gwyneth is trying seduce me. She came down to my apartment, smelling like expensive perfume and invited me to a Halloween party."

Morgaine's eyebrows shot up. "Halloween? Are you sure she said that?"

"Yes. I asked if she meant the solemn holiday I know Wiccans celebrate this time of year, but…"

Sly was still talking, but Morgaine was too angry to make out his words. Gwyneth, her scheming, coquettish cousin, who could have any man she wanted, wanted the only person Morgaine thought she might already be in love with.

Steam must have been pouring out her ears, because Sly had stopped talking and was watching her intently with his mouth slightly open.

"Are you all right, Morgaine?"

"I'll talk to her," she said.

"Maybe I should have done it myself, but I didn't want to insult her. And I didn't want to give her the wrong idea by coming up to her apartment. The truth is, I just don't think of her that way."

Did that mean he didn't think of either of them "that way"? Morgaine's heart crumpled, but she forced herself to calm down. "It's okay. I understand. I'm sure she wouldn't want to lose your friendship or make a fool of herself. I'll let her know you won't be coming to her *Halloween* party."

───※※※───

"Oh boy, this is gonna be bad," Chad muttered.

Morgaine leaned against her door, opening and closing her fists. Before she left her apartment, she turned the radio up loud. "Chad, don't you dare say one word to Gwyneth. This is our business, and I'm asking you nicely to stay out of it."

"Thanks for asking nicely, but I don't plan to warn her. What would I say? 'Look out. Witch on the war-path'? Heck, no. I don't want to spoil the surprise."

Morgaine inhaled deeply and said, "Okay, Sly's

inside his apartment with the door closed now." She threw open her door and marched across the hall.

Chad watched as Morgaine pounded on Gwyneth's door. The decorated broom hanging on it jumped with each blow. *"Hey, see if you can knock that thing off. I hate it, and it's still my apartment. I just let Gwyneth crash here so you two wouldn't kill each other last summer. Obviously, that didn't help."*

"Gwyneth! Open the door."

Chad stuck his head through the oak door and saw a blasé Gwyneth putting a chilled bottle of white wine back into the refrigerator.

A few moments later, she sauntered to the front door of her apartment and opened it a few inches. "Why, Morgaine, what's got y'all madder than a bottle full of bees?"

"You know damn well."

"No, I'm afraid I don't. Y'all are the powerful psychic. I'm just a student, green as a gourd, standing in the shadow of your greatness."

Uh-oh. "Gwyneth, I wouldn't shake that jar of bees if I were you."

"Stay out of it, Chad," they both said at once.

"Fine. Go ahead. Turn each other into toads. See if I care."

Gwyneth said, "Using magic to harm another is considered black magic and boomerangs on the sender. I can't turn her into a toad unless I want warts on my face."

Morgaine pushed on the door. "Aren't you going to let me in?"

Gwyneth wasn't prepared for the hard shove and the door flew open, revealing two wine glasses and several lit candles around the apartment. Soft music was playing in the background.

"This might not be as bad as it looks, Morgaine. Don't jump to conclusions."

Morgaine crossed her arms. "Are you expecting someone?"

Gwyneth turned her nose up in the air. "That's none of your beeswax."

"If you're trying to seduce Sly, I have a news flash for you."

Gwyneth shrugged one shoulder casually. "Oh?"

"Yeah, he's on to you… and he doesn't appreciate it."

"I don't see him up here tellin' me to stop. I just see a jealous older woman about to have a stinkin' fit."

Morgaine said, "I know I can't use magic to make my point, but…" She flew at her cousin and knocked her over. Gwyneth yelped and then grabbed Morgaine's hair and gave it a hard tug.

Oh, man. I saw this coming, and I'm not even psychic.

Morgaine threw a couple of punches. Chad hadn't known she had it in her.

"Come on, girls. Stop this. As Gwyneth would say, y'all are like two cats in a sack right now. Wait until you cool off."

Gwyneth tried to connect with Morgaine's face and missed. She tried again and missed again. It was as if her fist slid off an invisible barrier. Morgaine laughed and got up.

"I see you didn't bother putting the protection spell I showed you in place."

Gwyneth scrambled to her feet. "I'll show you how worthwhile your protection spell is…" She grabbed a lamp and heaved it toward her cousin. Morgaine leaned back and the lamp missed her—barely. "You only protected yourself from people, not inanimate objects."

Morgaine's eyes and lips thinned, and she trembled as if she were about to erupt. She grabbed the base of the lamp that hadn't shattered, and just as she was winding up for the pitch, Gwyneth's image slowly faded into invisibility.

Morgaine's mouth dropped open.

A door downstairs opened. Jules, the super, called up through the stairwell, "What's going on up there?"

"Oh! Uh, it's nothing, Mr. Vernon," Morgaine called back.

"Just a little spat is all," Gwyneth added—*from somewhere*.

"Well, take it outside. I don't want to have to replace the wallpaper or light fixtures."

"Sorry, Mr. Vernon. I think it's over now." Morgaine glanced around the empty hallway.

"We'll be quiet," Gwyneth answered.

"Good," Jules said, and slammed his door shut.

Morgaine crossed her arms and stared at Gwyneth's open door. It didn't move. Eventually, she whispered, "Where are you, Gwyneth?"

Gwyneth faded in. When she was fully formed, she stood there blowing on her fingernails with a smug look on her face.

"Where did…? How the…?" Morgaine, never at a loss for words before, just stared at her student cousin.

"Didn't think I was as powerful as y'all, didja?" Gwyneth touched the red spot on her cheek where she'd been hit and winced.

"I, uh… I always knew you had it in you. We're both hereditary witches from the same stock. I just didn't think you were spending as much time studying as I was."

"Well, guess what? I was." Gwyneth swept a hand over her cheek, and the red spot disappeared. She smiled, looking quite satisfied with herself.

"You didn't seem that interested."

"And you didn't seem to give me credit for all the hard work I did to catch up."

"Okay, witchy chicks. This seems to have ended in a stalemate, so why don't you shake hands and try to cool it for a while."

"For once, Chad's right," Morgaine said.

"I agree."

They shook hands and went back to their respective apartments.

"For once? What does that mean?"

Chapter 5

PUNGENT EVERGREEN SHRUBS OUTSIDE THE APARTMENT windows scratched Vorigan's face. Why couldn't they have planted a nice, soft yew? But he needed the cover since the subject of his fascination could see and smell as acutely as he did. So he'd have to endure spruce needles up his nose.

Sly Flores sat in a rocking chair inside the apartment, reading in the dark. He had opened the window blinds fully, perhaps to take advantage of the streetlamps. Vampires needed very little light to see well, but complete darkness would make reading impossible for anyone.

Vorigan wondered how the vampire he'd turned twenty-six years ago had managed to elude him for so long. He'd caught whiffs of the guy's scent from time to time and had tracked him like a wolf would track a rabbit. But his efforts had always led to dead ends.

Long ago, he'd spotted the handsome Latino walking with a pregnant woman along a quiet street in New Bedford, Massachusetts. He'd shadowed them until he was able to stop them in a secluded spot and ask for directions. As soon as he had their attention, he'd used his powers of mesmerism and led them to an even more secluded place inside a warehouse.

His mesmerism had held until he'd fed on the woman and she'd lost consciousness. For some reason, the handsome, virile male had snapped out of it at that point and begun begging for his wife and baby's lives. The sheer strength of will that took made Vorigan realize this man was someone special. Perhaps someone who could become his equal lover sometime.

So, he had promised to help the guy by turning him. Vorigan had explained that becoming a vampire would give the man powers of speed and strength beyond his comprehension—enough to get his wife and unborn baby to the hospital in time to save them. No matter how the man had begged Vorigan to take her there himself, he had refused. Why should he care about them? The only human he was interested in at that moment was this fascinating, drop-dead gorgeous man.

At last, the male had allowed Vorigan to turn him in exchange for safe passage to the nearest hospital. And Vorigan had kept his word. He'd stayed out of the man's way as he went through the change from life to death to undead. Vorigan had explained that the change would be swift if the guy didn't fight it.

Despite the pain, the brave husband had gone through the transformation faster than Vorigan had thought he would or could. The man had lifted his pregnant wife and run so fast that Vorigan wasn't sure he could keep up with him. But he did. Right up until the woman was taken from the emergency room up to the delivery-operating room.

Vorigan had planned to wait in the hospital lobby until morning if he had to. He had told the man that, as a vampire, he would fall asleep wherever he was when the sunrise began and had warned him to get to the lobby before that. Vorigan had said he would protect the fledgling vampire and teach him what he needed to know about his new life. *And Vorigan's loneliness would be at an end*.

Only something had gone wrong. Vorigan had waited until the very last minute, but no vampire had appeared. He barely got himself to ground in time. Then as soon as the sun went down, he took up his post again. No matter how vigilantly he watched the hospital over the next week, the new vampire never appeared. Vorigan hadn't even learned his name! Somehow his protégé had given him the slip.

Now here he was—finally. He'd have to pay for leaving him like that. Oh, yes. He'd punish the guy, but only until he understood how much better his life would be if he kept Vorigan happy.

Things would be better than ever before. He'd introduce his protégé to the delights of the dark world. First, he'd help him discover his latent bisexual tendencies and hone them. It would be no use pretending he didn't have them. All vampires did. At least, all the vampires Vorigan had ever known.

He stepped out of the bushes carefully and returned to the sidewalk. Now he had to find a way in. He surveyed the building and found the right side of the building on the second floor was lit. So, someone was home there. Both sides of the building's third floor were lit. Best bet would be an apartment on that floor, so he strolled up the steps to study the buzzers.

P was labeled only with initials—M.J.F. It must have referred to the penthouse, and chances were that the resident wanted privacy. An empty name slot on the second floor indicated a vacant apartment. 2B said

J. Vernon, so Vorigan deduced that the right side of the second floor was 2B, and J. Vernon was home. If like in most buildings, there was some sort of order as far as the labeling of apartments, perhaps under 2B was 1B?

1A said N. Nourie, but the left side was dark. Perhaps he was out. And even though there was no name next to 1B, the vampire's presence and furniture made it clear that the B side of the building was occupied. Perhaps he hadn't been able to put his name on the mailbox yet. Damn. Vorigan still didn't know his name.

3A was labeled G. Wyneth, and 3B said M. Morgaine. *Odd names. However, I'm not interested in seeing them anyway.*

He pushed the buzzer on the right, 3B. A female voice answered a millisecond later, as if waiting next to the intercom. "Do you have an appointment?"

"Er, uh, no. I was just wondering if—" A quick pop and silence let him know he'd been cut off.

"Damn." He should have had a simple speech rehearsed. But the query about an appointment threw him. All right. Time to try again.

He buzzed 3A and waited. Eventually, a lovely female voice drawled, "Who is it?"

"Hello. I'm here to see Mr. Vernon, but his bell doesn't seem to be working. Could you buzz me in?"

"Not by the hair of my chinny chin chin…"

"Excuse me?"

She giggled.

"His lights are on, and I know he's expecting me. If you would be so kind as to buzz me in, I could knock on his door."

"Well, we're not supposed to do that, but if the super's doorbell isn't working, he'll never know you're here. Y'all probably came to see the apartment for rent, right?"

"Yes, exactly. I—uh, I have an appointment."

"All right, sugar. Just mosey on up to the second floor. It's the door on your right."

That sounded enough like an invitation to satisfy the "rules." Once again, he wondered why vampires had to be invited in when a human burglar did not. Clearly the powers-that-be were prejudiced against the dark ones.

The outer door buzzed, indicating it was unlocked, and Vorigan snatched it open before the young woman could change her mind.

Once inside the hallway, he paused long enough to listen for doors opening. Hopefully the young woman hadn't decided to alert anyone to the presence of a stranger in their building. The halls remained quiet.

Fortunately the apartment he wanted was easy to locate. He knocked on the door marked 1B in brass letters, just to the right of the front door.

He waited—and waited.

No fuckin' way. The guy's a squatter? It was the only explanation. If he had no electricity and no name on the buzzer...

He knocked louder. "I know you're in there."

Finally the door flew open. The guy started to say something that sounded like, "Sorry," but he froze when he saw Vorigan. He was as handsome as Vorigan had remembered. But then, he would be. Vampires didn't age, so wrinkling skin and gray hair never entered the equation. *He should be grateful, right?*

As his protégé's handsome, almond eyes rounded,

Vorigan spoke quickly. "Hello, old friend, you may not remember me, but—"

"Oh, I know who you are all right." The soft brown eyes turned black and cold.

"You remember me? I'm flattered."

"Don't be," the guy said, and slammed the door.

"Oh, now, come on. Don't be like that. I'm here to help you."

The door didn't reopen. Vorigan knocked again, realizing his effort would probably be met with the same refusal, but he had to try.

Just then, he caught a lucky break. Someone was unlocking the outer door and wheeling a bicycle inside. Vorigan grabbed the door and opened it wide to help the young man in.

"Thanks," was all he said. He wheeled his bike to the apartment across the hall. He had to be the N. Nourie whose name was on the buzzer.

"Excuse me, I was wondering if I have the right apartment. I'm looking for a friend of mine who lives across the hall."

"Who, Sly?"

At last—a name. A weird name, but it was more than he'd had. "Yes. It looks like he's home, but he's not answering the door. Do you know him well?"

The stranger shrugged. "I know him well enough to know he can hear you. So, if he's not answering, he probably doesn't want to be disturbed. Now, if you'll excuse me…"

Vorigan grabbed the young man's arm. He tried to make eye contact, but blasé Mr. Nourie simply looked at his arm and said, "Take your hand off me."

Vorigan squeezed the arm, hoping the man would look up. He didn't.

"I said, get your friggin' hand off me, or I'll be forced to attack."

Vorigan laughed. "I'd like to see you try."

The young man heaved a bored sigh. "You asked for it."

Before Vorigan realized what was happening, the arm shrank, as did the man. A black bird easily slipped out of Vorigan's grasp and flew out of the limp shirt he was left holding. His eye received a hard poke.

"Ow! A fuckin' shapeshifter?" He swatted at the brazen bird but missed. When he opened the uninjured eye, he saw the damn thing flying up the stairwell.

He could easily follow. A giant leap and he'd make it to the first landing. But would the effort be worth it? He hadn't wanted to alert the other residents to his presence. If he left now, he could return without being recognized by the majority of them. Perhaps he could even try to rent that vacant apartment. It was a sensible plan.

So, holding the offended eye, which was already healing, he threw open the heavy oak door and trotted down the steps into the night.

———

Sly waited for his maker to leave. As soon as he saw the vampire disappear down the block, Sly tore upstairs to Morgaine's apartment and knocked frantically.

She opened the door with a concerned look on her face. "Sly, what's wrong?"

"May I come in?"

"Of course." Morgaine stepped aside and closed

the door behind him. "I've never seen you like this! What happened?"

"My maker just showed up at my door. My *apartment* door, which means someone invited him inside."

"It wasn't me... Someone buzzed, but he didn't have an appointment and I sensed he was up to no good, so I cut him off. Dear Lord and Lady! What did he want?"

"I didn't listen long enough to find out. No matter what he wants, I want nothing to do with him. He's a liar and a killer. He manipulated me and my wife all those years ago. He's responsible for her death and for Merry *almost* not making it into the world." He began to pace.

"Oh, Sly. I'm so sorry. Is there anything I can do?"

He halted and faced her. "Is there any way to un-invite a vampire once he's been let in?"

Morgaine bit her lower lip and looked at the floor. Eventually, she shook her head. "I don't know of anything that would work for sure, but I might know someone who can help. First we have to figure out who let him in."

"I guess the logical place to begin looking is with the residents. Probably someone who's here now. So, process of elimination..."

"I saw Merry and Jason go out earlier."

"Nathan just came in as the guy was leaving. If I'm not mistaken, he drove him out. I overheard a brief conversation—about me, heard a scuffle, and then the asshole yelled in pain. A moment later he shouted, 'Damn shapeshifter,' and ran down the steps."

"Good for Nathan. You're right. It sounds like he's in the clear. That leaves Jules and Gwyneth."

Sly raked his fingers through his hair. "I doubt the

super let a random visitor in since he's so concerned about excess foot traffic…"

"That leaves…"

At the same time, they glanced out Morgaine's door and said, "Gwyneth."

Morgaine left her apartment, marched across the hall, and banged on Gwyneth's door. A moment later, Gwyneth opened it and said, "What's got you upset now? Did they cancel *American Idol*?"

Morgaine jammed her fists on her hips. "Did you buzz someone in tonight? Someone you didn't know?"

Gwyneth paused before she answered. "You mean the guy who came to see Jules about the vacant apartment?"

"Oh, no! Gwyneth, that was no potential renter. You let in Sly's maker, and he's still after Sly even all these years later."

Gwyneth gasped and put both hands over her mouth. "Well, snap my granny's garters! I let in a vampire?"

"Yes, and now we have to find a way to reseal the building and keep him out. Or, more specifically, you do."

"Look, I had no idea he was a vampire… anyone could have done—"

"I'm not blaming you, Cousin. It's just more apt to work if the one who invited him in reseals the door."

"Oh, all right. I'll do whatever I need to. Just tell me what that is."

Morgaine let out a deep breath. "I was hoping you'd say that. I think you're going to have to make a trip to Salem."

"Salem, Mass.? Nuts. That's an hour bus ride, and…" She looked at Sly's face and didn't finish her sentence. "Of course I'll go. What do we need that we don't have here?"

"We need Laurie Cabot."

Gwyneth had called Laurie Cabot, the powerful Salem witch, and was granted a personal consultation. Thank the Goddess, Sly's confrontation with his maker had happened several days after Samhain and Laurie had time to see her. She'd head to the bus station early the next day, but meanwhile she and Morgaine had to do a locator spell to find Sly's maker. Later they'd devise a way to get rid of the slippery bastard—for good.

"It will have to be during the day so we'll have the advantage," Morgaine said.

"I can do the astral projection thing y'all taught me to get inside and figure out what his lair is like afore we go bustin' in."

"That's a good idea. But, first we have to find it. Hopefully he's there now and I'll astral project tomorrow when he won't see me."

"It's a good thing y'all can travel by astral projection. Otherwise you'd never see nothin' but the apartments and hallways of this here buildin' due to that agra... angora... well, hell. That thing what makes y'all afraid of going outside."

Morgaine didn't want to respond to that. "I'll grab my map and compass."

"I have mine right here..."

"No, I'll need to cleanse the tools after we expose them to evil energy. It's better if we use mine."

"How do y'all know he's evil?"

"Well, he sounds like a psychopath at the very least—the way he didn't care if Sly's wife and baby died. That's evil enough for me."

"Yeah. Now that you mention it…"

Gwyneth waited for Morgaine to gather the items for the locator spell and followed her down to Sly's apartment.

"Sly said he knocked on his door," Morgaine thought out loud. "So right outside his apartment we should find the largest concentration of the evil vampire's energy."

"Better warn Sly that we're out here. Y'all don't want to spook him. For all we know, he's got a loaded shotgun full of silver buckshot on the other side of that door."

Morgaine chuckled. "I doubt it."

"*I* would."

"Okay, okay. You're probably right that we should tell him what we're up to—just to be considerate." She knocked on Sly's door.

When he didn't open it right away, Gwyneth called out, "It's just little ol' us, Sly. No big baddies out here."

He opened the door and glanced around them up and down the hall. "Sorry, girls. I just had to be sure he hadn't compelled you."

"We understand," Morgaine said. "We'd like to do a locator spell to know where your maker's lair is. We need to do it here in the hallway in front of your door—while his energy is fresh."

Sly frowned. "I hate calling him my maker. I hate calling him 'my' anything, but we don't even know his name."

"We could call him Asshole," Morgaine said.

That made Sly laugh.

"And pretty soon," Gwyneth added, "A-hole won't be able to get into the building, don't you fret. Sorry, but I don't like to swear—except when doin' phone sex.

Tomorrow I'm headed off to Witch City—Salem, Mass. I'll find out what to do there."

Sly sighed. "Thanks. I appreciate any help you can give me."

Morgaine turned to Gwyneth and said, "We may be able to do more."

Sounding hopeful, Sly asked, "Like what?"

"I'll tell you what we discussed after this."

"Great. Mind if I watch my two favorite witches in action? Or is that against some kind of Wiccan rules?"

Gwyneth smiled. "It ain't agin' no rules I know of."

"It's fine if you watch, but..." Morgaine spread out the Boston street map. "Stay inside your apartment. I don't want to confuse your energy with his. Especially since I may have to call him 'the vampire' and the divine ones can be very literal."

"Sure. Of course." Sly took a step back but left his door open and stood there, riveted to the scene.

The women sat cross-legged on the cold floor on either side of the map. Morgaine placed the compass on their present location. As expected, it pointed due north.

They closed their eyes and held hands. Then took three deep breaths.

Together, they chanted, "God and Goddess, hear our plea. This intention bound shall be to cause no harm nor turn on me. As by your will, so mote it be."

Then Morgaine spoke alone. "Please use these tools to help us locate the source of evil energy that stood here tonight. We come here with pure hearts and a singular purpose. To protect ourselves, our neighbors, and especially our friend, Sylvestro Flores."

They let their eyes drift open and watched as the arrow on the tiny compass twitched at first. Finally, it moved slowly but with purpose in a singular direction. It stopped, pointing southeast.

Sly let out a whistle. "I wouldn't have believed it if I hadn't seen it myself."

Morgaine held up one hand to let him know they weren't finished. She slowly moved the compass toward the southeast. She stopped street by street until the arrow began to move again. She slowed her forward progress until the arrow spun.

"Gotcha!" Gwyneth clapped her hands.

Morgaine looked closer. "It's between Clarendon and Dartmouth Streets. I'd say it's close to the corner of Commonwealth and Clarendon. What's over there?"

Sly cocked his head. "A residential neighborhood, like this one. It's only a few blocks away. Haven't you explored your own neighborhood in the city?"

"Uh, I—uh, don't get out much," she said, her cheeks heating. As she rose from the floor, she deduced that he didn't know about her agoraphobia. "Thanks for your help, Gwyneth." She reached down and helped her cousin up. "I couldn't have done it without you."

Gwyneth waved away the compliment. "T'weren't nuthin'."

"It's nice to see you two getting along again," Sly said. "I heard you arguing the other night. I know you turned up the radio so I couldn't hear what it was about. It was none of my business, after all."

Gwyneth folded her arms. "I wish everyone would mind their own beeswax."

Morgaine squinted at her. "Don't start."

Sly cleared his throat. "Um, would you mind coming in? I think I need to tell you something."

Chapter 6

GWYNETH BREEZED INTO SLY'S APARTMENT, BUT Morgaine remained in the hall.

Sly wondered if she was hesitating because she was worried about what he had to say. "Aren't you coming, Morgaine?"

"I-it's awfully dark in there. Would you mind turning on the lights?"

"I'm afraid I never hooked up the electricity."

Gwyneth sighed. "Morgaine's afraid of the dark. Have you ever heard such a silly thing? A witch afraid of the dark?"

Morgaine folded her arms and glared in Gwyneth's general direction.

"Oh, come on. He might as well know since his place is *always* dark."

When Morgaine didn't respond, Gwyneth continued, "I can bring some candles down."

She let out a deep breath. "I can get some. And it isn't silly. It's an actual condition called nyctophobia."

"No need to leave," Sly said. "I have candles here. I'll be right back."

While he was in the kitchen, he overheard Morgaine say, "Did you have to tell him I'm afraid of the dark? Couldn't you have said it's harder for us to see in a dark apartment than it is for him?"

Gwyneth whispered, "Y'all are bein' silly. It's Sly,

after all. Not someone y'all have to impress. In fact, y'all might as well tell him about your agga... agriv... whatever that condition is called. The reason why I came up North to help y'all in the first place."

Morgaine whispered, "Agoraphobia. And, no thank you. I'd rather not tell anyone if I don't have to."

"Oh, for pity's sake. What are y'all gonna do if I'm not around and y'all need something from the store?"

"Wait until you get back."

Gwyneth let out a big sigh. "I do declare. Y'all are helpless as a Yankee at a grits-eatin' contest without me. Either get over this, or find someone else to help. I won't be here forever."

Sly returned to the living room with a couple of jar candles Roz had left for him. She'd said they weren't allowed to burn candles at the school, even in the resident apartments, but he suspected that was a ruse. The thought was appreciated and, as it turned out, handy as well.

The witches settled on the couch once illumination was flickering around the room. Sly placed the candles in the empty fireplace. "I hope you don't mind cinnamon scent."

Gwyneth smiled slyly. "We don't mind at all. Cinnamon inspires lust. Did y'all know that?"

Morgaine elbowed her.

Sly leaned against the mantel. "Well, that's sort of what I wanted to talk to you about."

Gwyneth's eyes popped. "A three-way?"

Sly almost burst out laughing. *Said with the innocence of a phone-sex actress.* "No. Actually, I thought before anyone got the wrong idea, I should explain why I'm not interested in a sexual relationship right now."

Gwyneth's face fell. "Y'all don't want a three-way? Y'all must be the only man on the planet who don't."

Morgaine leaned over and covered her face. "Where's a black hole when you need one," she mumbled.

Sly figured he'd better jump right into his explanation. "Gwyneth, Morgaine, you're both beautiful women, and any man would be lucky to have you—separately or, uh, together, but I'm afraid I just wouldn't feel right about that."

"Why? Because you're still hung up on your wife? She's been dead for about a zillion years," Gwyneth protested.

"Twenty-six. It's not that. I don't want to come between you two. I'd like to date one of you, but I'd hate to hurt the other's feelings. There's one thing I know about women—none of them want to feel like second best."

"Ain't that the truth," Gwyneth said. "So, which one of us are y'all choosin'?"

"Morgaine and I seem to have more of a connection, Gwyneth. I don't want to insult you, but I think she and I might really hit it off." Was he imagining it, or did Morgaine's eyes widen as if she were shocked?

Gwyneth rose. "Well, I won't be botherin' y'all anymore, Sly. I know when I'm beatin' a dead horse… so to speak."

Morgaine bolted upright. "Gwyneth, you'll still help Sly by going to Salem, right? I mean, he's still our friend—even if he doesn't want to have a romantic relationship."

"Of course. What do y'all take me for? I ain't someone who turns her back on a friend." She turned her pert little nose up. "I'll even help him set up and run the still, just like I promised."

Morgaine visibly relaxed. "Good."

"Well, Sly. I guess I'll mosey on. Y'all let me know if…"

Morgaine sent her a head shake.

"What? I was just gonna say—"

"I know what you were going to say."

Gwyneth threw her hands in the air and walked out muttering something about how folks have the right to change their minds.

Morgaine moved toward the door but stopped before she got there. "Did you mean what you said about me, or were you just saying that to discourage any more advances?"

Sly strolled over to her and took her hand. "I absolutely meant it."

She smiled shyly and then glanced up the stairs. "I'm sorry about my cousin. I don't know if she has the maturity to understand completely. I'll explain that it wasn't personal."

"Can you stay for a few minutes?"

"Sure."

Sly closed his door and led her back to his couch. "I don't have much to offer in the way of refreshment, but I do have that champagne Merry gave me. Would you like some?"

"I thought you didn't have a corkscrew."

He chuckled. "Champagne doesn't need a corkscrew. I was just making a joke. I didn't really want to open it then."

"But you do now?"

He tipped his head and shrugged. "Why not? Unless you don't want it since it's not chilled. No electricity means no refrigeration."

She hesitated a moment, then mirrored his gesture and said, "No, I don't mind. Sure. Why not?"

She waited on his couch while he strolled to the kitchen. He watched her stare into the candle flames as if in deep concentration.

This witch fascinated him. He could read the other one like a book. A book with two pages, including an index that referred every item to page one. *Not that she's shallow or anything…*

Morgaine was far more complex and raised questions he would love answered. Prying wasn't in his nature though.

He grabbed a couple of glasses and set them on the counter. Then he pulled the champagne out of the fridge and ripped off the foil paper to open the bottle. When the cork popped, Morgaine jumped.

"Are you okay, Morgaine?"

She chuckled. "Yeah. I just forgot about the pop when opening the champagne. I should have been ready for it."

Jeez, she has quite a startle reflex. Sly strolled over with the glasses and the open champagne bottle. "Are you nervous?"

"No. I was just… far away. Sometimes looking into flickering flames puts me right into a trance."

"I see." He poured a glass and handed it to her. "Is it all right if I sit next to you?"

"Of course, silly. You and I have sat next to each other before." She took a big sip of champagne.

In a few moments, she appeared relaxed and comfortable again. *Good.*

"Do you ever see things in the flames?" he asked.

"Yes. How did you know?"

"I've heard it's one way psychics scry. Is that the right word… scry?"

She grinned. "Yes. I'm surprised you knew that." Another long sip of champagne, and her posture relaxed some more.

He shrugged one shoulder. "I'm full of surprises. I spent many evenings at the Boston Public Library reading anything and everything that caught my interest." Setting down his wine glass, he rubbed his hands together, hoping the friction would take the chill off.

He took her hand in his. "I have a confession to make."

She sat up a little straighter. "Confession? I'm a priestess, not a priest. We don't generally hear confessions."

He laughed. "Not that kind of confession."

"Oh." She looked slightly embarrassed.

Her blush sent shivers straight to his loins, as had her earlier smile.

"Morgaine, I asked you to hang back because I'd like to get to know you better."

Her brows knit. "In what way? We've known each other a long time."

"I might be undead, but I'm not—dead. Know what I mean?"

She shook her head slowly. "No, I don't follow."

He rubbed her hand gently with his thumb. "I've noticed you in a whole new way recently. And it isn't because of the makeover. Well, maybe softening the hard edges opened up the idea of..." He struggled for the right words. Why, oh why, hadn't he rehearsed this speech?

"What is it, Sly? What have you noticed?"

"You're a caring, nurturing person. You're the one who thought of room-darkening shades for me. And even before that, you took such good care of me when

I hurt my fang. You didn't even tease me about my lisp until I was feeling better."

She dropped her head and blushed.

"Put it this way, I miss being married, and I think the right woman might be able to ease the loneliness."

She lifted her head and stared at him. "Are you coming on to me?"

He chuckled. "What I'm saying is that, for some reason I can't explain, I'm attracted to you. I wasn't looking for a relationship, and yet you confuse me. Well, that's not exactly right."

"My, I feel so flattered," she said, deadpan.

"Sorry. What I mean is, I've always liked you, but recently I've liked you more…"

"More than what? A kick in the head?"

He leaned back and stared at the ceiling. "I don't blame you. I'm making a mess of this."

"Would you mind if I tried something to clean up the mess? It might help."

"Sure. What did you have in mind?"

"Hold both of my hands and let me read you."

"You're not talking about mind reading, are you?"

She chuckled. "I wish. That would make things a whole lot easier. No, I'm just talking about gleaning whatever I can psychically. My mind forms pictures. Then maybe you can fill in the blanks."

He nodded. "What do I need to do?"

"Just hold both my hands and face me."

Sly adjusted his position on the couch and grasped both her hands. She did the same.

"Now lean forward until our foreheads are almost touching, and close your eyes."

He followed her directions. "Am I supposed to be thinking of something? Or should I try to empty my mind, like in meditation?"

"Just let it wander," she said softly. "Relax and let your mind go wherever it wants to." Her voice was almost hypnotic.

Despite hoping it wouldn't, his mind went straight to his cock. He pictured himself and Morgaine lying next to each other, facing each other, on the rug before the fire. Her long, blonde hair splayed out behind her, and then the romantic scene in his mind's eye rolled into an intimate embrace, a long kiss... *tenderness, that's it*.

That's what he felt for her. Tenderness. It wasn't exactly love, but more than like—a step between, perhaps.

His eyes drifted open. Hers were still closed, but she was smiling. Sly let go of one of her hands and cupped her jaw. The thought of compelling her to kiss him flitted across his mind. But no. He wanted her to want to. What good was it otherwise?

Her eyelids fluttered open. "Is everything all right?" Her lips remained slightly parted.

He didn't answer her, at least not verbally. He simply drew her to him and kissed her—tenderly. Thankfully, she responded in kind. They kissed for a good, long time.

—⁓—

Bundled in her black cape, Gwyneth rode the bus to Salem. It was still early morning, but Sly would be fast asleep by now. She didn't bother to say good-bye to Morgaine, either. How dare her cousin think she would let Sly down? She realized Morgaine was a lot sweeter on Sly than she was. Maybe he had picked the right cousin, after all. She'd find another guy, and then everyone would be happy. That's what she really wanted.

She was going not only to find out how to reseal the front door against vampires but also to ask Laurie Cabot if she'd heard about the vampire wine cure. Perhaps the high priestess knew the right ingredients. Then if she and Sly could figure out how to make the stuff, they could bottle it in the moonshine and it would keep practically forever.

Forever… that's what Sly was facing as a vampire. How could he stand the idea of going on without a woman's companionship—without sex—forever? Even if he did find someone to love again, it would be awful to know that person was going to grow old and die before his very eyes. She still couldn't imagine how he stood it, but the more she thought about it, the sorrier she felt for him. So, why didn't he see the obvious? A little casual sex could scratch the itch without the complications of a full-blown relationship.

Staring out the window, she watched as the bus made its way through the seaside town of Lynn, remembering the old adage she'd heard about the town: "Lynn, Lynn, city of sin, you never come out the way you went in." She didn't relax until Salem rolled into view.

A mix of old and new greeted her. Many small New England towns were the same. In Salem, fishing shacks and weathered boathouses along the water vied with a small but modern college campus only a few streets over. Prettier homes that may have belonged to ship captains back in the day were just a block away from cheaper digs like three-deckers.

Eventually, she made her way from the bus stop on foot around Pickering Wharf and found The Cat, The Crow, and The Crown, Laurie's shop. Gwyneth's nerves began to zing with excitement. How often does one get to visit with the most famous living witch in the whole country?

She strolled up the few steps to the front door. It was still early; otherwise the shop would be busy. Laurie's shop was a popular stop on Salem witch tours.

Suddenly, the scent of roses met her nose. Roses? In November? With her hand on the doorknob, Gwyneth glanced around. Inside the window, she saw roses twining across the bottom of the display shelf. How odd that she could smell them outside! Then again, look where she was. She was in the presence of the woman who made it snow in Salem, Massachusetts, *in July*.

The door opened as if of its own accord. Gwyneth realized she'd been standing there for quite some time. Perhaps the powerful witch had realized that her visitor needed a touch of encouragement.

She slowly entered the shop. Behind the counter stood a kind-looking young man. He smiled at Gwyneth immediately.

"Hi, there. I'm Jon. Are you Laurie's 10 a.m. consultation?"

"Yes, Gwyneth Wyatt."

At the sound of her name, a door to the far right opened. An attractive older woman with black and gray hair, and wearing a long black dress, strolled into the main shop area. "Merry meet, Gwyneth," the woman said.

"Are—are y'all *her*?"

The woman smiled. "I'm Laurie Cabot."

"Should I bow or kiss your ring or anythin'?"

Laurie stared at her a moment. Perhaps she needed to know if Gwyneth was sincere. She imagined the woman must take some ridicule from ignorant tourists.

"I'm not bein' a smart ass or anythin'…"

"We're all sovereign, Gwyneth. Please come into my sacred space."

Light-headed, she followed Laurie into the small room from which she had emerged. Sweet-smelling incense burned in a brass censor. Crystals decorated the table, and a witch cord hung down one wall. Gwyneth had made one and hung it in her kitchen, where she did most of her spells. Each was a nine-foot braided cord with nine knots, every one holding a symbol of the spell it represented.

The rest of the room was just as fascinating. A portrait of a black cat hung on the back wall. Laurie's armchair, covered in gold brocade, sat kitty-corner to the left with a hand-painted table in front of it. Whimsical *Alice in Wonderland* colored-ink drawings and a white rabbit statue added to the decor. Gwyneth imagined the tourists knew what Alice felt like in a place like this.

Of all things, a pink Christmas stocking lay against the back of Laurie's chair. Seriously? The greatest Wiccan of modern times celebrates Christmas and puts a stocking out this early? Maybe it was just a suggestion to the tourists that they could buy their Christmas gifts at the store. It sold everything from jewelry to homemade incense, spell kits, and candles.

"Y'all must do a lot of spells."

"Wicca is not only a religion, it's an art and a science. As with any art form, practice improves one's results."

"Pardon me for sayin', but I think y'all must be an expert by now."

Laurie smiled. "Living Wicca includes practicing our craft even after it becomes second nature. As long as we're alive, we don't have to stop growing."

Gwyneth nodded slowly. This sage woman seemed like Morgaine in some ways. Maybe she should listen to her cousin a little better in the future.

Laurie gathered a few ingredients and laid them on the table. A black candle in the shape of a man, a package of powder labeled "Vampire Slayer," and some iron nails.

"Have you made a protection potion yet, Gwyneth?"

"Yes, ma'am. That's the first thing my cousin Morgaine taught me to make for myself. Even with all that iron powder in it, the stuff stays mixed and doesn't settle to the bottom of the jar. That's when I knew magic was real."

"Good. You'll need to use your protection potion as you would normally to protect yourself while working with any magic and also on the door as you reseal it against the vampire. Do you know his name?"

"No, ma'am. Even our friend who he's after don't know his real name, yet. We just call him Sly's Maker for now—or Asshole."

Laurie nodded. "That will have to do. If in the meantime, you discover any details like his name or date of birth, etch those on this wax figure." She handed Gwyneth the black wax doll.

"I've used a doll like this in bindin' spells. Is that the spell what y'all recommend for a vampire?"

"That and more. Like these iron nails for your entrance. You can't overuse protection magick when it comes to vampires."

Gwyneth shifted uncomfortably. "Now, that brings up an itty-bitty problem."

Laurie cocked her head, listening.

"Our friend Sly—the one we're protecting... He's a vampire too."

"Oh, dear."

"But he's a good un'."

"Then it'll be doubly important to specify on the wax figure exactly who you mean to bind."

"I understand. 'Cause if we just said, 'Bind the vampire,' the powers-that-be could get the wrong one."

"Exactly. It seems as if you've learned to word your spells well. Have you ever had one backfire when you worded it incorrectly?"

Gwyneth tried not to laugh remembering some of her early blunders. "Yes, indeedy. I don't know if y'all can tell, but I'm from the South."

Laurie smiled and nodded.

"Well, we sometimes have colorful ways of puttin' things. It's just how we talk, but there was this once I was really mad and I called my ex-boyfriend a flea-bitten dog."

"Oh, dear. Let me guess... you witnessed him scratching his skin raw?"

Gwyneth couldn't hold it back any longer. She burst out laughing. "How did y'all know? He even took a flea bath!"

"I teach my students to avoid using magick in anger. Careless words can easily backfire on the witch."

"Yeah, I think that happened—even with all my

self-protection stuff. I couldn't get the smell of wet dog out of my nose for a solid week."

Laurie covered her mouth as if trying to hide a smile. Eventually, she cleared her throat and refocused the conversation. "Could your friend Sly be mistaken for someone called 'Maker' by anyone who doesn't know him?"

"He never made another vampire. I'm not sure if makin' other stuff counts. I know he made a daughter before he was turned."

"Better be specific and only refer to the wax figure as 'the vampire Sly's vampire maker' until you find out his real name. If your friend is also barred from the residence, you'll know it wasn't enough of a differentiation."

"And what would we do in that case?"

Laurie shrugged. "Simply invite him in again."

"Oh." Gwyneth hit her head with the heel of her hand. "Duh."

Chapter 7

"This better work," Morgaine muttered.

Gwyneth, who had been kneeling by the front door, rose and placed a hand on her hip. "Or what?"

"Or Sly will probably be afraid to leave his apartment."

Gwyneth huffed and returned to her work. She had made the ointment according to Laurie's directions and was now filling the cracks around the door with it like caulk. "Cain't one vampire settle things with another vampire in a fair fight?"

"Something tells me Sly would be the only one fighting fair. Besides, he was made twenty-six years ago and is considered a child in the vampire world."

In some ways, Gwyneth struck Morgaine as a child in the witches' world. Since Gwyneth was five years younger and hadn't been practicing Wicca seriously until she moved to Boston, Morgaine had felt it her responsibility to help her cousin catch up.

"How old is his maker?"

"I have no idea, but Sly seems to think he's ancient. I think some vampires lose their humanity over time, and this one seems to have none left."

"I wish I was as psychic as y'all, Morgaine. I shoulda known he was evil while I was speakin' to him—even over the intercom."

"It's the same principle for witches. The longer we practice, the more psychic we become. I think everyone is psychic to an extent, but some try to develop it and some don't. You just haven't been at it as long as I have."

"Yeah, I wasted a few too many years trying to get dear, drunk Dwayne off his inebriated ass. Thank the Goddess I didn't marry him."

"I don't think anything is wasted, Gwyneth. You did your best to help him, but some people are determined to self-destruct. You can feel good about your role in that relationship. You did everything you could. It was time to walk away."

Morgaine thought about how she might take her own advice. She had taught Gwyneth as much as she could for as long as the younger witch was willing to learn. But when the willingness had stopped, so had the learning.

"Yeah, an' I thought I was helpin' Dwayne for a while."

"When did you know it was hopeless?"

Gwyneth finished spreading the ointment around the door and wiped her right hand on a towel. "Long about the time he came home drunk with another drunk woman and told me to shove over so he'd have room to fuck her right next to me. Said he was tired of sneakin' around."

Morgaine shook her head. "You don't deserve that, Gwyneth. You deserve someone who loves you so much he wouldn't want to be with anyone else."

"I know that—*now*. Do y'all think Sly feels that way about you?"

Morgaine shrugged. "I don't know. It's too soon to tell." *If not now, maybe in time.*

"Well, let's knock on his door and get him to help us with that still. There's no way I can open that heavy secret door all by myself."

—␣␣—

"Are you sure this is what you want to do?" Morgaine asked. It was a new-moon night, and the candle she held made only a dent in the darkness as it flickered in the drafty basement air.

Sly barely heard her as he concentrated on the still Gwyneth was putting together. With the false wall opened up and the windows cracked, everything seemed safe enough… as long as no one called the health department. Sly pulled a large spider web out of the way and wiped his hand on a rag they'd brought down to catch spills.

"I haven't come up with any better ideas yet," he said absently. "Have you?"

Morgaine let out a long sigh. "No."

Gwyneth stuck out her hand. "Sly, honey, hand me that wrench, please."

Sly picked up the tool from the floor and gave it to Gwyneth. "Are you sure I can't do more to help?"

"We're almost done, sugar." She tightened the last of the bolts. "Speakin' of sugar, is everything set as far as the mash is concerned?"

"I followed your directions to the letter." He reached down and helped her up. "Has it fermented long enough?"

Her long black skirt was covered with dirt, dust, and who knew what else. She brushed it off and blew a few strands of dusty red hair out of her face. "Yep. Like I said, this recipe is quick."

Morgaine stepped back with one hand on her hip. "Now what?"

"Now we take this still for a spin," Gwyneth said excitedly. "Let's go upstairs and get the mash Sly made up.

My mouth's already waterin' for some good ol' home brew. This is the smoothest whiskey you'll ever taste."

"Don't forget we're trying to adapt the vampire wine cure we've heard about," Morgaine reminded her.

"But Laurie had never heard o' that."

Sly smiled at Morgaine. He hoped she wasn't jealous of her younger cousin anymore. He'd spent a lot of time with Morgaine and had done his best to put those fears to rest.

"Of course I haven't forgot. Have y'all discovered what the secret ingredient is?"

"Um, no. Not yet."

Gwyneth elbowed Morgaine out of the way and headed toward the stairs. "Then don't go givin' me no warnin's."

"I wasn't giving you a warning. I was giving you a reminder."

"Y'all was naggin' like a preacher gettin' the town drunk to church."

"Ladies," Sly interrupted. "Let's keep our eyes on the prize. First a drinkable batch of whiskey and possibly later a cure for vampirism."

Morgaine sighed. "You're right. I'm getting ahead of myself."

As the three of them traipsed up the stairs to Sly's apartment, Gwyneth whispered, "Can y'all see any of the sludge I painted around the front door? The last thing I want is for someone to come along and wash it off before it sets."

Morgaine said, "I'll take a closer look, but I thought you did a good job with it this afternoon."

Sly glanced at the door frame, which appeared to

glow faintly around the edges. "Can either of you see that? It's glowing."

"I can't see anything. It seems to have dried clear. We need to test it though," Morgaine said.

"Oh, that's right. I plumb forgot. Sly?"

"Uh-oh. What do I need to do?"

Gwyneth smiled. "Nothin' much. Just mosey on outside and see if y'all can get back in."

Something sounded suspicious. "What do you expect will happen?"

"Oh, probably nothin'. We just need to be here in case y'all need to be invited back in again."

"Are you saying you might have sealed me out of my own building?"

Gwyneth shrugged.

Morgaine blew out the candle and said, "We don't know the vampire's name, so Gwyneth decided to seal it against all vampires who don't live here. But sometimes the powers-that-be can be very literal. And since you're not alive…"

Sly finished her thought in his head. "Got it. So what happens if I can't get back in?"

"We just invite y'all in again."

"Are you sure nothing else will happen? I mean, I won't burst into flames if I try to walk through your barrier or anything?"

"Heavens no!" Gwyneth chuckled. "We're not firebugs."

"But you said you bought something called Vampire Slayer powder."

"I didn't use that on the door, silly. Y'all have to come and go. I'm saving that for your maker, if and when we can find him."

"I thought you already found him."

"We think so, but one of us," she glared at Morgaine, "has to go and look at the place in person."

"We agreed I'd astral project and Gwyneth would walk over there during the day. We can corroborate what we find later."

"So, are y'all gonna get over the willies or what, Sly? Go outside and come back in again. Morgaine, I'll deal with you tomorrow."

"Deal with me?" Morgaine's eyes grew a little larger, and Sly figured it was time to distract them quickly.

"Okay, here I go." He yanked open the door and stepped outside, letting the door shut. Then he reached into his pocket, pulled out his key, and unlocked the door. "So far, so good."

Sly took a giant step and slammed into an invisible barrier. "Ouch!"

Both women covered their mouths.

"Oops," Gwyneth said. "Sorry 'bout that."

"Well at least we know it works," Sly muttered.

"Please come in, Sly." Morgaine stretched out her hand. He grasped it and slowly stepped into the building with no more trouble than a human would have. "Whew."

"1 did it, Morgaine!" Gwyneth was so pleased with herself that she hugged her cousin. And Sly could tell that Morgaine was genuinely thrilled.

"Yes, you did. Did you have any doubts?"

"A little one, maybe. I was sure he wouldn't catch afire, but I was a bit worried he'd maybe get singed."

"Now you tell me? Forget it, I'm fine, and you've redeemed yourself," Sly said. Gwyneth's face fell, and he was immediately sorry he'd put it that way. He'd

have to remember how powerful these women were—
and that one of them had something called Vampire
Slayer powder!

———*w*———

The next morning, Morgaine crossed the hall to
Gwyneth's apartment. Before she knocked on the door,
she said a small incantation. It was more of a prayer to
the Goddess for help and direction. Then she knocked
and waited.

Gwyneth opened the door looking well rested and
refreshed. Good. She hoped her cousin would be in a
receptive mood.

"Mornin', Morgaine. Would y'all like to come in?"

"Please."

Gwyneth stepped aside, and Morgaine crossed to the
couch in Gwyneth's living room. "Is Chad here?"

Gwyneth cocked her head. "Chad?"

"Hello, ladies. Is there something I can do for you?"

"Uh, yes." Morgaine said nervously. "Can you give
us a few minutes alone?"

"You want to kick me out of my own apartment?"

"No. We can go to my place if you'd rather not leave."

"In other words, you just don't want me eavesdropping."

"Correct."

An audible sigh suggested that Chad was fed up.
*"What makes you think I won't just follow you and listen
in without telling you?"*

"Because I'm respectfully asking that you don't."

Another loud sigh. *"Oh, all right. You're taking all
the fun out of it anyway. I'll go see what Nathan's up to."*

"Thanks, Chad."

Gwyneth's expression turned to one of concern. "What's wrong, Morgaine? Y'all look like a pup that was left behind when the family went for a Sunday drive."

"I'm okay. I've just been thinking…"

"Oh. Well, that can't be good. Y'all want a glass of sweet tea?"

"No, thanks. I'd just like to talk to you for a little while."

"Of course." Gwyneth sat on the sofa next to her cousin. "What's got y'all thinkin'?"

"A couple of things. First, you know how much I rely on you for everything. It sounds as if you're starting to resent it."

"I'm sorry, darlin'. I don't mean to sound that way. I just worry about y'all. What if something happened to me? Back when Konrad and Roz lived here, I know y'all felt safe with them, but now they're gone."

Morgaine looked at her lap. "I know. I—oh, Goddess… This isn't easy. I don't want you to get mad."

"Spit it out, Cousin. I'm more apt to get mad if y'all keep dancing around the back door."

"I need to help Sly… and not just as a friend. But I need your help. Do you know what I mean?"

Gwyneth sat up straighter. "Oh! Y'all are sweet on Sly… More than a little, by the sounds of it. But what about his feelings for his wife? Oh, no wonder you look sadder than a broken swing."

Morgaine leaned back and stared at the ceiling. *Oh well, here goes nothing.* "He kissed me."

Gwyneth cocked her head. "Huh?"

"I know. I was confused too."

Gwyneth stood abruptly and balled her fists. "Well, now I know why y'all thought I'd get mad. But I'm not mad at y'all, Cousin. I'm mad at him. How dare he say all that stuff and then lead y'all on?"

"I-I don't think he's leading me on. Look, if you'll sit down and try to stay calm for a few minutes, maybe I can explain it."

Gwyneth dropped back down onto the sofa. "Fine. Try to explain, 'cause it sure don't make no sense to me."

"After you went back upstairs the other night, I stayed a little longer."

"I noticed that. I was thinkin' that was a good sign. It meant you were feelin' okay outside your comfort zone—especially seein' as how his place is always so damn dark."

Morgaine smiled. "Yeah, we talked about how we enjoyed spending time together, even though there's only a window of a few hours in the evening when we're both awake."

"And that's when he kissed ya?"

"No. Yes. I mean, after that."

"So what kind of kiss was it? Was it a peck, like kissin' Uncle Clarence?"

Morgaine shook her head.

Gwyneth's eyes widened. "A passionate tongue kiss?"

"Uh…" Morgaine shrugged. "It was nice. Soft. Sweet. Kind. Loving…"

Gwyneth stood again. "Then he *did* lead y'all on. I have a mind to go down there and—"

"No!" Morgaine put her hand on Gwyneth's arm. "Please, sit down. There's more I want to say."

Gwyneth lowered herself slowly and perched on the edge of the couch, apparently ready to jump up again at any second if she didn't like the way the conversation was going.

"We promised to help Sly, and I want to. Very much. I think if he and I keep getting to know each other better, maybe it will grow into something, and then you won't always be stuck with me. You have all kinds of opportunities to find nice guys. You can go out and socialize. You're *so* beautiful—"

Gwyneth raised her hand. "Y'all can stop now. I know what you're sayin'."

Morgaine studied her hopefully. It was hard to read what Gwyneth meant by that from her expression. "And?"

"And, I'll help. If y'all want Sly, I can teach y'all about flirtin' so he gets the message without feelin' like he's been hit over the head with a brick."

Morgaine laughed. "I wasn't asking you to help me flirt. I have the feeling he likes that I don't do that. I want your help finding a way to bring Sly back to the land of the living. If that means finding that cure for vampirism, I'll need your help. If that means defeating his maker, I'll need your help. Basically, whatever we do to help him will be dangerous, but if we do it together, we have a chance."

"And if there's a chance for more, y'all would like to be with him?"

"Yes."

"And y'all aren't scared?"

"I'm terrified."

Gwyneth smiled. "Good."

"Good that I'm terrified?"

"Good that y'all are terrified and willin' to try anyway." She nodded once, firmly. "I'm in. Now what do we do first?"

"Let's see if we can find his maker now that it's daylight. Bring your camera."

"Y'all are goin' with me? I thought I was goin' alone and y'all would astral project."

"No. If I want to be Sly's girlfriend, I have to stick my neck out for him. And if you're kind enough to help me, I need to be there to protect you."

Gwyneth put her arms around Morgaine and hugged her. "I always knew this day would come. I'm prouder of y'all than I'd be of a prize pig at the fair—oh, sorry. I didn't mean that to sound like I was comparing you to a pig. Y'all know what I mean."

Morgaine grinned. "Yes, I know."

—∿∿—

The witches located the basement apartment in the block where their compass had pointed. Morgaine set down her heavy canvas bag on the sidewalk.

Gwyneth studied the mailbox. "V. Malvant. That's a strange name."

Morgaine shivered and hugged herself. "There's something evil in there. I can feel a dark, twisted energy. Can you?"

Gwyneth closed her eyes. "Eek… now that y'all mention it, yeah. It's like barbed wire. All sharp and twisted."

Morgaine nodded and lowered her voice. "We need to be careful. Even though he should be completely unconscious and vulnerable, nothing says he might not have some kind of magickal alarm system."

"So that's why we're gonna astral project to get in there, right?"

"We can do that first, but eventually we'll have to find a physical way in. The more we know about him and his lair, the better."

"Know thine enemy an' all that, right?"

"Right. Now, according to the compass, there's an alley entrance too. When we actually break in, we should probably do it from the alley. I'm thinking we should astral project from there too. That way we'll see exactly what we're getting into."

"So, let's git back there so we can take him from behind. Ugh, that don't sound right."

"We're attacking his flank. Does that sound better?"

Gwyneth breathed a sigh of relief. "Much better."

"Can you take the bag? My hands are sweating."

Gwyneth hefted the heavy bag with an "Oomph," and the two women strolled to the side street and around the corner. As they entered the alley, Morgaine smelled garbage and urine. *Disgusting*. She stopped and her chest fluttered. *Maybe this was a bad idea*.

Their alley didn't smell like that. Of course, they'd had a werewolf and a vampire guarding the place for several years.

She reflected on how weird that was. She was more afraid of open spaces and panic attacks than she was of a werewolf and a vampire. Truth be told, she'd feel a whole lot better with her vampire and werewolf friends guarding her right now. At least it wasn't dark out, and she trusted her cousin to get her back to her own apartment safely in case she had to flee. She took a few deep breaths.

Since all the buildings on the block were connected, they counted the same number of buildings along the back and matched up the architecture. By that process, they had no difficulty finding the maker's apartment again. He had only one small barred window. A few steps led up to the back door. Morgaine felt the same malevolent energy, but she didn't detect any kind of magickal protection. Thank the Goddess.

"Back in the day, this musta been the servant's entrance," Gwyneth said.

"You're probably right. The back of the building was where the kitchen was usually located, with the parlor in front."

"That must be why the alley smells like garbage. But nothin' excuses the outhouse smell. I'm guessin' that might be from a homeless person."

"In this neighborhood?"

"They're all over the city, Morgaine. If I was homeless and had my druthers, I'd keep my cardboard box in a nice area like this."

Morgaine shuddered. "I can't imagine it."

"That's your agga… agriv…"

"Agoraphobia."

"Yeah, that."

Morgaine nodded but tried not to dwell on the thought. They had a job to do, and she wouldn't be able to do it if she stood there frozen.

She reached out and grabbed Gwyneth's hand. "I need your strength, right now."

Gwyneth squeezed Morgaine's fingers. "You got it, Cousin. It's time we get this cow to town."

"Huh?"

"Y'all would say, 'Get this show on the road,' I think."

"Oh. Yeah, let's do that."

Gwyneth shrugged the bag off her shoulder, and it lay in the alley. "Don't y'all want me to go alone first?"

Morgaine gulped and shook her head. "No. I can do

this." She squared her shoulders, closed her eyes, breathed deeply a few times, and went into her trance. She let her spirit soar above her body. Still holding Gwyneth's hand, she inserted her energy into the building.

Once inside, she stood in a hallway with a view of the front door and a banister to the right. A door on her immediate right probably led to the cellar. The building was set up much like her own, except narrower. Probably only a single-family home with a basement apartment.

She moved through the door to the right. Suddenly Morgaine froze. She was in total darkness. Her throat constricted.

I...I can't do this! Morgaine ripped her spirit out of the building and back into her body so fast her head spun. She tried to run, but her feet wouldn't move. Somehow, she lost her balance, let go of Gwyneth's hand, and fell on her ass. "Dear Lord and Lady!"

"I do declare!" Gwyneth stood over Morgaine as her cousin breathed into a paper bag. Gwyneth had helped Morgaine over to the next apartment's concrete steps, and they were partially hidden from the maker's apartment by a parked car.

Morgaine's breathing finally slowed and she said, "I felt a panic attack coming on. What did you want me to do? Lose my shit in there?"

"You wasn't even in there. Not for real. It woulda made a mess in your panties though."

Morgaine rolled her eyes. "It's just an expression."

"Just tell yourself it's not real."

"It was real enough. Look, sometimes I have panic

attacks for no goddamn reason at all. Suddenly I'm in a vampire lair in total blackness—and, surprise, surprise, I freak out. You would've too."

"Nope. I didn't inherit the freak-out gene. Didn't y'all say your mamma thought she was goin' crazy a few times?"

"Yeah." Morgaine hung her head. "That's why she moved to a big city. Too many small-town people knew her business."

Gwyneth sat beside Morgaine on the steps. She patted Morgaine's arm as if comforting a child. "Don't pay it no never mind. Y'all are perfectly safe. Ya hear?"

"I-I guess so."

Gwyneth let out a big sigh. "So, this is kind of a pickle. If all went well with the astral projection and there was no magickal alarms or booby traps, we was plannin' on going in for real."

"I don't think that'll happen."

"Why not? I can understand y'all not wantin' to, but *I* can still go."

Morgaine grabbed her wrist. "You can't go in there by yourself! That's really crazy."

"I'll be fine. As long as it's daylight, he's dead to the world... so to speak. Plus, we lugged all these supplies down here. Flashlights, candles, matches, a wooden stake, a camera..."

"So? We'll just take them back home."

"Do y'all really want to give up on Sly? 'Cause if you do, I doubt his maker—or V. Malvant, as we now know he's called—will give up."

Morgaine braced her elbows on her knees and covered her head with her hands as if she was expecting bombs overhead.

Gwyneth sat quietly and let that sink in for a bit.

At last, Morgaine sighed. "I'd still like to help Sly, but…"

"But what? Y'all are a powerful witch, Morgaine. If anythin', V. Malvant should be afraid of *you*!"

Morgaine chuckled. "Yeah, and a few minutes ago the big, powerful witch was breathing into a paper bag."

"Look, y'all can stand outside with the door open, and I can go inside. If anything happens you can hear me. But nothin's gonna happen!"

"I can't let you go alone."

"Then are we both goin' in, or are we givin' up?"

Morgaine glanced over at the next apartment where the vampire lay dormant. "I'll try it. If I start to flip out—"

"Y'all won't flip out because there are only two options. Help Sly, or don't help Sly. And if he means so much to y'all, we'll help him."

"He means the world to me, but I don't get why *you're* doing this."

"Because *you* mean the world to *me*. Even though we've had our differences, we're kin. And I want y'all to be happy."

Morgaine smiled at her. "I love you, Gwyneth. You know that, right?"

"A' course I do. And I love y'all too, knucklebrain."

Chapter 8

JULES VERNON GLANCED OUT THE WINDOW AND spotted the pretty Asian woman he had been expecting. While she pulled up to the curb in the moving van, he hopped up onto the ledge of his giant fish tank and watched the water sluice off his tail. As soon as his lower body shifted back to legs, he jumped down, grabbed the towel on the shelf beside him, dried off, and put on his robe.

Watching her out the window again, he was happy to see Lillian Chou helping the movers carry some of her things upstairs to her new apartment. Good. She wasn't lazy. Perhaps she wouldn't be high maintenance and could fix a leaky faucet herself.

He strode to the bedroom to get dressed so he could greet her and fill her in on some of the finer points of living in their neighborhood.

So far, Jules had been lucky. Nothing in the old building had broken, and no one had needed much of anything. But to get the job as the building's super, he'd had to pretend to be handy. God forbid something really went wrong.

She had received her keys from him when she'd seen the place and given him the security deposit and first month's rent in lovely, spendable cash. How was he supposed to check references with a thick wad of crisp Benjamins in front of him? Besides, she looked nice enough. Who needed a background check when the babe had a great backside?

Jules zipped up his blue jeans and threw on a dark green T-shirt that brought out the color of his green eyes. Women often commented on his eyes.

A quick look in the mirror, a fluff of his black hair, and he was ready to greet his new tenant. Almost... he grabbed the air freshener to mask the fishy smell in his apartment and sprayed it all around like a cloud of perfume. Just for good measure, he walked through it and scented himself with April freshness.

When he opened his door to the hallway, he had to wait for the movers to struggle by with her heavy wrought-iron bed. It reminded him of some of the balcony railings in New Orleans. Ornate scrolls imparted a feminine vibe. He fantasized himself handcuffed to those iron rails and almost chuckled. He was such a naughty fish.

Lillian, or Lily, as she had told him to call her, was hauling a suitcase up the stairs, so Jules trotted down to meet her and take it up the rest of the way.

"Hello, Lily. Welcome."

"Oh, thank you so much, Jules," she said when he grasped the heavy bag. "I am paying the movers by the hour, so I save money by helping."

She had a hint of an Asian accent, but her English was quite good. She said she had lived in San Francisco for several years before moving to Boston.

"So, it's just you and the movers? No friends or family signed up to help today?"

"No. My family is all in San Francisco. I'm so new to this city I have no friends and only one or two potential clients, so I had to hire help."

"Listen, I may have forgotten to tell you something important when you came to look at the place. Our landlord is a recognizable celebrity and doesn't want his whereabouts known."

"A celebrity? Who is he? A rock star?"

"No, bigger than that—at least in Boston. It's Jason Falco."

"Who's that?"

Jules's eyebrows shot up. "Only the star pitcher of the Boston Bullets."

"…and my son-in-law," Sly added as he ascended the stairs silently.

Jules startled. "Where did you come from?"

"More importantly," Sly said, "where did *she* come from?"

Lily flushed bright red. Jules thought he saw a wisp of steam waft from her ears.

"This is our new tenant, Lillian Chou. She goes by Lily. And, Lily, this is Sly."

Eventually, Lily recovered enough to nod in acknowledgment and asked, "So, Mr. Falco lives in the building?"

"Yes, in the penthouse. You might not see him very often," Sly said.

Jules shifted his weight from foot to foot. "He rides the elevator to the first floor and exits out the back usually. But if a lot of people come and go all the time, he's more apt to be discovered and recognized, and then his nice private home could become a media magnet. Just do me a favor and keep visitors to a minimum."

"My clients come one at a time, and I try not to have too many, but I do work from home. I hope that's not a problem."

"No, it shouldn't be as long as they don't hang around in the hallways."

"Aw, no." She laughed. "They never hang around."

"Good," Sly said.

"Everything should go well then. Where do you want your suitcase?"

"In the bedroom is fine."

"Nice to meet you, Lily." Sly waved and left as silently as he'd come.

Jules lugged the bag to the bedroom and set it next to the queen-size mattress. "Well, I guess I'll leave you to it. I just wanted to welcome you to the building." He stuck out his hand, and she looked at it hesitantly.

Eventually, she took it in her hot fingers and gave it a quick shake. *Cripes, she's scorching.* And he didn't mean that in a good way. Jogging across the hall, he couldn't wait to plunge his hand into his cool saltwater tank.

Morgaine felt immensely better. Stronger. Her panic attack had lasted only five minutes. Sometimes the attacks went on for half an hour and she felt like she was dying. Sweating, chest pains, the whole nine yards. Just now, even with the stress of invading a vampire's lair, her symptoms were fairly mild and short lived.

She stood, lifted her canvas bag, and said, "For Sly."

Gwyneth nodded. "For Sly."

They marched over to the vampire's apartment again. Morgaine set the bag down and fished out what she needed. She handed Gwyneth the candelabra and a stake. She set the camera on the stoop and grabbed the flashlight and matches, plus a powder meant to unlock doors.

Gwyneth stood to the side while Morgaine positioned herself in front of the lock. She shook some of the powder into her hand, then blew it right into the keyhole. Standing, she closed her eyes, muttered her incantation, and heard a soft click. The door opened a couple of inches on its own.

"I'll be jiggered," Gwyneth whispered.

Morgaine put her finger to her lips, tucked the small plastic bag of powder into her pocket, then picked up the camera, turned on the flashlight, and crept inside.

Gwyneth followed silently.

Morgaine repeated the process at the door just inside, the one they had determined would lead to the vampire's basement lair. After that door softly clicked open, Morgaine took the matches and lit Gwyneth's candelabra.

Gwyneth pointed to herself and then to the door, meaning that she wanted to go first. Morgaine shook her head.

Gwyneth nodded frantically, as if insisting.

Morgaine finally acquiesced and stood aside. She supposed Gwyneth didn't want to be mowed down like the last standing pin in a bowling alley in case Morgaine decided to run. Paralysis was more likely. If she lost her nerve again, Gwyneth might have to yank her out of there. *Don't think about that. Think about Sly. This undead asshole wants to mess with my possible, maybe, future boyfriend. Well, screw him!*

Morgaine took the first few steps down to the basement apartment. The air was warm, unlike Sly's unheated place. Other than hers and Gwyneth's quiet footfalls, all was silent. At the base of the stairs, an opening to the right revealed a tiny European-style kitchen. All of the appliances and counter space lined one side. She bypassed that and continued down the hall until thick carpet replaced the hardwood under her feet.

Her flashlight highlighted certain spots, but when Gwyneth's candelabra entered the room, Morgaine saw the entire luxurious living room. They stood on a large, expensive-looking Oriental rug over dark hardwood floors. Gothic decor was evident, along with a touch of elegance. The room boasted Victorian velvet-covered furniture—not imitation stuff, either. Morgaine recognized the large, round ottoman as similar in style and quality to the one in the private sitting room at the Isabella Stewart Gardner Museum.

Anger boiled under her skin to think about this jerk living in opulence while Sly had hidden behind a wall in a cold cellar for years. Even now, Sly lived a Spartan existence by comparison, but he didn't seem to mind. Perhaps she shouldn't have encouraged him to move into the first-floor apartment after all. Maybe this guy wouldn't have discovered Sly if he'd stayed in his hidey-hole. But that was a moot point. He *had* located him, and Sly wouldn't run from his daughter's building—even for his own self-preservation.

Pictures. She needed pictures to remember the layout when all three of them returned to stake Sly's stalker. *If* they could find and bottle the cure for Sly's vampirism.

Morgaine found the light switch and flicked it on. She quickly took several shots of the apartment from the back all the way to the front door. A small corridor led back to two closed doors. Probably the bedroom and bath. She hoped a camera flash or turning on a light wouldn't wake the undead. Probably not, but the anxiety she was trying to ignore invaded the pit of her stomach and she wanted to run.

She looked to Gwyneth and pointed to the back entrance. Gwyneth nodded and turned around. As Morgaine was passing the kitchen, something caught her eye. A map of the city on a bulletin board. She crept closer to take a better look. Pins were stuck in a few places, most of them near or on their block. Then she saw something else. A slip of paper with hearts all over it, pointing right at their corner.

Dear Goddess. I knew I might not be the only one who liked Sly, but I never thought my competition would be a vampire!

Suddenly thoughts of losing Sly to her cousin paled in comparison to what a vampire might do to take him away from her. Prickles crawled up the back of Morgaine's neck. She zoomed around Gwyneth, forgot about hitting the light switch as she passed it, and tore up the stairs.

In Morgaine's apartment, the witches uploaded the pictures of V. Malvant's lair to Gwyneth's laptop. They'd show them to Sly as soon as the sun went down.

"Don't y'all need to call your friend in New York about that wine he makes to cure vampires?"

"I'll call Mikhail now." Morgaine flipped through her Rolodex. "How's the new mash coming?"

"I'm sorry about gittin' the recipe wrong the first time. It should be ready for the still tomorrow. I'll check it afore I pour it."

"Good. If he can tell us the secret ingredient, we can try it in the very first batch!"

"Provided it don't have to ferment all over agin."

Morgaine located the number and picked up her phone. "What if it's some kind of special grape? We can't mix whiskey and wine."

"No, but we could drink the whiskey and make brandy next time."

"Figures you'd want to drink the whiskey. I thought you were going to let Sly sell it to make some rent money."

Gwyneth whapped herself upside the head. "Oh, yeah. I forgot that part. I just got my mouth all set for a taste."

"Well, you can taste it. In fact, we both should just to be sure it doesn't burn our throats like rocket fuel."

"Don't be silly. It goes down smooth as honey." Gwyneth rubbed her hands together. "Just like Daddy used to make. It should be, least ways. I'm using his recipe. There's just one part I didn't tell Sly about."

"What's that?"

"You gotta burn a piece of wood and toss it in at the end to get the right color."

"Why didn't you tell Sly about that?"

"Because he's a vampire, and they don't like wooden stakes or fire. I figured he could do without knowin' that part."

Morgaine stifled a snicker. "As long as you don't sharpen it to a point and light it on fire under his nose, I'm sure he'll be okay with it. I think the sun's gone down. You want to check on the mash while I call Mikhail?"

"You trust me to be with Sly alone?"

Morgaine's jaw dropped. "Shouldn't I? I thought you wanted me to pursue—"

"I *do*. I just didn't know if you'd be jealous anyways. I promise I won't try nothin'."

Morgaine remembered what Sly had said about Gwyneth and smiled. "It's fine. I don't have a problem with it." *Thank goodness. That's one worry I don't need.*

After Gwyneth left, Morgaine dialed Mikhail's number. She hoped it didn't matter what time of day she called since he probably used his own wine cure. The phone rang three times before he picked it up and said, "Hello."

"Mikhail?"

"Who's asking?"

"I hope you remember me. We met in Baltimore. My name is Morgaine."

"Morgaine! The goth witch. Of course I remember you."

She chuckled. "Good. But I've changed my look. I'm not doing the goth thing anymore."

"Really? What do you look like now?"

"I went back to my natural blonde hair and pink lips. I still wear some black though. Witches usually do."

"Yeah? Why's that?" Mikhail asked.

"It's the culmination of all colors. Very protective. Pulls in energy rather than reflecting it out like light colors. Plus, I like it."

"That's reason enough. Are you in the city? Can we get together and catch up?"

"Uh, no. I'm living in Boston now. But I'd love to catch up over the phone. How's everything with you?"

"Fine as wine," he said and chuckled.

"Speaking of wine, I specifically called to ask about your wine that cures vampirism."

"Vampire Vintage? It's not a cure, Morgaine. It's more like temporary relief from sun sensitivity and blood lust."

"Well, that's what I meant."

"Okay, so what did you want to know about it and why?"

"I need it for a friend of mine."

"Boyfriend?"

"Uh... maybe? We're both interested."

"Hey, that's a start. So, you're okay with dating vampires?"

"Yes... well, nice ones."

"If only I'd known that back in Baltimore." He chuckled.

"Are you still single?"

"Nope. Happily committed. It's quite a story. You should come down sometime and meet her."

"I—uh... I don't leave the apartment much."

"Why is that?"

"I have a home business."

"Really? What are you doing these days?"

She giggled. "I'm a phone-sex actress."

He let out a loud burst of laughter.

"Hey, come on. Is it that hard to believe? I've been told I have a nice voice."

He cleared his throat. "Oh, you do. I was just surprised, that's all. Has Internet porn cut into your business at all?"

"Yeah, somewhat. We also used to have a landlady who hated the noise. Some of the guys like us to sound like we're having the best orgasms of our lives."

He chuckled. "Give me an example."

"Of a typical call? I thought you were in a committed relationship."

"Not a call. Just let me hear your orgasm act. It is just acting, right?"

"Of course. I'll tell you what, I'll trade. I need to know the ingredient in your wine that cures vampirism."

"Oh, Morgaine… I can't do that."

"Why not?"

"Well, for one thing, it would be bad for business, but even more importantly, it's impossible to duplicate."

Morgaine's hopes sank like the Titanic. "Really? Are you sure?"

"Quite sure."

Morgaine mustered her resolve. She couldn't give up on Sly that easily. Maybe if she got hold of a bottle or two, she could reverse engineer the formula.

"So, how much do you charge per bottle?"

"It's pretty expensive. I doubt you'd be able to afford it if your business isn't doing well. How well off is your boyfriend?"

Morgaine groaned. "Worse off than me."

"Really? That's unusual for a vampire. We're usually stinkin' rich since we learn ways to accumulate wealth over the centuries. Does he have a gambling problem?"

"Oh, no. Nothing like that. Actually, he's quite young in your terms. He lives simply and considers crime fighting his contribution to society. There are precious few jobs for the absolutely nocturnal."

"Ain't that the truth. So he probably has to take advantage of others to get what he needs. Be careful, Morgaine. I wouldn't want to hear he's using you."

"I'm sure he isn't. We've been friends for years. If he was going to do that, it would have happened by now."

"I'm sorry to hear he has financial problems, but isn't his maker helping him?"

"That's another problem. His maker is an asshole.

He killed Sly's wife, and he almost prevented his daughter from being born during the attack. That's a long story. Let's just say his maker is after him for his own selfish reasons, and Sly will never forgive him for what he did."

"Understandable. Well, chances are… Sly is his name?"

"Short for Sylvestro."

"Ah, well, don't worry. He'll find a way to make some cash. Then with some smart investments…"

"That's why we were hoping you'd tell us what the secret ingredient is. My cousin knows how to make moonshine, and we've set up a still. Sly figured he could sell the moonshine for more if we could adapt your recipe, and instead of making wine, we'd make whiskey. He can still just tend the still and sell it as is."

"Smart. Unfortunately, it won't work. But I wish him the best of luck. Hey, since you brought up the idea of bargaining, maybe you can trade your talent as a witch for a case of my private stock. I have a little problem, but you may need to come to New York to handle it."

Fear sliced through Morgaine. "New… New York?"

"Yeah, that's why I'm offering an entire case of Vampire Vintage for it. I know it's inconvenient."

Inconvenient? That's an understatement. With this friggin' agoraphobia, it's damn near impossible!

"Morgaine? Are you there?"

"Uh, yeah. Why would I have to come to New York?" *Please, Goddess, let him be wrong! Let it be something I can do from here!*

"I need you to remove a curse from my warehouse. A vampire who practices black magic managed to get in and hex the place. I've had all kinds of workplace accidents, and there's nothing stopping him from coming in again. Do you know how to undo all that?"

"A whole case, huh?"

"Absolutely."

"How much would that ordinarily cost?

"About ten thousand dollars."

"Yikes!"

"It's well worth it to me."

Shit. She did have to go there. At least she knew how to remove hexes, and now she even knew how to reseal doors against vampires. "I, um... I'll see if I can get someone to take over my calls for a little while. It'll depend on that." *Among other things.*

Chad and Morgaine "sat" together at her kitchen table. More to the point, Morgaine sat while Chad hovered. Sometimes being nothing but spiritual energy was damned inconvenient.

She stared in his direction but her eyes didn't focus on his. "Chad, I know you have good reason not to leave the building, but do you think I'm lame for having agoraphobia?"

"Does it matter what I think?"

She sighed, sounding resigned. "I guess not. If feeling stupid cured our fears, I'd be bulletproof by now."

"Come on, kid. Don't be so hard on yourself. You have lots of strengths."

She had developed her psychic sense well enough to see him. Or a shadowy version of him. That was a welcome change from people staring at the ceiling when they spoke to him. As if he was on his way to heaven but had bumped up against the ceiling and stayed there.

She smiled sadly and shrugged. "I guess so. There are certainly things I can do that would be impossible for average people, so why should I be upset when everyone and his brother can do something I find difficult?"

"It's not that you can't, Morgaine. You know you can. It's just a matter of psyching yourself up for it. Look how you managed to get to the Isabella Stewart Gardner Museum last spring."

"Yeah, that's because I thought I might be able to crack the FBI's cold case and there was a five-million-dollar reward egging me on. Besides, it was right in our own backyard—relatively. New York is a hell of a lot farther away."

"So? The point is you did it. You had to go with a trusted person, but at least you always had a friend like that willing to help. I doubt anyone I know on the other side, or wherever most dead people go, cares enough to come back for me."

"I wish I knew more about the other side so I could help you, Chad. I tried, but..." She tossed her hands up.

"I know, and I appreciate that. To be honest, you know more about it than anyone else since you can communicate with spirits."

"It's been frustrating for me too. Usually all I have to do is tell a spirit to go into the light, and off they go."

"I don't think it's that simple. I think a lot of it depends on the spirit. Maybe they have to be welcome over there and, at the same time, want to cross over. After all, Reginald didn't leave the museum when you tried to get him to go."

"True. If anyone wouldn't be welcome somewhere, it would be him. Too bad that beautiful art museum is haunted by such a nasty-ass ghost. But you've changed. You should be able to cross over if it depends on good behavior."

"Why, thank you for noticing."

"How could anyone *not* notice? You used to be angry, surly, sarcastic, rude—"

"Okay, okay. I get your point."

"I don't really think it's based on behavior. Maybe you're attached to this place because you like and care about the residents."

"Ha. I doubt it. Most of you can go fuck yourselves as far as I'm concerned. You're the only one I almost care about. And that's debatable."

She smiled. "On the other hand, maybe it *is* based on behavior."

"Oh, yeah? Well, screw you and the broom you rode in on."

Morgaine laughed. "Thanks, Chad. I needed a good chuckle."

"Sure. Any time, kid."

Chapter 9

A KNOCK AT SLY'S DOOR FILLED HIM WITH MOMENTARY trepidation. Even though the witches had resealed the building against Malvant, some chucklehead might have let him in. Although, wait a minute—the front door hadn't opened so it must be someone from the building.

As he strolled to the door, he hoped it was Morgaine. He hadn't seen her for a couple days and he missed her. Gwyneth had come by once to pick up his mash and show him how to use the still, but thankfully, she had stopped flirting with him.

Upon opening the door, he grinned. "Morgaine, it's good to see you. Come in." She looked especially pretty. She had on a short black skirt and a pink blouse. Her embroidered black denim satchel was draped over her shoulder.

"Thanks." As she made her way to his couch, she commented, "I'm glad you're using candles now. I love the ambiance of candlelight."

"I have to. Knowing my maker's out there, I've kept the room-darkening shades closed. Thanks again for thinking of those."

She smiled. "I'm glad I did. This way Vorigan Malvant can't see in, either. At least, I hope not! Has anyone checked from outside yet?"

"Nathan did, and no, he couldn't see in even with several candles lit."

"I brought you more candles, by the way." Morgaine dug into the big bag she held in her lap. "I figured you'd be stuck inside most nights now that Vorigan knows where you are."

"That's very thoughtful." He leaned over and kissed her, then took the candles to the kitchen and returned. "I meant to ask Gwyneth how you discovered his name."

"It was on the mailbox outside, and a piece of mail was lying on his end table next to the door. I didn't notice it at first, but when we enlarged the photos, we could read it. It was blurry, but I'm pretty sure that's what it said."

Sly sat next to her and put an arm around her. "So, he's been here a while if he's receiving mail."

"Presumably." She leaned against him and rested her hand on his thigh. "There are a couple of things I need to talk to you about. They're important."

He shifted so he could see her eyes. She looked anxious, expectant. "What is it?"

"Well, I figured Vorigan has curtailed your crime-fighting and blood-drinking activities. How are you feeling?"

"Like shit." Sly hung his head. He didn't want to admit he'd wanted to snack on her since she'd entered his apartment, but he didn't want to lie, either. He'd been purposely avoiding the temptation to stare at her carotid artery.

"I figured. Are you… um…" She squirmed a little bit and averted her gaze. Whatever was on her mind obviously made her uncomfortable.

"Spit it out, Morgaine. Whatever you want to ask is perfectly all right."

"Are you able to stop before hurting someone? In other words, can you just take a little sip?"

What's she getting at? She couldn't be offering her-self—could she? After a brief hesitation, he said, "Yes, I can do that. I might be tempted to continue if I'm famished and the bastard deserves it, but if there's a good reason to stop, I can."

"H-how long can you go without feeding? That's what you call it, right?"

He shrugged. "I guess so. Feeding, drinking, whatever. And I'm not sure how long I can last without it. To tell you the truth, I tried suicide by not drinking at all for a while. It didn't work. I just went mildly crazy."

She looked horrified.

He held up one hand. "It was a long time ago. You have to understand, after my wife died and my daughter was taken from me, I sank into a deep depression. I'm not talking about days or weeks. I mean it lasted months. I don't know how long I went without blood. A couple weeks, at least."

"Are vampires even able to commit suicide? I thought you were immortal."

"I am—apparently. Having been a Catholic, I believed committing suicide was a mortal sin, but I had voluntarily become undead so I figured I was on my way to Hell anyway. Just in case I wasn't, I didn't want to do anything completely selfish like walking around in sunlight until I fried or falling on a broken chair leg. I could have made it look like an accident, but God would have known better."

"So you went without eating? And you didn't think God would be able to figure that one out?"

"It wasn't exactly like that. I hadn't been able to eat because I was so depressed. After a week or so, I became disoriented, weak, and even more apathetic. Letting it continue didn't seem like an active suicide attempt."

"I-I'm sorry you went through that."

He shrugged. "Morgaine, you've awakened my humanity. I've never thanked you for that."

"What do you mean? You've always been humane."

He smiled and focused on his lap as he spoke. "I mean human. I thought sexual interest in an attractive woman was a thing of the past. Now I know it isn't."

Morgaine smiled and nodded slowly. Then she looked pensive for a moment. At last she gathered her hair in one hand and swept it over her opposite shoulder. "Here. If you can stop before it gets dangerous…"

She *was* offering herself! He didn't know what to say. Yes, he wanted it—*needed* it! "Are you sure?"

She nodded more deliberately. "Yes. I don't want you to suffer."

He let out a deep breath and hesitated, giving her a moment to change her mind. Leaning in slowly, he whispered. "I can't thank you enough for this. I hate that it's going to hurt."

"That's okay. I have a high pain threshold. I may be chicken about other things, but not a little bite."

Sly placed his fangs over the pulsing artery in her neck and carefully bore down. When the blood hit his tongue, it was like finding water in the desert. Despite his relief, he had to keep himself in check. *Only a sip,* he reminded himself.

He drank. With tremendous effort, he pulled away and licked the holes. They stopped leaking immediately.

He licked his lips and squelched the impulse to say something stupid like "Mmm, mmm good."

"You didn't even flinch."

"I told you I have a high threshold for pain."

"As evidenced by at least three piercings in each ear. Do you have any I can't see?"

"You'll have to find out." She winked.

---~~~---

Oh, my Goddess! Did I just say that? And wink? No wonder he's grinning. Quick, change the subject!

"I, uh… have something else to talk to you about."

"Can it wait?"

"I guess so. Why?"

Sly cupped the back of her head, leaned in, and delivered the most toe-curling kiss Morgaine had ever experienced. Not that she'd had many.

When he finally let go of her lips, she leaned back and stared at him—stunned.

A look of concern crossed his face. "Did I overstep?"

"No! I mean, you just surprised me."

"Is that all?"

"Yeah. Well, that and you just gave me the best kiss of my life."

He laughed. "I'm glad. Can I do it again sometime?"

A thrill rippled through Morgaine's lady parts. Even though she was a phone-sex actress, she tried to think of herself in more respectful ways. "Anytime. Right now, if you want to."

He looked at her with desire burning in his eyes. "Oh, I want to."

It was about time she tipped her hand. *Be brave. You can do this.* "Do you want more? More than a kiss?"

He hesitated. "Do you?"

"Good Goddess, yes!"

He reared back and laughed. A moment later he straightened up and effortlessly lifted her in his arms. She grasped him around the neck and let him carry her to the bedroom.

When he set her down on the bed, her nerves began to get the better of her. "It's been awhile. I hope I don't disappoint—"

He placed a finger over her lips. "It's been a while for me too. Quite a while. Twenty-six years, to be exact."

"So you haven't been with anyone since your wife died?" He nodded.

"Well, I hear it's like riding a bike."

He chuckled and brushed a lock of hair away from her face. "Hang on then. It might be a bumpy ride."

It was Morgaine's turn to laugh.

Sly didn't waste the opportunity and dove for her open mouth. She had never kissed a vampire before and wondered if his fangs would come out. A second later, she didn't care if they did.

Their tongues met as if magnetized. He slanted his mouth over hers and their lips fused. His hand found her breast and fondled.

Dear Lord and Lady, my vaginal muscles are clenching.

More long-forgotten feelings invaded her abdomen. Something fluttered around her heart chakra. Warmth flared. If she had been over forty or forty-five, she might have thought she was having a hot flash. Nope, she was only thirty. Funny how a chilly vampire could generate so much heat.

She pulled in a ragged breath.

His head raised and his lips brushed over her

temple, her cheek, and found her mouth again. Morgaine wrapped her arms around his neck and pressed her body to his. Sly's embrace was strong, but it only made Morgaine feel safer. He deepened the kiss. Everything else fled to the far recesses of her mind.

His tongue swept over hers, creating a jolt of excitement in her core. They'd both been celibate far too long. Morgaine needed him… inside her. Needed to feel his strength plunging into her channel.

The passion he had sparked burned hotter. She rubbed her breasts against his chest and ground her pelvis into him.

Sly broke the kiss and groaned. He stared into her eyes. "I want you." His voice rasped, adding to her arousal. The possessive look in his deep brown eyes fueled her lust as much as his words did.

"Take me." Her hands slid over the hard wall of his chest. "I want you too."

His eyes darkened and almost glowed. "Tell me exactly what you want."

Her inhibitions started to melt away, replaced by a sense of safe exploration. The hand she had placed against his chest descended. Her fingers slid over his rippled abs through his thin shirt. Hunger overtook her. A raw, desperate need stole her breath as she came upon his hip bone. Her heart pounded, but she slid her hand inward to where their bodies met. At last, she gripped his hard shaft through his pants and squeezed. He let out a low growl. There couldn't be any doubt about what she meant.

Sharp waves of desire caused her pussy to throb. Her nipples tightened behind the cups of her lace bra.

When she spoke, her voice sounded low and throaty—seductive even to her own ears. "Ravage me, Sly. I need you to tear my clothes off and fuck me. Like you can't wait another moment. Like *we* can't wait— because I can't."

His eyes blazed with an internal fire that seemed to heat his skin. Or perhaps he had just absorbed enough of her intense heat that he was radiating it back to her.

Without breaking eye contact, he gripped the top of her blouse. "Say it again."

"Fuck me. I want you to tear off my clothes and ravage me. Don't make me wait any longer."

He groaned. His fingers curled around and gathered a handful of cloth just above her breasts. With one quick yank, he ripped the line of buttons open, sending them flying and plinking in all directions. They both kicked off their shoes and let them plop on the floor.

His hand cupped her breast and squeezed, and then he teased the nipple through the rough fabric of her bra with his thumb. When he leaned over and pulled the nipple into his mouth to suck, Morgaine's head fell back and she moaned. The blissful sensations bordered on agony. She thought she might come right then and there.

His sharp fang hooked through the lace and tore, freeing her breast. Her sharp intake of breath made him hesitate.

"Don't stop," she begged.

At last, he seized the fabric between them and tore it loose. He descended on one breast and then the other, hungrily suckling each one. He was careful his fangs did no more than graze her skin. This is exactly what she had wanted… what she'd pictured when she allowed herself to have fantasies of Sly making love to her.

"Touch me everywhere," she rasped.

He leaned back and, in one motion, pulled her short skirt over her hips and down her legs. Fortunately, there was elastic in the waistband, so he didn't have to tear it. She reached for his zipper. Before she could get it down, he freed the button, and in seconds, his jeans lay on the floor next to her skirt. He grabbed his shirt hem, pulled it over his head, and tossed the shirt across the room.

Morgaine lay in a pile of tattered clothes, so he raised her back an inch and pulled out the remnants of her blouse and bra, sending them to the floor as well. Finally, they were both gloriously naked.

Sly caressed her from her ribs to her waist and down to her sensitive thighs. He slid his hand around to cup her bottom and squeezed. She shivered from the thrill.

His eyes were molten. He leaned over her breasts again. His tongue swiped one taut nipple and Morgaine jumped. Her ultra-sensitized nerve endings sprang to life wherever he touched, licked, or caressed her.

He sucked hard, pulling more of her breast into his mouth. She arched and moaned. "Oh, Goddess, yes." She greedily tangled her fingers in his hair and pulled his head closer. When he had thoroughly ravaged one breast, he gave the same amount of attention to the other.

Meanwhile, his hand roamed freely over her lower half. Touching her everywhere but not in that special spot. Morgaine was half out of her mind with wanting him. All of him. Inside her, pounding hard. Quelling the ache.

At last he took possession of her mouth, and his

fingers found her clit at the same time. She gasped and the vacuum sealed their lips together. They kissed and groped frantically.

Finally, Morgaine couldn't stand it anymore. "Please, Sly. Now. I need you inside me. I *have* to feel you."

He didn't hesitate. He positioned his thick cock at her entrance. She was wet and slick and more than ready for him. He plunged deep inside in one thrust and held her for a moment. She sighed with pure relief.

He let out a deep breath too. "Jesus, Morgaine. You feel so good."

"You too," she whispered. "Fuck me."

With that, he began his rhythm. He thrust hard and fast, causing Morgaine's pulse to race. "Oh, yes, that's it," she encouraged.

He cupped her ass and drove himself deeper, pounding into her and obliterating reality. She savored the sensations, clinging to him with her arms and legs. Before she expected it, her inner muscles clenched. As she cried out in blissful release, a pulsating orgasm ripped through her.

Sly didn't let up. He continued to piston into her, unleashing his own desire. He possessed her. Took her. Not only did it turn her inside out, but it made her hotter and wetter for him. Perspiration broke out on her forehead as she built to another fevered peak.

"Come with me, Sly. Please. I need to feel you come."

It took no more than her request. He let out a low groan, and her name ripped from him as he jerked with his own release. Warmth shot inside her as he climaxed. Suddenly another orgasm of her own hit. She spasmed and shook, her inner muscles milking him of every last drop.

At last they collapsed and lay panting, Sly still inside

her. Morgaine knew that part of them would remain connected. She felt him in her soul.

———〰———

Sly, Gwyneth, and Morgaine watched the clear liquid drip, drip, drip out of the copper pipe and splash into the nearly full glass jar.

"I thought this was whiskey," Sly said. "It looks more like vodka." The smell of ethanol had overwhelmed him as soon as he'd opened the false wall. Now it was beginning to dissipate but he wondered if it was wafting upstairs.

"I know y'all expected it to be brown or amber colored, and it will be by the time it's ready for sale, but we thought we'd try the spell on the purest form first."

Morgaine smiled. "We can call it Vampire Vodka if this spell works." She bumped Sly playfully.

He put an arm around her and kissed her temple. "From your lips to G… the Goddess's ears."

"Now you're getting it." She nipped his ear and he growled low.

Gwyneth folded her arms. "If all y'all can pay as firm attention to the spell as to each other, this should work just fine."

The new lovers chuckled.

"Okay, I think we've got enough," Morgaine said. She picked up the empty Mason jar and swapped it for the nearly full one. She set the clear liquid on the floor between them and held out her hands. Gwyneth grasped one and Sly the other, then Gwyneth and Sly joined hands so the three of them made a triangle around the liquid.

"Sly, just concentrate on the outcome y'all want while Morgaine and I chant the spell."

He had purposely waited until his blood lust was back in full force to measure the success of the spell. He tried not to think of its failure.

"Wait just a doggone minute," Gwyneth said. "It might help if we had the spell."

Morgaine chuckled and let go of her hand. "Good thinking."

Gwyneth dug a folded paper out of her pocket. They set it on top of the jar. Morgaine closed her eyes first, and Gwyneth followed suit. The witches took some deep breaths. They had explained to Sly that they'd need to go into a trance to recite the spell, and all he needed to do was keep the circle connected and visualize a positive outcome.

The two women opened their eyes and gazed at the Mason jar. They stood perfectly still and read, "Lord and Lady, hear us now. We repledge our faithful vow. With this spell we help our friend. Your healing power, his way send. The treatment for his vampirism, with this liquid will be hisn."

His eyebrows rose. *Hisn?* Was that a word? Oh well, he figured the witches knew what they were doing.

"Let our will be granted as read, and help our friend, live un-undead. If for the good of most, so mote it be."

They closed their eyes and stood silently for several seconds. He was just beginning to wonder if their minds had gone somewhere never to return when their eyelids fluttered open.

They smiled and nodded to each other. Then Morgaine said, "Blessings and thanks to the spirits attending our circle. We release you until we meet again."

Sly glanced around nervously, half expecting to see shadowy figures floating away.

Morgaine continued. "The circle is open but not broken as we send it skyward. Blessed be." They raised their arms and released their grasps.

"There. That ought to do it," Morgaine said, sounding confident.

Gwyneth picked up the jar and grinned. "I'll drink to that." She took a big swig and wiped her mouth with the back of her hand. "Ahhh... that's the stuff, all right."

Handing it to Morgaine, she said. "Y'all enjoy."

She lifted the jar like a mug of ale in a silent toast. "Down the hatch." She took as big a gulp as Gwyneth had and almost choked. "Holy shit!"

"Ain't it though?" Gwyneth giggled.

Morgaine gagged.

"Now don't y'all go spittin' it out. That's good moonshine and not ta be wasted."

"Dear Lord and Lady, that stuff should come with a warning label!"

Gwyneth frowned and crossed her arms. "Like what?"

"Like, 'caution, may eat through your stomach lining.' That's probably why they call it rotgut."

"This ain't no rotgut whiskey. It's just a little stronger than y'all are used to. Try sipping it next time."

"What next time?" Morgaine held the jar out to Sly.

"Don't listen to her, sugar. She's a wimp about all kinds of things. Why should liquor be any different?"

Morgaine suddenly yanked back the Mason jar without releasing it.

"I beg your pardon? I'm not a wimp just because I like my internal organs." She took another sip, squeezed her eyes shut, and swallowed. "Yeah, it's better in small doses."

At last, she handed it to Sly. He winked at her. "At least I don't have to worry about this stuff killing me."

The girls giggled.

"To your health." He raised the jar in a toast and drank. *Hmm… that's not too bad. Maybe the cure will outweigh the curse after all.*

The witches watched him expectantly.

Morgaine spoke first. "Anything?"

Sly tried to think of blood without getting thirsty. Damn. He needed to feed worse than ever. Disappointment descended like a heavy cloud.

Suddenly, Gwyneth pointed to him and the witches gasped.

"What?"

"Y'all are red as a tomato!"

Sly lifted his hands and was temporarily stunned speechless. His skin was lobster red.

Morgaine ripped the piece of paper out of Gwyneth's hand. "Let me see that."

It may have been torn, but apparently she could still read what it said. She slapped her forehead. "Dammit! We asked the cure be granted as read. R-e-a-d."

"Yeah, so?"

"The powers-that-be must have thought we meant the color, r-e-d!"

Gwyneth stamped her foot. "Shoot." Then she snapped her gaze toward the ceiling. "No, *don't* shoot! Sorry for the confusion, Goddess. Can y'all fix it—please?"

Sly watched as the color faded from his skin. When he was his usual pasty shade, he let out a sigh of relief. "Whew. I wouldn't mind having a little pigment again, but I'd prefer my Latino tan to lobster red."

"What about your other symptoms?" Morgaine asked. "Are you still, um, thirsty?"

Sly nodded sadly.

"Oh, no."

Gwyneth started toward the stairs. "Let me go up to my place and try again."

"No!" Morgaine and Sly said at once.

"Well then, let me get a paper and pencil, and we can write it together. That way it'll be triple-checked to make sure we get all the kinks out."

Morgaine looked at Sly. "Do you want to try again?"

"If you're sure you can guarantee the worst that'll happen is no cure for this bad case of the munchies."

Chapter 10

THE WITCHES TRIED ANOTHER, SIMPLER SPELL. Morgaine had high hopes for this one. It didn't rhyme, but it specified exactly what they wanted to happen. Remove Sly's blood lust and allow him to stay conscious and safe in daylight.

Morgaine handed the jar to Sly. "Well, are you ready to try it again?"

He took it from her. "I think so."

"I'll go first if y'all want a guinea pig." Gwyneth grinned like she couldn't wait to chug it down. Well, why not? She seemed the most able candidate to handle it.

Sly passed it to her. "By all means. Ladies first."

Gwyneth took a huge gulp and smacked her lips. "I just can't get over how good this is. It just might be better than Daddy used to make."

Morgaine rolled her eyes. "If you say so." She took the jar from her and sipped. "Whoa! That still burns like gasoline—after putting a match to it."

Gwyneth sighed. "What can I say? Some people just don't appreciate the finer things in life."

Sly took the jar from Morgaine, held it near his mouth, and said, "Over the lips and past the gums—look out, stomach, here it comes."

As he sipped, Gwyneth turned to her older cousin and said, "See? Sly knows how to rhyme."

They all waited anxiously for something to happen. Sly held out his hands. "Well, I'm not turning bright colors this time."

"Is your thirst decreasing?"

Sly hesitated a moment. Then he shook his head. "Not yet."

"Well, maybe y'all need a little more. Let's keep passin' it until it's gone. We got more collectin' in the bucket over yonder."

Gwyneth pointed with her thumb toward the still where indeed the bucket held at least another jar full.

Sly gazed at Morgaine. "What do you say? Do you think it's worth a try?"

She shrugged. "Having never done this before, it's anybody's guess. Maybe it does take a certain amount to be effective. Like medicine."

"I'm game if both of you are." He handed the jar to Gwyneth.

"Y'all know I'm in favor." She took another swig.

"So, while we're sitting here drinking, we might as well talk about our Plan B," Morgaine said.

Gwyneth stole an extra sip before handing the glass jar to Morgaine. "You mean going to New York?"

"New York? Who's going to New York?" Sly asked.

Just the thought of it made Morgaine jittery, and she took a large swallow. "Plauhh!" She took a few deep breaths, hoping to cool the molten lava sliding down her throat. At last she answered him. "If I live through this, you and I need to go to New York to see my old friend, Mikhail."

"Is that the guy who makes the Vampire Vintage?"

"Yes. I called him but he wouldn't give me the secret

ingredient. The one thing he said he would do is trade
me a case of it for a little magick."

Sly gave her a sidelong glance. "What kind of magic?"

Gwyneth sat up straighter. "Why Sylvestro Flores,
are y'all jealous?"

"N-no. I was just… curious."

Gwyneth slapped her knee. "Don't deny it. Y'all are
jealous. I know the signs."

Morgaine had to intervene, although it secretly
pleased her to think Sly might be a little possessive.
"Gwyneth, 'mind your own beeswax,' as a certain witch
I know would say."

Gwyneth jumped up and said, "Fine. I feel like
dancin' anyway." She whirled away, trying to pirouette
across the basement.

"I was hoping you'd come with me, Sly."

"Oh? Wouldn't Gwyneth have to go? I can't travel
in daylight, and you can't travel at night—or period."

"I have to go. Mikhail doesn't know Gwyneth, and
he's very cautious of people he doesn't know. He wants
to meet you for the same reason." She leaned toward
him and whispered, "Besides, he needs me to remove
a curse and set up a sigil. It's a type of magickal warning system, and that's rather advanced. I don't think
Gwyneth can do it yet."

"Okay. So how do we proceed?"

Gwyneth twirled past them. "I can teach y'all about
takin' Morgaine out into the scary world."

Morgaine sighed. "I'm all right as long as I'm with
someone I trust."

"Yeah, but y'all need to know what to do if she has
a panic attack."

"I'll learn all I can about your condition and how to help you with it, but are you really willing to do this, Morgaine? For me?"

She stroked his arm. "Call me crazy, but I wouldn't do it for anybody else."

Sly leaned over and kissed her senseless.

Gwyneth recited, "Sly and Morgaine sittin' in a tree... y'all have stupid names." Then she became giddy and couldn't finish the rhyme.

—⁓—

When the super opened his apartment door, a suspicious chemical smell assaulted his nostrils. Maybe it had wafted in from outside? Jules followed the strange odor downstairs. It seemed a little stronger on the first floor. He sniffed outside apartments 1A and 1B. It didn't seem to be coming from either of the men's apartments—and it didn't smell like dirty gym socks anyway.

He opened the front door, and the odor vanished. *Nope. It's definitely coming from inside. Great. Just what I need—a Unabomber in my building.*

Maybe the smell was coming from the basement. As he neared the basement door at the back of the hall, the scent became stronger and a little more distinct. *Alcohol?* When he opened the door, the smell intensified.

Jules heard the sound of scurrying feet followed by girls giggling. *Holy crap. What am I walking into?* He thought about calling the police for a moment, but Jason Falco, the landlord and his boss, had made it clear that he wanted to avoid drawing attention to the building at all costs. Well, the culprit didn't seem to be a Unabomber, so that meant investigating giggling girls fell to Jules.

He switched on the light at the top of the stairs and tiptoed past a few cobwebs. Yeah, he'd have to brush those away later. Nearing the bottom step, he glanced around. A light was on in the laundry room, so he checked there first. It was empty.

A few snickers led him to the storage side. He looked past stacked boxes and old furniture, but he couldn't see anyone.

"Okay, girls, I can hear you. Come out, come out, wherever you are."

Peals of laughter gave them away, and the two women from the third floor came stumbling out into the open. They may have been giggling like little girls, but they swayed like a couple of old drunks.

"Isn't this a strange place to have a party?" he asked.

The young redhead sidled up to him and grasped his arm. "We was just… My, what big muscles y'all have!"

Proud of his swimmer's body, Jules flexed his bicep.

She gasped and stroked the sizable bulge under his shirt sleeve. "I do declare! Y'all must be strong as a bull. Do y'all work out?"

"I'm a swimmer."

"Well, I'll be. Who knew swimmers could get so virile?" She leaned in closer to him. "I bet y'all could help me move my bed with one hand tied behind your back." He smelled alcohol on her breath—not that he needed much confirmation of what she and her cousin had been up to.

"Gwyneth, isn't it?"

"Uh-huh, and y'all are Jules, right? Jules Vernon?"

"Yes, and I'm afraid that as building super, I need to ask you and your cousin to move your party to your private residences."

"Well now, we was just about to do that anyways. Y'all want to come with us? They say three's a crowd, but I druther think of it as three's a party!"

Jules relaxed his guard. He knew she was flirting with him, but she was so darned cute. Who could get mad at her? The other one watched silently, but he couldn't complain about that, either. He liked his women cute and quiet.

"Thanks for your kind offer, Gwyneth, but I was just investigating the smell of alcohol coming from down here. Do you girls know why it's so strong?"

Gwyneth giggled and said, "Well, we may have had a tiny bit to drink." She pinched her index finger and thumb almost together. She widened the gap, giggled harder, and eventually managed to admit, "Okay. A little *more* than a little."

"So why are you down here?"

She shrugged. The other woman jumped in. "It's neutral territory. My cousin and I had a spat recently, but we managed to talk it out down here and we were just shelebrating—I mean celebrating."

"Well, I'm glad you worked things out." He glanced down at the cute redhead, and she gazed up at him, batting her eyelashes.

"I'll bet y'all have lots of swimmin' medals, Jules, like those Olympic athletes." Her eyes seemed to glow—or maybe that was just the low light hitting her glazed green irises. "Would y'all like to show them to me?" She wrapped her hands around either side of his arm.

"I don't have any medals, but that's because I never really competed."

"Well, I'm sorry to hear that. Y'all woulda had a houseful of trophies by now, I bet."

He simply smiled. Too bad having races with his fellow mermen didn't count.

"Listen, I'm feelin' a bit wobbly. Would y'all mind helpin' me climb them stairs? Y'all don't mind if I monopolize him, do ya, Morgaine?"

"No, not at all. You go have fun. I'll head up in a minute."

Jules tipped his head toward the stairs. "How about now?"

"Sure. Now's good." Morgaine maneuvered her way around the boxes, brushed off the bottom of her long skirt, and followed them up the steps.

Sly heard a knock on his door and hoped it was Morgaine. He hadn't seen her since the super had caught them in the basement. He had managed to encase himself behind the false wall with the still before Jules discovered it, but he'd almost keeled over from the fumes in there. Fortunately he had been able to slip out after he'd heard their footsteps climb the stairs.

Opening his apartment door, he found his lover looking up at him and smiling shyly. She carried a jar of clear liquid and a candelabra that lit her face and eyes with a soft golden glow.

"Hi, Morgaine. You look especially beautiful tonight. I was hoping you'd come to see me sooner rather than later."

"Yeah, we need to talk."

"Uh-oh. Conversations that begin that way are never good."

She smiled. "It's not one of *those* conversations. Don't worry."

"In that case, come in." He stepped aside.

Morgaine had the most graceful way of moving he'd ever seen. If not for the swish of her hips, she'd almost appear to float. He caught a whiff of her patchouli oil scent. She had been toning it down since he'd mentioned it made his head swim. Maybe it wasn't the fragrance. He felt a little light-headed just looking at her in the candlelight.

He recognized the scent in the glass jar too. It was their Vampire Vodka.

She set the candelabra on top of his bookshelf. The entire living room flickered in the candlelight. She sat on his couch, and he settled in next to her.

"So what did you want to talk about?"

"This." She raised the jar of liquid.

"Do you want to try another spell on it?"

"No. I don't think it's that simple, or it would have worked the first or second time. Have you fed recently?"

He nodded. He wasn't proud of it, but he refused to be ashamed of it, either. When it came to live human blood, he did what he had to do and coped with it the best he could—by looking for criminals—and he did the city a favor.

"Why did you bring the moonshine if it doesn't do anything?"

"I thought you might like something to drink since we finished your champagne. And I thought we should talk about the idea of selling it."

"Oh." He chuckled. "I never thought of it as just a beverage." She handed him the jar, and he took a sip. "Sheesh, that's strong. I'll have to buy something to mix with it."

"That's probably a good idea. I think this stuff has killed off a few too many of my cousin's brain cells."

"Oh, no. What's Gwyneth done now?"

"Nothing. I just meant… in general."

Sly smiled and leaned over to give Morgaine a kiss. She still seemed to need reassurance that he loved *her*, not Gwyn. *Huh?* Had he just used the word "love"? Even if it was only in his head, the idea shook him.

He broke the kiss a little quicker than he had planned. *Be careful, Sly. You don't want to hurt her or yourself. This is only your first relationship since Alice died.*

Deciding to get back to the subject at hand, Sly said, "The super came pretty close to discovering what we were up to. What do you think he'll do if he finds the still?"

Morgaine winced. "I checked into the legalities. I'm afraid moonshine is very much illegal to make and sell. I suppose he'd have to call the health department and have it shut it down."

Sly shook his head. "We should have anticipated that before we considered it a possible income for me."

"I don't think we should give up yet. It really seems plausible that if wine can be made to temporarily cure vampirism, all we need to do is figure out the missing ingredient and preserve it in the moonshine. Besides, I know you really want to pay Merry rent, and you need stuff like electricity and heat. I got so mad seeing how opulent your maker's apartment was compared to yours."

Sly raised his eyebrows. "What's wrong with my

place? I have what I need. Maybe you'd enjoy more decadent surroundings when you come to see me?"

Her jaw dropped. "Of course not! How can you think that?" She swiveled away from him and crossed her arms.

Shit. She didn't deserve that. Was he picking a fight with her to establish some distance?

"I'm sorry, Morgaine. I really am. You've been nothing but thoughtful and kind. I didn't mean that."

She twisted back to face him and sighed. "You're an idiot if you think I need that stuff."

He smiled. Then he reached out and stroked her cheek. "Yeah, I know. I might be an idiot once in a while, like it or not. But let me ask you this, what *do* you need?"

She turned into his hand and closed her eyes. *Uh-oh.* That soft smile indicated she was already having feelings for him.

"This," she said.

"What do you mean?" Sly thought he knew what she meant, but he didn't want to assume. If she asked for more than he could give, he'd have to tell her to slow down. But if he'd learned anything about women in his fifty-six years on earth, it was not to try to guess what they were feeling or thinking. Few men, if any, had them all figured out.

"Trust."

Trust? Her answer puzzled him, but he wasn't about to start an in-depth discussion about their relationship. He didn't think they were "there" yet.

"I need to trust a person in order to venture out of the building with them. And I trust *you.* That's why I'm going with you to New York."

"So, you've decided? You're sure?"

"I think the sooner we go, the better. Gwyneth will keep an eye on the still and answer the business calls while we're gone."

"Is that what you call phone sex? Business calls?"

"Well, yeah. That's what they are."

He relaxed slightly. "Morgaine, I've been hesitating to confess what I think of that for a little while, but I should probably get this off my chest."

She arched her eyebrows and leaned back as if to get a better look at his facial expression. "Okay. Share."

He smiled, hoping to lighten the mood. "I know it's none of my business, and we've only been sleeping together for a short time…" He paused. How should he say this?

"But?"

"But, I'm not sure I want other guys talking to you like that."

She waited, but he had no follow-up.

At last, she looked puzzled and asked, "Why? Or maybe I should say, 'Why not?'"

Shit. He shouldn't have begun this conversation until he understood it himself. Maybe he should change the subject? He chewed his lower lip until he noticed his fangs starting to protrude and tasted blood. "Ouch." *Fuck, it bothers me just to think about it.*

"What's the matter?"

"Oh, nothing. I just fanged myself." He swiped his tongue over the spot that was beginning to bleed and it stopped. "I'll live. Pardon the irony."

She chuckled. "Okay, so let's get back to the other thing. Why do you have a problem with my business?"

Damn. Not enough of a distraction. Maybe I should have set myself on fire? "Can we forget I said anything?"

"No. At least *I* can't. Look, whatever you want to say, it's okay to say it. It might not change anything, but you can tell me what's on your mind."

Suddenly he had a crick in his neck. He rubbed the spot until it eased. "Fine. What if someone finds out where you live? You could be putting yourself in danger."

"We've got that covered. That's not what's really bothering you, is it?"

He gazed at the ceiling. "Oh, the joys of dating a psychic…"

She laughed, then crossed her arms and pretended to get tough. "Okay, you. Even psychics can't read minds. Spit it out."

"Thank God." He sighed. "I'm not exactly sure what it is that bothers me about it. It's not exactly jealousy. I just don't want you treated that way."

"Oh." She appeared to ponder that for a few moments. "Thanks, I think."

"Don't your skills as a medium and psychic pay well enough?"

"Not by themselves. We really need to supplement our income with *something,* and as they say, 'Sex sells.'"

"Is that why Gwyneth was writing erotica?"

"Yes, but she's lost her enthusiasm for it. She claims she needs a new research partner, but I think she's uncomfortable with her grammar. Joe used to take care of both for her."

"I can imagine."

"Look, don't tell her I said that. Her ego has taken

enough of a beating. To be honest, the still is the only thing she's been excited about for quite a while. That's why I'm not asking her to dismantle it and why I didn't say much to discourage her cockamamie idea in the first place."

"Is that the only reason?"

"No, of course not. I had hoped we'd be able to bottle a vampirism cure for you."

"Why do you think it didn't work?"

"Mikhail said there was some kind of secret ingredient. Even though he refused to tell me what it was, I'm hoping if we spend some time with him and I help with his magickal needs, maybe he'll decide he can trust us with it."

"That's a big 'if.' At least he's willing to give us a case of the stuff. Maybe we can reverse engineer it."

"That's what I was thinking."

"Great minds…"

"Yeah." She smiled and looked down at her lap.

Damn. He wanted her every time she gave him that shy smile. Reaching out to cup her cheek, he drew her closer. "I can't thank you enough for agreeing to help me. I know traveling to New York might be hard for you."

"It might also be good for me."

He kissed her straight nose. "That's the brave woman I'm proud of."

Morgaine hadn't expected to end up in the bedroom that evening, but she was glad they did. Sly was an incredible lover—surprisingly gentle, considering his vampiric strength. He also had great—ahem—endurance.

He made sure she was completely satisfied before reaching his own destination. And his recovery time might as well be measured with an egg timer.

She was still huffing and puffing from her second climax when he rolled up onto his elbow and gazed down at her.

"Want to go again?"

She laughed between deep breaths. "You've got to be kidding. Don't you ever get tired?"

"Sex exhausts me about as much as a Sunday stroll." He bent over her and kissed her forehead, nipped her nose, and then claimed her mouth with a fierce possession she hadn't experienced before—ever.

She held onto his shoulders and returned his kiss with the same fervor. Their tongues met and swirled. He tasted slightly like the Vampire Vodka she'd given him, but another flavor mingled with it that she'd come to know as Sly's very own.

Without realizing it, her hands began to wander. When her nails raked down his back, it only inflamed his passion more. He climbed on top of her, and she felt the unmistakable hardness of his staff nudging her entrance.

She parted her legs and allowed him access. Without breaking the kiss or waiting for permission, he rammed himself home. She gasped and he wrenched his lips away.

"Fuck! Are you all right? Did I hurt you?"

He began to pull out until she grabbed his ass. "No, I'm fine." She hauled him toward her until he was fully seated again. "Now let's do that first thing you mentioned."

They both grinned.

He began his rhythm while they stared at each other.

She moaned with wonderful sensations as he filled her. Her eyes closed on their own. "Goddess, that feels good," she said, breathily.

"Yes, it does." His voice lowered and he leaned closer, kissing her temple. "You know what else feels good?"

She paused. "What could feel better than this?"

He raised himself up on one hand and locked his elbow. Balancing like that, he used the other hand to locate her clit. The moment he touched her pearl, she arched and let out a loud moan.

Heightened sensations zinged through her, rippling outward. "Oh, my Goddess!"

His strength was definitely an asset in the bedroom. He wasn't even breaking a sweat. He continued to pump in and out of her as he rubbed her supersensitive button. She writhed with the powerful pleasure of it. Barely conscious of making odd sounds, something primal emanated from deep inside her.

She was skyrocketing toward a higher climax than ever before. Even with all her squirming, Sly stayed right on her clit. He stroked it quickly, and the glorious vibrations led to a shattering orgasm.

Morgaine bucked and screamed. He didn't let up and she kept coming. Electric jolts shot through every cell and nerve ending. Her thighs shook uncontrollably.

At last, he let go and landed on his elbows over her. He jerked and spasmed with his own release and blew out a deep breath.

"You're amazing," she whispered hoarsely.

He pushed back the hair from her face. "You too."

"How? All I do is let you play me like a piano."

He chuckled. "You've got a great keyboard."

She would have laughed, but she didn't have enough breath.

He withdrew slowly and flopped onto his back. After a few moments, he asked, "Do you want to stay the night?"

Morgaine was barely aware of his question or her obvious nonverbal answer as her consciousness slipped away.

Chapter 11

MORGAINE AWOKE THE NEXT MORNING FEELING WELL rested, refreshed, and... blind! Oh, my Goddess! She felt her eyes with her fingers. Yes, they were open. But no matter which direction she faced, she remained in total blackness. Could the myths possibly be true? Could sex make you go blind?

"Where the Hell am I?" Her heart squeezed.

"Relax, pumpkin. You're okay."

"Chad? Is that you?"

"I'd say, 'In the flesh,' but... well, you understand."

"Oh, thank Goddess, I'm not alone!"

"Really? Wow, I think this is the first time you've ever been happy to see me. Usually you tell me to get lost."

"I-I'm really sorry about that. I don't mean to sound—"

"Forget it. Listen, you're not alone anyway. Sly's right next to you."

She patted around the mattress until she hit an arm. "Oh!" She tried to shake him awake, but he didn't move or make a sound. "Sly? Are you okay?"

"Nah, he's out cold. You won't be able to wake him until sunset—unless you set him on fire or something."

She was too freaked out to laugh. "Chad, can you help me? I need to find the door. I've got to get out of here."

"Sure, but first you might want to slow your

*breathing. If you keep hyperventilating like that, you'll
pass out before you get there."*

She deliberately took some slow breaths. "Okay. I
think I'll be all right long enough to reach the door if
you can help me find it."

"Stand up and I'll guide you."

"Wait. I have to find the floor first." She covered her
chest with the sheet, leaned away from Sly, and felt for
the edge of the bed. When she had it, she dragged her
feet over and set them on the hardwood. She tugged on
the sheet, but she couldn't pull it free. "Okay. I—uh, I'm
not dressed. You won't look, will you?"

*"How the hell can I guide you out of the room if
I can't look?"*

Morgaine mentally rolled her eyes. "Okay, you have
a point, but don't stare."

"Fine," he said, sounding bored. *"It's nothing I haven't
seen a million times."*

She gasped. "You've seen me naked a million times?"

He laughed. *"No, but I got your mind off what's happening, didn't I? Now stand up and I'll put my hand under
your elbow. We'll walk around the bed to the door."*

Morgaine chewed her bottom lip, but she forced herself to stand, leaving the safety of the mattress behind.
Good to his word, Chad applied gentle pressure on the
underside of her arm, near her elbow. She shivered at his
cold touch but was grateful for it.

"Ready, set, walk with me."

She tentatively advanced a few baby steps at a time.
"I thought you promised to stay out of our bedrooms.
Does my waking up and finding you here mean you're
not doing that?"

*"Not at all. I just noticed you didn't make it back to
your place last night, and knowing how freaked out you
get in the dark, I figured you'd be in deep shit when you
woke up."*

"Uh, yeah. I guess everyone knows my little secret
now. Thanks."

*"What? That you're afraid of the dark? Please. Any
thirty-year-old who sleeps with a night light on is either
afraid of the dark or thinks she's five."*

Eventually she ran into something soft with her foot.
"Oh! My dress." She bent over and scooped it up with
her free arm. "Thank the Goddess. Now I have something to wear when I get out of here."

"Damn," Chad said.

"Don't tease. I'm about a hair away from losing it."

"Okay, okay. Relax. We're almost there."

She walked a few more steps completely blind and
stubbed her toe. "Ow!"

*"Sorry, I should have warned you. You made it. That
was the door."*

"Oh!" She fumbled around until she found the handle.
As soon as she twisted it, relief washed over—only to be
replaced by despair when she discovered that darkness
lay on the other side of it too.

"Shit. The living room is blacked out too. Now what?"

"I've got you. I'll just take you to the other door."

"Wait. I need to put my dress on."

Fortunately, it was a peasant-type dress with elastic
around the neckline and bodice, so all she had to do was
slip it over her head. Once she had it on, it felt funny and
she tried to adjust it.

"You have it on backwards."

"Oh, for Goddess's sake." She blew out a frustrated breath.

"What's the matter?"

She heaved a deep sigh. "Screw it. Just get me to the hallway door."

"Aren't you even going to say, 'Please'?"

"Sheesh! Fine. Please take me the rest of the way."

As he took her elbow and guided her, she pondered out loud, "I wish there was something I could do to repay you."

"I'm sure I'll think of something."

She clamped her lips together, realizing she should have kept her mouth shut.

―――――∾∾―――――

Merman Jules enjoyed splashing around for several minutes in his saltwater fish tank before he relaxed and gazed outside his front windows. What was going on? He'd seen people filing in and out of the building all day. Now several people were traipsing up the walk together. Mostly related by the looks of them. Was somebody having a family reunion?

Fortunately, the landlord and his pregnant wife were out of town, but if they had been home, all these guests would have put them at risk for discovery. Since his job included protecting the landlord's privacy as well as his property, Jules had warned everyone to keep visitors to a minimum. So who was ignoring the rules?

Jules's super-sonar hearing picked up the vibration of the buzzer as someone let in the whole troop. *Damn.*

He hopped up onto the wall of his tank and waited for the water to sluice off. When his body sensed he was no longer submerged, his tail divided and he jumped onto the hardwood floor, landing on his bare feet.

He grabbed a towel off a shelf, wrapped it around his waist, and trickled water all the way to his bedroom. When he had changed into blue jeans and a "Save the Mermaids" T-shirt, he ventured into the hallway.

To anyone else, it would have seemed quiet. He fine-tuned his sonar until he could have heard blips passing through the air instead of through water. The group had apparently wound up on the third floor. He jogged up the flight of stairs and listened. The sounds were coming from the right. Ah, Morgaine Marlowe's apartment.

He stood outside with his ear to the door for a few moments. Suddenly all the chatter and movement inside stopped. He heard someone taking deep breaths and then more quiet. At last a single voice said, "He's here."

He? Me? Crap. He knew the girls were rumored to be psychic, so he backed away from the door. Suddenly he heard a scream across the hall.

Rushing to the opposite apartment, he tripped and fell before he reached the door. He glanced around his feet but didn't see a thing he could have tripped over. *What the hell is going on up here?*

Suddenly the door he had been running toward opened. Gwyneth Wyatt, the pretty redhead who lived there, gazed down at him. She held a phone in her hand and looked like she was just finishing a call.

"All right, sugar. I'll be here if y'all need me." *Click.* Reaching down, she took his arm and helped him up. "Why, Jules! What on earth happened to y'all?"

"I—uh, heard a scream coming from your apartment.

I was on my way to make sure you were all right, but I tripped."

Gwyneth looked at the ceiling. "Hush, Chad. That wasn't funny. Y'all could've killed the man."

Jules looked up and saw nothing, even though he glanced all around. Eventually she filled him in.

"That was our ghost you tripped over. Chad thinks it's funny to see people fall down—now that he can't." Then she set her hands on her hips and aimed a stern expression at the ceiling again. "But t'ain't funny a'tall, Chad. Not cool, as y'all would say."

Jules's spirits plummeted. He'd thought the redhead might be relationship material or, at the very least, a good romp in the sack. *Why are the prettiest ones always the total nut jobs?* "So what was the scream about?"

"Y'all want to come in? I can explain everythin'."

"Uh, no. I have a… thing… to do… downstairs…"

"Oh, that's too bad. I was gonna tell y'all about our phone-sex business."

He raised his eyebrows but managed to hold his reaction to no more than that. She continued on as if she'd just said she worked as an accountant.

"Yeah, well, me an' my cousin, Morguine, we started the phone-sex thing to pay the rent here. Y'all know we're witches, right?"

Yup. Nut job. "No, I didn't realize that."

"Yes, well, it's agin' the Witches' Rede to charge money for magic, and my cousin goes by the letter of the law when it comes to the Rede, so she started the phone sex as a home business. She don't like to leave the apartment."

"She's not doing phone sex over there now, right? There's a whole crowd visiting, from what I saw and heard—unless..." *Oh no, she couldn't be...* "She isn't having an orgy in there or anything, is she?"

Gwyneth burst out laughing. "My uptight cousin? Naw, y'all just saw the folks who came for the séance. She's a first-class medium too."

Séance? Medium? Nut jobs must run in the family. "Well, it's been nice talking to you, Gwyneth. I wish I could stay and visit."

"Y'all come back now. I'll put on the kettle, and we can have a fine ol' time."

"Oh, sure. Sometime when I'm not so busy..." *Suuuure...*

He turned to leave, then thought he should ask while he was talking to her: "Do you remember when I found you and your cousin in the basement, drunk out of your minds?"

Gwyneth's spine straightened. "We was *not* drunk. Just a little tipsy is all. My gran-pappy used to say, 'As long as y'all can hold on to one blade of grass and not fall off the face of the earth, you ain't drunk.'"

"Oh, I see. Well, then, do you know why the cellar still smells like alcohol?"

"Huh? It do?"

"Yes, it do... I mean, does. Any idea why?"

She scratched her chin and squinted like she was pondering hard. Then she snapped her fingers. "I got it. I bet y'all just got the smell up your nose and now you cain't get it out. That's happened to me when something stinks real strong. Like skunks and gasoline."

Jules shook his head. "No, I—uh. Never mind." *Total. Nut. Job.* "I'll see you around." Then he dashed back downstairs.

As he was passing Lillian's door, he almost bumped into a guy who was leaving in a hurry. He was still tying his tie.

"Oh! Sorry."

The guy just gave him a frantic look and said, "Be careful. She's hot!" Then he rushed down the stairs and out the front door.

What did he mean by that? Maybe all the women in the building were beautiful crazies. Or was it more? He remembered Lily's sizzling handshake. Jules stood there for a few moments, trying to decide whether or not he should check on his tenant in 2A.

"Nah, screw it," he said out loud. Returning to his apartment, he figured that dating neighbors wasn't the best idea anyway.

"You're probably worried for nothing." Chad floated over her bed as Morgaine packed her suitcase.

"What do you mean, probably?"

"You know. There are no guarantees in life. Now, death on the other hand…"

"Chad, shut it. I'm nervous enough as it is." She folded her favorite cashmere sweater, running her hands over the soft, comforting fabric before moving on to the next item.

"Why are you nervous? You'll be with a vampire. A big, bad, bloodsucking killing machine, who can use mesmerism to make people do whatever he wants."

"For fuck's sake, Chad!" Morgaine threw her black satin nightgown at his frothy image. It passed right through him and fluttered to the floor.

"Why are you throwing your lingerie on the floor?"

"Why are you still here?"

He vanished, then reappeared on the other side of the room. *"Man, if you let every little thing freak you out like that, you'll be a wreck before you even leave the building."*

She blew out a deep breath. "Tell me about it."

Chad scratched his head. *"I don't get it."*

"Don't get what?"

"The agoraphobia. Why that?"

"It's not exactly like I had a menu to pick from." She held up the piece of paper on which she'd printed the hotel's address and phone number, flipped it over to the blank side, and studied it. With her finger on her chin, she said, "Hmm... let's see... should I take the paranoid schizophrenia or the multiple personality disorder? Oh, I know! I'll get the agoraphobia and nyctophobia. They're having a two-for-one special on those today."

"Yeah, yeah. Very funny."

"It totally isn't. How would you like to be plagued with panic attacks and feel like you're about to keel over and die?" She thought about what she'd said and snickered. "Sorry."

Chad shrugged. *"Forget it, man. See how easy that is? I don't get all strung out over little things."*

"Goody for you... and stop calling me 'man.'"

"Sorry. I have a hard time giving up the vernacular from my time. I miss it. You never hear anyone say 'groovy' anymore."

"Thank goodness."

"Look, I was trying to help you see there's nothing

to be afraid of, but if all you're going to do is insult me, I might as well leave."

Morgaine sighed. "I appreciate the thought, but it isn't working. There's a powerful vampire out there who's gunning for Sly." She grabbed three pairs of lacy underwear out of her drawer and forcefully threw them into the suitcase. "I finally find someone I lo... I mean, like, and who likes me, and —"

"Ah! I caught that. You were going to say 'love,' weren't you?"

Morgaine slapped her hands over her face. Heat invaded her cheeks, but it was too late. Chad wouldn't miss her blush, and she knew it.

He chuckled. *"Look, ordinarily, I'd start razzing you right about now, but I'm really not that much of an ass. You're a good kid, and I just hope you don't get your heart broken."*

"Jeez, first you call me a man, now a kid. I'm neither one. Do you think you could just call me Morgaine?"

"You're all kids to me. Hell, I'm even older than Sly. At fifty-six, he's just a baby vampire. Who knows how old ghosts get. So what does this other vampire want from him?"

She plopped down onto her bed. "I'm not sure, but it isn't good. He's obsessed. I've sensed his presence around our building almost every night."

"Bummer. So how are you two going to get past him?"

"We haven't figured that out yet."

"Shit. Sounds like you need my help."

"Your help?"

"Well, of course. Who else can distract him without getting themselves killed?"

Morgaine sat up straight, and hope flooded into her again. "Do you think you could?"

"I can try. Maybe if I use my telekinesis to throw rocks at him, he'll be too busy trying to figure out what's happening to focus on you two slipping out the back."

"That might actually work. We'll have to disguise our scents though."

"Easy. Just soak yourselves in cheap wine. You'll smell like a homeless couple who scored a bottle of Mad Dog 20/20."

She had no idea what Mad Dog 20/20 was, but if it helped cover their scents long enough to escape Vorigan Malvant, she'd bathe in it.

Stretched out on their sectional sofa with her head in Jason's lap, Merry was reading *What to Expect When You're Expecting* and Jason was reading a biography of Sandy Koufax. Merry had some questions her book wouldn't be able to answer.

"Honey?"

"Mmm?" Jason answered absently.

"When will we know if our baby inherited your shapeshifter genes?"

Jason placed his bookmark between the open pages and set his book down. "Well, I imagine we'll have to wait until sometime after he or she is born."

She rolled her eyes. "I know that, silly. I mean, are there any signs we should be watching for?"

He half smiled. "Other than an empty crib and a baby falcon flapping around the apartment?"

Her eyes widened. "Are you kidding me?"

"Yes." His eyes twinkled, letting her know he was teasing.

She growled and gestured pulling out her hair.

His expression turned more serious. "Sorry. All kidding aside, I was told my brother and I didn't show any signs of it for a few years. We were five or six, my mother said. I think I'd just lost my first tooth."

"Oh, good. I was wondering how that would impact early childhood development. According to—"

Jason's cell phone rang.

"Hold that thought." He answered it with his usual businesslike greeting. "Falco."

She watched as his face slowly fell.

"Crap. Are you okay, Mom?"

Merry pushed her heavily pregnant body to a sitting position and waited for what seemed like bad news.

Eventually he said, "Yeah, we'll be—Oh, wait a minute. Merry was told not to fly this late in her pregnancy."

"What is it, Jason?"

"My dad had another heart attack. This one seems more serious."

Jason didn't say, *he might not make it this time,* but he didn't have to. His furrowed brow said it all.

"Oh, no. You go ahead. I'll be fine. Roz is all prepared to be my backup. If anything happens, I'll call both of you right away."

"Are you sure?"

"Absolutely."

"But what if she can't get here quickly enough?"

"Then we have a whole building full of tenants I consider friends."

He nodded, then turned back to the phone. "I'll be on the first flight I can get, Mom. Where will you be?" After a short pause, he said. "Good. I'll meet you at Mayo Clinic as soon as possible."

When he hung up, Merry threw her arms around him and squeezed. "I'm sorry about your dad, but if he's at Mayo, he's in the best possible hands."

"I know. Are you sure you'll be all right?"

"Positive."

"Good. Can you pack my bag while I call the team's travel agent?"

"Of course." She smirked. "I'm just glad you're using the airlines."

Sly appeared at Morgaine's door that evening. "Are you all packed and ready to go?"

She sighed. "As ready as I'll ever be."

Something about her expression concerned him. "Look, you don't have to do this for me. I've lived this way for two-and-a-half decades." He shrugged. "What's a few more?"

She straightened her spine and put a determined smile on her face. "No, it'll be good for me too. I need to know I can face challenges and succeed."

That sounded a little too rehearsed. He just hoped she meant it deep down. He would make sure she *did* succeed. If anyone could keep her safe, he could.

"That's my girl." He leaned in and kissed her.

She hit her forehead with the heel of her hand. "Where are my manners? Would you like to come in."

"No, I still have to, um, find myself some dinner. I

figure it'll be a long trip, and I ought to fill up before we leave."

She nodded. "Sure. That makes sense. Well, give me a yell when it's time to go."

He hoped they'd be able to slip away quietly. Yelling wasn't his style.

Chatting casually with his next victim, Sly enjoyed a rare cigarette. It wasn't like he had to worry about lung cancer. The guy had tried to sell him a bag of heroin or cocaine. It was some kind of white powder that Sly assumed wasn't baking soda. He wouldn't feel too bad about biting this one.

Sly just hoped the dealer was only selling and not using the stuff. Getting a contact high through the dealer's blood would sure mess up his and Morgaine's plans for the night—and they were important plans. As soon as he fed, they'd be on a train bound for New York.

"So, you deal drugs in this neighborhood often?"

"Not usually. I was thinking about it though. Lots of college students live around here, right?"

"Yeah, but you wouldn't want to get them hooked on this stuff, would you? I mean, their lives are just beginning. Addiction could ruin everything before they even get started."

The guy shrugged. "That's not my problem. If they're stupid enough to use the shit, they probably don't belong in college anyway."

Good. This one seems like a nonuser and a despicable human being who knows full well what he's doing to others and doesn't care.

Sly clamped one hand around the guy's wrist and the other on his shoulder so he couldn't escape. Then he looked into the drug dealer's eyes and put him under his thrall.

"You'll stand very still, and you won't make a sound."

The guy nodded.

Sly's fangs descended, but before he could sink them into the tempting, pulsing carotid artery in front of him, a blur flashed before his eyes. Gelling into focus on the other side of the victim's neck was Vorigan Malvant.

"Mind if we share?"

Sly let go of the drug dealer and stepped back. "What do you want from me? And I know it's more than just my dinner."

His maker's mouth turned up in an evil-looking grin. "What's wrong with a dinner date?"

When Sly didn't respond, Vorigan continued. "I'd like to do what I didn't get a chance to do all those years ago when we first met."

"Oh? And what was that?"

"Make you mine."

"What the hell does *that* mean?"

"I think you know, but just in case you're not as intelligent as I thought... First I made you a vampire. The next step was to make you my *lover*."

Sly cringed. "I'm taken," he said through clenched teeth.

Vorigan cocked his head and smiled in a way that could only be called *evil*. "I can fix that."

Sly's eyes narrowed, and his lips thinned and hardened. "You'll stay away from her... and everyone I know."

"Then you'll come with me quietly?"

All I need is to get inside the building. He probably

thinks he can follow me right in. "Just let me get a few things first."

"Excellent! Lead the way." Vorigan swept a hand in the direction of Sly's neighborhood. They were less than a mile away. Should he try to outrun the older vampire or continue with the ruse and simply outsmart him?

Sly stuffed his hands in his pockets and walked at a brisk pace toward Beacon Street. Vorigan kept up and chatted blithely.

"You were slippery all those years ago. Why didn't you trust that I'd look out for you?"

"Maybe because you didn't do such a superb job of looking after my wife and unborn daughter."

"The daughter you gave up?"

Don't lose it. That's what he wants. Don't let him get to you. Stay focused.

Vorigan strode beside him and continued talking. "You wouldn't want to be saddled with a wife and child after becoming a vampire. That would spoil all the fun."

Sly couldn't handle it any longer. Almost of its own volition, his fist reared back and flew smack into older vampire's face. Vorigan hit the ground. Sly suspected that the older, stronger vampire was only temporarily disabled. He'd need to run as fast as he knew how to reach the safety of his building before Vorigan retaliated.

For the first time since he'd become a vampire, Sly flew. He'd heard of vampires who could fly, but he had never done it before. He'd never *had* to. Aware of his surroundings despite the blur they had become, he managed to stop when he reached the front steps of their building on Beacon Street. *Home.*

He'd no sooner unlocked the door and rushed inside

when Vorigan came up behind him and slammed into the invisible barrier. Apparently, Gwyneth's resealing worked. The building was impenetrable to all uninvited vampires—in other words, all vampires except Sly.

Seeing the stunned vampire on his ass on the front stoop, Sly burst out laughing. He couldn't help picturing Vorigan in a cartoon with stars and birdies circling his head.

Chapter 12

As she and Sly rushed toward the train station, Morgaine hoped Chad was right, and the smell of moonshine would disguise their scents. She'd poured some in an atomizer and spritzed it on like perfume, hitting all her pulse points. Sly didn't have much of a pulse, but he sprayed plenty on his black slacks and coat. Now they smelled like a couple of drunks—lovely.

They had slipped out the back, and only the lights of the city and an occasional security spotlight broke the darkness. Their connected hands kept her grounded, but Goddess forbid he release her—even for a second. This test couldn't be more challenging. Here she was, out in the open in the dark of night!

I'm safe. I'm with Sly. I'm safe.

Sly carried a small duffel bag and Morgaine's suitcase, insisting the train station was too far for her to carry it herself. She knew he wanted nothing to slow them down. They purposely avoided Vorigan's block. The logical route to the Back Bay station would have brought them close—too close, so for obvious reasons they took the longer way around.

"Almost there, babe." Sly squeezed her hand. She liked the nickname he'd begun using for her. They hadn't taken three more steps when he froze.

"What's wrong?"

"Shit," he muttered.

She glanced around until she saw him. It was her first glimpse of the evil V. Malvant, and although she could only see him from the back, she recognized his warped energy right away. His black, stringy hair lay over thin shoulders like the dark, jagged aura that hung over the rest of him.

"Quick, down here." Sly yanked her arm toward the subway entrance. Before they disappeared down the steps, she saw the other vampire turn and smile cruelly. Yellow light from the streetlamps glinted off his fangs.

"Hurry!" she cried.

They took the steps two at a time all the way to the bottom. A train waited at the platform, but Morgaine doubted they could make it before the doors closed.

Sly scooped her up in his arms, vaulted over the turn-stile, and had them safely ensconced inside when the doors shut. Vorigan, seconds behind them, slammed into the windows. Morgaine gasped. Vorigan's face distorted as he slid down the glass.

As the train pulled away from the station, she heard Sly chuckle. She joined him as he laughed harder. By the time they were well on their way to the next station, they guffawed in cathartic relief.

At last, wiping the tears from her eyes, Morgaine asked, "Now what?"

"Now we take the subway to the next station and change lines. We can board the train at South Station."

She blew out a deep breath. "So, you think we've lost him?"

"Unless he anticipates our next move."

Suddenly a horrible thought occurred to her. "You don't think he's following us, do you?"

She tried to see out the back window, but all was black except for the occasional signal light flashing by.

"No, even he's not that stupid. The one thing no supernatural creature wants is to be found out."

"Why is that?"

"I imagine we'd be tazed, drugged, and dissected."

She shivered.

"Are you cold, love?" He placed an arm around her shoulder and pulled her closer.

"N-no." *Did he just call me "love" instead of "babe"?*

———

At last, Sly and Morgaine arrived at South Station. The place was brightly lit, so he imagined she'd feel more secure. The light bothered his eyes though. Would she feel safe enough if he let go of her sweaty hand to allow him to hunt? Since he hadn't fed for days, and his previous dinner plans had been rudely interrupted, the blood lust was making his head ache. He imagined this must be how someone with low blood sugar felt if he or she skipped a few meals, times a thousand.

After purchasing their train tickets without any money, thanks to his power of mesmerism, Sly led Morgaine to a bench in the waiting area.

"Morgaine, I need to um... find some nourishment. Will you be okay sitting here for a few minutes by yourself?"

Her eyes widened. "I guess so." Quickly, she added, "Or maybe you could just take a little from me?"

Touched by her willingness, he smiled. "Not this time, love. I'm famished and I need more than a snack."

"Oh." She heaved a huge sigh. "In that case, I guess I'll *have* to be okay." She released his hand. "Go ahead. I'll be fine."

"Are you sure?"

She nodded, but her smile seemed strained.

"I'll be back as soon as I possibly can. The train leaves in thirty minutes." He bent down to give her a quick kiss, then took off before she could change her mind.

Stepping out into the night air, he stopped for a moment and sniffed. All he smelled were humans and fuel from cars and trains. No hint of Vorigan. Good. Hopefully they had seen the last of him for a while.

Sly thought he remembered an area nearby where some homeless people hung out. He wasn't fond of feeding on them—especially if they had booze in their blood, but this was an emergency and he didn't have time to watch and wait for a serious crime to be committed. Loitering was a crime, right?

Striding along the tracks, he came to a bridge. Yup. They were there. Huddling around a trash can fire.

One of the three men looked him over with suspicion. "You're a cop, aren't you?"

Sly chuckled. "Far from it."

Another guy looked him up and down. "Well, you're too clean to be one of us."

"Hell, he's too well dressed to be a cop," the third guy said. "So, if you're not a cop, you got any money?"

Sly looked directly into each of their eyes.

"Hey, your eyes are changing…" The man's words trailed off as he fell under Sly's thrall. Sly knew his eyes turned from brown to blue to violet when he mesmerized people. At least that's what he had been told by onlookers before he'd wiped their memories afterward.

One after another, he compelled the men to do his bidding. Taking some from each of them allowed him his fill without depleting a single individual. The tanginess hit his tongue like a welcome first bite from a long-awaited meal.

"Ah…" He burped. "Much better."

He spoke to the men once more. "I have no money for you. You don't see me and won't even remember I was here." Turning to leave, he released them from his mesmerism with a snap of his fingers.

"Guess I was hearing things," one of them said.

The guys turned back to their fire and ignored him.

He trotted back to the station, hoping to find Morgaine waiting calmly exactly where he'd left her. As soon as he entered the noisy waiting area, he spotted the bench—empty.

Shit.

———ᴡᴡ———

Sly found Morgaine huddled on the floor of the ladies' room, struggling to breathe.

He sat beside her and grasped her trembling hand. "Babe, what's going on? Are you all right?"

"Panic attack." She rocked slightly, clutching her chest.

"Here, look at me." He tipped her chin up so she was looking directly into his eyes. *Mesmerism didn't work the first time I tried it on her, but what the hell… try, try again, right?*

She did as he said, but for some reason his mesmerism didn't seem to work on her. *Damn.* Her eyes still blinked and didn't take on a glassy look. Was he losing his touch, or was she just immune? He had never met a human immune to him before, but Morgaine wasn't just anyone. She was a powerful witch, and who knows... maybe she was more powerful than he was.

"Your eyes! They change color."

He sighed heavily. "So I've been told." Realizing he wouldn't be able to use his favorite trick to get her through this trip, he'd have to come up with other ways to relax her.

"What can I do? Would you like a glass of water?"

"Don't leave me."

"I'm not going to leave you. We might have to leave the ladies' room though. I don't think women would appreciate my being here, despite my charisma." He grinned, hoping to joke her out of it.

She didn't crack a smile, but her breathing changed. "Don't worry about visitors." She pointed toward the door and swept her arm in a wide circle. "There. We won't be disturbed now. Breathe in through the nose... out through the mouth..."

Sly pulled a lock of hair away from her face. "What brought this on, love? Was it just my being gone for a few minutes?"

"Not completely." She loosened her fist and let go of the bunched-up dress fabric over her breasts.

"What else factored into it?"

"Some old guy was hitting on me."

He smiled. "You're a beautiful woman. And in case you've forgotten, I'm an old guy."

"You are not. You're only fifty-six."

That made him smile.

At last she turned toward him. "I'm so embarrassed."

"Don't worry about it. If you can accept my embarrassing moments, I can accept yours." He squeezed her hand.

"You don't have any."

"Sure I do. I'm embarrassed that I don't have any money and have to compel people to give me whatever I need."

She shrugged one shoulder. "I guess. It doesn't matter much to me."

He lifted her hand to his lips and kissed her knuckles. "You're amazing. You deserve someone who's equally amazing."

Her eyes widened. "Are you dumping me?"

"No!" He shook his head emphatically. "I'm not breaking up with you. I'll stay around as long as you want to put up with me."

She snorted. "And how long are you going to want to put up *with me*?"

Sly placed his hand on her cheek and leaned in to kiss her. She pulled away.

"What's wrong?"

"I-I need to know something."

"Okay…"

"All the endearments. Are you just being charming? Are you using them to keep me calm? Or are you telling me what you think I want to hear?"

"None of the above."

Morgaine stared at him, waiting… What could he say to her? *He* didn't even know why the pet names flowed so naturally.

"Look, it's been a long time since I've been involved

with anyone. I don't know if what I'm doing is right, wrong, or…" He searched for better words. There *must* be words to explain himself.

She ran her fingers over his thigh to his knee and back. "Maybe it's just lust?"

The gentle pressure of her fingers felt so good that he groaned. "Morgaine, if you don't want me to lift you up and fuck you against the wall in this public bathroom, you'll stop that."

She smiled sadly. "And there's my answer."

"No. Don't do that. Don't put words in my mouth."

She dropped her gaze as well as her hand.

Baffled, Sly sighed. "What's going through that pretty head of yours?"

When she glanced up at him, tears shimmered in her eyes.

He grasped her chin gently and turned her to face him. She tried to twist away, but he wouldn't let her. "Tell me what's bothering you."

"I tried not to fall for you," she said. "I really did. I don't want to get hurt, but I guess my heart had other ideas."

Sly couldn't help but be surprised. *She loves me?* The thought might have caught him off guard, but it didn't scare him.

He stroked her cheek and leaned in to kiss her again. This time, she didn't pull away. She met his lips with a tentative tremble. He kissed her once, tenderly. Then something inside him insisted he go for more. He slanted his head, cupped the back of hers, and dove in for a deep kiss. She wrapped her arms around him and returned his fervor.

Yes, he could get used to this. In fact, he was damn

lucky to have found someone to take a chance on him at all. How many women want a sterile, nocturnal partner on a permanent liquid diet? How many would let him sink his fangs into their necks and trust he'd take no more than he needed? And how many women could he trust with his heart like he knew he could this one?

Their lips had parted automatically. He swept the inside of her mouth with his tongue and found hers. She returned his French kiss but avoided his fangs. Swirling their tongues and tightening their embrace, Sly almost forgot where they were.

The doorknob rattled, bursting their little bubble.

"Damn. Somebody wants to come in." Sly leapt to his feet and extended his hand to her. "Come on, dar…" What should he call her if not "darling"?

She smiled like she had come to some sort of peace with herself. "It's okay, Sly. You can call me sweet names. I kind of like it."

"Good. Are you ready to get out of here now?"

She took his hand and stood, then pointed her finger at the door and circled her arm the other way.

He grinned. "You're amazing."

She shrugged. "I'm a witch."

"And all woman."

Morgaine had slept with her head in Sly's lap most of the way to New York. They took a cab to their hotel, thanks to Sly mesmerizing the driver.

The city was decorated for Christmas. She thought it was still early, but perhaps since they were in the commercial center of the universe…

Now he was going to try his mesmerism on the desk clerk. Fortunately, the hotel was pared down to a skeleton crew at four o'clock in the morning, so there was no one but Morgaine to witness it.

Sly made eye contact with the man and held his gaze for a few seconds before saying, "I called about the corporate suite. Is it still available?"

The desk clerk answered him cheerfully. "Yes, sir. Do you have a credit card?"

"But the place is already paid for."

"Of course, but we need a credit card for incidentals."

Sly reached into his inner coat pocket and withdrew an invisible wallet. He went through the motions of looking for something. "I'm sorry. I must have left all my cards at home. That shouldn't matter though, right? The company will pay for everything."

"Very true, sir. We prefer a card for identification but if you don't have one, you'll need to fill out this form." He handed a slip of paper to Sly and returned to his computer while Sly filled out only the top portion asking for a name. He scribbled in the other spaces, then slid the form across the desk.

"Thank you, sir."

Sly acted like he was extracting some money from his billfold and slid nothing across the counter. "A tip for your trouble."

"Thank you, sir." The guy smiled at both of them and said, "I hope you have a pleasant stay, Mr. and Mrs. Flores."

Mrs. Flores? Had Sly registered that way? Or did the desk clerk just assume they were married? She hadn't paid much attention to what name or names he had actually written. She supposed he could have gotten away with registering as Mickey Mouse with the desk clerk under his thrall.

On the way up to their suite, she became curious and had to ask. "Sly? Have you ever done that mesmerizing thing on me?"

He wrapped an arm around her waist. "Nope. I tried it when you had the panic attack, but it didn't work."

"Damn. It would have been easier."

"Yeah, that's what I thought."

"Why didn't it work on me?"

He kissed her temple. "I'm not sure, but I'm glad it didn't. For one thing, it's a trick. Whatever a person says or does isn't real. You're taking away their free will. If you want to know what they'd really say or do—who they are—you can't manipulate them."

"That makes sense, but what if I gave you permission? Like in an emergency."

"I suppose…"

The elevator stopped, and the doors whooshed open. Sly picked up her suitcase and followed the corridor to their suite. He used the key card to open the door for her.

Morgaine strolled inside and flicked on the lights. On the thick carpet sat a stately tan sofa, two overstuffed armchairs, and some mahogany end tables, plus a coffee table polished to gleaming. "Pretty!"

"Yeah, it's almost too nice. Maybe I should ask for another crappier room."

She whirled on him. "Why?"

He laughed. "I was kidding."

"Oh." She felt silly whenever she didn't recognize his humor. Oh well, she'd catch on eventually.

"Getting back to why I didn't mesmerize you…"

"Yes?"

"If I hadn't let you talk, I wouldn't have discovered some important information."

She stopped admiring the artwork and turned to face him. "What information?"

He set the suitcase down, crossed to her, and grasped her shoulders gently. "That you love me."

She glanced up at him coquettishly. "Did I say that?"

"Sort of." He drew her in and held her close.

She tensed.

"What's wrong?" he asked.

"Nothing." She let out a deep sigh. "Okay, there is something, but it's no big deal."

"Spill it."

She hesitated a moment, then mumbled, "You didn't say it back."

He stroked her hair. "That doesn't mean I won't."

"So, I'm in this alone for now?"

"You're not alone. I'm just…"

She looked up at him, expectantly.

"I don't know how to explain it. Maybe I'm still not used to the idea of being *with* someone other than my late wife. Or I've been missing Alice for so long, I have to let go of that first. Or maybe I'm just being cautious. I don't really know. I'm sorry. I guess that's not really helping."

She nodded but didn't speak. She didn't want her voice to tremble or crack. *It'll be okay. He'll come around—I hope.*

Suddenly, Sly's body slid out of her grasp and fell to the floor.

"Sly!"

She looked at the heap and couldn't fathom what had happened. Kneeling next to him, she shook his wilted body.

"Sly! Wake up!" His chest wasn't rising and falling. *Oh, no. Is he dead?* A moment later, she rolled her eyes at herself. *Well, of course he's dead. He's been undead for twenty-six years. He told me once he only takes a few breaths per hour.*

Suddenly it occurred to her—the sunrise. It must be sunrise! She rushed to the window and spied a faint purplish-pink sky and a golden glow behind mostly dark buildings.

"Oh, crap. Now what do I do?"

She had to protect him from the sunlight. He had explained that a suite would afford them a room they could darken while she remained in another room with the sunbeams streaming in during the day.

This schedule sucks.

She had to act fast. There was no way she could drag him across a carpeted living room all the way to the bedroom, avoid the growing light, then lift him onto the bed and seal the curtains shut before the sun caused him to burst into flames. *I could close and tape the curtains first... No, that would take too long, and meanwhile the sun is rising!*

Thinking fast, she grabbed his wrists and dragged his lifeless body into the bathroom. *No windows in here at all. Perfect!*

But what if she had to go?

She pondered that for about a minute, then realized he wouldn't wake up if she sat on his stomach and played solitaire all day. "Okay, I guess you're safe from the sun." *And I'm safe from embarrassment.*

She strode to the bedroom, pulled a blanket and pillow off the bed, then returned to the luxurious, spa-like bath and tucked him in.

Did it always happen like this? Passing out no matter where he was when the sun rose? *That could be quite inconvenient.* That's when she realized that he needed her as much as she needed him.

Chapter 13

MERRY POUNDED ON THE DOOR OF APARTMENT 3B FOR the third time. "Morgaine!" *Where the hell is she?*

Gwyneth was jogging up the stairs. "Merry? What on earth's going on? I ain't never heard you yellin' like that before."

"Oh, Gwyneth, do you know where Sly and Morgaine are?"

"Yeah, they went to New York City for a spell."

"A spell? Morgaine had to go all the way to New York for something to do a spell?"

Gwyneth chuckled. "Well, yes and no. I meant they went away for a while. A spell is just another way of saying 'a while.' As it turns out, Morgaine is givin' a friend some magickal help too."

"Oh… Oh!" Merry clutched her pregnant belly and doubled over with the pain of another contraction.

"I do declare, Merry. Are y'all are in labor?"

She did her Lamaze breathing and nodded.

"Oh, dear. Where's Jason?"

When the pain eased, Merry straightened. "At his parents' house in Minnesota. His dad's had another heart attack. We decided that since it's about three weeks before my due date, I shouldn't fly. Roz is my backup, but I can't get ahold of her."

"Oh, my goodness. Well, what did you have planned? Was you doin' a home birth or hospital?"

"Hospital. I can't drive myself though. Can you drive?"

"I ain't got a driver's license, but I'm sure I could figure it out if y'all have an automatic transmission and I don't have to shift the thingy."

Merry laughed. "No offense, but driving in this city isn't a piece of cake for experienced drivers. Never mind. I'll think of something else."

"Maybe Nathan can drive. Let me run down and ask him."

"Let's take the elevator."

"Too slow. Y'all can take it—or better yet, wait here and I'll call up to ya with what he says."

Merry worried about another contraction coming on, so she just nodded.

Gwyneth took off running down the stairs. She disappeared from view, and Merry heard her footsteps fade as they tapped out a staccato beat on the marble steps.

She braced herself through the next contraction and barely heard Gwyneth talking to the resident of Apt 1A.

After a brief wait, Gwyneth yelled up the stairwell. "Nathan don't drive neither, but he says he'll take y'all on the back of his bicycle."

Merry laughed and called down. "No, thank you."

Gwyneth's feet tapped up the stairs again. "Let me try Jules or Lily."

"Never mind. I'll take a cab."

When Gwyneth finally reached her, Merry was panting. "I'll go with y'all."

"That's sweet, but you don't have to."

"Y'all need a birthin' coach, right?"

"Have you ever witnessed a birth before?"

"Sugar, I'm from the hills of Tennessee. I've seen my

share of home births. A hospital with doctors and nurses helpin' should be a piece of cake, as y'all would say."

Gwyneth wouldn't have been Merry's first choice, or even her third or fourth, but at this point she couldn't be picky. "Thank you. I'll need my suitcase."

———————

In the Admissions waiting room, Gwyneth paced while Merry waited patiently. How could she be so cool, calm, and collected? Maybe it was just the relief of knowing she was at the hospital. She probably felt comfortable here, being a nurse and all.

"Gwyneth, why don't you sit down?"

"Sorry, Merry. Hospitals make me as nervous as a cat in a room full of rocking chairs."

"Everything's going to be fine. Take a seat."

"Did y'all call Jason?"

"Yes."

"Is he flyin' back?"

"Yes, but flights were all booked up. He won't get here until tomorrow at the earliest."

A wave of relief washed over Gwyneth. "Thank the Lord and Lady. He'll be here in plenty of time."

Merry squinted at her. "What do you mean? You don't think I'll be in labor *that* long, do you?"

"I wouldn't want to second-guess Mother Nature or nothin', but this is your first baby. I knew a girl what went seventy-two hours, screamin' and pitchin' fits."

Merry's eyes rounded and she blanched.

"Oh, but don't worry, sugar." Gwyneth strode over to her and patted her shoulder. "I'm sure y'all will be just fine."

"Uh… me too. Oddly enough, I haven't had a contraction in about ten minutes. Maybe they're Braxton-Hicks."

"Who? I ain't heard tell of them hicks. Are they from West Virginny?"

Merry smiled, then coughed. "No, those are the names of the two people who scientifically studied false labor."

"False labor? Y'all faked this whole thing? Why?"

"No, I didn't fake anything. Sometimes it just happens. A woman has contractions for a few hours, then they stop. You've never heard of that?"

"Hell, no. Back home if a woman starts grittin' her teeth, y'all better boil some water and get out the clean towels. There's no fakin' allowed."

"It's not faking…" Merry took a deep breath and sighed. "Never mind."

Gwyneth patted her hand. "It's all right. I don't blame y'all fer bein' scared. I've heard some horror stories about birthin' babies, and y'all have probably heard them too.

The woman behind the glass window called Merry's number.

"Oh, thank God."

"And I'll thank the Goddess. Now let's go have that baby, and no more stallin', ya hear?"

In the restaurant's horseshoe-shaped bench seat, Sly stretched, trying to get the crick out of his neck. He probably got it from sleeping on cold tile all day, but he wasn't about to complain. Morgaine had probably saved his life. Plus she had spent the day all alone, except for one phone call to Mikhail to set up this meeting.

The waiter at the French restaurant seemed to know

Mikhail well. His "special wine" was brought to the table without his even ordering it.

"Does Monsieur wish to share his owner's reserve with everyone?"

"No, Pierre. Just the other gentleman and myself will be drinking my special vintage tonight. The lady can order whatever she likes."

Morgaine smiled and asked for herbal tea.

The waiter said, "Very good," and left.

Delicious aromas teased Sly's palate, but naturally, he wouldn't be able to partake. At times like this, he envied the living.

Over the chatter from other patrons, Morgaine had made introductions. Mikhail seemed like an affable fellow. Tall, dark, and aristocratic but without the arrogant air Sly had expected from the older, more experienced vampire.

"Tell me how you like it." Mikhail nodded toward Sly's glass.

Sly took a sip. The smooth red wine slid down his throat and was like nothing he'd ever tasted. A moment later, his blood thirst was gone!

"Amazing," he breathed. "I feel—better." He glanced around the restaurant to be sure no one could overhear. "Is it always like that? Instantaneous, I mean?"

Mikhail shrugged one shoulder. "It depends. If you haven't fed for a while, it might take longer. And if you have to spend prolonged periods in sunlight, you'll probably need more. But be careful. It's potent."

Sly swirled what was in his glass. "Have you ever gotten drunk on it?"

Mikhail grinned. "Tipsy maybe, but not drunk."

Sly took another tentative sip and smiled. *A cure! At last!* "Are there any other things I should know? Will it sap my strength or dull my senses?"

"No. That's why it's so popular among our kind. It removes the negative effects of our condition, while allowing us to keep the positive."

Sly shook his head in wonder. "It's a miracle."

"You might still need sunglasses and sunscreen. I imagine it's been a long time since you've been exposed to sunlight."

He sighed. "Twenty-six years."

"Only twenty-six?" Mikhail didn't appear to be joking or sardonic.

The waiter returned with Morgaine's herbal tea. She had been studying the menu and was probably starved after all day in the hotel room.

"Would the lady like to order?" the waiter asked.

"Yes, please. I'll have the coq au vin, spring greens with the house dressing on the side, and do you bring rolls or bread to the table first?"

He grinned. "Only the best warm wheat rolls in the world."

She licked her lips. "Hurry."

The waited bowed slightly and rushed off.

Sly chuckled. "Hungry?"

"Famished."

Mikhail crossed his arms. "Aren't you taking care of my dear, old friend?"

Sly saddened. "I would have, but I'm afraid sunrise snuck up on me this morning. Had I thought of it before I passed out on the floor, I'd have urged her to order room service." He took her hand. "Why didn't you?"

"I didn't want to add any charges to the bill since you'd paid up front and didn't have a credit card."

"Oh, sweetheart…"

The waiter returned with a small basket of rolls that smelled freshly baked. He set a tiny crock of butter in front of Morgaine, and she dove into the appetizer.

"How do you two know each other?" Mikhail asked.

"We live in the same apartment building. Our friendship goes back to the night she moved in—what was it, nine years ago?"

"Ey," she mumbled with her mouth full.

The guys chuckled.

Sly changed the subject. "So, if you don't mind my asking—how old are you?"

"About six hundred," Mikhail answered casually.

"Six hundred! I can't fathom six hundred years on earth. Think of the changes you must have witnessed over the centuries."

Mikhail swirled the wine in his glass. "The last century was the most impressive as far as change, but people are the same."

Sly tipped his head. "How so?"

"Greedy, acquisitive, then surprised when all that doesn't make them happy. But technology has certainly changed. We used to need a horse for transportation. Now we have trains, planes, and automobiles."

"Not to mention the communication devices," Sly added.

Mikhail chuckled. "So little to say, so many ways to say it. I think I was content as soon as we had the telephone."

"Seriously?"

"All right, maybe the cell phones, email, and ATMs

weren't bad, but don't talk to me about half the crap on TV and the Internet."

Morgaine nodded her head emphatically, then mumbled around her bite of roll. "'At's right." After gulping down the mouthful, she continued. "There's so much misinformation about magick, it makes me nuts. If you don't have proper training, you're asking for trouble."

Mikhail leaned closer. "Speaking of which, do you know what to do about my little problem?"

"I want to see the space and I still need to write the spell, but I'll do that after you fill me in on the specifics. I brought the ingredients I'll need. It sounded as if you knew the identity of the evil magician."

"Oh, yes."

"Good. That will help. You don't happen to know what kind of hex he used, do you?"

"I'm sorry, no. But I know he brought in some kind of paper and left without it. We caught him on security cameras."

"He may have burned it. That's what witches usually do with spells."

"Could he have planted it somewhere?"

Morgaine thought briefly. "He could have left it. Or he could have tucked it in his pocket before he left. What did it look like?"

"It looked like a small scroll. Unfortunately, our cameras only cover certain areas. There were places he could have left it without our knowing it."

"Okay. I can make the wording pretty general and still break almost any curse. However, if he left an object behind, we should try to find it. Then we'll bury it in the earth and neutralize it."

Sly couldn't help being impressed. She was so knowledgeable and didn't hesitate to share that knowledge with others. It was a shame her friend didn't feel he could return the favor. Or, maybe he could. Perhaps he just needed a bit of convincing.

Sly cleared his throat. "Mikhail. My lady here is being very generous with her skills, knowledge, and information. I wonder if you could share with us a little something about the special product you make. At least tell us *why* it works. It seems only fair."

Mikhail sighed. "It is, but even if I tell you what's in it, you'd never find it again in a million years."

"I'm awfully curious, Mikhail," Morgaine said.

Mikhail straightened as if gearing up for a long lecture. "You've heard of the stigmata, right?"

They nodded. Sly couldn't help wondering where this conversation was going.

Mikhail continued. "Well, Joan of Arc, while in prison, received the mysterious wounds on her hands and feet where Christ was nailed to the cross. The rags used to bandage the wounds and stanch the flow of blood were saved by one of the guards who believed in her sainthood long before she was canonized. He sold them as souvenirs after she was burned at the stake."

"That seems crass," Sly said. "But enterprising."

"Whether it was or not, if I hadn't obtained a small sample of her blood, you and I wouldn't be drinking this now." He raised his glass of wine and swirled the red liquid.

Morgaine snapped her fingers. "Of course. Joan of Arc, burned at the stake. Two things vampires are deathly afraid of. Fire and wooden stakes. I see the connection. So, is she the patron saint of vampires or something?"

"Or something," Mikhail confirmed.

"I see." Sly was still hoping that some secret would slip out. "So how do you add her blood to the wine?"

Mikhail shifted uncomfortably, then checked his watch. "I'm awfully sorry. I just remembered a previous engagement." He reached into his pocket and produced a card. "Here's the address of my warehouse. I live in the penthouse in the same building. Stop by tomorrow sometime in the afternoon."

Sly gaped at his glass of wine. "One glass will protect me all day tomorrow?"

Mikhail tipped his head. "Hmm… maybe. Finish my glass as well as your own just to be sure."

"Won't he be tired if he's up all night and all day too?" Morgaine asked.

"Tonight, you'll sleep like you used to. You may even dream."

"Wow. And tomorrow you'll give me more of this fantastic stuff?"

Mikhail laughed. "Don't worry. I'll have a glass ready and a bottle open. If Morgaine keeps her promise, I'll have a case waiting for you to take home."

Morgaine straightened and looked slightly offended. "I always keep my promises."

"Of course. I didn't mean to infer you wouldn't. Forgive me."

Sly shook his head in wonder. "I can't get over the power of this wonderful product of yours. It seems like I'm dreaming already."

"Morgaine, Sly, enjoy my fair city, and bring your

magick mojo with you tomorrow afternoon. Meanwhile, I'll try to search the places not covered by cameras and see if there's anything hidden." He stood and bowed slightly to Morgaine. "It was wonderful to see you again. Sylvestro, nice meeting you."

Sly rose and shook his hand. "Likewise."

"I'll see you both tomorrow." With that, Mikhail strode toward the coat room.

Morgaine watched as he left. "That was odd."

"I know. I think he was changing the subject and leaving before we could change it back and find out too much about making his special vintage."

She nodded slowly. "That's exactly what he was doing. Which makes me think we might be able to duplicate it."

"Would he refuse to help a friend?"

"He hasn't seen me for eight years, and he just met you. Why would he hand over his trade secrets?"

"Good point."

Morgaine and Sly took in some of the famous New York sights after dinner. After a horse-and-buggy ride through Central Park all snuggled together, they walked hand in hand and window-shopped down Fifth Avenue, which was well lit, thank the Goddess. They even took a short bus ride to Greenwich Village. The whole time Sly kept Morgaine safe and anchored. More importantly, he didn't make her feel like a freak.

She was so happy that she didn't want to think about their private time together ending. But eventually they'd have to return to their lives in Boston, darn it.

"You should probably go to sleep at a reasonable

hour so you're not exhausted tomorrow," Sly said. "I wonder if maybe I should too?"

Morgaine grinned. "Is that your sneaky way of getting me into bed with you?"

"Do I need to be sneaky?"

She laughed. "Not at all." After a short pause, she decided to risk a little more intimate information. "I love making love to you, Sly."

He smiled down at her and squeezed her hand. "I love making love to you too."

They continued their walk in companionable silence until they reached their hotel. The young man behind the desk who had checked them in glanced up and then went back to his work as if he didn't even see them.

Sly let go of her hand, but only to wrap a possessive arm around her waist.

As soon as they were ensconced in the elevator and the doors whooshed closed, Sly pulled her into a firm embrace and kissed her soundly.

They didn't pull apart until they reached their floor and the doors opened. An older couple stood there. They smiled knowingly as they exchanged places. Morgaine glanced back over her shoulder as she strolled away and caught the other couple moving closer to each other. Affection inspired affection, apparently.

Morgaine just knew Sly loved her. She'd wait patiently for him to say it though. Forcing the words would do no good and might push him away. That was the last thing she wanted. She felt more secure with him than with Gwyneth. Actually, she trusted him more than anyone in recent years—and he was a vamp! *No*, she decided. He was Sly. And Sly just happened to be a vampire.

Once in their room, Sly took her hand and led her to the bed. Morgaine stepped away from him and found the zipper at the nape of her neck. She dragged it down as far as she could, then turned around. Without needing to be asked, he opened her black dress the rest of the way. She rotated back to face him and let it slip off her shoulders and puddle on the floor around her feet.

His breath hitched.

That was the reaction she'd been hoping for when she'd dressed braless and pantyless. He hopped out of his black trousers and peeled off his shirt, tossing both to the floor. His erection jutted out proudly.

"You go commando a lot," Morgaine noted.

"Does that turn you off?"

"Not hardly! It turns me *on*."

He grinned. Then without warning he tackled her.

She shrieked, then laughed as they bounced on the bed. "Someone's feeling playful…"

Sly leaned over her. "Sex should be fun. Don't you agree?"

She nodded, though part of her thought sex should also be passionate and loving. *Never mind. He'll get there.*

As if he'd read her mind, he swooped in for a long kiss. She opened her mouth, and their tongues sought each other immediately. His very shallow breaths grew deeper and more frequent. Soon he undulated on top of her and a fevered heat seemed to take over.

Her mind clouded. She couldn't concentrate on anything but his drugging kiss. Good Goddess! She'd never been kissed like this.

He flipped both of them over until she lay on top of

him. His hands were everywhere. He stroked her back, then squeezed her bottom. She felt his hard shaft prodding her belly.

When she rolled slightly to one side so she could grip his erection, it filled her hand. She squeezed and stroked until he growled into her mouth.

She lifted her head and sat astride his hips. "I want you inside me so badly, I think I'll lose my mind if you aren't fucking me soon."

He smiled. "Whatever the lady wants…"

Morgaine sighed with relief and rose onto her knees. She took his cock in her hand and positioned herself over it. As she impaled her slick channel, they both moaned.

He grasped her hips and began thrusting. She leaned over him and offered his mouth her breast. He took the pebbled nipple between his lips and sucked. At the same time he added a clit rub. She gasped and braced herself on his shoulders to survive the erotic onslaught.

Every nerve ending trembled with electricity. "Oh, Goddess!" Before she could say more, a powerful orgasm ripped through her. Sly had to let her breast pop out of his mouth. She spasmed over and over again. Her clenching inner walls set off Sly's climax. He went rigid and jerked into her core. They finished together, and she collapsed on top of him.

He wrapped his arms around her. "There now, wasn't that fun?"

She let out a weak chuckle, but as she caught her breath, her laughter grew. "It certainly was. Was it good for you?"

He shrugged. "Passable, I guess."

She tried to smack his shoulder, but he caught her wrist. "You know that was the answer you deserved for asking such an inane question, right?"

"I suppose. But I-I've never experienced anything like this. And I know you have. Can you blame me for wondering?"

He was quiet for a moment. When he finally spoke, his voice was barely a whisper. "That's why I thought you might have a hard time with this. Knowing how much I loved my wife, I knew you'd wonder if you measured up."

She rolled off him and tried to face the other way. He stopped her and pulled her close. Looking into her eyes, he brushed back her hair. "You don't need to worry. You're wonderful. Our relationship is different from my marriage, but it's neither better nor worse." Taking her chin between his finger and thumb, he held her facing him.

She quickly averted her gaze. "Are you trying to mesmerize me?"

He cocked his head. "No, but it would only be fair."

"Fair? How?"

"Because you mesmerized me." He drew her lips to his and gave her a long, tender kiss that told her how special she really was.

Chapter 14

MEANWHILE, BACK AT HOME, GWYNETH KNOCKED ON the door of the new neighbor who was living in the apartment directly below hers. She had been anxious to welcome the newcomer to the building. Since Merry had been diagnosed with those Braxton-Hicks contractions and sent home, Gwyneth was off the hook for a while. *Whew*.

A petite Asian woman opened the door a few inches and peeked around the opening.

"Howdy, I hope I'm not interruptin' anythin'. I'm Gwyneth—your neighbor from upstairs."

"Ah, I'm pleased to meet you. My name is Lillian, but you can call me Lily." She didn't open the door further or invite Gwyneth in.

Puzzled, Gwyneth asked, "I don't normally invite myself, but do y'all mind if I come in?"

"I…" Lily glanced over her own shoulder nervously. "The place is a mess. I'm just moving in."

"Oh, y'all don't have to make no fuss, bless your heart. I don't need no impressin'."

"I—uh, well…"

What a silly woman. Did she think a few unpacked boxes would matter to a neighbor? Lily looked behind her again. When she let go of the door, Gwyneth pushed it open, ready to reassure her that her place was no more a mess than any—

"I do declare! What in tarnation happened here?"

Lily hung her head in shame. Gwyneth wandered through the apartment, openmouthed and wide eyed. Scorched furniture and rugs were scattered over the blackened hardwood floors.

"I-I'm sorry. I haven't worked in a couple of days."

"Worked? What's work got to do with it? Unless you're a professional firebug. In which case, I want to know. I live right over y'all."

"No, it's nothing like that. I… I have this problem."

Gwyneth took Lily's hand and patted it. As she led Lily to the charred sofa, Gwyneth said, "Maybe I can help."

Lily sank down onto the couch. "I doubt it."

"Now, come on, sugar. Y'all can tell me anythin' and I won't breathe a word. We all have our little problems."

"Not like this."

"Try me."

Lily heaved a deep sigh. "I might shock you."

"Oh, honey. I'm a witch and a phone-sex actress. How shocked can I be?"

Lily bolted up straight. "Really?"

"Uh-huh. Now come on. Out with it."

Lily bit her lip, then offered the strangest explanation Gwyneth had ever heard.

"I'm a dragon. I sneeze fire. The only cure for it is regular sex. So I'm a call girl, but because I just moved to this city, I have no clients and haven't worked recently."

"A dragon? But y'all just look like a pretty girl to me."

Lily smiled. "Thank you. You're looking at my human form. If I need to protect myself, I shift into my dragon form, but that's only as a last resort."

"I see. So you're a shapeshifter?"

"You've heard of us?"

"Oh, honey. Y'all have no idea. But back to the sex thing. I think I get it. That's how y'all blow off steam— so to speak."

"Exactly."

"Well, I'll be jiggered. Can't y'all find a dildo? I have several upstairs. What's your favorite color?"

Lily chuckled. "Thank you, but vibrators don't work. I need the real thing."

"Well, there's got to be somethin'…"

"Perhaps there is, but I don't know of anything else and haven't any clients yet. I just moved here from San Francisco."

"Why, that's clear across the country. What made y'all pick up and move so far away?"

"I-I'd rather not talk about it."

I wish Morgaine was here. She's way more psychic than I am, and this lady is just confusin' the hell outta me.

"Well, there's gotta be somethin' I can do to help. I can't let you set the building on fire."

Gwyneth could think of only one solution. It wouldn't be her favorite thing to do, but this was an emergency.

She moved closer to Lily and draped an arm around her. "Now, I don't usually swing this way, but for the sake of my neighbors…" She pursed her lips. "Pucker up, darlin'. Looks like we're gonna have to get cozy real fast."

Lily shoved her off the couch, and Gwyneth landed on the hard floor with a thud.

"Ouch! Why'd y'all go and do that? I was just tryin' to help!"

Lily crossed her arms. "I don't swing that way either, and I don't want to start now."

Loud laughter echoed all around them. Gwyneth shook her fist at the ceiling. "Chad! Y'all know it's impolite to eavesdrop."

"Yeah, but I wouldn't have missed that for the world."

Gwyneth's lips thinned. "What in blazes—er, I mean, what in tarnation are you doin' here anyway?"

"I wanted to meet the new neighbor too."

"And how long have you been here?"

"I was right behind you, oooo…"

She glanced at Lily, who was giving her the oddest look.

"Oh, sorry. Y'all don't know about our ghost, I guess." She picked herself up off the floor and brushed off her skirt. "He can be a smart-ass, but he's basically harmless."

Lily glanced around the room, nervously. "Basically?"

"He only pulls pranks on people he don't like. I'd say not to worry, but y'all burnin' down the place he haunts might really tick him off."

Lily covered her eyes and wailed, "What am I to do?"

"If only I had a body…"

Gwyneth snapped her fingers. "That's it! I know exactly who can help y'all, Lily."

She lifted her eyebrows. "Who?"

"Yeah, who?" Chad asked.

"Nathan! He lives in the apartment right under y'all's. I don't think he's ever had a girlfriend in his life."

Lily sounded doubtful. "He isn't gay, is he?"

"Nope. I remember some reporter tryin' to make it look like he and Jason had a thing for each other, but from what I hear, they was both pretty horrified at the thought."

Lily folded her hands in her lap. "Would this Nathan be understanding of my—um, real nature? As understanding as you are?"

"Oh, heck yes. He's a shapeshifter too. That's why I thought y'all would be good together."

"Oh! Is he a dragon?"

"No, but I wouldn't feel right tellin' you all his secrets. Why don't I go talk to him and if he's interested, he can tell you himself."

"How can I ever thank you?"

"Don't burn down the building. That'll be thanks enough."

"Sly, dear. It's me, Alice."

"Alice?"

Sly bolted upright and saw his late wife sitting at the foot of the bed. She looked as young and beautiful as the day they'd met. "But how can you be here? You're…"

She smiled. "Dead?"

"I was going to say a dream."

"I know. I had to come and see you one last time. This is the only way I could."

"Why? Are you going somewhere? Or, somewhere else?" Sly scratched his head.

"No, I'm where I'm supposed to be. I had to visit you though. I have something important to tell you."

"I'm listening." He reached for her hand.

She laid her palm in his and curled her fingers around

his hand. He was amazed by the warmth and pressure. She actually felt real, but how could that be?

"I want you to stop holding onto the past. I've seen you struggle and resist the changes in your life. It's time for you to move forward."

"What do you mean?" He glanced at the other side of the bed, but it was empty. Where was Morgaine? "Do you mean with someone else?"

"Yes. You've brooded for too long. It's time to enjoy life again."

He stared at his lap. "If you can call what I do living."

"You have a lot to look forward to. You've been re-united with our daughter, a grandchild is on the way, and you have the wholehearted love of a good woman. But you could miss out on that blessing if you don't open your eyes and your heart."

"Is that why you're here… to tell me it's all right to fall in love again?"

"It's not just all right. I want you to."

"Seriously? But you had a jealous streak when we were dating… sometimes even after we were married."

"It's not like that anymore. Things like envy, jealousy, greed, and fear… we let them go here. As it turns out, all we really have that matters is love."

Sly smiled. "You were always the wise one."

"You're wise too. You simply have to believe in yourself and trust your instincts. She's right for you. Allow the love you already share to blossom."

He looked to his side again, and there was Morgaine, sleeping with an angelic look on her face. A blonde curl crossed her cheek and lay on the pillow next to him. Warmth flooded his heart. He wanted

*more than anything to touch that curl, but he didn't
want to wake her.*

"Alice?" He glanced back toward the foot of the bed,
but she was gone.

How odd. Why hadn't Morgaine been there a few
moments ago when Alice appeared? Now Alice was
gone and Morgaine was beside him. He knew dreams
took strange turns and often represented the dreamer's
subconscious thoughts.

It didn't take a genius to figure this one out.

Sly blinked in the glare of the first sunrise he'd witnessed in twenty-six years. When his eyes adjusted to
the light, he noted the beautiful colors reflected in the
windows of the high-rises. New York City was beautiful
at this time of day—and almost quiet. He wondered how
many others woke up to this view and didn't even notice
it. A lump formed in his throat.

Morgaine came up behind him and wrapped her arms
around his waist. "Are you enjoying the view?"

He couldn't speak, so he nodded.

As if she understood, she remained quiet and let him
stand there and lean on the window sill for a long time.
Morgaine was the perfect person to share this moment
with. His late wife, Alice, would have been chattering
away, completely unaware of the spiritual impact this
was having on his psyche.

He turned in Morgaine's arms and hugged her
close. "I never appreciated this time of day like I do
right now."

"It's beautiful, isn't it?" Morgaine whispered beside

his neck, her breath warming him. With even more joy, he realized that although he could hear her blood coursing through her veins, he had no desire to drink from her—or anyone else.

He pulled away far enough to see her face. "This morning is unbelievably beautiful, and so are you."

She gave him her shy smile and looked down.

"Why do you do that?"

"Do what?"

"Hide your eyes when I give you a compliment."

"I don't know. Maybe I just want to savor the moment privately. I'm not used to it, you know."

He sighed and shook his head. "Yes, I know and I don't understand it. You must have had boyfriends at some point."

Her expression saddened immediately.

He placed a finger under her chin and held her gaze. "What happened?"

"How can you tell something happened?"

He smoothed her hair down her back, hoping to soothe her. "I just can."

She let out a deep breath. "Date rape put a stop to my social life. I thought it would be temporary, but the longer I went without a relationship, the more comfortable it became."

Profound anger invaded his gut. He could tell there was more to this story, and it was hard for her to talk about. Controlling his voice, he asked, "There's something else. What is it, babe?"

"I almost died—Natalee Holloway style. Only I managed to escape and swim to shore."

"Shit! No wonder you're scared. Look, you don't

have to tell me any more if you don't want to, but I'm here to listen if you'd like to talk it out."

"I think it's enough to know I'm safe with you. Years ago, when it happened, I talked about it with counselors and the police. I got a lot of support, and the guy went to jail for a long, long time."

"Is that why you moved away from Baltimore?"

"Yes. Boston reminded me of Baltimore, somewhat. I lived in a little row house there, and the Back Bay has the same kind of historic vibe—but on a slightly larger scale. And even though it snows more in Boston, the summers aren't quite so hot and humid."

"Is that when the agoraphobia started?"

"Shortly after that. It took every ounce of self-control I had not to hex the Hell out of the guy."

Sly enveloped her in a strong hug. "Oh, honey. I'm so sorry that happened to you. If he ever gets out, let me know. Okay? I'll pay him a little visit."

That made her smile. "I'll bet. But you don't have to defend me. It's just nice to hear you say you want to. I love you, Sly."

Fuck. Could he say it back yet? She certainly needed to hear it. But did he mean it? He thought he did. He wanted to. Her expectant eyes shifted to her feet. If he hurt her, he'd never forgive himself. *Better wait until I'm sure.*

Gwyneth pounded on apartment 1A's door for the third time. "I know y'all are in there, Nathan. It's just lil' ol' Gwyneth. Now open up."

Several clicks on the other side of the door said he was unlocking what must have been Fort Knox-like security.

Finally the door opened and Nathan peeked around it.

Gwyneth jammed her hands on her hips and sputtered, "Jeezum Crow. Y'all would think there's martial law and chaos out here or somethin'."

"What do you want, Gwyneth?"

"Well, for starters, how about some manners? Where I come from, when a neighbor comes to call, y'all invite her in."

Nathan hung his head and stepped back, opening his door wider. She understood that was the only invitation she was likely to get and breezed inside.

He closed the door behind her and relocked it, but only by the dead bolt. He looked handsomer than usual. His black slacks and black shirt were nicely pressed, and his hair, though wet, looked good slicked back that way.

"So, aren't y'all gonna offer me some hospitality, like a place to set a spell?"

Nathan shrugged, then gestured to his sofa. "I suppose you want a cup of coffee too."

"If it's not too much trouble. That would be most kind of y'all."

Nathan shuffled off to his kitchen, and while he was gone, Gwyneth wandered around the living room, appraising the only apartment in the building that she'd never seen. Other than the necessary furniture and a large-screen TV, there was very little in it.

As expected, the raven had a lovely hand-carved perch next to his big bay window. "I wonder if he'd rather be his human or bird form?" she mumbled to herself.

"Oh, he definitely prefers his raven form. I envy his ability to fly on the wind and have some control

over it. Me? I wind up halfway down the block with the slightest gust."

"I didn't know y'all was here, Chad."

"Yeah. I followed you downstairs and came in behind you. So, if you were a shapeshifter, what kind would you be?"

"If I was a shapeshifter, a bird would be the type I'd choose. Not like Nathan or Jason or Morgaine's owl, Athena. I'd be a beautiful swan or a Canada goose, able to glide across water or air currents equally good."

She settled on Nathan's comfortable distressed-leather couch and crossed her ankles in an attempt to look ladylike. However, no lady would propose what she was about to ask him.

"Chad, would y'all mind leavin' us alone for a bit? I have somethin' personal to discuss with Mr. Nourie."

Chad sighed. *"I suppose. Although I'd love to see him squirm when you ask him to be Lillian's booty call."*

"Oh, hush, you."

Chad laughed.

Nathan returned with two mugs and handed her one filled with steaming, dark brown liquid.

"Yeck, black coffee. You should have asked for tea."

In as sweet a way as she could muster, she asked, "Do y'all have a speck of milk or sugar? I'm not used to drinkin' my coffee black."

He rolled his eyes and schlepped back to the kitchen.

Why did he always seem so sad, she wondered. He had a good job—not one she'd ever want, but he seemed suited to it. He lived in a lovely place. But something was definitely missing. If she had to guess, she figured it must be companionship. The thought of fixing him up with Lily lifted Gwyneth's spirits a little. Even with all his oddities, she liked him.

He returned with her mug and handed it to her.

"Thank you kindly, Nathan." She blew on the steaming hot coffee and took a tentative sip. It wasn't bad. Not that a shot of moonshine wouldn't improve it one hundred and fifty percent, but at least she could drink it.

He stood stiffly in front of her as if he had no idea what to do next. She patted the couch cushion. "Set a spell, sugar. I won't bite."

He lowered himself hesitantly and perched on the edge of the couch, as if he might flit away any second.

"There's somethin' I need to take care of first. Chad? Did y'all leave like I asked?"

She waited a bit, and when he didn't answer, she said, "Oh, good. He must have honored my request for privacy."

"Nope." Nathan pointed to the door. "He's over there, leaning against the wall."

Gwyneth whipped her head around and stared at the space Nathan had pointed to, but it was completely empty. "You can see him?"

"Yes. I can't hear spirits like you can, but I can see them."

"So, y'all are clairvoyant and I'm clairaudient. Hey, between the two of us, he can't never hide nor talk nasty behind our backs."

Still staring at the door, Nathan chuckled.

Gwyneth squinted. "What's he doin'?"

"He's giving us the finger. But at least he's leaving." Nathan turned back to face her. "Okay, we're alone now. So what did you want privacy for?"

"I have a special request of y'all. It's kinda unusual and may take some explainin' first."

"I'm all ears."

She traced the shell of his outer ear. "Actually, y'all have cute little ears. And a bit of a beak-like nose. Even when you're not a bird, y'all kind of remind me of one—in a sexy, manly way, a'course."

He shivered at her touch. "Is that what you wanted to talk to me about? My birdlike appearance?"

"No, it ain't. I discovered we have a common problem since we live on the same side of this building, and y'all might be able to help with it."

"What does our side of the building have to do with anything?"

"Well, y'all know we have a new neighbor whose apartment is sandwiched between yours and mine."

"That's an interesting way of putting it."

"Well, for lack of a better description, I think the bread on our sandwich might be in danger of toastin'. Ya see, the fillin' has a tendency to explode."

His eyebrows shot up. "Explode? Is our neighbor some kind of anarchist who makes bombs in her bedroom?"

"No, but you could say she defuses them there. No, wait. I'm not doin' a very good job of this explanation."

"No shit. Why don't you skip the colorful language and just give it to me straight?"

"That's a fine idea. You see, Lily, our neighbor, is the fillin' in our sandwich."

"Yeah, I got that. Now, what about her is exploding?"

"Well, she claims to be a dragon. I ain't seen her like that, but I've seen her apartment. It's all scorched-like on the floors and furniture."

Nathan raised his eyebrows again. "You said I might be able to help. How?"

"Well, she needs to blow off steam or she'll sneeze fire. It's like some kind of weird allergy to clean livin', I guess."

Nathan looked confused and shook his head. "I don't get it. What do I have to do? Take her out drinking and gambling?"

Gwyneth laughed and patted his arm. "Bless your heart, no, silly. Y'all need to have sex with her."

Nathan reared back as if she'd slapped him. "What?"

"She says it's the only way she gets rid of the fire. If y'all could just help out until she gets her call-girl business set up…"

Nathan sprang off the couch. "No."

"Well, shucks. There's no need to be horrified. She's not an ugly toad or anythin'. In fact, she's quite pretty."

He faced away from her. "I've seen her. Still not interested."

"Oh! I'm sorry. I didn't know you was gay. I got the distinct impression you wasn't when that paparazzo reporter tried to make it look like you an' Jason…"

"I'm not gay."

Gwyneth threw her hands up. "Then what's wrong? If y'all ain't gay and she ain't ugly—is it some kind of bird thang?" She stood. "Birds of a feather fuck together?"

"No, I can have sex with humans when I'm in my human form."

She crossed her arms. "Then enlighten me. I'm tirin' of this guessin' game."

He took a deep breath and let out a sigh. "Gwyneth. I'm in love with someone else."

"Oh! Well, I'll be jiggered! Y'all got a girlfriend. I had not one clue. Who is she?"

He snorted. "She's not my girlfriend. I've been trying to get up the nerve to ask her out for a long time, but…"

"Oh, you poor man. You're shy. How long have y'all been like this?"

He gazed up at the ceiling. "Give me strength."

Gwyneth sidled up next to him and wrapped her arms around his. "Maybe I can help. I'm a girl. Y'all can practice on me."

He turned toward her slowly. "Gwyneth? Will you go out to dinner with me?"

She beamed. "You see? That wasn't so hard, was it?"

"Well, will you?"

She frowned. "Y'all don't want to be pushy with the woman. If she says yes, you make plans. If she says no, y'all say somethin' nice like, 'Oh well, maybe another time.' Give her the option to change her mind."

He hung his head. "Okay. Well, maybe another time."

"But I didn't say no."

He looked up again, hope glimmering in his eyes. "Then you'll go?"

She bit her lip and stepped back. "Wait a minute. Y'all are confusin' the heck outta me."

He slapped his hands over his face and looked like he was about to scream. She waited until he composed himself.

"Maybe it would help if y'all tell me somethin' about this woman."

He stared at the floor, but nodded.

"Y'all must know her pretty well… You're in love with her?"

"Desperately."

"And how do you know her?"

"She lives in my building."

Gwyneth's jaw dropped. "Why, that means it's got to be someone I know..."

Nathan rolled his eyes. "She has long red hair, a smattering of freckles across her nose, and the cutest armpits I've ever seen. Oh, and she's a witch. Not a very psychic witch, apparently."

Gwyneth's knees went out from under her, and she caught the edge of the sofa just before she hit the floor. Nathan was beside her in a second.

"I'm sorry. I knew I shouldn't have told you." He averted his gaze and stared at the floor. "Please forget I said any—"

"No! I will not forget it. I just needed to find my voice is all."

He helped her up. "You don't have to say it. I understand."

"No, apparently you don't." She launched herself into his arms and kissed him on the mouth.

Chapter 15

MIKHAIL'S APARTMENT WAS A LOFT OVER HIS WAREHOUSE. He'd said he lived with his lover, and Morgaine noticed that a woman's touch had softened some of the modern industrial feel. One wall was brick, but sage silk curtains and a thick ivory rug covering part of the dark wood floors warmed the place considerably.

"Where's your significant other?"

Mikhail chuckled. "I can't get used to that term. She owns a shop in Soho and should be there at the moment. Why?"

"Well, she may not like this, but I need you to put my name on the deed to your warehouse temporarily. In order for me to reseal the doors and invite you back in, I need to have some type of ownership of the property."

"Temporary, you say? How temporary?"

"You can take my name off the deed as soon as it's done."

"In that case, she doesn't need to know. It's in my name only and willed to her in the *very* unlikely event of my death. I'll probably tell her after the fact just for fun."

Sly stood by the large expanse of windows, watching the sun set. It was as if he couldn't get enough of it. And with good reason. If Morgaine couldn't reverse engineer the curative powers of Vampire Vintage, his days would be numbered and his nights never ending.

"I'll take care of the deed and get some wine."

Mikhail excused himself. Morgaine psychically knew he was heading for his safe. She returned her gaze to his computer monitor. The more she watched it, the less she paid attention.

Concentrate, she scolded herself. Mikhail had the security tape playing in a loop so Morgaine could see the vampire black magician at work. They hadn't found the scroll, so Morgaine figured it had been taken out of the warehouse to be burned or buried.

She kept all of her parchment ashes and released them on the wind each Samhain. The vampire might do the same. This year, however, Samhain had come and gone without much fanfare. She and Gwyneth had barely spoken that day. She shook her head and realized her mind was wandering again.

Eventually, she called out, "I think I've gotten all I can out of this tape, Mikhail."

He returned with two glasses of red wine and handed one to her. "Okay. I'll shut it off. Is there anything else you need?"

"Just a place to set up my altar."

"Here or in the warehouse?" He moved smoothly over to Sly and handed him the other glass. Morgaine's glass had a purple stem, and the other one was clear. She imagined that was so she didn't get mixed up and accidentally drink the vampire stuff. *Blood. Ick.*

"The warehouse would be best. I can reseal the door after breaking the curse. You'll need to be invited in again after that, along with any other vampires you want to allow access to."

Mikhail stuffed his hands in his pockets. "I'd prefer to keep my warehouse sealed to all but myself."

"Oh! Then Sly can't come with me?"

Sly turned and watched them. He might have jumped in and offered to go with or stay away. Any kind of hint would have been nice, but no. He was letting her decide what she wanted and needed.

"I-I guess I can let him stay here," Morgaine said. "Or better yet, wait just outside the warehouse door. He can try to come in after I seal it. Then you'll know it worked."

"Or didn't."

"Oh, it'll work," she said, slightly affronted. "If there's one area I'm competent in, it's magick."

"I'm sure you're competent in many things, and I apologize if it sounded like I doubted you, but I've never seen your work before…"

She took a deep breath. "I understand. There's no need to apologize. I'm just a little touchy right now."

"Oh? Is anything wrong?"

She glanced at Sly. He remained as he had been—just watching and waiting for things to play out however she let them.

"No. I'm fine. Let's go." She rose and gathered her satchel, which she jokingly referred to as "Have altar; will travel."

Together they tromped down to the refurbished elevator and rode it to the main floor. Sly took her hand and gave it a squeeze. When she glanced at his face, she saw pride shining there. She smiled and whispered. "Don't worry. I can do this."

He leaned close. "I know you can."

The warehouse had two entrances, one on either side of the polished travertine corridor. "He came in this door," Mikhail said, as he pointed to the left.

"It won't matter which door he used. I'll need to seal them both. Do you know who invited him in?"

"No, I'm afraid I don't. No one would own up to it. I was pretty pissed, and I can be an intimidating guy when I'm angry."

Morgaine could only imagine it. Mikhail was dark but not swarthy. He could probably get red in the face if he'd fed or had enough wine.

"Sly, you don't mind waiting right here, do you?"

"Not at all." He gave her a quick kiss before she and Mikhail entered the warehouse.

Row upon row of wine racks were filled with product. *How in hell did he manage to make so much with a long-ago dried drop of blood on a tiny piece of ancient cloth?*

Mikhail gestured to his space. "Where would you like to do this?"

The rows of wine racks were fairly close together, but the perimeter allowed for a nine-foot circle. "Right at the bottom of the steps should be fine."

As she was preparing her altar and arranging the four woods to break the hex, the way to make the wine occurred to her in a flash of vision. They no longer needed the rag. They used a bit of wine from one bottle to pass on the cure to the next. It was like sourdough bread. She almost gasped aloud when she realized she'd uncovered Mikhail's precious secret. Now all she had to do was earn her case of wine and start adding it to their own concoction. Hopefully, it would take. At least they'd have plenty to experiment with until they figured out the ratio.

"Morgaine, are you all right?"

"Huh? Oh, um, yeah. I just need one more thing and we can do this. I gave it to Sly for safekeeping. I'll be right back."

Mikhail frowned, and his eyes followed her as she left.

She didn't care if he was suspicious or not. She had to let Sly know about this new revelation before she began messing with hexes, just in case something happened to her.

She opened the warehouse door, but before she closed it, she asked Mikhail, "Will this lock if I let it close?"

"Yes. Why don't I go with you so I can let you back in again?"

"No! Uh, no. I'd rather you keep watch over my altar. I'll prop open the door with my shoe." She whipped off her black half boot and stuck it in the door as soon as she was on the other side.

Sly had been looking out the glass panel in the front door. He turned, arching one brow in curiosity. "Is everything all right?"

"Yeah, I just had to come get that…" She winked. "…ingredient I tucked into your pocket this morning."

Apparently he followed her ruse and just said, "Ah."

Hurrying to his side, she whispered in his ear, "Can Mikhail hear us if I whisper?"

Sly shrugged.

She had to make a quick decision. Possibly let Mikhail know she'd discovered his secret or take the chance of Sly never knowing…

Finally she just said, "If anything happens to me, tell Gwyneth to use the principles of sourdough bread."

His brows knit. "What do you mean, if anything happens to you?"

"Look, magick can be dangerous. You already knew that, right?"

He reared back. "No, I didn't. You'd better rethink this."

"I can't," she said a little too loudly. She coughed, then lowered her voice. "I doubt anything will happen. I just had to let you know—in case…"

"In case what?"

Exasperated, she blew out a deep breath.

"Fine. But will she know what that means?" he whispered.

Morgaine nodded. Then she grabbed him and kissed him hard. "I love you." With that she whirled on her remaining heel and ran back to the warehouse before he could stop her.

Mikhail was pacing. "What was that about?"

She smiled innocently as she put her boot back on. "What was what about?"

I heard you say, "I can't."

"Oh, you heard that, huh? Did you hear anything else?"

He hesitated, then shook his head. "What's this about, Morgaine? Is something wrong?"

"No. Everything's fine."

Sly opened the door. Apparently the lock wasn't strong enough to hold the door closed against vampiric strength, but he didn't enter. "Everything isn't fine." His expression was stern. "She just told me this could be dangerous. I don't want her risking her neck for you or me or anyone."

Mikhail stared at Morgaine. "Is that true? Could you harm yourself if you do this?"

"It's very unlikely. I mean, how would he know you'd find a witch to remove his curse? And I'm not sure he *could* do anything to stop me even if he did know."

"And what was 'I can't' in response to?" Mikhail asked.

"I wanted her to reconsider," Sly answered for her. "Mikhail, invite me in."

"No, don't." Morgaine had to stand up to these two men. Otherwise the whole trip would have been for nothing. "Please, Sly. Tell you what, I'll do a spell to increase my own strength first. Now, close the door and let us continue."

"No." He folded his arms and planted his feet shoulder-width apart.

She rolled her eyes. "Well, then, I'll just have to do this with you watching."

"Mikhail, if she looks at all unwell, you'll stop her, right?"

"Absolutely." The two stubborn he-men nodded to each other.

Morgaine threw her hands up. "Fine. Now, let's get this done." She shoved a box of sea salt at Mikhail. "Start on the opposite side of the altar. Pour this salt around us, and don't leave the circle once it's been cast."

He glided around her in a wide circle, spreading the salt. When he finished, he moved to the spot she'd indicated and stood across from her, hands clasped behind his back.

Morgaine picked up her wand and pointed it at the north until blue light flowed out of its tip. Then she rotated in place and drew the circle over their heads chanting, "We stand in circles of light that nothing may cross."

She remembered her promise to increase her own strength and lay down on the floor.

"Is she okay?" Sly shouted.

"I'm fine. It's part of the ritual. Now, please stop worrying and *don't* interrupt—no matter what, okay?"

Sly didn't respond. She'd just have to hope he behaved himself. At least Mikhail still hadn't invited him in.

She lay with her hands crossed over her chest as if dead. Closing her eyes, she went into a trance, then slowly sat up and mumbled, *"On, Oron, Doron."* She raised her voice as she rose. *"Radoron, Gorradoron, Rogoradoron!"*

Next she took the small ball of parchment paper on which she'd written the spell and set it on fire in her censor. Holding the twigs she'd brought with her over the smoke and taking in a deep breath, she looked up and cried out, "Goddess, hear me. Turner be turned, burner be burned. Let only good come of this wood."

She spit on the sticks, broke each in turn, and tossed the pieces into the fire. Then she said, "The curse will die with the fire's death. So mote it be."

She watched the fire in a trance until the last flicker had disappeared and a few tendrils of smoke rose from the glowing embers. "It is done."

She opened the circle and came out of her trance.

Mikhail still looked vaguely uneasy. "Let me try something just to be sure the curse has been broken and we don't have to worry about freak accidents anymore."

"Of course," Morgaine said. "What did you have in mind?"

Mikhail strode to a workbench and plucked a pair of scissors out of a drawer. Jogging up and down the aisles of wine racks, he shouted to some unknown power, "Hey, I'm running with scissors here!"

When he returned unharmed, he and Morgaine laughed and shared a congratulatory high five.

———

Back in their room for the night, Sly was filled with a combination of victory and relief. Morgaine had succeeded. She'd lifted the curse, resealed both doors, and more than earned the respect and gratitude of her friend. He hoped she was as proud of herself as he was of her.

"You did it," he said as they slipped into bed.

She grinned. "Yes, I did. Now I hope both of us will *do it*, if you catch my drift."

Sly laughed and pulled her soft, naked body against him. "I think I know what you mean, but just to be sure, why don't you show me?"

One side of her lip raised in a knowing smile, then she feathered the tip of her tongue down the column of his neck until he groaned.

"I could let you do that all night, but you're the one who deserves something special."

She lifted her head and smiled. "Oh? Like what?"

In one smooth motion, he had her positioned on her back with her legs spread. He knelt between them and scooped up her ass, lifting her mound to his face.

"Like this, love." Sly's tongue flickered softly along her labia.

She arched and moaned.

Her eyes dilated and her heartbeat quickened as she watched him continue to explore her. Morgaine pulled in a shuddering breath when he slid two fingers inside her, slowly and gently. Moaning, she ground her hips against his hand.

He mimicked a rhythm of fucking as he stroked in and out of her core. After several moments of caressing her intimately, he lowered his head and found her clit with the tip of his tongue. She bucked and gasped. Good. She was almost as sensitized as he wanted her to be.

He whirled his tongue around her clit and she quietly whimpered. He could have teased her like this longer, but he sensed she needed release.

He zeroed in on her clit and flicked his tongue as fast as a hummingbird's wings. She cried out and climaxed. Her legs vibrated uncontrollably as she alternately screamed and emitted unintelligible sounds.

Finally, after her body's powerful reaction disintegrated into a weak, panting quiver, Sly settled gently on top of her. His cock nudged her opening, and he tingled with the contact.

"You're wonderful," he whispered. "Beautiful." With a gentle thrust, he pushed the swollen head of his erection in and stopped.

She caught her breath.

"Are you all right, sweetheart?"

"Goddess, yes. It feels so good."

He smiled. "It does for me too, love."

Sly braced himself on either side of her with his hands pressed into the mattress. He'd massage her clit with his pelvis as he moved in and out of her. He began his thrusts, escalating a bit faster each time.

The friction rubbed her already sensitized area, and she moaned with her head tilted back. His cock throbbed with pleasure too. As if she wanted to increase his joy, she squeezed her lower muscles around his shaft.

He groaned and pumped faster.

She lifted her legs and wrapped them around his waist, softly moaning as he rode her. Suddenly he reached his peak. His balls drew up and he cried out as his cock pulsed inside her. She buried her face in the crook of his neck and followed him over the edge. Hoarse from her previous orgasm, her voice took on a lower, raspier sound as she cried her blissful release.

The tension had run out of his body. His damp skin fused to hers. He gently lowered his full weight onto her boneless torso and covered her mouth with a long, deep kiss.

Yeah, I could get used to this.

Chapter 16

CHAD MISSED MORGAINE. AFTER GWYNETH AND Nathan had summarily dismissed him, he had no one to talk to. *Just like the old days*, he grumbled.

Maybe he could drop in on the two newest residents and test their psychic sensitivity. After all, he hadn't discovered Morgaine's ability to communicate with him until he'd followed her around for a while insulting her.

He chuckled to himself as he remembered the exchange. He had been mocking her goth makeup and coloring—black hair, pale skin—as well as her all-black wardrobe, when she'd suddenly whirled around and shook her fist at the ceiling.

"Cut the shit, you damn spook," she'd yelled.

Chad remembered laughing so hard that, *if* he'd had an ass to fall on, he would have stumbled backward and landed on it.

A quick visit to the strange fish-man might prove interesting.

Chad floated down the stairs and pushed his way into the super's apartment.

Just as he had suspected, Jules lay in his giant fish tank. Fingers locked under his head, he floated on his back, gently agitating the water with his large tail fin.

Here goes nothin'. "Hello there, fish breath."

Jules didn't react. His eyes closed, and a slight smiled played across his face.

"Wet enough for ya?"

Nothing.

"I wish I knew why you decided to become a landlubber."

When no reaction to that followed, Chad figured the super was completely unaware of his presence. He was about to leave when he realized he could use other means to communicate besides telepathy.

Let's see… I could use my telekinesis to move the toaster out of the kitchen and across the room and then dump it in his fish tank. Naw, it wouldn't be worth the effort without a massively long cord. The threat of electrical shock would get him to spring out of that water, and wouldn't that be fun to watch?

Hmmm… there must be something I can do to get his attention.

Chad eyed two rolled-up towels on a shelf near the tank. *Ah, those must be what he uses to dry off. I know! Wouldn't it be fun if dry towels weren't so handy and he had to drip across the floor all the way to the bathroom?*

Chad concentrated on the towels until they floated off the shelf and hovered in midair. When he was ready, he mentally directed them over the tank and dumped them into the water.

The disturbed surface tension alerted Jules, and he opened his eyes. "Hey!"

Grabbing the waterlogged towels, he glanced around the room in confusion.

Heh, heh. That was fun.

"Very funny, Chad," the super said.

Huh? He knows about me?

Chad cleared his throat and yelled, *"Hey, Jules. I'm over here."*

Jules ignored him and climbed onto the edge of his tank. He wrung out the wet towels and waited until his tail turned into legs.

I'll try telepathy one more time. "Hellooo... Your momma's a guppy."

Jules pattered across the floor, leaving a wet trail behind him.

With no real satisfaction in the effort, Chad let out a deep sigh. *Okay, cross another resident off my list of intelligent conversationalists.*

Sly had made love to Morgaine twice. They lay side by side, holding hands, basking in the afterglow. The way he whispered endearments to her while he was fucking affirmed the loving nature she knew he had.

Making love. Yes, those were the right words— not fucking. He loved her. He must. She'd made him nuts by taking a risk to her own safety. He had said she was like Alice in that way. His dear departed wife had driven him out of his mind by attending rallies and protest marches despite his worry that violence might break out.

He hadn't said the words to her yet, but she was sure he'd find the right moment.

"I don't want you putting yourself in that kind of danger again, Morgaine."

"Oh, come on, Sly. Don't kill the mood. I did good, right?"

"Yes, you did."

After she had resealed the doors against vampires and invited him in again, Mikhail had been so impressed, he'd offered her two cases of wine. His cases were actual briefcases lined with plastic foam in the shape of his bottles. Each one carried only three precious bottles. They now sat at the foot of the bed.

"And I 'saw' how we can make more so you'll always have your cure. That vision probably wouldn't have happened if I hadn't been in the warehouse."

"I know, sweetheart, but Jesus, you almost gave me a heart attack!"

"Like that would have killed you?"

He chuckled. "You're right. It wouldn't have. Otherwise I'd be dead."

She rolled up onto one elbow and stared down at him. "Well, I'm glad you're not. And by the way, why do you call on Jesus? I didn't think vampires could be Christians anymore."

He shrugged. "Why not? I was raised Catholic and was never excommunicated. It's r.ot like I chose to become a vampire. I don't think there's a manual that says vampires have to surrender their rosary beads. Is there?"

She chuckled. "Forget I asked."

Just as she was scooting down the bed, getting ready for a third round, the phone rang.

Damn.

She groped for the receiver on the nightstand. On the fourth ring, she answered it.

"Hello?"

"Well, howdy, y'all. Did I interrupt anythin'?"

"Hi, Gwyneth. Uh, no. As always, your timing is impeccable. What's up?"

"Y'all are never gonna believe this. Guess who I made out with last night? Go ahead, guess. You'll never—"

"Nathan?"

She heard Gwyneth's gasp. "Well, fiddlesticks! Y'all probably got a psychic news flash. Sometimes that ability spoils all the fun."

"No, it had nothing to do with the sight. I figured he'd make his move eventually. He's been in love with you since the first time you met."

"That's what he said! But how did y'all know that?"

"By the way he tries not to look at you but can't help himself. And he becomes totally awkward around you—more than usual. It doesn't take a psychic to figure it out."

Sly cleared his throat. "What doesn't it take a psycho to figure out?"

His eyes twinkled, and she knew he was just trying to get a rise out of her.

With her hand half over the receiver, she answered, "Psych-*ic*, sweetheart."

"Oh, so y'all are callin' each other pet names now?" Gwyneth giggled. "I reckon things are goin' well with Sly."

Morgaine glanced over her shoulder at him. He smiled and winked. *Damn that acute hearing of his. He's getting every word of this.*

"Yeah, well, I'm more interested in talking about *your* new development."

"I think we're good together, Morgaine. I make him laugh. I never seen that boy laugh before."

"And what does he do for you?"

"Well, I know he'd never cheat on me, and I guess you'd say he keeps me grounded. Least ways he gets me to look afore I leap."

"Thank the Goddess," Morgaine mumbled.

"What?"

"Um—that's good. And the chemistry? Is that there?"

She giggled. "I guess that's the biggest surprise of all. I can't get enough kissin' when I'm with him."

"Do you think you'll start seeing him in earnest?"

"Who's Earnest?"

Morgaine stifled a laugh. "I mean, are you taking his feelings into account? Or are you just messing around with him? I don't want to see anyone in our building get hurt."

"I'm no cock tease, Morgaine."

"Good."

"So I have your seal of approval, I guess?"

"Is that why you called? You wanted my approval?"

"Heck, no. We're in a bit of a pickle now and I wanted to ask all your opinion. Sly too."

"Okay, let me put you on speakerphone." Probably completely unnecessary, but whatever… Morgaine pushed the button marked "Speaker" and said, "Go ahead."

"Well, first off, don't go gettin' all rattled right away. It takes a bit of explainin'."

Morgaine took a deep breath. Whenever Gwyneth began by telling her not to get upset, it meant she *was going to* upset her. "Uh-oh. What happened?"

"Well, nothin' yet, but… I went to Nathan hoping he could fix it, but, well, he couldn't."

"What is it? If there's a plumbing problem or something, that's what the super is for."

"It ain't no leaky faucet, Morgaine. Apparently our new neighbor, Lily, is a she-dragon."

"That's not a very nice thing to say about someone."

"No, I mean, she's a real-life, actual dragon. She needs sex to blow off steam."

Sly sat up and Morgaine sensed sudden tension coursing through him.

"She used to control it by being a call girl in San Francisco. Now that she's moved here, she ain't got no clients yet. I tried to get Nathan to sleep with her and, well, he refused, sayin' he was in love with someone else. So, that's how I discovered—"

Sly interrupted. "Gwyneth, skip to the problem at hand."

"Well, to make a short story shorter, if she don't have sex, she sneezes fire. It's some kind of weird allergy to abstinence or somethin'. Her whole apartment's scorched. If she don't get sex pretty soon…"

Sly jumped off the bed. "She'll burn down the building. *My daughter's* building. Jason could shift and fly to safety, but Merry… Morgaine, start packing. We have to get home, now!"

"Just a second. Gwyneth, have you told Jules?"

"Well, no. I didn't want to get Lily in trouble. She's a real nice girl, and t'ain't her fault she was born a dragon."

"You *have to* tell Jules! He's responsible for everything that happens there. Besides, do you want our home to go up in flames? For Goddess's sake, Gwyneth!"

Sly shouted, "Shit, the *still*! That would turn any fire into an inferno."

"Okay, okay. That's why I called, dagnabit. I thought you might come up with somethin' other than tattlin' on her. But if I have to tell Jules, I'll just tell him."

"Tell him now. We'll be back as soon as we can, but

promise me you won't do another thing until you talk to Jules."

The phone went dead.

"Gwyneth?"

Sly tossed their clothes and toiletries into Morgaine's suitcase so fast he whirled like a tornado. "Come on, we have to go."

"Gwyneth? Are you there?"

No sound from the other end. *Holy shit. Did she take me literally, drop the phone, and run to the super's apartment, or did a fire just eat through the electrical and phone lines?*

"Fuck. The line's dead."

Sly zipped up Morgaine's suitcase, then picked her up off the bed, tossed her over his shoulder, and grabbed one of the two cases of vampire wine. "If I have to carry all of this and you out of here, I will."

"Put me down. I'll help carry the stuff."

"Then hurry."

"No! You *can't* evict me. Please… I have nowhere to go. No one…"

Jules didn't want to toss his beautiful new neighbor out on her keister. But when Gwyneth from upstairs said Lily had been setting small fires in the apartment right below hers… well, what was he to do?

"I'm sorry. If you have a problem—I mean, if you're a fire starter and you want help, maybe I can find—"

"No, that's not it at all." Fat tears rolled down her soft cheeks. "Please, let me explain…"

He paused. There was no real harm in letting her talk.

After all, she wouldn't set a fire in front of him. Her behavior had him baffled. An explanation might not change anything, but he'd sure like to hear it.

"Please?"

"All right."

"Come inside. I'll get you a cup of tea."

He followed her inside and appraised the damage as she went to the kitchen. Scorch marks on the hardwood that would have to be sanded and re-stained. It looked as if some drapes had caught fire, and the trim around the window would need to be replaced. Other than that, it was her own furniture that looked and smelled like it had been set on fire and put out.

Jules sat on the only chair that looked relatively unscathed. "Don't make any tea for me. I have a bottle of water." His ever-present plastic bottle carried salt water with him wherever he went. Something she ought to do.

She poked her head out. "Oh. I guess I won't bother, then."

"You can go ahead and make some for yourself. Don't let me stop you."

She smiled and said, "I'll be just a minute."

As soon as she disappeared again, he rose and softly stole to the kitchen entrance and peeked around the corner. She held a cup of water in her hand and dropped a tea bag in it. Then she blew on the cup and—*fire came out... of her mouth!*

"What the hell?" Jules strode toward her but stayed out of blowtorch reach.

Her body froze in fear, but her eyes were wild. "Oh, no. What did you see?"

"What do you think I saw? Look, lady. I came in

here for an explanation, and I want it more than ever now. I just saw you heat that cup of tea with your breath like a fire-breathing…"

She smiled innocently and shrugged.

He reeled back as reality hit him. "You're a dragon?"

She nodded. Then she lowered her head in shame. "I-I have a certain condition. There's something I need on a regular basis, and if I don't get it, I have the tendency to sneeze—and fire comes out. I…"

She glanced up at him, then must have decided not to continue. He realized he must be wearing a very stern look. He could feel his brows bunched together and knew he was frowning. Her tears returned, and his heart ached for her.

"Look, if it's something I can help you find, like medicine, just say the word. There's a pharmacy right down the street."

She shook her head and covered her eyes with her hands.

"Hey, let's not have any more of that. There's no need to be embarrassed. Tell me what I can do to help."

She looked up, and hope shimmered in her dark eyes. "You're so understanding. I thought you'd call me a freak and have the cops take me away."

"You'd be surprised how understanding I can be. Now, why don't you tell me more about this thing you need. What is it?"

She hesitated a good long time. Finally, she hung her head and muttered what sounded like the word "sex."

"What did you say?"

"Didn't you hear me?"

"It sounded like you said, 'Sex.'"

"I did. I need sex to stop sneezing."

After a few moments, he realized he had been staring at her. "Oh." He scratched his head. "Well, I might be able to help with that…"

She straightened and looked him in the eye. "Really?"

He chuckled. "Why not? I mean, it's not exactly a hardship."

"And… and I can stay?"

"Hmmm…" He folded his arms and thought about the consequences. "I guess that depends."

"On?"

"On whether or not it works." He reached for her hand. "Come with me."

She took a step back and eyed his hand cautiously.

"What's wrong?"

"I might be a little warm blooded for you right now. I don't want to burn you."

He snapped his fingers. "I have an idea. Come."

That was all he said and all he intended to say until he showed her the kind of *steamy* sex he knew they could have. He left her apartment and marched across the hall to his own. He didn't turn around to be sure she was following until he reached his door.

She paused in her doorway. He opened the door to his own place and swung it wide. She must have seen all the fish tanks, because her jaw dropped and she entered slowly as if mesmerized. Once she was inside, he locked the door behind her.

"Watch this," he said. He strolled to his human-sized tank and stripped down, figuring that if she was willing to sleep with him she wouldn't be shocked to see him in all his glory. The next part might surprise her a bit, but he hoped that since he'd shown her understanding, she'd afford him the same kindness.

Her gaze swept over his body, and a small smile curled her lips. *Good. She likes what she sees*. Then he vaulted over the wall of water and his tail formed almost immediately.

She gasped.

He grinned at her and leaned back, then clasped his hands behind his head. He floated with his tail gently treading water.

"You're a merman!"

"In the fin."

She giggled and asked, "What happened to your...?"

"It's still there. Come on in, the water's great! It'll cool you down, and as soon as I can 'handle you,' we'll get out and try it."

She glanced all around. "Where? I don't see any furniture?"

"I have a bed, but maybe this first time we could try it in the shower." He winked. "Think of all the steam we'll generate!"

She laughed, stripped off her clothes quickly, and jumped into the tank. Sure enough, generous plumes of steam rose from the surface. "Ah... I feel better already."

"Great. Well, I can feel the temperature rising, so I'll get out and meet you in the shower whenever you're ready."

"You don't have a tail in fresh water?"

"Nope." He hauled himself up onto the side and let the water run off. "You've never heard of lake-men have you?"

She smiled. "No, I guess not."

When his lower half became human again, he hopped down onto the floor and leaned over the tank. "There's an old saying, 'When a bird and a fish fall in love, where will they live?'"

She nodded.

"I guess they'll have to live at this address." He cupped her face and brought her lips to his for their first kiss. One of many, he hoped.

Sly saw Morgaine's breath in the cold late November night as they strode from the Copley Square subway station to their Beacon Street neighborhood. He hadn't calmed down much since leaving New York.

"Now is when a cell phone would come in handy," Morgaine muttered.

"I won't feel better until I get there and see for myself that everything's all right. After that I plan on having a chat with our hot new neighbor—and I don't mean 'hot' in a good way."

Morgaine let out a weak chuckle.

They passed beneath a streetlight, and he glanced over at her. "By the way, I'm proud of the way you handled this whole trip. I hope you're proud of yourself too."

She grinned at him. "Yeah, I really didn't know if I could do it. Having you beside me the whole time made it possible. Thank you."

"Hey, you were the one doing me a big favor. Going with you was the least I could do."

"How are you feeling, by the way? It's been a while since you had any wine."

"I'm okay. I'd much rather use it conservatively until

we know we can make more of it." He didn't want to tell her that his blood lust had returned. He could control it until they reached their destination safely. The last thing he needed was to be stopped and hassled for public consumption of alcohol.

"It's pretty quiet tonight," she remarked. "Of course, it's the wee hours of the morning."

"Plus it's probably too cold for most people. I smell snow."

"You can actually smell snow?"

A sudden movement from above caught him by surprise. Vorigan Malvant landed on the sidewalk right in front of them.

Morgaine yelped.

"Shit!"

"Is that any way to greet your maker?" Malvant asked in his oily way. "I had hoped you'd be happy to see me."

Sly stepped in front of Morgaine. "Why the hell would I be happy to see you?"

"Because of all the wonderful things I have to teach you, of course."

"Go fuck yourself."

Malvant sighed. "I didn't want to do it this way, but you leave me no choice."

"What way?" Sly took a swing at Malvant, who shoved him off the sidewalk.

Sly lost his balance on the curb, and while he was busy landing on his ass in the street, Vorigan Malvant grabbed Morgaine, took a giant leap, and disappeared with her over the rooftop.

Her scream shattered the night.

Sly tossed his precious briefcases of wine into the

bushes. He tried to follow, but Vorigan was too fast and too clever. When Morgaine's protests became muffled, then stopped altogether, Sly realized in horror that he'd lost them.

Chapter 17

MORGAINE'S WILD RIDE OVER THE ROOFTOPS FINALLY ended in the back alley she recognized from her trip to Malvant's basement apartment. He had shoved something in her mouth and held her wrists so tightly that he was cutting off the circulation. She struggled to get away, even though she doubted anything would come of it besides more pain.

When he finally wrestled her inside and down to his lair, he shoved her into a dark room and slammed the door. She couldn't see a thing. Her arms prickled with pins and needles, and she smelled something foul and rotten. Probably coming from whatever cloth was in her mouth. *Ewww.* She yanked it out and began screaming and pounding on the door. She heard him laugh.

"No one can hear you. This place is soundproof, and the owners are away in Europe."

Morgaine slid down the wall and started to cry.

"Oh, relax, will you? I'll find your boyfriend tomorrow night, and I'm sure he'll offer himself up in exchange. Then I'll wipe your memory of his and my existence, and you'll be free to go."

"You don't mean that."

"You're right, I don't." He laughed. "I'll eat you for dinner and maybe even share you with Sly. We'll be sharing so many things throughout the coming millennia."

That thought didn't comfort her. She knew he was

right. Sly would sacrifice himself for her, and she couldn't let that happen. She swiped the tears away and took some deep, slow breaths.

If only she could communicate with Sly or Gwyneth! Or if Chad could find her, he might be able guide her out while the others created a diversion. But all of them putting their heads together like that was highly unlikely.

She tried to calm herself, but the completely dark room closed in on her. Her heartbeat had been racing ever since she was abducted, but now she could hear it pounding in her brain. Her chest constricted. She broke out in a sweat, and her mouth went dry.

Get control over yourself, Morgaine! Remember, Sly has secret weapons. A glass of Vampire Vintage will allow him to break in during the day. Gwyneth knows where Malvant's lair is. All they have to do is wait until daylight.

Yeah, they wouldn't wait and she knew it. They'd walk right into Vorigan Malvant's trap. She had to find her own way out of here before they tried anything.

Despite her heart hammering against her ribs, Morgaine forced herself to stand and feel along the perimeter. She needed to locate doors and windows. How could a room be so dark if it had windows? She prayed to the Goddess that the windows were just so light tight that she couldn't see them. She placed her hands against the wall over her head. They were in a basement, so windows would have to be small and high.

Eventually she made her way back to the door without finding another egress. Dammit. Didn't he know a bedroom without an escape window wasn't to code? Oh, Hell. What did he care about legal apartments? And for all she knew, she might be locked in what was supposed to be a walk-in closet.

A new emotion took over. *Anger*. And it was helping combat her overwhelming fear of the dark. *Yes! Hang on to the anger*.

"You fuckin' asshole! Let me out of here!"

She was met with silence.

"Damn you to Hell! I hate your guts."

Still no response.

"When I get out of here, I'll stake you where your heart should be a thousand times! But I doubt you have a heart."

"Well, now that's just rude," he called through the door.

Her shoulders slumped. He wasn't the least bit worried about the consequences of his actions. He probably expected her to be angry and was completely unfazed by her threats. She wanted to burst into tears. *Keep it together, Morgaine. You can do this*.

She wasn't going to let her loved ones walk into a trap. Her panic wouldn't help anyone. More than ever before, she needed to focus. *Think. You're a powerful witch, dammit!*

Ah, that was it! She needed a spell. But what would be powerful enough?

Frig. Even *if* the right words opened the door, Malvant was still on the other side. How could she get out, overpower a vampire, and run away before he went after her? *That's a hell of a lot to ask of a spell*.

Wait a minute. She could astral project. Maybe she could create her own diversion and mislead him into thinking she'd escaped. If she could find a way to open the door, she'd really escape while he was chasing her image.

That would be a crapshoot if ever there was one. But something about astral projection stuck in her mind as the answer. There was one thing she could do. She could intercept Sly if he came looking for her before morning. She couldn't speak to him in that form, but she could find some way of waving him off. *Hopefully*.

———

"Please, Gwyneth. You're the only one who knows where his lair is. You've *got* to help."

"For pity's sake, Sly. Quit jarring your preserves." Gwyneth jammed her hands on her hips. "Chargin' over there at night when there's a way to sneak in during the day is just pure stupid." *He's wound up tighter than a fat lady's girdle at an all-you-can-eat breakfast*.

"If he hurts her and I do nothing, I'll never forgive myself."

"He ain't gonna hurt her. She's his way to get y'all to come runnin', and he knows it. So should you."

Sly shook his head and stared at the floor. "She must be freaking out, at the *very least*. I can't stand the thought of her going through that."

Gwyneth grabbed his hand and talked as she led him down the stairs. "Yeah, her cheese is probably slidin' off her cracker, but y'all know as well as I do, she ain't gonna die. She may think she is, but she ain't. Now quit frettin' and git some of that vampire wine. We're gonna add some to the moonshine and see if it works like Morgaine reckons it will. Y'all must be hungry now, right?"

"The blood lust is back, yes. But I don't want to waste time."

"Well, we need to try makin' it anyway, so y'all

won't be wastin' time. Then we can go after her during the day."

"Meanwhile I'll be going crazy."

"My granny used to say, 'To act is easy. To think is hard.' It's especially hard when your thinkin' is as cloudy as the sky in a thunderstorm, and this is your rainy day."

"Gwyneth, do you honestly think he'll be understanding when Morgaine falls apart? She *needs* me—now!"

She stopped and considered the wild look in his eyes. "I ain't never hit a vampire afore, but if it'll knock some badly needed sense into y'all, I might just clock y'all upside the head."

He narrowed his eyes and frowned.

She eyed him for a moment and decided he wasn't going to attack her, so she continued her rant. "I know my cousin wouldn't want y'all gettin' yourself killed. She's in love with y'all, Sly, and wouldn't forgive herself neither."

"Did she say that?"

"Does she have to? I do declare. Men are so stupid sometimes."

He sighed. "How sweet."

"Hey, some folks have tact. Others tell the truth. And it ain't the beard that makes the philosopher."

"You're right," he mumbled. "Whatever you said."

—◆◆◆—

In the basement, Sly and Nathan opened the false wall and revealed the still. Everything seemed to be in order, so it must not have been discovered—yet.

Gwyneth had argued that the wine should go into the finished product and not the still in case the process of distillation destroyed the blood. It made sense to Sly, so they brought an empty Mason jar with them to get some of the fresh product.

Sly took the container from Gwyneth. "Why aren't we just using the moonshine we made before Morgaine and I went to New York?"

"Because this is fresher."

"I thought whiskey was better aged."

"Naw, my motto is 'Fresher is almost always better,' isn't that so, Nathan?"

Nathan chuckled. "I guess it has to be since we drank what was left of the last batch."

She slapped his arm with the back of her hand and he laughed. Sly had never seen Nathan so happy. They really did seem good for each other.

He poured some moonshine from the bucket into the jar until it was about three-quarters full, and then he handed it to Gwyneth.

"Seems like the proper time to collect it anyways. There's room at the top to add some of your wine cure. What's it called agin?"

"Vampire Vintage."

"Okay. So how much of this Vampire Vintage should go into our Vampire Vodka?"

He shrugged. "I don't know. Morgaine said to tell you something about sourdough bread. Does that make sense?"

Gwyneth snapped her fingers. "It sure do. Let me think for a minute. If I can figure out how much starter goes into my sourdough bread recipe, I can probably figure out how much wine to put in the moonshine."

"Like a ratio?" Nathan asked.

She looked at him blankly, then said, "Uh-huh, I guess. Now here's the recipe."

> ¾ cup cracked wheat
> 1 cup hot water
> ¼ cup margarine, melted
> 2 tablespoons molasses
> 2 tablespoons honey
> ¾ cup nonfat milk
> ½ cup flax seed
> ½ cup raw sunflower seeds
> 2½ cups sourdough starter
> 2 cups whole wheat flour
> 3½ cups bread flour
> 1 egg, beaten

"Add up all that except the starter, and what's it come to?"

Sly rattled off, "Almost ten cups of ingredients, plus one egg."

Both Gwyneth and Nathan stared at him openmouthed.

"What?" he asked.

"Nuthin'. So y'all are saying it's about twelve and a half cups of everything including the starter?"

"Correct."

Gwyneth splayed her ten fingers on the floor and then said, "Sly, will you put two and a half fingers next to mine?"

He shook his head, smiling. "I think it might be easier to find the ratio on paper. Or, better yet, let me just tell you it's a fifth."

Gwyneth gasped. "A fifth! Well, now that can't be right. Ain't a fifth a big-ass bottle?"

Sly and Nathan both burst out laughing. Nathan extended his hand and helped Gwyneth up.

"What in tarnation is so dang funny? I'm tryin' to help Sly, and y'all are laughin' at me."

"Sorry, hon. He was just saying that the ratio is twenty percent, or one-fifth. If you divide the whole bottle into five parts, you'd need to add one of those parts of wine to the bottle to get the right ratio."

"Oh. I do declare, Sly, how'd y'all know how to do that? Are you some math genius like Good Will Huntin'?"

Sly shrugged. "I was an engineer before the incident."

"I see. So runnin' trains takes math?"

"I wasn't…"

Nathan put a protective arm around her and gave Sly a quick head shake.

He took one look at her confused face and said, "Never mind." Explaining what an electromechanical engineer did might make her head explode.

Nathan gave her a side hug and said, "You know what, Gwyneth? I think you may be on to something. A job Sly could do."

"Really? What's that?"

"Math tutor."

Sly straightened. *Math tutor?* It made sense. "I could tutor kids after dark. Now that I have an apartment, they could come to me or I could meet them somewhere."

"And there's all kinds of schools around. I'm sure some of them have math dummies like me," Gwyneth said.

"And me," Nathan added quickly. "That's what made me think of it. I needed a tutor in trigonometry to get through high school."

Gwyneth's eyebrows rose. "Trigger what?"

"Not trigger…" He pronounced it slowly. "Trig-ah-nom-e-tree."

"Oh. I thought with your Boston accent you were sayin' trigger-somethin'."

Nathan chuckled and kissed her on the nose. "You're too adorable for words."

Sly huffed. "So now that we have one of my problems solved, let's see if we can get back to the other one."

"Oh, yeah." Gwyneth slapped her forehead. "We need to add one fifth of the Vampire Vintage to the Vampire Vodka. Let me see that." She extended her hand, and Sly passed her the open bottle of wine.

She held the Mason jar at eye level and poured the Vampire Vintage slowly until the amount looked right. Then she swirled it gently until the red and clear liquids mixed and resembled a rosé wine.

She handed the mixture back to him. "Down the hatch."

He lifted the jar and said, "Cheers." After taking a careful sip he waited. When nothing happened, he took another.

"Well?" she asked.

"Nothing yet."

"Take a big swig of the stuff, not a little sip. How much wine did you have to drink in New York to cure you?"

"It seemed to work almost instantly. But because it's watered down, you might be right. I'll need more." He took a large gulp. As soon as it hit his stomach, he knew something was wrong. It began to roil. "Whoa, that went down hard." A wave of nausea swamped him.

Nathan squinted. "Are you all right?"

"I-I'm not sure. I feel kind of…" *Oh, no*. He recognized the unmistakable feeling of his guts about to empty. He glanced around wildly, looking for a receptacle of any kind. All he saw were residents' boxes holding treasures too important to throw away. He'd never make it to the laundry room sink in time.

Gwyneth must have recognized the symptoms because she grabbed the container and held it over her head. "No barfin' in the moonshine, whatever you do!"

At last, he simply bent over and yakked up on the floor.

Nathan snorted. "Who knew Vampire Vintage plus Vampire Vodka would equal Vampire Vomit?"

"Dang," Gwyneth said. "Y'all are super pale an' look like you been drinkin' Clorox."

Morgaine had managed to calm herself enough to astral project. She lay next to the door and sent a quick plea to the Goddess.

"Dear Lady, help me succeed in my efforts to warn away my boyfriend and cousin. Let no one I love walk into this evil trap."

She tamped down her nerves one more time before going into a trance. Once she had reached the appropriate level mentally, she let her spirit rise from her physical body and walk through the wall to the next room. Malvant lay in wait, peering out the peephole in the front door, just as she had thought he would be.

While he's occupied there, I'll slip out the back.

She had decided that rather than try to escape without a decent plan, she'd prepare Sly for a daylight assault. She'd need his strength to break down the door. Without it, she pictured herself just bouncing off it a few times until she gave up, bruised and battered—and no better off.

Morgaine gathered her energy in an about-face and traveled to the back entrance. Once she'd pushed her way through, she ascended up and out. At last, she hovered over the dark alley. She had to remind herself that she was safe. In a weird way, Malvant's locked room provided safety from him and an a peaceful place for her body, while allowing her spirit to travel free.

Unencumbered by her body, Morgaine allowed her consciousness to float above the buildings. Looking down, she hoped to intercept any well-meaning but foolish attempt at her rescue.

The city slept while streetlamps twinkled below her. Enough of the sidewalks were illuminated to show only a lone dog walker. It had to still be cold since she could see his breath. Other than that, an occasional car moved down the streets, but she saw no Sly and no Gwyneth— *thank you, Goddess*.

While she was in astral form, perhaps she could track them down. She didn't know if Sly could see her. Probably not. But she might be able to catch Gwyneth in a trance… a light sleep state in which spirits can visit and even communicate with the living. Most people would dismiss it as a dream.

Wait. Communication with spirits… Maybe Chad can help?

Morgaine floated two blocks over and three down, then located their building. As she descended, she couldn't help taking a peek in the windows.

Merry was snuggled in bed. The next window she

passed was Gwyneth's bedroom. It was empty. Sly must have gone to her for help. They were probably hatching a plan to rescue her. Hopefully she hadn't missed them somehow. What a disaster that would be! She *had* to stop them.

She continued her descent past the window on the second floor. The new neighbor snored softly in her bed. Tiny curls of smoke emanated from her nostrils with each exhale. And who was that in bed with her? Oh well, she couldn't afford to get sidetracked now.

She passed Nathan's bedroom window and was surprised to find his bed empty too. Okay, a three-way in Sly's apartment was just out of all realms of possibility. But maybe they were over there putting their heads, and not their bodies, together.

At last she let her consciousness enter the building. She was approaching Sly's apartment when a familiar voice said, *"Morgaine? Is that you?"*

"Chad?"

"Yup."

"Where are Gwyneth and Sly?"

"They're in the basement. With Nathan. Boy, will Gwyneth be glad to see you!"

"Why is that?"

"Why? Well, duh. You were kidnapped by a vampire."

Morgaine mentally rolled her eyes. *"Do they think I'm dead?"*

"Not really. Gwyneth's just been having a hell of a time convincing Sly to wait until dawn before they go after you. She dragged Nathan out of bed, hoping he could hold Sly back physically if necessary. I doubt a raven is any match for vampiric strength though."

"You're right. Both of them together couldn't hold him. Can you help me communicate with Gwyneth? I've got to warn them."

"Sure, my witchy friend. But be glad you weren't here ten minutes ago.

"Why?"

"Because, as Nathan put it, Vampire Vintage plus Vampire Vodka makes Vampire Vomit." He laughed.

"Oh, no."

"Don't worry. It's all cleaned up now. Let's go."

The two descended right through the floorboards.

"Pretty cool traveling this way, huh?"

Morgaine chuckled. *"Personally, I can't wait to get back in my body and take the stairs like a normal person."*

Sly whipped his head in their direction. "Did you just hear that?"

"Hear what?" Nathan said.

Gwyneth looked up. "I think I heard Chad. Is that you, roomie? Did you get worried about ol' Gwyneth bein' up so early?"

"It's me all right. Me and Morgaine."

Gwyneth gasped. "Morgaine's here? How did she…"

"Tell her I'm not really here, Chad. I'm astral projecting. I think she thinks I escaped."

"She's not here in body, just in spirit. Much like myself."

Gwyneth turned white and fainted. Before she hit the ground, Nathan caught her.

"What did you say that for? Now she thinks I'm dead."

"Hey, I didn't realize she'd take it so literally."

Sly was wandering toward them, squinting as if he could almost see something. "Morgaine, honey?"

"I'm here, Sly. Well, not really. I'm astral projecting.

My body is still alive and well in Malvant's place. Can you see me?"

He shook his head. "I can't see you, but I can hear you."

"Can you hear Chad, or just me?"

"Just you."

"Are you sure? Chad, say something."

"Something."

"Did you hear him? What did he say?"

Sly shrugged. "I don't know. I didn't hear him. But I can hear you! Are you all right, darling?"

"Yes, but I came to warn you. Do not go after Malvant. It's a trap."

"That's what Gwyneth said. Are you all right though? Will you be okay until we get there?"

"Yes. He has me locked in another room." She glanced past him to Gwyneth, who was slowly moving into Nathan's arms. *"Please tell Gwyneth I'm alive. I think she got the wrong impression from Chad's poorly worded greeting."*

"Sure, blame me. That's what I get for trying to be nice."

Sly held up one hand. "I'll tell her." He wandered back to Gwyneth and Nathan. "Are you okay, Gwyneth?"

"A' course I'm not okay. My cousin's a ghost! That means she's—"

"Alive," Sly interrupted. "She's astral projecting."

"Is that what Chad told y'all?"

"No, I can't hear Chad at all. I can only hear Morgaine."

"Really?" Gwyneth scrambled to her feet. "Y'all can hear her?"

When he nodded, she hugged him. "Oh, my! I'm so

grateful to hear that. Not just that she's alive, but that y'all are her beloved."

He cocked his head. "What are you talking about?"

Gwyneth chuckled. "A beloved is a vampire's one true love. Listen to me, tellin' y'all about vampire lore."

"Hey, you probably know more than I do. Everything I've learned has been by trial and error. So how do you know she's my beloved? Because I can hear her?"

"Yup. It's called telepathy. Y'all are lucky. Some vamps never find their beloved—ever, and that's a long, long time to go without true love. I think that's what makes most of them so cranky."

Sly scratched his head. "Okay… Morgaine, are you hearing this?"

Morgaine couldn't respond. A lump had lodged in her throat. This was heady stuff. Sure, she knew she loved him, but she hadn't been sure he loved her. Oh, she'd hoped, but… he'd never told her so. Now she knew.

"Morgaine?" Panic filled his eyes.

"I'm here." She sniffed.

"Are you crying? What's wrong?"

She didn't answer. At last Chad said, *"For cryin' out loud. She's a woman. Does she need a reason?"*

"Shut up, Chad. I-I guess I just hoped to hear it from you, not my cousin."

"Oh, honey. If I could hold you and destroy Malvant, I'd tell you right now. In fact, I wish I could."

She giggled. *"I can wait until dawn. I hope you can."*

Nathan had been staring at Sly. At last he shook his head in wonder. "Weird stuff goes on in this building. My girlfriend lives with and talks to a ghost. Her cousin has a vampire called a 'beloved,' and they know this because he can hear her over some kind of invisible long-distance telephone line."

Gwyneth leaned into him. "It's telepathy, but that's about the size of it."

He wrapped an arm around her shoulder. "And people think *I'm* the weird one. So, since I can't hear anyone but the two people standing next to me, is anyone talking about a plan to get her out of there or what?"

"Well, so far, Cousin…" Gwyneth faced the direction Sly had been facing when talking to Morgaine. "…all I've done is refuse to tell Sly where Malvant's lair is until daylight."

"Good. Smart girl, Gwyneth."

"She can't hear you," Chad said.

"I know, but Sly can. Sly, sweetheart, tell Gwyneth I said that was smart."

He sighed. "Not until I have you in my arms again."

Chapter 18

Morgaine sensed time passing. When she heard the click of a door opening and the creak of what she imagined might be a coffin, she figured daylight must be near. Malvant would be unconscious soon, and she could attempt her escape. If she could get out before Sly got in, she'd turn on the lights and check for traps Malvant might have set for anyone who tried to rescue her. Besides, she couldn't just sit there and do nothing.

Malvant still didn't know about their secret weapon—the Vampire Vintage—so he wouldn't be expecting Sly. He also didn't realize the witches knew where his lair was. Maybe the place wouldn't be booby-trapped at all. But she had to know for sure.

When everything was quiet, she astral projected to the street and confirmed for herself that it was sunrise. *Thank the Goddess*. It was now or never, but first, she had to be sure Malvant was out cold.

She returned to her body. "Hey, jerk face!"

No sound answered her. It looked as if the circumstances were right, but just to be sure, she yelled, "Your mother was a werewolf!"

Still no response. *Good*. It was time for a lock-opening spell. Since she didn't have her moonwort powder with her, she'd have to hope the words alone would do the trick.

Feeling around the door, she formulated the words in

her mind. When she located the doorknob, she kneeled in front of it.

"Lord and Lady, hear my plea... Out of this room, I shall be."

She concentrated as hard as she could, visualizing the door open and herself stepping over the threshold. When she tried turning the doorknob, it clicked. Surprised, but delighted her simple spell had worked, she rose and pushed open the door.

"Yeeeuck." Something disgusting assaulted her nose. The odor smelled like rotting meat. Morgaine held her breath until she absolutely had to let it out and take another. Meanwhile, she felt her way around the door frame and along the wall. She hoped she'd run into a light switch eventually. *Come on, Morgaine. You can do this. You're Sly's beloved. Don't you want to hear him say it?*

Then she remembered that she knew exactly where the light switch was. When she and Gwyneth had been in the space, there was a switch at the bottom of the stairs. Morgaine turned in that direction and felt along the opposite wall until she had it. *Oh, thank Goddess!*

She flipped the switch, and bright light stabbed her illumination-deprived eyes, almost blinding her. *Freakin' vampires and their dark hidey-holes!* She blinked a few times until her vision adjusted to it. Thank goodness, she could see again.

Casting her gaze around the room, she didn't see any obvious signs of a trap. Perhaps if she opened the front door, she'd better be prepared to run.

First, she threw open the heavy black curtains that

covered the light-blocking shades. Once she opened those, daylight streamed into the room. Still no sound from Malvant. *Now's my chance.*

—∾—

Nathan and Gwyneth sat on Lily's charred sofa while Sly stood to the side sipping his second glass of wine—the special kind. He was feeling a little tipsy, but that might not hurt considering what he was about to do. He needed all the liquid courage he could get.

Lily scratched her head. "So, how do you kill a vampire again? And why are you telling me this?"

"Y'all need to burn, stake, or behead him. All three just to be extra sure he never comes back."

Sly shifted uncomfortably as Gwyneth outlined their plan. He had thought it was brilliant ten seconds ago.

"And what do you need me for?" she asked.

Nathan laughed. "You're kidding, right? Look, it's simple. Sly stakes, I chop." He pulled his long coat aside to reveal an ax. "And you burn the pieces."

"But why me? I…"

Nathan rolled his eyes. "We all know about your special—condition, Lily."

Her jaw dropped. A moment later, her shoulders slumped and she gazed at the floor.

"It's nothin' to be ashamed of, sugar. We're all a little peculiar in different ways. It's just that your… fire-breathin' would come in mighty handy if y'all are willin' to lend a hand—or a sneeze."

Lily smiled for the first time since they'd entered her home. "I suppose I could help. I wouldn't be setting the whole building on fire, would I?"

Gwyneth sat up proudly. "No, ma'am. That's where I come in. I'll carry the fire extinguisher."

"And he's a really bad vampire?"

"Most are," Nathan said. "Sly here is the exception, but he hasn't been a vampire long enough to get cocky. We're still hoping he doesn't turn into an ass."

Sly chuckled. "Some might say it's too late."

Gwyneth waved away the comment. "Pshaw. Y'all are the nicest vampire I know, Sly."

Nathan's eyebrows shot up. "How many vampires do you know?"

She counted on her fingers. "Well, let's see. There's Sly, Vorigan Malvant, Morgaine's friend Mikhail, and Dracula—but I don't really know the last two, I just heard o' them."

Nathan looked relieved, then amused. "So, are we going to do this thing or not?"

Outside his maker's lair in the alley, Sly began to quake in his wing tips. He was here to do murder, plain and simple.

He wasn't used to the hustle and bustle of daytime traffic and exhaust smells. What if someone saw them break in? What if Malvant woke up and shrieked? Or worse, what if he didn't? Would staking an unconscious, defenseless vampire in his coffin feel worse than killing a vampire able to fight back?

Sly tried to clear his head, but his brain was foggy from all the wine he had just consumed. *Remember, Morgaine is in there. You need to protect her and the rest of the world from this evil bastard—if she's still alive.*

He didn't want to entertain thoughts to the contrary, but Gwyneth had said she couldn't sense Morgaine's energy in there.

"How do we get in?" Nathan asked.

Gwyneth smiled. "Hold this for me, darlin'." She passed him the fire extinguisher. Then she kneeled in front of the door and took a small glass vial out of her skirt pocket. Shaking a bit of powder into her hand, she mumbled a few words, then blew the powder into the lock.

Click. She rose and tried the door handle. When it opened, she grinned. Lowering her voice, she whispered, "Sly, y'all go first, followed by Nathan, then Lily, and I'll be in the rear. I mean…" She blushed the peach shade of a natural redhead. "I'll be the caboose on this vampire-huntin' train."

Sly nodded and entered silently. She had told him the door to Vorigan's lair would be on his right as they first walked in. He held the stake in his other hand as he tried to open the door, but it was locked.

Gwyneth muttered, "Fiddlesticks." Then she pushed her way to the front of the line and poured more powder from the vial into her hand. She blew the herb into the keyhole and mumbled, "Open says me, you S.O.B."

Those are the words of her spell? When the door clicked and she was able to open it, Sly gave a mental shrug. *Whatever works, I guess.*

She stood aside and waited while the rest of the line advanced.

Sly was touched that three of his neighbors—even one who didn't know him well—were willing to stick their necks out for him and Morgaine. Probably more for Morgaine since she was the one held captive in there—he hoped. Why was it so quiet? And why were the shades open, letting light into the living room?

A door to the right of the kitchen stood open. As he hurried over to it, he noticed her scent, but she wasn't there. She *had been* though.

"This is the right place," he whispered to the others. "So where is she?"

"Why don't y'all ask her?" Gwyneth suggested.

"Ask?" Suddenly he knew what she meant. "Telepathically?"

Gwyneth nodded.

Morgaine? Honey? Are you hiding somewhere?

"*Sly. I'm lost!*"

Lost? How did you get lost in Malvant's apartment?

"*I'm not in his apartment. I managed to get out and I ran. Now I don't know where I am.*"

Don't panic. I'll come for you. First, I need to take care of Malvant—once and for all.

"*Be careful! Did you drink enough Vampire Vintage to be safe outside for a while?*"

I *hic* certainly did.

He heard her chuckle.

I'll let you know when it's done. Meanwhile, look around for landmarks so I'll know where you are.

"*Okay. Good luck!*"

"She's safe." Sly let out a deep breath. "Let's just get rid of Malvant and get out of here."

"Wait." Lillian held up a hand. "If she doesn't need to be rescued, why are we still after this guy?"

"He won't give up. He'll just come after us again and again—only we might not be as lucky next time."

Gwyneth put a hand on her hip. "I don't know

about y'all, but I'm not crazy about the idea of bein' vampire food."

"Sly's the only one with matching vampiric strength," Nathan explained. "We need him to have any hope of pulling this off."

"And he doesn't have an unlimited supply of his temporary curative wine, letting him be out during the day," Gwyneth added. "I reckon it's now or never."

"I don't know that my strength *is* a match. Vorigan's centuries old and seems to have me at a disadvantage. But right now, with daylight and Gwyneth's Vampire Slayer herbs, *I* have the advantage, so I've got to take it."

"Oh." Lily nodded and seemed satisfied with everyone's explanations.

Gwyneth pointed to the far partition wall. "I think his room must be around that side."

The group crept quietly behind Sly as he advanced farther into the apartment. Sure enough, a door came into view. It must be where Malvant spent his days. Sly held the stake he'd brought with him above his shoulder, ready to attack if faced with any threat on the other side of the door.

He tried the doorknob. It didn't budge. "Damn. It's locked."

Gwyneth moved to the front of the line and shook the last of the vial's powder into her hand. She blew it at the doorknob and said, "Open says me, you S.O.B."

Miraculously, the lock clicked and Sly opened the door easily. The windowless room was dark and smelled disgusting. He flipped the light switch, but it must have been faulty or disconnected. Only the daylight streaming in from the hallway illuminated the area. Even so, it was impossible to mistake what he was seeing for anything else.

A coffin sat in the center of the otherwise empty room. Wait a minute… it wasn't empty. A half-decomposed body lay heaped in the corner, chains around its ankle bones. *That has to be the source of the disgusting smell. I wonder if he kept someone to feed on over and over, but went too far one time.*

———— ⁓ ————

"Ouch!" Vorigan's eyes flew open of their own accord. If the searing pain in his chest wasn't enough to piss him off, now he was looking up into the faces of four strangers—here in his private lair.

He recognized only one, his sexy dark playmate, Sly… or he *would be* his plaything if he'd just cave in and realize the futility of defying him. Vorigan looked down at the spot that throbbed. "What the hell? Did you just stake me?"

Sly's jaw dropped. "What the hell? Did you just survive?"

Vorigan rolled his eyes. "You missed." He yanked on the stake a few times, but it was stuck and he remained pinned to the floor of his old wooden coffin.

One of the women, a redhead, rested her hands on her hips and smirked. "What's the matter, vampire? Are y'all too weak during the daytime to pull out a little ol' stake?"

Vorigan growled. "Dammit. Why did you have to go and do something dickish like that? Now, as soon as I get up, I'll have to kill you."

"Not if we kill y'all first," the redhead taunted.

The only other male elbowed Sly and said, "I don't think I can chop off his head. The sides of the coffin are in the way."

Vorigan chuckled, folded his hands behind his head, and crossed his ankles. "Well, I guess I'm safer just lying here and laughing at your incompetence."

"Not really," said the young Asian chick. "I feel a sneeze coming on."

"Hang on," the other woman shouted. She poured something powdery on him.

"Oh, you wouldn't. You're going to cover me in germs and saliva spray, on top of whatever this green crap is? That would be disgusting!"

"No. That's not the way I... I..." She took in deep breaths after each attempt to finish her sentence. Like she was about to—

"Chooooo!" Fire roared out of her mouth and nostrils.

The pain he felt in his chest was nothing compared to the harsh sting that spread from his head to his neck and shoulders, then down the length of his body. "Crap. That smarts!"

Suddenly he smelled charred flesh mixed with burning wood. *Fuck.*

Sly crossed his arms. "Shall I try again and make it a merciful death?"

Vorigan sighed in defeat. "Whatever."

Sly took the ax from his friend, broke off the head of the ax, and drove the wooden stake straight through Malvant's heart.

Sly excused himself as soon as Gwyneth had emptied

the fire extinguisher's foam into what was left of the coffin and the last curl of smoke had dissipated.

"Where are y'all goin'?"

"To find Morgaine."

"She ain't home? I thought that's where she'd go if she managed to escape."

Sly shrugged. "Apparently she panicked, got disoriented, and ran in the wrong direction. Or maybe she was so afraid of his following her home that she purposely went the other way."

Gwyneth smirked. "Knowin' my cousin, it were a little bit of both."

"Well, I've got to go find her. She's wandering around the city somewhere, trying hard not to lose it."

"Do y'all want any help?"

Sly shook his head. "I know this city inside out. All she has to do is describe the area, and I'll find her. Why don't you give me a minute and I'll demonstrate?"

The others seemed interested, well, all except Nathan, so Sly closed his eyes and concentrated.

Morgaine? Can hear me, babe?

"Yes, I'm here."

Have you found a landmark or street signs or anything you can describe to me?

"I'm outside a bus station. It's on St. James Street."

That's almost all the way downtown. How did you get there?

"I bolted—and ran—and ran—and walked—and pooped out here."

Sly laughed. He turned to his companions and said, "I know right where she is. We'll see you in a few hours."

Nathan exclaimed, "A few hours? How far did she get?"

"Not that far. But I want some alone time with her—if you know what I mean…"

Nathan chuckled. "I understand. Sometimes when you face death, it makes you want to live more fully right away."

Gwyneth folded her arms and didn't seem all that happy about it. "I can hold off the party until tonight, I guess…"

Sly smiled. "That would be much appreciated."

Nathan draped an arm around Gwyneth's shoulders. "Fine by me."

She looked up at him and said, "I suppose you want to fool around too?"

His smile lit up his whole face. "Well, I *did* risk my life."

She let out a chuckle. "Nice try. See y'all tonight, Sly. Tell my cousin I'm glad she's okay."

He grinned. "I will."

Without waiting for good-byes, Sly turned and ran down the alley. He wanted to go at top speed, but people might notice a black blur so he held himself to a fast jog that *was* humanly possible.

Five minutes later, he spotted her. *I'm here, darling.*

She turned in his direction. As soon as she saw him, she began running toward him. *"Thank the Goddess!"*

They came together in the middle of the street, and he swept her up in a tight embrace. He whirled with her in his arms and set her down as cars and buses honked at the lunatics playing in traffic.

As they made their way safely to the sidewalk, she said, "Thanks for coming to get me."

He touched his forehead to hers. "Would I ever desert you?"

She gave him a quick peck. "No way."

Chapter 19

THEY STRODE HAND IN HAND FROM THE SUBWAY STATION to the block where their building stood without saying a word. One would occasionally glance over at the other and smile. Morgaine knew exactly where they were going and what they would do, and she didn't need to be psychic for that.

When they reached their stoop, Sly dropped her hand to retrieve his keys and let them in. They entered his apartment and stripped off their clothes on the way to his bedroom. They moved in complete silence. It seemed as if words would break the spell.

Standing beside the bed, she stared at him. His molten brown eyes held an intoxicating mixture of relief and desire. No. It was more than desire. He *needed* her.

He gazed at her a moment longer. "I thought I'd lost you." Sly leaned in and closed his mouth over hers. Her eyes fluttered closed. Lust simmered from his mouth to hers and she took an instinctive deep breath, fusing their lips together. Heat passed between them, and their tongues found each other. They met and swirled, and a murmur of delight escaped her.

Morgaine broke the kiss and sighed deeply, and her body dropped onto the mattress still holding him. They landed on the bed, bounced, and laughed. He nuzzled her neck.

"I love you," he whispered.

He said it. She had been dying to hear those words. Elated, she felt as if her heart would burst. Suddenly, all their passionate feelings for each other concentrated into nonverbal communication with more and deeper kisses.

Their tongues tangled sensuously. She embraced him and felt the warm flexing of his broad back. They rolled toward the pillows, then back toward the foot of the bed. They hadn't even turned lengthwise yet.

He slid his hand up her rib cage to capture a full breast and kneaded it. She offered him complete access and moaned when his mouth found her nipple.

He suckled her briefly, then maneuvered their bodies lengthwise and toward the middle of the bed. When she felt his bare chest on top of hers and his hard erection nudging the juncture of her thighs, she basked in his erotic promise. His passion would penetrate her to the core.

She bucked her hips against him. The friction of his cock against her clit made her wild. Her mind melted into an oblivion where only the two of them existed. The light coating of black hair on his chest rubbed her nipples into stiff peaks.

His tongue massaged hers in hungry strokes, and he slipped one hand around to cup and squeeze her buttocks. A warm shiver passed through her.

He lifted his swollen lips from hers. Every nerve ending tingled. He lowered his head over one breast, and his ebony lashes hid his eyes as he captured the nipple in his mouth and sucked. She arched and moaned, unable to help herself. His clean, musky scent filled her senses. He slipped his arm around her back, encircling her completely. He was so strong and yet so impossibly tender.

He swirled the tip of his tongue around the sensitive nipple. Morgaine arched her back, trying to push her breast further into his mouth. He seemed to understand her silent plea and sucked deeper, harder. White hot ripples radiated from her breast to her core. Her womb clenched. She opened her thighs wider, inviting him to take her. Instead, he kissed a hot trail to her other breast and suckled that one thoroughly too.

She was sure she was going to come from his relentless attention to her breasts alone if he continued that way. Several times the tug of pressure on her nipples sent a jolt of heat into her core. She ground her hips against his. His cock seemed to grow even larger and harder, if that were possible.

At last he lifted his lips and looked into her eyes. His gaze held a bone-melting, hungry look she'd never seen before.

"I want you," he whispered. He rose onto his knees and reached out.

Grabbing his waist, she pulled him toward her mouth. "Not yet. I have something for you first." She licked her lips.

He grinned and walked up on his knees until his cock was poised in front of her. She grasped the base with one hand and massaged his balls with the other. He leaned back and groaned.

Then she took him into her mouth and sucked. He undulated with the beat of a primitive drum only he could hear. She'd never wanted to do this for any other man, but for Sly she didn't think twice. She wanted to give him as much pleasure as she could—to show him a fraction of how happy he made her.

He reached behind and ran his fingers over her slick, aching folds. She pulled in a shuddering breath but continued to suck until he said, "Stop. No more."

He backed down the bed until his mouth was level with hers. He leaned over and crushed her lips in a brief but hot kiss. Then he continued to back down between her legs until his mouth reached her most intimate spot.

He ran his tongue up and down the ridges of her labia. She whimpered and pleaded with him incoherently. At last he zeroed in on her clit and lapped it repeatedly. The pleasure zinged through her, pushing her higher and higher.

At last she shattered. Crying out, ripples of joy sped through her shuddering body.

As soon as she had begun to breathe normally again, he settled gently on top of her. The head of his cock nudged her slick opening.

Morgaine caught her breath softly. Her mind spun and her body tingled. A few hours earlier, she hadn't known if she'd ever see Sly again. Now she was going to be joined with him in the most intimate way possible.

With a small thrust, he pushed the head of his cock inside her and stopped. He lowered his face and kissed her softly. She sighed and surrendered willingly. He pushed his hips forward a little more but stopped again. She was getting impatient. She wanted him. All of him. All the way.

"Please, Sly. I need you. All of you."

He smiled and pushed ahead slowly until he was fully seated. He caressed her cheek with one finger and reached between them with the other hand to where they were joined. He rubbed little circles around her clit as he withdrew and thrust. If he kept going slowly like this, she'd go mad.

As if sensing her frenzy, he coated his finger with her juices and rubbed quick strokes across her clit while he increased the tempo of his thrusts. She moaned her gratitude and sensed the building tension in her core.

Finally, the pleasure peaked and shock waves erupted, radiating from her core to the top of her head to her fingers and toes and back again. She quivered and shook, trying to be quiet but unable to stop a scream of ecstasy as it tore from her lips.

She screamed and bucked and screamed some more as Sly stayed right on the root of her pleasure until every last drop of bliss had been wrung from her. He came with a few uneven jerks and gasps. At last, he dropped next to her as she lay spent.

She curled into the crook of his arm and he held her. Softly, she murmured, "I love you, Sly."

He kissed the top of her head. "I love you too. I always will." A smile entered his voice. "After all, you're my beloved."

A wave of contentment filled her. "You're mine too."

That evening, as Jules opened his door to the hallway, the strong smell of alcohol almost knocked him over. "Don't tell me they're partying in the basement again. And even if they are, why the hell does their booze waft way up here?"

He was about to take his trash out to the Dumpster, so he figured he'd swing by the basement on his way and check on things. He jogged down the flight of stairs to the first floor, leaned his trash bag by the wall, and opened the basement door. A wave of crisp ethanol-scented air hit his nostrils like the deep chill of swimming through a cold spot in the ocean.

"What the hell?"

He flipped on the light switch and took the cellar stairs double time. "Ladies? Are you down here?"

All was quiet. Except for a small dripping sound. Afraid something in the laundry room might have sprung a leak, he went there first. He checked the deep sink, the pipes beneath it, and the space behind all the washing machines. Everything was dry.

Whew! I can skate by on my false claims of plumbing expertise for a while longer.

"So where are that damn dripping and strong smell coming from?"

He moved to the other half of the basement and peered around the boxes, half expecting to hear female giggles again. Not this time. Just that infernal dripping sound. It sounded like it was coming from the back wall. As he approached, he noticed something he hadn't seen before. A crack spanned the length of the wall right at the bump-out.

That's weird.

He grabbed the flashlight he kept on a shelf and returned to the suspicious spot in the wall. He illuminated the crack and noticed a space behind it. Then something glinted in the light. Something copper.

What the hell is that? With my luck, it's some new plumbing I haven't seen before and it's leaking, dammit.

With a crowbar and a hard pull, a hinge creaked and the crack opened. A metal contraption with copper pots and tubes came into view, with a clear liquid dripping from it into a bucket.

"Is that a still?" he said out loud.

Of course no one answered him, but they didn't have to. This explained everything. The smell. The girls partying in the basement. Everything. Should he report it to the board of health? Heck, no. That would call attention to the ballplayer's building. They'd probably want to talk to the owner.

He sighed. "This might explain the extra foot traffic too. They're probably selling it."

Well, they wouldn't be selling any more. He'd have to drain and dismantle the enterprise. But should he squeal on the residents? He began looking for the shut-off valve and decided that would depend upon how much of a pain in the ass the still was to take apart.

Sly held Morgaine's hand and knocked on the door of apartment 3A with his free fist. She'd noticed that his skin warmed whenever he had some of the vampire curative wine in his system. He was still plenty warm from that morning's dose.

Lily had come up the stairs right behind them and waited along with them for Gwyneth to open her door.

Eventually, the door swung open wide.

"C'mon on in, all y'all!" Gwyneth stepped back and allowed her guests to enter. Country music played in the background. It had to be Gwyneth's favorite radio station or a CD she'd recently bought. Morgaine had never heard the song before.

She had seen Gwyneth's girly apartment plenty of

times, but the other two probably hadn't. Their gazes wandered around, taking in the decidedly feminine decor. White wicker furniture with pink-and-white striped cushions and loads of unmatched floral pillows dominated the room.

A pink tablecloth and a vase of flowers graced the dinette table. Also on the dinette were a platter of crust-free sandwiches cut in triangles, cheese, crackers, fried okra, and peanuts. Gwyneth's version of party food.

Nathan rounded the corner of the kitchen with a Mason jar of what looked to be the finished moonshine whiskey. It was a pure amber color.

Morgaine pointed to it. "Is that the um..." She glanced at Lily. *Oops.* "Is that what I think it is?"

"First batch," Nathan said proudly. "Gwyneth and I finished it up while we were, ahem, waiting for you and Sly to, ahem, relax after your ordeal."

Sly smirked. "Badly clogged throat you've got there, Nathan."

Morgaine dropped Sly's hand and strolled toward the windows. She gazed outside at the fierce snowstorm. *It must have begun snowing as we were, ahem, making love.*

Nathan noticed her by the windows. "Big snowstorm out there. It's times like this when I'm glad I don't have a car."

"Amen to that," Sly said.

Gwyneth piped up. "If I had a car out there, I think I'd just let it set until spring."

Nathan strolled over to her and casually wrapped an arm around her waist. "Until the city made you move it so they could plow. Thank goodness for public transportation."

"Are you two…" Lily pointed from one to the other and back again. Her question wasn't hard to figure out.

Gwyneth chuckled. "Not just yet. I'm gonna make him wait a bit. That way he'll appreciate me."

"I already appreciate you."

"I know, I was just teasin' is all."

"You're a tease all right."

He tickled her. She shrieked and tried to squirm away.

Morgaine noticed Lily watching the scene with a serene smile.

"Lily, how are you doing?"

"Fine now, thank you."

Nathan looked over at her. "No more fiery sneezes?"

"No. I saw Jules before coming up here." She blushed.

"Why didn't y'all bring him to the party?"

"I didn't know if he was invited."

"Of course he is."

"Now, wait a minute, Gwyneth. This is my pad too. Shouldn't you ask me if I'm okay with him being here first?"

"Oh, fiddlesticks, Chad. What could y'all possibly object to as far as Jules is concerned?"

"Well, I think you might want to avoid him for a while."

"Why's that?"

"He's dismantling your still as we speak."

Gwyneth and Morgaine gasped.

"Not the still," Gwyneth wailed.

Sly had been gazing longingly at the food on the table, but he whirled around and stared at them. "What about the still?"

Gwyneth collapsed on the sofa and covered her face with her hands. "Chad just said Jules is dismantling it."

"Shit! Now what are we going to use to preserve the…" He trailed off and gazed at Lily.

Morgaine knew what he was going to say, but he probably didn't know Lily well enough to trust her with his secret yet.

Suddenly Gwyneth lifted her head. "I know. We can make wine. I don't know why I didn't think of that afore. It don't require no still."

Lily looked confused. "You have a still? Can't you afford to buy alcohol when you want some?"

"Um…" Morgaine had to say something before Gwyneth spilled any more beans. "No, not really. Our finances are pretty low right now."

"Oh. I'm sorry to hear that. I have some money saved…"

"No, please, don't worry about it. We'll manage."

"Are you sure?"

A knock at the door interrupted their conversation.

"Now who could that be?" Gwyneth wondered out loud.

"You might not want to answer it."

She hesitated, then rolled her eyes. "Pshaw. Don't be silly, Chad. I can handle Jules."

"It's not Jules. It's Merry, your landlady."

"Well, why wouldn't I want to talk to Merry?" She strode to the door and opened it. "Why Merry, what a pleasant surprise. Were we makin' too much noise? We was just havin' a little gatherin'…"

"No, not at all," Merry said. "I'm sorry to bother you—again, but I think I'm in labor for real this time."

Sly rushed over. "The baby's coming? Now?"

Gwyneth's jaw dropped. "Goodness. Ain't Jason home yet?"

"No, the blizzard hit Minnesota before he could get a flight out. Now it's here, so even if he could take off, he couldn't land."

"Oh, dear. And Roz?"

"I didn't call her. I don't want her to drive all the way from Newton in this storm."

By this time, Morgaine had joined them. "Merry, I can help you. I've been trained in midwifery."

"You have? Awesome!"

"So, where do y'all want to do this? We can kick everyone out and use my apartment…"

Merry looked horrified. "No, goodness no! I already called a cab. I just wanted someone to go to the hospital with me… you know, in case something happens and I get a cab driver who doesn't know how to deliver a baby."

Sly stepped forward and took her hand. "Morgaine and I will both go to the hospital with you, sweetheart. Don't worry about a thing. Now, let me get your bag."

"Thanks, Gramps. It's upstairs." Merry winked at him, and he gave her as big a hug as he could around her belly.

"I'll just grab my coat," Morgaine said and hurried across the hall.

Gwyneth rushed after her. "Morgaine, wait."

Morgaine stopped. "What is it?"

Gwyneth leaned in and whispered in her ear. "Talk to Merry about our little problem in the basement while you're waiting with her."

"Oh, Lord and Lady, Gwyneth. Now's not the time."

Chapter 20

As Merry began her fourteenth hour of definite, genuine labor, she found it hurt less when she was positioned on her side. Or maybe it was the low back rub Morgaine was giving her that eased the pain. Sly sat on the opposite side and held her hand.

"How are you doing, honey?"

"I'm fine," both women said at once. Then Morgaine let out a nervous giggle.

Merry suddenly realized Morgaine had been standing in one spot for a long time. "I'm sorry, Morgaine. You don't need to keep massaging me if you're getting tired."

"I'm not."

"Oh, thank goodness, because it feels really good."

Sly chuckled. However, it was the kind of nervous noise that relieved an awkward moment.

He voiced what Merry had been hoping ever since her labor pains had sped up to every two minutes. "I'll bet Jason will be here any minute."

"Is it still snowing?" she asked.

"I doubt it," Sly said. "It's almost morning, and it began yesterday afternoon."

Morgaine stopped massaging just long enough to stroll around the curtain to the window. Merry was glad the semi-private room had been the only one available when they checked in. Sharing her experience with someone else who was going through it had helped with sympathy. Her roommate had gone to the delivery room an hour earlier.

"It's stopped," Morgaine said.

"Finally! Maybe Jason's plane has landed and he'll get here in time for the birth. Although I'd feel kind of bad for the two of you having gone through all these hours of labor with me only to miss the grand finale."

Morgaine returned to Merry's side and resumed her low back massage. "Don't worry about us, Merry. We'll be in the waiting room if we can't go in with you."

"I can't thank you both enough—" Another pain was coming. She began to moan, and concern filled Sly's eyes. In some ways, he seemed more nervous than she was.

She squeezed his hand and knew that if Jason was here, he might *not* be holding her hand. He wasn't allowed to do certain things that would risk his ability to pitch. She remembered him telling Roz that skydiving was strictly forbidden. But, she imagined him trying his hardest to make it to the hospital and bailing out over Boston General. He *could* shift into his falcon form and fly, after all.

At last, the contraction eased and she took a deep breath, relieved it was over—for a couple of minutes.

A nurse's aide entered the room. "How are you doing, Mrs. Falco?"

"Okay," she said, tentatively.

"Good. Be sure to use the buzzer if you need anything."

When she left, Sly asked, "Do you know any of these nurses from working here?"

"No. I was in pediatrics. Nurses from different departments don't usually get chummy unless they were friends before."

Just then a stretcher holding her exhausted-looking roommate rolled in.

"Hey, Anna. How did it go?"

Her husband grinned. "We had a healthy baby girl."

Anna snorted. "Yeah, *we* were in labor for six hours. I'm just glad it's over."

"Congratulations. I'm happy for you both."

Morgaine seemed genuinely interested. "This is your second, right?

Anna nodded. "I don't mean to be rude, folks, but I've got to take a nap."

"Of course," Merry said. "We'll be quiet—unless I start screaming."

Just then Jason sailed into the room. "Who's screaming?"

"Jason!"

He rushed to her outstretched arms.

"Looks like I made it," he said.

"Thank goodness. How's your dad?"

"Much better."

"Good. Sweetie, can you take over for Morgaine and rub my back with your non-pitching hand?"

"I'll be glad to. Have you been at it a while, Morgaine?"

"About fifteen minutes."

"More like forty-five," Merry corrected. She imagined her friend didn't want them to feel as if she'd been working too hard for too long.

"Thank you for taking such good care of my wife in my absence." Jason rounded the bed and relieved Morgaine.

Another person entered the room. A different nurse this time. "I need to check to see how dilated you are," she said. "Your husband can stay, but I think your visitors ought to leave for a few minutes."

"That's okay." Sly smiled. "We'll be nearby."

"Maybe we should go to the waiting room at this point," Morgaine said. "I have a feeling it won't be much longer before she delivers." She winked at Sly.

The nurse looked over at Morgaine. "Are you a nurse or a midwife?"

"I took some classes in midwifery."

Merry was about to explain that Morgaine was her father's girlfriend, but another contraction hit and the information seemed superfluous.

Jason paused. "Are you all right, honey?"

"Will be. Keep rubbing," she said.

Jason returned to his task.

Sly reluctantly let go of Merry's hand. "Good luck, sweetheart. Jason, be sure to let us know how she's doing as soon as you can."

"Will do." He reached over her and shook Sly's hand.

Morgaine closed her eyes briefly and murmured something just under her breath. When she opened them, she must have noticed a puzzled look on their faces.

"Just offering a prayer to the Goddess for the best possible outcome," she said.

"Why? Is anything wrong," Jason asked.

Morgaine quickly interjected, "No. Nothing at all. I just figured it wouldn't hurt."

Merry smiled at her. "That's perfectly fine. In fact, all prayers and good wishes will be gratefully accepted."

Sly walked Morgaine to the waiting room. A couple of

other people were there reading, so he whispered to her. "Did you really say a prayer or were you doing a spell?"

"They're pretty much the same thing."

He took a seat, even though he felt more like pacing. Morgaine settled into the chair next to him.

Keeping his voice low, he continued. "You are so talented in magick, I imagine you could make good money at that alone, if you wanted to."

"What are you saying?"

"I just think you could let Gwyneth take over the phone-sex business and you could become a full-time witch. You know… doing spells for people like you did for Mikhail."

"First of all, witches aren't supposed to sell their magick. We can charge money for tarot, palm, or tea-leaf readings, but when it comes to spells, we have to be asked. We can trade favors as I did with Mikhail, but anything else is against the Witches' Rede.

"Why do you think there are no signs that say, 'Spells R Us'? Magic is not to be used lightly, and it's definitely not for fools. If you don't know who you're helping and what they're up to, it can be very dangerous."

Her voice took on a slightly hissed, higher pitch as she whispered. The other people looked up from their magazines.

"Hey, what's the matter? I was giving you a compliment."

She folded her arms and huffed. "I suppose."

"Then why are you pouting?"

"I'm not pouting."

There was that raised voice again. Something was bothering her.

"Morgaine, if you have something to say, just say it."

"I could say the same to you," she snapped.

"Shhh…" He looked over at the other visitors, but they continued reading, hopefully tuning out the argument. "Excuse me?"

Leaning toward him as if wanting to get her point across while she tried to keep her voice down, she said, "This *isn't* about my magick, is it? It's about my phone-sex business."

He shrugged. "I just don't understand why you'd continue doing that if you had another option."

She narrowed her eyes. "Maybe I'm talented in more than one area."

What was going on? Did she *like* talking dirty to strangers? Sly had been thinking of discussing marriage with her, but now he wasn't so sure. He let out an exasperated breath.

Maybe she was just used to relying on this type of interaction to feel attractive to the opposite sex. Well, he'd have to let her know she didn't have to. He'd more than fill that bill.

"Morgaine, I don't want to fight. I love you."

She sighed. "I know. I love you too. I suppose it's normal to feel a little jealous of my customers."

"Jealous? Don't be ridiculous." He laughed.

She jumped to her feet and began to walk away. Her eyes looked like storm clouds had just rolled in.

Uh-oh. That was the wrong reaction. "Morgaine… honey." He rose and strolled toward her. Then his head spun and the odd sensation of falling into a hole engulfed him.

―᳝᳝―

"Sly! Oh, my Goddess." *What happened?*

He had been walking toward her when suddenly he'd swayed and sunk to the floor. The other people watched as she rushed over to him. One of them rose and joined her.

"Is he all right?"

The Vampire Vintage must have worn off—and it's sunrise. But how could she explain that to strangers? Before she could think of an explanation, the gentleman grabbed Sly's wrist and checked for a pulse.

"Uh-oh. Your friend's in trouble. I'll stay with him. Go call a nurse."

"No, you go. I'll stay with him."

The man looked puzzled, but he got up and strode out of the waiting room in the direction of the nurse's station.

Now what? Thank the Goddess he hadn't landed directly in the shaft of sunlight filtering through the windows, but he was near enough to make her nervous. She grabbed Sly's arms and dragged his lifeless body toward the restroom.

The remaining woman rose. "I'm pretty sure you're not supposed to move someone after a fall."

Stay out of it, lady, Morgaine thought. *What do you know about vampirism?*

A "code blue" was announced over the loudspeaker, and a nurse came running. She kneeled next to Sly, tilted his head back, and placed two fingers on one side of his neck. Another nurse joined her shortly, towing a large red cart. When she plopped a container with paddles onto the floor next to Sly's lifeless body, Morgaine figured out what it was for.

Oh, no. A defibrillator. What would that do to him?

She had to think quickly, yet her mind was frozen.

The nurse with the defibrillator had turned it on and was poised over Sly's chest with paddles in hand.

At last Morgaine came up with something. "Stop! He's a Christian Scientist. And he has a living will. He doesn't want any medical treatment, even in an emergency."

The nurse without the paddles had opened the cart and was retrieving something with a plastic mask and a large oblong balloon attached to it. She stared at her.

"But we might be able to save him. Don't you want us to try?"

Yeah, they might be able to kill him too. Morgaine bit her bottom lip. "I-I think he'd want us to respect his wishes."

The nurses looked at each other openmouthed.

I could kick myself. We were so focused on Merry that I never thought about Sly's condition. Dearest Goddess, please let Nathan be working in the morgue tonight.

Nathan Nourie flew to his workplace carrying a pillowcase containing a bottle of wine in his strong beak. Luckily, Sly had left in such a hurry, he hadn't locked his door and Morgaine was able to direct Nathan to the briefcase holding the stuff Sly needed.

And everyone says self-medicating with alcohol is a bad thing.

Never had he thought his job as a morgue attendant would help save someone. Least of all a friend. It occurred to him that for the first time in a long time, he had friends—not just acquaintances. Sly was someone he'd plow through snowy sidewalks for. And he knew Sly or

Morgaine would do the same for him. And Gwyneth… just thinking about her made him smile.

He had to shift into human form and dress quickly. Fortunately, he had found a spot outside the hospital where he could keep a change of clothes. There were the inevitable days when he overslept and had to literally *fly* to work to get there on time.

Nathan dug his clothing out of the hidey-hole and hopped into his black pants. He struggled into his shirt and ran toward the entrance, still buttoning.

Morgaine had sounded frantic. As he skidded around the corridor, he hoped he'd arrived in time to prevent the daytime attendant from doing any damage. He strong-armed the door to the morgue and strode inside.

Morgaine was draped over a sheet-covered body, wailing. The attendant seemed perturbed and was trying to pry her hands off the gurney.

"Stop," Nathan ordered.

They both looked up at him, openmouthed. Morgaine's cheeks were streaked with real tears. She wasn't just acting.

Oh, no. Am I too late?

Morgaine gazed at the ceiling and said, "Thank the Goddess!"

"Nathan? What are you doing here?" the attendant asked.

"Taking over." Nathan grabbed a pair of latex gloves on his way to the supply cabinet. He gathered what he'd need to infuse the wine intravenously. On his way to the hospital, he'd realized that would be the only way to get some of it into Sly's system.

The other attendant scowled at him. "What the hell are you up to?"

"Saving this man's life." Nathan pushed him aside and peeled back the sheet.

Sly lay there immobile and pale. Nathan worked quickly before the other attendant could call anyone or interfere. Fortunately, he didn't move. He simply stared at Nathan as if he'd lost his mind. Perhaps he had. How would he explain this later?

There was no time to worry about that. Nathan shoved Sly's sleeve up and located the large medial vein in the crook of his arm. He quickly took a syringe with the longest, thickest needle he could find and stuck it right through the cork. Then he drew the syringe full of wine and injected it directly into Sly's vein.

Nothing happened for a few seconds. Just as Nathan was beginning to despair, Sly sat up and opened his eyes.

The other attendant reeled backward. "Jesus Christ!"

Sly blinked a few times and looked around. Then he glanced down at his bare torso and the sheet covering him from the waist down. He yanked the sheet up over his bare feet and saw the toe tag. "Fan-fucking-tastic."

He slid off the gurney and walked, butt naked, toward the frightened attendant.

"What the hell are you, man? A zombie?"

Sly held the attendant's gaze for a moment, and the guy's jaw went slack. "You did *not* see a body on that gurney. You did *not* see a woman or one of your co-workers here this morning. Everything is as it should be on this quiet morning in the morgue."

He turned toward Nathan. "Now, where are my clothes?"

Nathan pointed at what amounted to a laundry hamper. Sly walked over to it, fished out his clothes, and put them on.

"Thanks, Nathan. Morgaine, I assume you were responsible for calling him, so I owe you a debt of gratitude too."

She burst into tears and hugged him. Then she rushed to Nathan and hugged him too. He gave her a few awkward pats on her back.

"There, there." Isn't that what people were supposed to say after a crisis? What else should he say? "Everything's all right now."

"Thank you," she whimpered. "Thank you so much. I'll never forget this."

"Please don't get mushy." He didn't know what to do with that. He had never saved anyone before. It felt pretty good though. Damn good, in fact.

Chapter 21

BACK AT THEIR BUILDING, SLY HAD TO MAKE A DIFFICULT phone call. He didn't know what Jason and Merry might have been told about his highly exaggerated demise.

Oh, well. I shouldn't put this off.

Nathan couldn't wait to tell Gwyneth about his heroism, so he pivoted left at the top of the stairs while Sly and Morgaine entered her apartment on the right.

"Is it okay if I borrow your sex phone to make a local call? I mean, it won't come up as 1-900-Sex-Kitty or anything, will it?"

She snorted. "No. It'll come up as a private number."

"So, can I use it to call Jason? I imagine Merry's a little busy right now."

"Of course. How are you going to tell him what happened? It's not like you can mesmerize him over the phone…" Her eyes rounded. "Can you?"

He smiled. "No, I can't. And I don't know what to say, but I want to know how Merry is."

She sighed. "I understand. Why don't you let me call? At least the nurses won't flip out if they hear my voice."

"I was going to call Jason's cell phone."

"Oh, do you think he left it on?"

"If not, I can leave a message. That might be better since I wouldn't have to explain anything until they get back…"

"And then you can erase their memories," she finished for him.

"Yeah."

She led him to the phone and said, "Mind if I listen in?"

"If you want."

She didn't say anything else, but just perched on the arm of the chair after he sat and dialed.

They waited through three rings, and at last Jason picked up.

"Falco," he said.

"Jason, it's Sly."

"Sly? Why are you calling? Aren't you in the waiting room?"

Morgaine smiled and said telepathically, *"Thank the Goddess, he doesn't know."*

Sly nodded to her. "No, we had to get home."

"Oh. Well, you'll want to know that Merry's in the recovery room and doing well."

"The recovery room? What happened?"

"As soon as you left, the nurse checked her and confirmed that our son was double breech. Upside down *and* backwards. She had a C-section."

"A son? Is he all right?"

"Perfectly. They said if they hadn't performed an emergency C-section, he might have broken a shoulder on the way out. I hope he's not always this uncooperative."

Sly laughed. "I hope not too. But if you ever need a break from the little guy, let me know. I'd be more than happy to baby-sit."

Morgaine grinned. She leaned toward the phone. "What are you naming him?"

"Max, after Merry's father. I mean—her other father." Jason sounded vaguely uncomfortable, but Sly couldn't be happier. Not only because he had a biological grandson, but because his son-in-law seemed to finally accept that Sly was Merry's real father, despite looking so much younger than he should.

"Her dad's nickname is Mac—for MacKenzie," Jason finished.

"I remember Merry telling me that. I like the name Max. It's a good strong name."

"I'm glad you approve. Merry's other dad is on his way here now. He and her younger brother had to wait until the roads were cleared."

Sly heard Merry in the background asking, "Is that Sly?"

"Yes, would you like to talk to him?"

"Please," she said. A moment later, he heard her loud and clear. "Hi, Gramps."

"Hi, honey." Despite the lump in his throat, he asked, "How are you feeling?"

"Like a wrung-out dishrag."

He laughed. "Good."

"Good?"

"Yeah. If you didn't say something like that, I'd know you were lying."

"I'd never lie to you, Sly. Just like I won't keep things from my husband."

A jolt of panic whipped through him. "But, that would mean he knows I'm a..."

"Vampire? Yes, he knows."

Sly was so shocked he didn't know what to say.

Jason returned to the phone. "So, you have to admit... that trip to the morgue was pretty funny."

Morgaine's jaw dropped. *The hell it was!*

Sly chuckled. "I don't think Morgaine would agree with you."

"True. I wasn't there. Someday you'll have to tell us exactly what happened."

"Just that the sun came up. What did the nurses tell you?"

"A doctor pulled me into the hallway and said my dear father-in-law had died from a heart attack, and not to tell Merry until everything was over."

"And you thought that was funny?"

"Considering…"

Sly snorted. Then it occurred to him that Jason was taking his condition fairly casually. "So, you're okay with a vampire in the family?"

"Why wouldn't I be? Merry says you take care of your needs elsewhere and keep the city's crime rate down at the same time."

"That's true. How about my living in your building? Is that a problem?"

"If I had a problem with every paranormal and strange neighbor in my building, I'd have to evict everyone — with the possible exception of Merry."

He heard her laugh.

Sly chuckled. "You're one in a million, Jason. I'm glad Merry found you."

"Me too." He heard the smile in his son-in-law's voice and then a loud kiss between the happy new parents.

As soon as they hung up, Sly scooped Morgaine into his arms and carried her to her bedroom. She couldn't help giggling at the way he took charge.

"I think it's time we christened your bed with our lovemaking, don't you?"

She chuckled. "You're constantly horny, aren't you?"

"Are you saying you don't want to?"

"Heck, no! Of course I want to. I was just teasing."

He smiled and laid her on the bed. "Whew. I'm glad your sense of humor is returning, but I was afraid you were tired of me."

"I'll never get tired of you, Sly. I love everything about you."

The hunger in his eyes spoke for him as he unbuttoned her blouse. She reached for his belt buckle, and they undressed each other simultaneously.

When at last they lay next to each other, skin to skin, he cupped her cheek and stared into her eyes. "Those were real tears you shed this morning. Were you afraid something would happen to me when I was incapacitated?"

"Are you kidding? I was terrified. I figured if I didn't stop them, they'd try to perform an autopsy."

"But you didn't let them."

Her brows knit as she remembered just how tightly she had held on to the gurney all the way to the morgue. "The orderly tried to convince me to let you go, but I wasn't about to leave your side until and unless they pried me off with a crowbar."

He chuckled. "I knew I could depend on you to keep me safe. And I'll always protect you too. We're good together, don't you think?"

"Yes, I do. In all kinds of ways."

He captured her lips in a long, deep kiss. Meanwhile, his fingers traced a path down the column of her neck to her chest and kneaded her breast. She moaned into his mouth.

He broke their lip-lock and kissed his way down the

same path his hand had taken until he latched onto a nipple and suckled her.

She arched and moaned. The deep sensations rippled through her and tugged at her core as if he'd pulled an invisible string.

His hand and mouth traded places so that he cupped and squeezed the breast he'd been sucking and paid equal attention to the other one.

How she loved this man... vampire... no, man. Whatever he was didn't matter. He was hers.

He inched his way down her torso, feathering more kisses along her heated skin. When he reached her thighs, he ran his tongue along the ridges of her labia. She shivered.

"Cold?"

"Not hardly."

He chuckled and went to work licking, nipping, and sucking her most sensitive area.

As the fever built, she anticipated an earth-shattering orgasm.

"Oh, Sly!"

Each time they coupled, she thought she couldn't possibly feel more satisfied than the time before, yet somehow he managed to top his performance without trying. Perhaps it had to do with how much more she fell in love with him each day.

Before she knew it, Morgaine's climax crashed over her, taking her on the ride of her life. She cried out and grabbed the sheets with both hands as if she might levitate any second. He didn't stop until he had wrung every last aftershock out of her.

Panting for breath, she said, "Wow."

He grinned. "I'm glad I can still wow you."

When she could speak again, she giggled and said, "...and how." As she reached for him, he scooted up beside her and leaned into her embrace.

"I love you, Morgaine. I never thought I'd love someone this much again."

"I never thought I'd love someone this much at all."

As he kissed her, she felt a shared deep emotional connection. She could have let him kiss her all day and night, but it was his turn for satisfaction and she dearly wanted to give it to him.

At last, Sly broke the kiss and tapped her knees. She parted them. He climbed over one leg and kneeled in the V she made for him. She held his hooded gaze as he entered her. An unspoken bond had them moving together in one fluid motion.

How did I get so lucky? I found the love of my life right under my nose.

Sly's rhythm sped up and she knew he was close. She twined her legs around his back and let him take her however he wanted to.

Eventually his motions became irregular and his gasp told her he had found his peak. He stilled, then collapsed on top of her.

"Thank you," he whispered in her ear.

She giggled. "Anytime, stud."

—◈—

Spending a week in bed was something Morgaine had never pictured doing... at least not without being ill. She and Sly had been constant companions ever since they'd returned from the morgue and had barely made it out of the bedroom long enough to avoid starvation. Gwyneth gladly took over the phone-sex calls.

Sly had said he would make love to Morgaine until she understood he really believed her to be the most beautiful woman in the world. She enjoyed being convinced thoroughly.

Other than setting up the wine-making operation in Sly's kitchen, they hadn't accomplished a thing.

"Sly?"

He propped himself on his elbow and dragged a finger over her torso. "Yeah."

She shivered. "Don't start that again."

"Why not?"

She chuckled. "Because I'm getting sore."

He snatched his hand back. "Why didn't you say something?"

"I just did."

"Oh." Sly's expression turned from one of concern to playfulness. He took a lock of her hair, curled it around his finger, and kissed it. "Imagine if we were both vampires. We'd never have to worry about too much loving. Even if we went at it like out-of-control jackhammers, you'd heal in seconds."

Morgaine raised her eyebrows. She'd have reacted more forcefully, but (a) she didn't have the energy and (b) she'd been thinking the same thing.

"Would you really want me to be undead with you?"

Sly shook his head sadly. "No. I wouldn't wish that on anyone. It's just that—"

He didn't finish his thought. He simply levered himself to a seated position on the bed. Bending over her, he took her hand in his and caressed it.

"I love you, Morgaine. I never thought I'd love again, but God or the Goddess or whatever powers-that-be must have decided to give me a second chance."

She opened her mouth to speak, but he placed his finger against her lips and whispered, "Shhh. I have more to say… much more."

"All right."

He kissed her knuckles and took a deep breath. "Before we got close, I liked you. I thought of you as a friend and a woman I admired."

"And now…"

"Now, you're all I could ever want or need. You truly *are* my beloved. My equal. My soul mate."

He paused a little too long, so to encourage him, she said, "I feel that way about you too. Is there more?"

"Yes. Part of me thinks about losing you some day, and I picture the pain as insufferable. I don't know if I could survive it. Physically, yes, but emotionally?"

Morgaine smiled weakly. "People can survive all kinds of things, Sly. Even losses we can't imagine going through."

"I suppose… but I'm not like most people. I'll have to go through centuries, maybe millennia with only memories."

"I know," she whispered. "And even before that, you'll have to watch me grow old while you don't age a day, if we stay together."

"Don't you worry about that."

"How do you know I'm worried?"

"I know women well enough to know what you're thinking."

She chuckled. "Maybe you do."

"You're my beloved. I'm never going to trade you in for a younger model."

"So you say now."

"Morgaine, I'm serious. I've given this a lot of thought…"

Looking at his face, she realized he was holding something back. It was something important so she'd better shut up and let him finish.

He ran a finger up her arm, making her tingle.

"Whatever you have to say, please say it before we get sidetracked."

He grinned. "We do get sidetracked easily, don't we?"

She smiled. "Yup."

"Okay, no more beating around the bush. I was about to say that while I still have a believable birth certificate, I'd like to apply for a marriage license."

Morgaine gasped. She knew she should say something, but the words got stuck in her throat.

"Will you marry a fifty-seven-year-old vampire, Morgaine? Will you be my wife?"

She still couldn't speak so she merely nodded.

He grinned and dove for her. Scooping under her torso, he rolled until she lay on top of him.

"You just made me very happy," she said with tears in her eyes. "I'll do my best to make you happy too."

"I already am."

They shared a long kiss.

When at last Morgaine came up for air, she asked, "When did you turn fifty-seven? I thought you were fifty-six?"

"Well, actually my birthday is next month, but I figured I'd get used to the idea."

"Whew. I thought I'd missed it. There's still time to think of a gift."

"No need. You just gave me everything I wanted."

———~~~———

Gwyneth opened her apartment door to let in the landlord's wife. "Thanks for comin' to visit me, Merry. Take a load off."

Merry stuck a hand on her hip. "Excuse me?"

It took a moment to realize what might have upset her. "Oh, I didn't mean y'all are a load or anythin'. It's just an expression that means 'set a spell.'"

Merry chuckled. "I knew that. I was just joking." She gingerly seated herself on Gwyneth's flowered couch. "Since Max was born, I've lost about twenty pounds, but I still have another ten to go. I can't help feeling heavy. But my old jeans will fit again—some day." She sighed.

Gwyneth offered a dismissive wave. "Oh, pshaw. You look wonderful. So, can I get y'all some sweet tea?"

"How about a small glass of milk, if you have it."

"You got it." On her way to the kitchen, Gwyneth asked over her shoulder, "How's the little bundle of joy doin'?"

Merry chuckled. "He's full of piss and vinegar, as Sly would say."

Gwyneth laughed. "That's prob'ly truer than it's meant to be."

She quickly poured the milk and arranged some cookies on a bamboo tray. She put the pitcher of sweet tea and an extra glass in the middle, just in case Merry changed her mind about the tea. Maybe she was worried about caffeine. Most new parents needed all the caffeine they could get after waking up a couple of times a night with a baby hollering for attention.

When she returned to the living room, Merry smiled. "This is the first time I've gone anywhere in a week. It was nice of you to invite me."

"No need to go thankin' me yet. Not that it isn't nice just to share a snack and some gossip with y'all, but I kinda need to ask a favor too."

"A favor? Sure."

"I ain't asked it yet."

Merry chuckled. "I mean, sure, you can ask. If it's something I can do, I will. What do you need?"

"Well, I was hopin' y'all could talk to Jules. You see, that favor is for Sly, but Jules didn't know what we was tryin' to do and he kinda undid it."

"Oh. Can you be more specific?"

Gwyneth took a deep breath. "Well, Morgaine and Sly went to New York right before Thanksgiving to get a cure for his vampirism."

Merry's posture straightened, and her eyes popped. "A cure? I didn't know there was one."

"Well, it's only temporary, but it cures the worst parts of bein' a vampire. I guess it takes the place of blood and Sly could walk around in sunlight without passin' out or burnin' up."

"Wow. That sounds awesome. So what can I do to help?"

"Well, Sly's probably too proud to ask and Morgaine thought we should let you rest and recover a little longer, but I saw no harm in askin'…"

"Sure. Go ahead, ask."

"Well, it's crazy expensive, but Morgaine figured out how to make more from what we got."

"That's great. And?"

"It's like a sourdough-bread recipe. You know how they make it with starter?"

Merry nodded.

"Well, y'all have to add some of the old wine to new-made wine before it gets bottled."

"Okay... so what do I need to talk to Jules about?" She sipped her milk.

"Well, Morgaine and I found a big wooden vat, and we'd like permission to stomp grapes down in the basement. Then we can put the stuff in bottles with the vampire cure and let it age where it's the right temperature. We're fixin' to buy some wine racks too, if we get y'all and Jason's okay. We want to make it as close to the real thing as possible."

Merry shrugged. "I don't think that would be a problem. You said Jules undid something you'd tried to do before?"

"Well, yeah. We had a still down there back when we was tryin' to add the vampire wine to some moonshine. The idea was to make it stretch more and preserve it in a recipe my daddy used. Unfortunately, Jules found the still and took it apart. Threw out some perfectly good whiskey too, I reckon."

"Well, that's too bad."

"It's a damn shame. If the still weren't illegal in the first place, I'd call it a crime."

Merry raised her eyebrows. "So is making wine illegal?"

"Nah. Not for your own use. To sell alcohol is illegal, but that's a racket the government's got goin'. They want their tax money. If everyone made and sold their own under the table, the liquor stores would lose a lot of business and the government would lose out on all those taxes."

"I suppose that's true." Merry mulled that over, then asked, "So how do you make your own wine?"

"Oh, it's dead easy. It's just sugar, water, yeast, and grape juice. When it's all good an' mixed together, y'all just pour it in a glass bottle and fix a balloon over the top."

"A balloon? What does that do?"

"Well, it blows up with the carbon dioxide. You gotta make a few pinholes in the balloon to let it out."

"Wouldn't that keep the balloon from inflating?"

"Nah, the balloon gets big anyway. When it loses all its poof and goes flat again, the wine's done. Y'all have to strain it through a pillowcase to catch the junk at the bottom, but the final stuff is plumb delicious."

"Speaking of plums, I've heard of wines being made with fruits other than grapes. Have you ever tried to make other kinds?"

"Oh, heck, yes. My momma made raspberry, peach, and cherry wine. Any kind of fruit juice will do—exceptin' orange or any other citrus."

"You know what? That sounds like fun. I should talk to Jason first, but I'll bet he'll be fine with it."

"Then y'all will tell Jules to leave it alone?"

"Yes. I'm sure he'll be on board with it if we are. I've noticed he takes his responsibilities very seriously."

"Let's just hope nothin' breaks. Morgaine sensed somethin' weird goin' on with him."

"Weird? Uh-oh. What constitutes weird around *here*?"

"She said she thinks he lies a lot."

Merry's jaw dropped. "What has he lied about?"

"Well, she thinks he lied about his whole résumé. She don't think he could fix a clogged sink with a bucket of Drano."

"Hmmm… Jason's Uncle Ralph recommended him. Said he had tons of experience, but I'll admit, no one checked."

"Oops. Well, I didn't mean to tattle on him. He seems like a right nice man, and he's been gettin' real chummy with Lily."

"You mean Lillian? That's the new woman, right?"

"Yeah. She just goes by Lily. Have y'all… met her?"

"Just once. I'm afraid I've been a little preoccupied between the end of my pregnancy, a false alarm, and then Max's birth. But that's no excuse. I should go down and see how she's doing."

Gwyneth jumped up. "Oh, no need to do that. She's just fine. Besides, Jules will take care of anythin' she needs. I'm sure of it."

Merry rose slowly. "Okay… I guess I could use a little more rest, come to think of it."

"Oh, yeah. You should get all the rest you can while Jason's around. He'll be too busy once baseball season starts."

Merry chuckled. "I hope I'll be back to normal before then."

"I'm sure you will, although I've known some women who've never—"

Merry held up one hand. "That's okay, Gwyneth. Thanks for the milk. I'd better get back upstairs before Max wakes up and wants lunch." She hefted her full breasts.

Gwyneth giggled. "I guess that's best, since y'all are carryin' around the restaurant."

———∽∽———

Merry sidled up to her awestruck husband, who was staring into the crib at his sleeping son.

"He really is a miracle, isn't he?" she whispered.

Jason nodded his head. "I never imagined..." His throat seemed to clog.

"I know. Me neither."

He pivoted and pulled her into his arms for a long kiss. When he released her lips, he didn't break their embrace. He simply tucked her head under his chin and stroked her back.

"Jason?"

"Mmm?"

"I need to ask you a few things."

He stepped away and took her hand. "Let's talk in the living room."

When they were settled on the sectional sofa, she took a deep breath. Exactly how would she explain everything Gwyneth had told her?

"Okay, this is going to sound weird, but I just learned a couple of things from Gwyneth."

"You learned from Gwyneth? That *is* weird."

She smirked. "Be nice. She's a lovely woman with a good heart."

"And has a ghost as a roommate."

"Be that as it may, she seems to know what goes on around here better than we do."

"Yeah? What's going on?"

"Well, first, they had a still in the basement."

His eyebrows rose. "A still? Like a thing that makes alcohol? Aren't stills illegal?"

"Yeah. They had a good reason… well, if what she said is true, and I see no reason for her to lie." She placed her arm on the back of the sofa and massaged his neck. He always loved it when she did that.

"Ahhh… that feels good. Go on."

"So, according to Gwyneth, there's a kind of cure for vampirism made by some guy in New York. He preserves it in wine. It's crazy expensive though."

"And?"

"And apparently Sly and Morgaine went to New York and brought some of it home. They planned to reverse engineer it and preserve it in Gwyneth's father's whiskey recipe. Apparently the still was something she knew how to set up and she did it to help Sly."

"Why didn't they just ask us to pay for the cure?"

"His pride. You know how he didn't even want to take the apartment for free. As far as I know, he's still trying to think of a job he can do at night."

"Too bad. I'd have bought the stuff for him just to have one less vampire in the building."

Merry gasped. "There's more than one?"

He chuckled. "No, not that I know of. But considering the folks that are attracted to living here…"

She blew out a breath. "Whew. You scared me for a minute."

"Sorry, so go back to the weird story."

"Yeah. They tried mixing some of the wine with the whiskey and it didn't go well. As Nathan put it… ick, never mind."

"So Nathan knew about it too? Did anyone bother to tell Jules?"

"Apparently he discovered it on his own and dismantled it."

"Good. Seems like it could have been more than a legal hazard."

"Yeah, but they're back to square one. Apparently Morgaine had a psychic flash and knows how to make it now. They have to make their own wine and add a little of the vampire cure to it. If it ferments together, the whole bottle becomes the curative stuff."

"Doesn't it get diluted though?"

"No. Apparently it's like sourdough bread in that way."

Jason's brows knit. "Huh? I don't bake, sweetheart."

She chuckled. "Oh, yeah. Well it's the same principle. If you add a little of the old mixture to the new, it keeps it going."

"And going and going and going?"

"Exactly."

"And you wanted to ask me something. No, let me guess. You want to know if they can set up a winery in the basement."

She grinned and batted her eyelashes at him.

"Oh, man. I know you so well."

"Not a whole winery. It turns out that making wine for your own consumption is easy and legal. And it isn't dangerous like a still would be."

"I like the sound of that."

"So do they have your permission to make the wine and store it in the basement? Apparently the cool temperature down there is ideal."

He leaned over and rested his head in his hands. "Will I ever be able to say no to you?"

"Maybe if you don't love me anymore."

"Then I'm doomed. Because that's never going to happen."

She leaned over him and hugged his back. "Good."

He sat up and gave her a real hug. Then he leaned back and looked her in the eye. "You said there were a couple of things…"

"Gwyneth told me something about Jules that was a little upsetting."

"Yeah? What?"

"Well, Gwyneth said Morgaine suspects Jules of falsifying his résumé. As Gwyneth put it, 'He couldn't fix a sink with a bottle of Drano.'"

"Oh, boy." Jason rose and began to pace. "It's a little late to check his references now, isn't it?"

"Did he give any references other than your uncle Ralph?"

Jason strode to his desk. "I barely glanced at his resume. I took Ralph at his word."

"And Ralph probably believed whatever Jules told him. What if he's a pathological liar? They can be very convincing. If something breaks…"

Jason pawed through the drawer until he found the folder he wanted. "Okay, under references it says he has twelve years of experience in apartment building maintenance at 70 Rowes Wharf. Why does that address sound familiar?"

"It sounds like it's down on the waterfront."

"It is." Jason opened his laptop. "Let me check it out."

A few minutes and keystrokes later, he said, "Ah ha!

No wonder that address sounded familiar. It's a seafood restaurant. One of the team's favorites."

Merry gaped. "So it's not an apartment building at all?"

"Nope. Apparently, ol' Jules did lie on his résumé. There's a contact name and number here. Maybe I'll call and ask about him just for kicks."

"Yeah, I think we should, just to be thorough before we speak to him."

Jason groaned. "Oh, crap. If it doesn't pan out, one of us will have to fire him. You know how much I hate confrontation."

"Maybe we should talk to him before we fire him. And if it comes down to that, don't worry, I'll do it."

Jason grinned at her. "You complete me."

"Yeah, yeah. Just dial the number."

He chuckled and used his cell phone to place the call. It must have rung a few times with no one picking up. Eventually Jason put his phone away. "The number he gave is disconnected."

"Oh, no."

"I guess we'd better go have a chat with him. Then we can start the happy process of looking for another maintenance man." He rolled his eyes.

Merry snapped her fingers. "Wait a minute. I have an idea."

"Uh-oh."

"Hey, when have I ever steered you wrong?"

He shrugged. "Never, I guess. Okay, let's hear it."

"Sly was an electromechanical engineer before he was turned. He wants to earn his rent. Why don't we ask him if he can do building maintenance?"

Jason's eyes lit up. "You might have something there. Why don't you find out, and then we'll have a talk with Jules."

Just then Max began to fuss in his crib.

"Okay. Right after lunch. It sounds like Max is ready for his."

"Can I watch?" Jason waggled his eyebrows.

"You'll do anything to get an eyeful of my massive jugs, won't you?

Jason chuckled. "You know it."

Chapter 22

SLY OPENED HIS APARTMENT DOOR AFTER A LOUD KNOCK. It was such a relief not to worry about Malvant being on the other side.

"Merry! How nice to see you. Come in. How's the baby. How are *all* of you?"

She smiled. "We're fine. I have to talk to you about something though. May I sit down?"

"Of course." Sly led her to his sofa in front of the fireplace.

"Would you like some heat? I can build a fire."

She chuckled. "That isn't necessary unless you want one for yourself and Morgaine. Is she here?"

"No, she's upstairs in her own apartment. She needed a... rest."

Merry smiled. "I'll bet."

If Sly could have blushed, he would have. Instead he changed the subject. "So, what's on your mind?"

"Well, we're not certain about this, so keep it under your hat..."

"Of course. What is it?"

"We think maybe Jules lied on his résumé. We're not sure he's qualified to do building maintenance."

"Seriously? What a weasel." He raised one eyebrow. "Shall I go have a talk with him?"

"No. I'll do that in a few minutes. I just wanted to ask. If it turns out we have to fire him, would you like the job? I was thinking, with your background as an electro-mechanical engineer, I imagine you're pretty handy…"

A job? Right here in the building? Something I can do and help out my daughter at the same time?

"I'd be delighted to do it. And as far as building maintenance, I maintained the home your mother and I lived in for five years. Plus, I'm ridiculously strong. I could lift the dryers to clean out the dust bunnies behind them."

Merry laughed. "No need to go crazy. I just thought I'd ask you first. You'd really be helping us out."

"And I wouldn't feel like such a freeloader. I actually came up with a part-time gig—well, Gwyneth and Nathan thought of it—but I can do it from here. I distributed some flyers around the college campuses offering my services as a tutor."

Her expression lit up. "That's great! Since the super's job comes with a free apartment, you'll have free rent and spending money too."

"Sounds good to me. When can I start?"

"Well, I have to talk to Jules first, and I imagine he'll need a little time to find another place. We won't just kick him out with nowhere to go. Meanwhile, I'll tell him about your wine cellar and ask him to leave it alone."

"You know about the wine?"

"Yes, Gwyneth told me everything. Sly, if you can make a cure that's great, but if you can't…" She shifted uncomfortably. "Well, just know that Jason is ready to pay for the stuff from New York."

"No." Sly held up one hand as if saying, *halt right there*. "I appreciate the offer, but it's more than I can accept. Besides, Morgaine is fairly certain this new batch will do the trick. It's almost ready. I'll test it tomorrow, just before sunrise."

"Terrific. Would it be okay if I visit during your test? I'll be up with Max anyway."

"Why not? Let's invite the whole gang."

"I really hope it works."

"You and me both."

⸺•••⸺

Merry found Jules not in his own apartment, but in Lillian's. The door was wide open. He wielded a hand-held belt sander and appeared to be trying to scuff the hell out of the hardwood floor.

"Jules? What are you doing?"

He whipped around and stared at her, wide eyed and openmouthed. "Uh, um, Mrs. Falco. I didn't see you there."

"I was about to look for you at your place, but I spotted you here. What happened to the floor?

He set down the belt sander and rose. "Oh, nothing. Just giving the floors a little freshening up."

"I may not know a whole lot about building maintenance, but even I know you're not supposed to use a hand sander on floors. How could you keep them even? Ever hear of 'the right tool for the right job'?"

He waved away her comment. "Ah, it's nothing. I've done it about a hundred times. Once you're that good at something, you don't need the right tools anymore."

Merry stepped into his space, and he backed away. She slid the toe of her shoe over the place he had sanded and felt quite a dip.

"Jules, I don't think you know what you're doing.

You've gouged this floor. And since when did it need freshening up? It was perfect when Lillian moved in."

He shifted his feet nervously. "Yeah, well, Lily had a little accident."

"An accident? Is she okay?"

Just then a moan came from the direction of the bedroom. "Oh, dear! She's hurt." As Merry dashed to the bedroom door and yanked it open, she started to ask Jules, "Why didn't you tell—"

She stopped short. Lily and some guy were kneeling on the bed, naked. If Merry wasn't mistaken, he was giving it to her doggy style.

Their gazes met for a moment, then the guy continued his rhythm.

Nope, I wasn't mistaken. Her cheeks heated, and she closed the door quietly.

She returned to the living room only to find Jules cleaning up and putting away the sander.

"Did you know they were in there?"

"Yeah. How else could she make the money to pay me with no job?"

Merry shook her head hard, trying to clear it. "Are you telling me that what I just saw was... is... Lily's a prostitute?"

Jules nodded slowly. "Why? Is that bad? I thought it was the oldest profession."

She crossed her arms. "It's only illegal and unhealthy. We can't let her break the law in our building."

"But the third-floor tenants sell phone sex. Why is this so much worse?"

"Because that isn't illegal and it doesn't spread STDs." Merry sighed. Obviously this guy hadn't the faintest idea where to draw the line and how to maintain a legal residence.

"Jules?"

"Yes."

"You're fired. And when you see Lily, tell her she can expect an eviction notice too. Now, if you'll excuse me, I'll be upstairs writing your final check."

"Huh?" Jules tipped his head, looking genuinely puzzled.

"Did you understand what I just said?"

"You said I'm fired, but it's Lily who's setting fires."

Merry stepped back and rested her palm on her hip. "Are you kidding me?" She pointed to the scuffed spots on the floor. "This is fire damage?"

Jules grimaced. "Uh, yeah. I thought you knew."

"Obviously not. Why...?" Merry paused, then remembered they lived in Freak Central. "I mean, how did this happen? What is she?"

Jules shrugged one shoulder. "She's a call girl—and a dragon. Sometimes she sneezes fire."

Merry's breath lodged in her throat. "Don't move." She ran for the door but stopped when she reached it and pivoted. "Unless it's to pack your things and get out."

⁓

Sly stopped reading, laid the book face down to hold his place, and strolled over to answer the knock at his door.

"Merry, you're back. Did Jules have anything to say for himself?"

Merry sagged against the doorjamb. "Oh, Sly. I hate to put you on the spot so soon, but do you think you could go upstairs and keep an eye on the second-floor apartments, just for a few minutes?"

"Sure. Why? Was he a jackass about it? Are you afraid he'll vandalize the place?"

"No. Well, not on purpose and no more than he already has."

Sly zoomed around Merry and up the stairs faster than she could say, "Please."

Morgaine was just descending the stairs, and they met in the middle. "Is everything okay?" she asked. "I sensed some very unsettled energy."

"Stick around. I may need you." He pounded on the door to 2B, Jules's apartment. There was no answer. *He must be at Lily's. That's why Merry said to keep an eye on both places.*

Sly strode across the hall and banged on 2A.

Lily opened the door a crack and peered through it.

"Step back," Sly said authoritatively.

Lily took a giant step backward and waited for Sly to come in. He couldn't enter without being invited, but did she know that?

"Aren't you going to invite me in?"

"No," she answered meekly and pulled her robe tighter.

Morgaine strolled over to Sly and placed a calming hand on his arm.

He relaxed for a moment, heard the sound of the elevator, and figured Merry must be heading back up to her apartment. Probably for some necessary paperwork. What had she told them? He should have waited for her to finish her sentence.

"Is Jules here?"

"Not anymore."

Sly glanced around Lily and spotted the ugly floors. It looked as if the finish had been partially sanded off in some places and the wood taken down to the nails in others.

He gestured to the floor. "What happened here?"

"Jules was sanding it."

"Damnation, where is he?"

Jules opened his door, and Sly whirled to face him. He pointed to Lily's damaged floor. "What were you trying to do here, Jules? Were you looking for carpet under the hardwood?"

Jules stared at his feet. He had a duffel bag slung over one shoulder. "I don't want any trouble. Mrs. Falco asked me to leave, and I will. I just wanted to stop here first and ask Lily to come with me."

Lily rushed to the door and gaped at Jules. "But the bird and the fish… where will they live?"

"You leave that to me," he said.

Sly narrowed his eyes. "I knew there was something off about you. You're a fish?"

"Sort of. I'm a merman."

"That makes sense," Morgaine said. "But why did you choose to live here? Why not in the ocean like the rest of your kind?"

"I was kicked out of my pod, so I won't be going back to the ocean. Safety in numbers and all that. It's especially true for mermen and merwomen." He smiled at Lily. "But as a human, I can manage just fine. What do you say, beautiful? Want to come with me?"

Sly frowned. "Wait just a minute. What about the damage?"

"I can take care of that," Morgaine said. She waved

her hand in the direction of Lily's floor and sawdust swirled. The spiral split into separate clouds and gathered in the crevices. The next thing Sly saw was a completely smooth hardwood floor, gleaming as if brand new.

He gazed at Morgaine. "You never cease to amaze me." They shared a meaningful smile.

Lily seemed more nervous than grateful. "I need to pack my things."

Jules focused on Lily. "Great. I'll call you as soon as I have a place for us."

Sly didn't hate the pair, but he would rest easier without them living in his daughter's building. "Want some help packing, Lily? I'll have you loaded into your moving van in no time."

"But I don't have a moving van."

Sly glanced at Jules. "I'm sure your man-fish can find one for you." He aimed an intense stare into Jules's eyes.

"I will." Then he turned toward Lily. "I'll be back tomorrow. If I don't have a place yet, I can take care of your, um, needs and then go out looking again."

Sly extended his hand to Jules. "Thanks for taking it so well."

Jules glanced down at Sly's hand, but he didn't shake it. "Taking what well?"

"Being fired."

"I wasn't fired. I quit."

Sly shook his head. *Sure you did, buddy.* "I wish you both Godspeed relocating." He narrowed his gaze to look intimidating. "If you need any *help*, I'll be right downstairs."

—⁓—

Sly poured the first glass of his homemade wine and said a silent prayer that it would work. He had purposely gone without feeding or having any of the Vampire Vintage so he could test the effectiveness of his concoction.

Morgaine answered the knock at the door and welcomed Gwyneth, Jason, Merry, and baby Max, who was sleeping in Merry's arms.

Gwyneth stretched and yawned. "What time is sunrise today?"

"It's in a few minutes. Why don't you all have a seat? Can I get anyone coffee or tea?"

"Not for me," Merry said as she settled herself in the rocking chair. "I don't suppose you have any milk?"

Morgaine sighed. "Not until there's electricity for the refrigerator."

Merry slapped her head. "That's right. What's wrong with me? I'll call the electric company today and get them to turn it on."

"I don't really need it," Sly said and winked so Merry could see him but Morgaine couldn't.

Morgaine gasped. "Why would you turn down electricity? It's a basic necessity, and you're earning it now since you're the building super, and—"

Sly laughed. "Don't worry. I wasn't about to say no."

"Whew." Gwyneth wiped her forehead with the back of her hand. "It may not be important to y'all, but it is for my cousin since she has nicto… nicta… Oh, hell, fear of the dark."

Merry's eyebrows rose. "You have nyctophobia? I didn't know that."

Morgaine smiled weakly. "Yeah, but it's getting better. I'm fine if I'm asleep and all cuddled up with Sly."

He strolled over and slipped his arm around her. "All the more reason not to hook up the electricity."

"Cut it out. I know you're only joking, but sometimes you make me crazy."

He laughed. "All right, I'll stop. But you're so fun to tease." He kissed her temple.

"Thanks. Then if your wine doesn't work and you pass out on the floor, you won't mind if I laugh my ass off."

"Ouch." He made a face, but underneath he was still smiling.

"Speakin' of which." Gwyneth pointed to the glass of wine in his hand. "Ain't it time to glug down a glass or two?"

He chuckled. "Yes, it is." His hunger gnawed at him. If it abated quickly, he'd know the wine was working.

"Here's to all of us," he said, and then he took the first long sip.

Nothing happened immediately. *Oh, no*. He took another sip, and sweet relief flooded him. His blood lust abated, then disappeared completely.

"I think it worked," he pronounced.

Everyone started to cheer, but not wanting to celebrate yet, he held up one hand. "There's one more test."

Sly crossed to the big bay window. The sky had changed from black to dark blue. The sun would be coming up any second. He stood in the open, sipped the rest of his wine, and waited. Morgaine came up behind him and wrapped her arms around his waist.

"Are you here to catch me?" he teased.

"Only if you need catching."

He glanced back at the twilight. "I think I'll be okay."

She nipped his earlobe. The sky lightened steadily and added the colors of a beautiful sunrise heralding a crisp, clear day.

He drained the glass and let out a deep breath. "It's official. The wine works."

"Thank the Goddess," shouted Morgaine and Gwyneth.

Jason clapped and Merry rose, handing the baby to Jason. Morgaine let go long enough for Merry to give Sly a big hug.

"What are you going to call your miracle cure, Sly?" Jason asked.

"I hadn't thought about it."

"How about Sly Wine?" Gwyneth suggested.

"I like it." Jason stuffed his hands in his pockets. "I asked because some of the guys on the team have a commercial wine made and named after them. I was asked if I'd like one too. They want to call it Jason Falco's Lefty Merlot. Does your cure affect non-vampires?"

"I don't know."

Gwyneth raised her hand. "I volunteer to try a glass, if y'all want to find out."

Morgaine and Sly stared at each other. At last Morgaine said, "I don't think that's a good idea. Mikhail wouldn't let me have any. I don't know if that's because it wasn't good for the living or if it was too precious to waste on us."

"That's fine," Jason said. "I just thought I'd mention it in case it could be mass produced. Then you wouldn't have to make it yourself."

"I don't mind making it," Sly said. "I don't know how you'd explain having to add a few ounces of old wine to each bottle of new stuff before it ferments."

"Besides," Morgaine said, "to make a commercial wine takes months. The recipe we got off the Internet is quick and easy."

Jason shrugged. "Oh well, it was just a thought."

"Thanks for thinking of it."

Merry rubbed her hands together. "You'll need wine racks for the cellar."

"And a big ol' wooden vat," Gwyneth said. "Morgaine and I can stomp grapes and make it from scratch when the summer comes. Maybe we can even plant a few grapevines on that little patch you call a lawn."

Sly laughed. "As much fun as that would be to watch, I think using frozen grape juice works just fine."

Gwyneth looked disappointed. "Dang."

Merry studied her. "What's the matter, Gwyneth?"

"It's nothin'. I was just hopin' for some extra income is all. I thought if we could make more than Sly could use, we might sell a few bottles to local vampires."

Jason snapped to attention. "You mean there are more?"

"Oh, I don't know about that, y'all. I just figured there might be."

Morgaine crossed her arms. "Gwyneth, don't go upsetting a young family with ideas of local vampires unless you know they exist." Then she focused on Merry and Jason. "If you like, we can find out for you."

Jason's eyebrows rose. "You can? How?"

"Well, we won't know their names or addresses, but we can scry with a greater Boston area map and see if anything comes up."

"Do it," Merry said. "No offense, Sly, but from what I hear, they're not generally as trustworthy as you are."

"No offense taken," he said.

Morgaine cleared her throat. "I'd like to know too. If my step-grandson is going to grow up here, I want to know he's safe."

Merry's eyes rounded. "Step-grandson... Are you two engaged?"

Morgaine giggled. "Oops, I let the cat out of the bag."

Sly tugged her to his side and kissed her cheek. "That's all right, love. I'm glad you told them."

"Yahoo!" Gwyneth yelled. "I feel another party coming on!"

Jason extended his hand to Sly. "Congratulations. Have you set a date?"

"Not yet." Sly shook his hand and winked at Merry.

Merry hugged Morgaine. "Do you know where you'll have it yet?"

"Well, we've ruled out a church wedding."

Gwyneth laughed. "Y'all got that right."

"Jason?" Merry nudged him with her hip.

At first he seemed confused, until she whispered, "The penthouse," in his ear.

"Great idea." He bent down and gave her a peck on the lips. "Sly, Morgaine, how about having your ceremony at our place?"

Morgaine grinned. "I'd love that."

Sly stroked her arm. "Then it's decided."

Later that afternoon, Sly flicked the light switch in his apartment.

The lights came on and Morgaine cheered. "At last! Heat, hot water, *and* electricity!"

He chuckled. "What a diva. Who knew you'd demand all these luxuries?"

Morgaine rested a fist on her hip and smirked. "Do you want to get through the winter without frozen pipes or not?"

"I suppose for the sake of the other residents I can deal with having utilities. But…" He strolled over to her and patted her ass. "My needs are simple. A loaf of bread, a glass of wine, and thou."

She tipped her head. "What are you going to do with the bread?"

"Feed you, of course. I may not eat, but you'll need to."

His thoughtfulness always impressed her. She could never picture him losing his humanity.

He continued to mosey to the kitchen where he retrieved a glass for his special wine cure. They had taken to calling it Sly Wine.

Morgaine looked down and shuffled her feet. "I need to discuss something with you."

"Sounds important."

"It is."

"You haven't changed your mind about marrying me, have you?"

"Goddess, no! That's not it at all."

Sly smiled. "Good. Come here, love." He set down the glass, took her hand, and led her to the sofa.

Morgaine perched on the edge so she could face him and took both of his hands in hers. "We only scratched the surface of this conversation before, but I need to finish what I wanted to say."

Sly nodded. "Of course. Go ahead."

"It's about my getting old and dying and you going on alone for who knows how long."

He hung his head. "Oh, yeah. That."

Morgaine threaded her fingers through his hair. "I love you, Sly. I'd do anything for you. I think you know that, right?"

He smiled and gazed at her. "Yes, I know."

A golden shimmer appeared in his eyes. She didn't think he was trying to mesmerize her. They had already established that he couldn't, and his eyes weren't changing from brown to blue and purple. The brown irises simply glowed with amber light.

"I… I want you to turn me."

His jaw dropped and he reeled back as if slapped.

She placed her finger against his lips to silence him. "Please don't say no."

"In that case, I'll say absolutely not." His eyes narrowed, and the rich brown faded to cold black. "How could you even suggest it? You know what I've had to do to survive. You know how much I hate my condition. I wouldn't wish this on my worst enemy."

"But I'm not your enemy. I'm your beloved. And from what I understand, I may be the only one you get. I *want* to do this, Sly. I want to be with you… forever."

Sly stood and paced, his lips clamped shut in a tight line. Morgaine waited. She was about to ask if he was okay when he finally spoke.

"My answer is still no. I can't ask you to do that for me."

"You're *not* asking. I am. If necessary, I'll beg."

He stopped pacing and held his head in his hands.

She couldn't see his eyes. He was silent so long it scared her. "Sly?"

He dropped his hands to his sides. "Morgaine, I love

that you want to be with me, but I really need to think about this."

"Why? Maybe you'd rather be single and free to date whoever you want after a while."

He stared at her openmouthed.

Oops. That might not have been the right thing to say. It sure wasn't the smart thing to say, considering how long Sly had gone without anyone.

"I'm sorry, Sly. I didn't mean that."

He shook his head. "I'm not ready to discuss this any further right now. Maybe you can give me a little space."

"Oh-oh. 'Space' can be a euphemism for I don't want to be with you anymore."

He gave her an intense look. "You have to get over this insecurity, Morgaine. I don't want to be with you right now. It doesn't mean I want you to go away forever."

She nodded sadly. "I understand." She rose and strode to the door.

He was beside her in a split second. "I love you," he said and kissed her.

When he released her lips, he escorted her to the stairs. As she ascended, she heard him lock his apartment door and go outside.

Chapter 23

"OH, GWYNETH, I'M AFRAID I BLEW IT."

"Of course you didn't. Any fool can see that Sly loves y'all with all his heart."

"He probably does have to think it over, Morgaine." Chad interjected. *"This isn't the kind of decision a man like him would take lightly. Now, if it were me, I'd say definitely not, because who wants to be saddled with the same ball and chain for centuries? Maybe millennia? Not me."*

Morgaine flopped backward in her chair. "Thanks, Chad. You're a big help."

"I'm just sayin'…"

"Don't listen to him, Morgaine. I *don't* think the problem is with Sly. Personally, I think y'all are nuttier than a tree full of squirrels for *wantin'* to be turned."

Morgaine questioned her own sanity for the umpteenth time. "I probably am. I don't know. It just feels so right."

"Let's pretend for a minute that he did it. He turned you. What would you get out of it?"

She placed a finger over her lips as she thought. "Hmmm… immortality. The chance to spend eternity with the man I love."

"Every woman's dream…to be twenty-nine forever."

"Thanks, I'm thirty, and so is Sly. He turns thirty again next month, and the year after that and the year after that…"

"Anything else?"

"Strength and speed, I guess."

"Okay, and what would you lose?"

"As long as we have Sly Wine, nothing."

Gwyneth planted one hand on her hip. "Which brings up a major point. What if somethin' happens and y'all don't have it anymore?"

"What could happen?"

"What if the building burned down and all you could do was get your asses out on the sidewalk. Or say a nuclear war started. Everything would be contaminated."

Morgaine huffed, annoyed. "Yeah, and what if a spaceship full of alien monkeys broke in and made off with it?"

"I don't know about the aliens, but a gang of teenagers might steal all the alcohol you have."

She threw her hands in the air. "Well, one good thing came out of this little exercise. Clearly we need to hide a fireproof safe somewhere with a separate supply in case of disaster."

"See? I'm good for something."

"I never said you weren't, Chad."

"Then why do you ignore me when I'm trying to reason with you? Oh, that's right, you're a woman."

Gwyneth wagged her finger. "That's enough female bashin', Mr. Chad." She cocked her head. "I'm curious. What happened to make y'all hate women so much?"

"I don't hate women."

"Then why do y'all criticize us every which way?"

"Because it's fun."

"Fun for y'all, maybe. Not so much for us."

"Turnabout is fair play. Why don't you get into the spirit and try some man bashing?"

Gwyneth laughed. "I can think of much better things to do with a man."

Chad groaned. *"It's times like this I really miss my body."*

"So, Gwyneth, how are things going with Nathan?" Morgaine asked.

She giggled. "Well, now... I'm havin' loads of fun with him."

"Really? That's a nice surprise. I didn't expect you two would have that much in common."

"Oh, we don't. But for some reason, it don't matter neither. I get more out of how he makes me feel."

"Really? How?"

"Well, I've never realized my full power as a woman before now."

Chad coughed. *"The hot, witchy Southern belle is just discovering she has power over men? God help us."*

"It ain't like that, Chad. I could take advantage, but I don't. I'm simply teachin' him how to treat a lady. That way if things don't work out for us, he'll be all prepared to find someone else to love someday."

Sometimes Morgaine thought she knew her cousin, and then Gwyneth would do something completely unexpected. "That sounds very altruistic of you."

"All true what?"

"Altruistic. Adjective. Unselfishly concerned for or devoted to the welfare of others as opposed to egocentric."

"Oh. Well, yeah. That's me all right. I'm as concerned and devoted to Nathan's well-bein' as I am for y'all's."

"Good." Morgaine smiled. "I'm glad to hear it. So how are you teaching him to treat women?"

"Well, today he's buyin' me a Christmas present."

"Christmas? But we don't celebrate—"

"That don't matter. He does. So I'm lettin' him buy me a gift. It's part of bein' all-true-istic."

Morgaine smirked. "Oh, is it now? I hadn't thought of it that way. So what are you buying for him?"

"Do I have to buy him somethin'? It ain't my holiday."

Chad snickered and muttered something about the blind leading the dumb.

Gwyneth jammed her fists on her hips. "You take that back, Chad. I am *not* dumb."

"I should say not. Any woman who gets a guy to buy her a gift without being expected to give one in return is pure genius."

"Crap," Morgaine said. "I just remembered Sly probably celebrates Christmas too. Gwyneth, will you take me shopping?"

Gwyneth's eyes brightened. "Shopping? Y'all want to go out *with* me to shop for presents?"

"Yes. If I made it all the way to New York and back, knowing there was an evil vampire out there waiting, I think I can make it to downtown Boston now that the danger is gone."

"Oh, that reminds me. Weren't we gonna check to see if there were any other vampires in the area for Merry and Jason?"

"I already did. There's a small faction in East Boston."

"Ain't that where the airport is?"

"Yes."

"It makes sense they'd hang out there. Cheap rent and they can sleep through the noise."

"With plenty of people coming and going, and no one aware of who belongs and who doesn't, it's a perfect

place to pick off a stranger once in a while. Someone who might not be missed right away."

"So how does that help Jason and Merry?"

"I don't know. On the one hand, their kids won't be playing there, but on the other, Jason has to travel."

"Doesn't the team travel together?"

"I imagine so. I'll just warn him not to go off by himself if he can help it."

"I guess he'll have to hold it until he gets on the plane and use the tiny bathroom onboard," Gwyneth said. "That's a shame. At least when women go to the bathroom, we go in groups. Who's the stupider sex now, Chad?"

―~~~―

Sly needed a long walk to clear his brain. This was a decision he couldn't make lightly. On one hand, he'd never be lonely again, and he wouldn't have to watch Morgaine age and die, but what if after a century or two, she just wasn't into him anymore?

What would she be getting out of it? Immortality? If she was right and vampires lost their humanity over the years, it might not be all that great. Strength, agility, the power to mesmerize others? She probably wouldn't use those assets anyway, unless for self-preservation. He'd want her to have those abilities if she ever needed them.

Perhaps they'd give her an added sense of safety and she'd be able to overcome her agoraphobia. But, oh Lord, what if something horrible happened and they no longer had the wine cure. How the hell would a nyctophobic vampire deal with a darkness-only existence?

As Sly wandered the Boston University campus, he snapped out of his obsessive musing when a scream shattered the evening. Charging in the direction of the distress, he realized his inner crime-fighter had become an ingrained habit. He no longer had to hunt down criminals to feed. What would he do with the perpetrator?

A young man dashed across the Quad with a purse. A female student was in pursuit but lagging behind.

Sly still could make a difference and would. It was crazy to think he'd lose his humanity. Just as it was crazy to think Morgaine could ever lose hers.

He spotted where the guy would resurface after rounding the corner of an old brick building. The nearby parking lot might be his destination, so Sly stationed himself between the building and the lot.

Sure enough, the purse snatcher cast a glance over his shoulder as he zoomed around the corner and ran headlong into Sly, who stood his ground as firmly as the brick building.

"Oomph!"

Sly picked up the guy by his jacket collar. "Hand over the purth." Oops. His fangs had descended out of habit.

The young man stared openmouthed but didn't release it. Not that he wouldn't have if he could make his fingers move.

Sly shook him. At last the purse fell out of his hand and landed on the ground.

Now, what to do with him? Sly had no desire to drink from him. He could retract his fangs and mesmerize him so all the young man would know was he had been bested by a freakishly strong older dude. That would work.

"What's your damage?" he asked the petty criminal.

"I need money. I-I can't feed my family."

Sure. Chances are he can't feed his coke habit.

Sly erased his memory and tossed him in the direction of the parking lot with a final bit of advice. "Get a job."

The female student approached carefully. "Mister, can I have my purse back, please?"

Sly smiled, picked it up, and handed it to her.

"Thanks. I don't have very much money in here, but I'd like to give you something for your trouble."

"Keep it," Sly said. "I've got everything I need." Realizing he was right, he sauntered off, whistling.

As Sly approached his apartment building, he spotted a couple at the top of the stoop. A very tall blond man and a woman with short, highlighted brown hair turned, and two pairs of blue eyes brightened, recognizing him just as he realized who they were.

"Konrad, Roz! What brings you here this lovely evening?"

"Sly." Konrad jogged down the steps and surrounded him in a man hug, thumping him on his back.

Sly returned the friendly raps and glanced up at his old werewolf friend.

Roz smiled and waited at the top of the steps. "I heard you have your own key now."

Sly chuckled as he ascended with Konrad. "Yeah, and my own apartment, but you knew that."

She cocked her head and stared at him quizzically… as if she didn't know.

"I may be giving it up soon though."

Roz sucked in a deep breath. "You're moving out? Why?"

"I'm getting married."

Konrad's jaw dropped. Roz glanced at Konrad and mumbled, "That was fast."

She may not have meant for Sly to hear it, but he did and laughed. "Why are you so surprised, Roz? I heard you were the one who suggested Merry offer me *the love shack*."

She giggled. "Oops. She told you, did she?"

"Yup."

"You're not upset about the matchmaking, are you?" Konrad asked.

Sly shook his head. "Far from it. Everything has worked out better than I could have hoped."

"You're with Morgaine, right?" Roz asked.

"Correct."

"We thought we noticed sparks between you two." Roz winked. "I guess you just needed a little push."

"Here, let me get you inside and we can talk some more." Sly fit his key in the lock and let them in to the building. "Who did you come to see?"

"Whoever's around," Konrad said. "We've missed everybody." He shrugged out of his jacket and helped Roz with hers. "We were in town for *The Nutcracker* and thought we'd stop by."

"Great idea. So if no one's expecting you, who do you want to start with?"

Roz and Konrad stared at each other as if communicating telepathically. Oh yeah, they probably were.

"Why don't we all go see Morgaine? You two can tell us about your plans."

Sly led the way to the elevator. "There's not much to tell. I just asked her. Merry and Jason offered their penthouse for the handfasting ceremony, and we agreed to take them up on that."

As they rode the elevator to the third floor, he asked, "So how about you two? Made any plans yet?"

"Not yet," Roz said. "We're still settling into the routine of private school life. All we've figured out so far is we'll have our ceremony next summer."

Konrad squeezed her. "But now that we have a two-week break, there's plenty of time to make reservations and stuff. I guess we'll have to plan on an evening so you can attend, but we'll be careful to avoid the full moon, of course. That could be awkward for Roz's relatives."

Roz raised her eyebrows. "To put it way mildly."

The old friends chuckled.

The elevator came to a stop, and they proceeded to Morgaine's door. Sly knocked. No footsteps sounded on the other side. *Could she be out and about? Nah*. He knocked again. When there was still no answer, he said, "She must be over at Gwyneth's."

They traipsed across the hall and knocked on the opposite door. Again, no footsteps. Another knock. No answer.

"That's strange. They must have gone out together."

Suddenly, the decorated broom hanging on Gwyneth's door jumped.

Konrad chuckled. "It looks like Chad's home."

Sly had never needed to communicate with Chad when Morgaine wasn't around, but it might be nice to try. "Hey, Chad, can you make the broom move up and down for yes and side to side for no?"

The broom lifted a couple of inches and fell back in place. "Okay, that looks like a yes. Are Morgaine and Gwyneth in the building somewhere?"

The broom swept the door back and forth until Sly interpreted out loud, "No." He turned to his friends. "Hmmm… That's unusual."

Roz shrugged. "Maybe they went shopping. Morgaine and I went a few months ago. She had all kinds of fun trying on new clothes."

Sly nodded. "She told me about your makeover. She really did have fun. That's probably where they went then."

He turned to leave but before he got far, he felt something soft whap him in the back of the head. Spinning back to face Gwyneth's door, he noticed the broom wagging back and forth.

"Do you have something to say to me, Chad?"

The broom lifted and fell. That meant yes.

Sly looked at Roz and Konrad. "Can either of you hear him?"

"No," they both answered.

Now what?

At that moment a door downstairs opened.

"Nathan?" Sly leaned over the railing and called down.

He couldn't see him, but it was Nathan's voice that answered, "Yeah, buddy?"

"Can you communicate with Chad?"

"Not unless he points to something and I happen to guess what he wants. Usually he just points to the TV and if I don't turn it on, he points to me with his middle finger."

Roz and Konrad chuckled.

"Who's up there with you?" Nathan asked.

"It's Konrad and Roz back to visit," Konrad said. "We were trying to find Morgaine but the girls aren't here."

"I know. They're Christmas shopping."

By now, Nathan had found the one spot where he could look up through the stairwell and make eye contact with the trio leaning over the third-floor railing.

Sly's eyes grew wide. "Christmas shopping? Like, for us?"

Nathan grinned. "Well, yeah. It's not like they buy gifts for each other at this time of year."

"Shit," Sly muttered. "I didn't get her anything. And tomorrow is the winter solstice. That's the holiday they celebrate. It's called Yule. If we're getting gifts for our holiday, we should reciprocate for theirs."

Roz spoke up. "You know what, Sly, you should go get something for her while there's still time. We can always visit Merry and the baby until you get back."

He thought it over and agreed. "Okay, I wouldn't just run out on you, but this is important. What should I get her?"

Roz tipped her head and tapped her bottom lip, as if she were giving it some thought. "Hmmm... Let's see. What do you give a woman you want to marry? Oh, I know!" She waggled her third finger on her left hand. The pretty little marquis diamond sparkled in the light from the sconces.

"A ring? Really? It's that simple?"

Roz smirked. "If you can afford it, you'll never have an easier no-brainer gift to get."

⁓

Only Sly *couldn't* afford it. The visitors had called Merry and were welcomed up into the penthouse, so Sly was on his own to figure this out.

Nathan waited at the bottom of the stairs, and Sly jogged down to talk to him.

"How do you know they went Christmas shopping?"

"Gwyneth stopped by and asked me all of my sizes, so I guess I'm getting clothes."

"Did you buy her anything yet?"

"Yes. She has pierced ears, so I got her a pair of earrings."

"Hmmm…" Unfortunately, Morgaine had about seven piercings, so Sly didn't know how to handle that. Would he have to buy three and a half pairs of earrings? And, with what? Would she want something he got with his charm, good looks, and powers of mesmerism?

Sly shook his head. "I have to think of something else. Got any other ideas?"

"I thought Roz told you what to get."

Sly hung his head. "I know. A ring. I can't afford anything, much less a ring. I haven't begun tutoring yet, but I dropped off some flyers around the colleges. If only I had another couple of weeks. Do you know when they're planning to do this?"

"You can borrow some money from me. I have a bunch saved, just in case I get evicted."

In case he got evicted? Who thinks about that when saving money? Oh, yeah. He was talking to Nathan… Mr. Gloom and Doom.

"I'm sorry, Nate. I couldn't take your money. Not that you'll be getting evicted or anything. It's just that to me, it would seem like *you're* buying Morgaine's ring."

"But I'm not marrying her."

Sly chuckled, trying to picture the unlikely pair. "No, you're not, so I should be the one to buy her a gift."

Nathan clapped him on the back. "I wouldn't want to be in your shoes, buddy. But I doubt Morgaine is the type to expect a big, fancy diamond ring. You could probably get away with a thin, silver band."

Ha. Silver. I might burn my fingers on it. And she might too, if I turn her. Then, it was as if a lightbulb lit up over Sly's head. Of course! "You're right. She's not the type to care about expensive material things. I know just what to get."

"Good. Glad I could be of help."

"I do have to do an errand though."

Chapter 24

GWYNETH'S KNITTING NEEDLES CLICKED AS SHE KNITTED and rocked. "Morgaine, are you sure a sweater is enough of a gift?"

"It is if you knit it with your own hands."

"I love the black wool we got, and the pattern is nice, but I haven't knit anything for a few years. Last knittin' I did was a flask cozy for Dwayne."

Morgaine chuckled. "A cozy for his booze?"

Gwyneth pouted. "It's what he wanted. The metal flask got cold in winter."

Morgaine had all she could do to hold in her laughter. Dwayne was still a sore spot for Gwyneth.

Suddenly, Gwyneth brightened and sat up straighter. "I know what he *really* wants. Yeah, that'll do it." She fell silent and returned to her knitting, but she sported a satisfied smile.

"Uh-oh. What are you thinking?"

"None of your beeswax. It's personal."

"What? A blow job?"

Gwyneth gasped. Morgaine waited for the indignant denial, but to her surprise, her cousin asked, "Have y'all learned to read minds now?"

Morgaine slapped a hand over her mouth, but she lost the battle and guffawed.

Gwyneth stopped knitting and leaned forward, her eyebrows scrunched. "What?"

Morgaine waved away the giggles. "Nothing. It's a great gift. Any man would be thrilled, especially one who loves you so much." An unexpected sadness came over her.

Gwyneth noticed her mood change. "What is it, Cousin?"

"I just wonder if Sly loves me that much. He seemed so shocked that I'd want to be with him forever. I thought that's what commitment was all about."

"Oh, sugar… y'all are lookin' at this all wrong. I thought me and Chad explained it to y'all already."

"Y'all… I mean, you did. I just wasn't quite in agreement."

At that moment a knock sounded on the door. "I'll get it," Morgaine said.

"Thanks, I know it's my apartment and all, but I'm all comfortable and covered with yarn so I'd be much obliged."

Morgaine opened the door and was surprised to see Sly standing there.

"Hi, hon. You're just the one I wanted to see."

How did he know she was here at Gwyneth's place? Oh, yeah. Superhuman hearing. *I guess I'll never know what that's like.*

"Nice to see you, Sly."

"Why so formal? Is everything all right?"

Gwyneth butted in. "She thinks y'all don't love her enough to turn her. Personally, I think she's crazy for wantin' it, but who am I to judge?"

Morgaine whirled on her. "Gwyneth!"

Sly put his hands in his pockets. "I thought as much. We need to talk."

Morgaine sighed. "I guess we do. Gwyneth, I'll see you later. You're still coming over for dinner and the burning of the Yule log, right?"

"Of course. I wouldn't miss it. Remember that cake Yule log I made last year?"

Ugh. Don't tell me she still has it.

"I just made another one exactly like it. I thought we could invite Nathan and Sly over for dessert. Well, wine for Sly."

Whew. The cake isn't stale and hard as a rock. "Sure. Sly, would you be interested in celebrating Yule with us tonight?"

"Absolutely. I was going to ask you when I could give you your Yule gift."

Morgaine sucked in a breath. "A Yule gift? For me?"

"Why are you so shocked? I heard you went Christmas shopping."

"Oh... I did. It won't be ready tonight though."

"That's fine. I'll give you your Yule gift today, and you can give me my Christmas present on Christmas."

She smiled sadly. "That would be fine with me, except your gift won't be ready for Christmas either. I tried, but it's kind of complicated."

"That doesn't matter. We can have a belated Christmas anytime."

She gave him a coquettish look. "I'll make it up to you."

Gwyneth laughed.

He grinned. "I'll look forward to that. So, can you come down to my apartment?"

"Sure." She waved to her cousin, called, "See you later," and closed the door behind her.

The night before, Sly had mesmerized a jewelry maker, telling her she would give him three pieces of white gold and he would pay her back as soon as he could. The cost wasn't prohibitive because they were raw materials and nothing had been designed from them yet. Sly knew exactly what he wanted to do.

He braided all three bands of gold, bent them around a dowel to meet, cut the ends to barely overlap, and then used his vampiric strength to fuse them together. On the flat section where he'd pressed, he used a sharp needle and, in his best cursive handwriting, inscribed their initials… SF & MM. It came out better than he had envisioned.

He was excited to show it to her and hoped it would mean more because he'd made it by hand just for her.

Morgaine appeared nervous while he unlocked his door. She shifted from foot to foot behind him.

"What's wrong, Morgaine?"

"Nothing." She slapped a smile on her face so fast that he almost didn't catch the worried expression it had replaced.

He opened his door and stepped aside for her to enter.

"Seriously, how are you, love?"

"I'm well. I suppose you are too, since you never get sick unless you come into contact with silver or sun. And now that you have your wine, you don't even have to worry about that."

"I don't know about silver yet. I haven't tried handling it."

Is she being sarcastic? No, that's not my Morgaine.

"I want you to know I'm rather proud of what I made for you. I hope you like it."

"You *made* something for me? That's so sweet."

All the jittery nerves and frosty formality seemed to disappear.

"Wait in the living room. I'll go and get it."

She grinned and strolled over to his sofa.

He had it in his bedroom, having been unsure when he'd have the opportunity to give it to her. He thought giving it to her before or after making love would be nice, but come to think of it, giving gifts while wearing nothing but underwear seemed a little unromantic.

He plucked it off the dresser and returned to her. On the way, it glowed. Maybe it was simply the way the light hit the metal. Perhaps he'd infused it with the light of love. That idea pleased him.

He curled his fingers around the ring and hid his hand behind his back.

Morgaine smiled. "You're not going to make me guess which hand, are you?"

"No." Sly sat beside her. "I just didn't have a box or wrapping paper. I hope that's okay."

She smirked. "No, absolutely not. I *must* have wrapping paper."

Sly knew she was joking but decided to play along. "Oh, never mind then." He started to rise.

She grabbed a fistful of his shirt and dragged him back down. "No, I'm kidding. I'll forgo the wrapping… this time."

He grinned and kissed her on the cheek. "I thought as much." Then he opened his hand.

Morgaine caught her breath. Her eyes grew wide, but

she didn't say anything. She picked up the beautiful ring and examined it.

"You made this?"

Sly nodded.

"It's beautiful." She stared openmouthed.

"Let me try it on you and see if it fits."

"Okay." She held out her left hand, then her right. "Which hand should I wear it on?"

"Well, now, that's up to you."

She grinned and dropped her right hand, keeping her left hand extended for him. He slipped it on her ring finger, and it fit perfectly.

"Wow, how did you know my size?"

"I didn't. I guessed."

"Good guess." She held up her hand and admired it. "I can't get over it. You made this?"

"Yup."

"How?"

"Brute strength. I suppose you'll be able to do the same thing someday soon… if you're still interested."

She whipped her gaze to his face. "Interested? In what?"

"Becoming my vampire bride."

She threw her arms around his neck and hugged him tight.

On Valentine's Day, the happily engaged couple sat in front of a cozy fire in Sly's apartment. After exchanging Valentines and kissing fervently, it was time for Morgaine to spring her big surprise.

"I hope you didn't mind waiting until now for your Christmas gift. It took a while to put it all together."

Morgaine admired her ring again. Every time she looked at it, it reminded her of the man she loved with all her heart. It still seemed like a dream that he'd fallen in love with her too.

"I don't mind at all. I admit I'm curious though. You and Gwyneth have been up to something."

She chuckled. "Yes, we have. But this gift is also from Merry and Jason. It's a little weird, but I think you'll be happy."

He glanced at her sideways. "Weird, huh?"

"You'll see."

She took him by the hand and led him out of his apartment to the basement door. "Do you want to go first or shall I?"

"Why? Am I going to trip over it?"

She chuckled. "No. It might surprise you though."

"Hmmm…" He bowed and swept his arm in a grand gesture. "Ladies first."

Morgaine couldn't wait to see the expression on his face when he saw the enterprise the four of them had set up. Gwyneth had suggested the idea, and then Merry and Jason hired some help to put the whole business together. Morgaine had insisted on paying for the supplies. Her biggest and best surprise she'd save until last.

She flicked on the light switch and descended the stairs with Sly behind her. At the point where he could see the actual layout, he halted.

"What the…"

Morgaine giggled. "Can you tell what it is?"

"I see a big wooden vat, some shelves that look like they're made for wine bottles, and a few other pieces

I'm not familiar with. It looks like a whole wine-making operation." He reached the bottom of the stairs and wandered through the setup.

"It is. Gwyneth figured Sly Wine would be better if made fresh. We researched the necessary process, ingredients, and environment, and then Merry and Jason helped us with the business plan. I even have a fireproof safe to store a few bottles, just in case. So we'll always have enough to hold us until we can set up the operation again."

"You're brilliant."

"There's more. Jason said I don't have to pay rent anymore."

"I see… sort of." His brows knit in confusion.

"I think you'll like the next part the best."

He tipped his head and waited without saying anything.

"I'm going to run the whole thing. If you're the super while I make Sly Wine for you… for us, I'll have plenty of money from readings and can give up the phone-sex business. Gwyneth's already said she'll take over the calls and help me stomp the grapes when it's not busy."

Sly's jaw dropped. "Really? You'd want to do that?" His expression softened. "You know I never asked you to. Is this really what you want?"

She smiled. "More than anything. I can still work from home, be sure our needs are taken care of properly, and show muwumfuoo."

She couldn't finish her sentence because Sly had grabbed and kissed her.

When he let her go, he laughed. "What was that last thing you said?"

"By doing this, I can show my love for you."

"Oh, honey." He held her tenderly. "This means so much to me."

She sported a grin he couldn't see. She just hoped he'd hear it in her voice. "I thought you'd like it."

"I love it. I love *you*. So much."

She couldn't speak around the lump in her throat as tears formed in her eyes.

———

A couple weeks later, the operation was in full swing. The girls were knee deep in the vat stomping grapes. Morgaine glanced up and spotted her beloved on the stairs.

"Hey, Sly," she called out when she saw him. "Want to join us?"

He chuckled. "No, I was actually hoping you'd join me, Morgaine. We have something important to take care of."

Gwyneth continued squashing grapes with her feet. "More important than making all your curative wine?"

Sly cleared his throat. "It's something we ought to do before the handfasting. You'll have to forgive me for borrowing your cousin, Gwyneth."

He moved to the side of the vat so fast that he created a blur. Then he lifted Morgaine out of it and carried her toward the stairs. She clasped him around the neck.

"Sorry for deserting you, Gwyneth. We'll see you later."

"Aw, don't pay it no nevermind." She waved them away. "I can finish this up without y'all."

"Thanks, Cousin," Sly said and winked.

That seemed to please Gwyneth immensely. It pleased Morgaine too, and she kissed him on the cheek.

Sly carried her up the stairs into his apartment and

gently set her standing up in the bathtub. "Let's wash off those feet of yours, and then we'll take care of that little matter I mentioned."

"Yeah, what is it we need to do that's so important?" She turned on the water and waited for it to warm up.

"Since it's going to be a late night, I thought you might prefer to go through the conversion first."

Her eyes rounded. "You're going to make me a vampire? Now?"

"Would you rather wait?"

She lowered herself to sit on the edge of the tub. "No. I guess I just thought we'd do it after or around the same time as the handfasting. There's two weeks to go."

Sly shrugged. "We can do it either way... or not at all. It's up to you."

"I still want to go through with it."

"Are you sure?"

"Absolutely, positively."

He smiled. "Okay, then. I guess we just need to decide when that should happen."

"Does it take some getting used to?"

"Oh, yes."

"Like how?"

"You'll have to learn to hold things gently. Anything you grip hard you could crush."

"Oh, dear. Is that why you've always been so gentle with me?"

"Exactly. When we're both vampires and I know I won't hurt you, we can play as rough as you want."

Morgaine laughed. "Let's see how it goes. Maybe we should let the mood decide."

"Agreed."

He twirled a lock of her hair around his finger and leaned down to kiss her.

After a long, sweet kiss, Morgaine said, "I think we should do this well before our celebration. I'd hate to give someone an enthusiastic hug and crush them."

Sly laughed. "That's what I thought."

She trailed a finger up his arm sensuously. "Can this conversion involve sex?"

"I was hoping you'd be open to that. I understand it's pretty hot that way. Your thinking of it makes me even happier."

She washed her feet quickly and dried them on the towel he handed her. Batting her eyelashes, she said, "Race you to the bedroom!"

Naturally, Sly beat her to it.

They seemed as perfect for each other in bed as they were in other areas. Morgaine understood his body and knew exactly how to turn him on. She felt every bit of her womanly power whenever he told her he'd go mad if he didn't have her. Maybe it was her psychic skills—or maybe she was just paying attention to his moans and groans of pleasure. Whatever it was didn't matter. He was the love of her soon-to-be immortal life, and she couldn't believe she'd ever found this much happiness.

"I never thought I'd get so lucky."

He held her gently, almost reverently, as he gave her a long, deep kiss. She snaked her hand down between them and cupped his balls through his pants. His groan betrayed a deep hunger. She felt it too. It invaded her chest, and she needed him naked now.

As if on cue, he said, "If you don't take your clothes off this minute, I might tear them off."

She giggled. "This is one of my few pairs of shorts, so I'd rather you didn't."

"Then get naked, woman."

She grinned as she rolled up to a sitting position and whipped off her periwinkle jersey. Then she shimmied out of her navy blue shorts, which she considered her grape-stomping outfit. With only her black lacy underwear on, she allowed him to appreciate her womanly curves.

"You're beautiful, Morgaine."

"You're not bad either," she quipped. "But you'd look a lot better naked too."

He chuckled and bounded off the bed. In a split second, he had geared down to his birthday suit and zoomed back to the place he'd just been lounging.

She sighed. "I can't wait until I can do that."

"Me too." He held out his arms. "Come to me, darling." Giving her a devilish grin, he said, "I've wanted to make love to you ever since you left my bed this morning."

She lay next to him and threaded her fingers through his silky dark hair. "Take me, Sly." Her lips grazed the pale column of his neck. "Make love to me as only you can."

He covered her body with his larger one, pressing her into the mattress. His hands scooped beneath her and roamed over her flesh, exciting myriad sensations.

"I love how you touch me," she said softly. "You know every inch of me now, yet you hold me like it's the first time. I hope we never lose that."

"We won't. If anything, we'll add more to our repertoire." He let out a low growl, hauled himself up in one swift, fluid motion, and flipped her onto her stomach.

She squealed, then laughed at her own surprise. Sly popped open her bra and lowered his body on top of her. His hands slid beneath her to her breasts and fondled them. She moaned, then lifted her bottom and pressed it against his erection. She felt his heat right through her lacy underwear. He'd obviously had his wine recently. Soon, they'd drink together and wind up tangled in the sheets.

His lips were on her neck. He kissed and excited her skin until it tingled in anticipation.

As if he'd heard her, he said, "Not yet." Perhaps he had. He teased her by drawing his fangs over the spot.

"Don't make me wait," she murmured. "I want this."

"Soon." He plucked her hard nipples before his hand eased down between her sweltering hot thighs. He slipped his fingers into her panties and rubbed her clit until the exquisite sensation built to a fevered peak. She crashed over the edge, yelling out her release. Except for his name and "Oh, my Goddess," the words were indecipherable.

Then he divested her of her bikini bottoms. He hooked an arm around her waist and hoisted her to her knees. Her bra straps fell off her shoulders and settled around her elbows. She lifted one arm, then the other, and flung the remaining garment. She braced her forearms on the pillows, and her bare bottom was completely exposed to him. A decadent thrill worked its way through her. She knew they possessed the same passionate nature, and she loved him all the more for it.

As his fingers eased inside her already wet channel, Morgaine felt the overwhelming need to have him inside her, filling her completely. He stroked her sensitive flesh, gently at first, then increased his strokes, inciting a raging inferno.

He pumped his fingers in and out of her, his thumb coming into contact with her clit each time. When she teetered on the edge of coming, he withdrew his fingers and thrust his hard cock inside her.

The moment he touched her clit with his finger, she came, letting out a series of sharp cries that filled the room. Her internal muscled clenched, and he tensed, holding on to his control.

"Oh, yes," he hissed. "I like it when you express yourself, sweetheart."

He let his finger slip away from her clit so she could recover. But she didn't want to recover. She wanted to come again and again, until neither of them could take any more. "Keep going, Sly. Keep it up until we come together."

He chuckled and didn't break his stride. As he surged into her, the heat grew again. She knew it would. She loved the feeling of him buried inside her, filling her. The erotic sensations made her body hum with life. It was no wonder she wanted eternal life with him. Only with him.

"Come on, Sly. Fang me, baby!"

He leaned over and just as he touched her clit again, he sank his fangs into her neck. She shot to the edge of oblivion, resulting in an out-of-body experience unlike anything she could have imagined.

Eventually, she stopped bucking and felt her life slipping away. When he'd brought her to the brink of consciousness, she slumped onto the pillows. He turned her head to the side and pressed his skin against her mouth.

"Drink, Morgaine." A tangy liquid passed her lips and hit her tongue. He must have opened a vein. A metallic smell filled her nostrils. She lapped at his life blood, lazily at first. Suddenly, a tremendous thirst hit her and demanded more. She sucked greedily at his offering until he yanked his wrist away.

"Enough."

Her head spun and then magically cleared. Something was happening. A profound awakening took over. All her senses were growing tenfold.

"I can hear the rustle of wind through the trees outside… and footsteps on the sidewalk." The smell of her herbal shampoo overwhelmed her.

"Remember, I'm here for you. I love you."

She heard his thought, muffled somewhat but audible, as if in a TV dream sequence.

"Oh, my Goddess. Sly, is this what it's like for you all the time?"

"Don't worry. You'll learn to moderate it."

"I hope so. Can you hear everyone's thoughts?"

He laughed. "Thank goodness, no."

Chapter 25

May 1st, Beltane

THE DAY OF THEIR HANDFASTING HAD FINALLY ARRIVED. Morgaine, Merry, and Gwyneth had made all the preparations. A quiet ceremony in the penthouse would be followed by a celebration feast. All the building's residents plus Konrad and Roz were invited.

To blow off some of her nervous tension, Morgaine had decided to join Gwyneth in stomping grapes in the basement. They removed their slippers and climbed into the large wooden vat.

"So, are y'all excited about tonight?" Gwyneth asked.

Morgaine giggled. "I'm beyond excited. I'm a nervous wreck."

"Well, this here's the best way to lose some of that nasty tension. Y'all are making what's needed to keep the bad vampire symptoms away. I still can't believe y'all are a vampire *and* a witch now."

"Hey, if anyone can handle being different, I think I can."

"That's not what I meant. I'm talkin' about the nyctophobia. It was funny enough for a witch to be that way, but a vampire afraid of the dark?" Gwyneth burst out laughing.

Morgaine rolled her eyes. "Well, at least you've finally learned how to pronounce it."

The two women grinned as they stomped the grapes,

creating a squishy pulp. In minutes Morgaine was relaxed and having fun.

"So, how are things with you and Nathan?" she asked.

"Great. He surprises me almost every day with some thoughtful gesture."

"I'm so glad. You've really brought him out of his shell."

"Yeah, and he's taught me a few things too."

"Like?"

"Like bein' realistic and acceptin' things. I don't get mad so quick anymore."

Morgaine chuckled. "I thought I noticed a more easygoing cousin. I just thought it was the great sex that relaxed you."

"Well, that sure don't hurt none." Gwyneth winked.

Morgaine sensed a presence on the stairs and glanced over her shoulder. Sly stood there smiling. His eyes glowed—the soft golden glow of love.

"Is it bad luck to see the bride before the handfasting?"

She chuckled. "Not at all. What's up?"

"I was about to move my stuff up to your apartment. I thought you'd want to be there so we could arrange our things together."

Morgaine held up one finger. "Hang on a second. I'll be right with you."

Her knees pistoned so fast her legs became a blur. The grape juice drained into the smaller vat as fast as it could, but the spigot couldn't handle that much volume so the juice backed up until she and Gwyneth were standing knee deep in purple liquid.

Gwyneth set her hands on her hips. "Show off."

Morgaine giggled, then vaulted over the side and landed on the towel she'd spread out on the floor.

As she dried her feet, she said, "Thanks for helping, Gwyneth."

"Like y'all needed my help."

Morgaine enjoyed her cousin's help even if she didn't need it. "It was good to talk and exercise. I feel much more relaxed now."

Gwyneth sat on the edge of the vat, swung her feet over the side, and dropped down onto the towel she'd placed on the floor near her exit point. "Well, that's good. I'm glad. I suppose I won't see y'all until the handfastin' tonight."

"Unless you want to help me with my hair."

"What are you plannin' to do? Some big beehive or somethin'?"

Morgaine laughed. "No, silly. I was just planning to brush it until it's nice and shiny, then weave some flowers around the crown."

"Sounds beautiful and perfect."

Morgaine tipped her head slightly. "What do you mean by perfect?"

"Laurie Cabot says we're sovereign, so y'all wearin' a crown is perfect."

"Oh." Morgaine smiled. "I guess you're right."

Turning to her lover, she launched herself into his arms. His split-second reflexes caught her as if he had been just standing there waiting to catch a flying witch. Vampire-witch. Vampitch. Or wampire. She chuckled as she thought up her new designation.

"What's so funny?" Sly asked.

"Oh, nothing. Let's get you moved in." She looked over her shoulder to Gwyneth. "See you tonight, Cousin."

"With bells on."

The penthouse furniture had been moved aside so the group could stand in a circle in front of the fireplace. The happy couple stood on either side of Lynne, the justice of the peace, who also happened to be a witch trained in performing handfasting ceremonies.

On Morgaine's left, Gwyneth stood with Nathan beside her. Konrad was on Sly's right, and Roz next to Konrad. Linking the circle at the back were Jason and Merry. Merry had placed five-and-a-half-month-old Max in his playpen. He looked on, making occasional baby squeals and noises, but other than that, the room was silent. Each guest held a candle.

The JP Lynne, who wore a black robe, spoke. "Friends, let us now gather within a circle of unity to celebrate and commemorate the marital intentions of Sylvestro and Morgaine. As we appreciate the gift of sharing this special evening, we call upon the elements of the ancients to symbolize the blessings that we wish upon this union."

Lynne stepped to the center and rotated to face the couple. Sly and Morgaine linked hands and smiled at each other. Sly had always thought her beautiful, but tonight she seemed to glow. Her green eyes reflected the soft candlelight, but it wasn't only that. She had parted her blonde hair in the middle, and it fell in soft waves well past her shoulders. Her long, soft ivory dress and the flowers in her hair conferred an air of Mother Nature herself. *How did I get so lucky?*

The JP said, "Would the engaged couple please take a step forward and allow the guests to form a circle around us?" As soon as they had all taken their places,

Lynne rotated about 45 degrees. Extending her hand, she said, "As we welcome the elements of the East, we call upon air, and ask that this couple be blessed with understanding and the ability to communicate freely with each other."

Then she swiveled again and motioned toward the south. "To the elements of the South, we ask that the fire of passion and desire always burn within this couple's hearts. May they always keep the sacred energy that brought them together."

She turned toward and gestured to the west. "As we observe the West and its element of water, we ask that this couple's love and commitment to one another always stays pure. May they find ways to renew the spirit and emotion of love that flows between them."

Finally, Lynne turned all the way back toward them and said, "To the element of North and in appreciation of the Earth, we ask that Sylvestro and Morgaine be blessed with abundance and fertility."

Fertility? Obviously, the good witch didn't know they were vampires or was unaware that dead sperm don't swim. Sly still couldn't believe that Morgaine was willing to give up the possibility of motherhood. They'd be loving guardians and friends to Max and potential future children of all the other couples here, but nothing more.

The JP continued on, "If children are desired, may they be healthy and happy always."

Yup, she didn't know. Oh, well. She didn't have to. Probably better if she didn't. How many JPs would show up to a vampire wedding?

Lynne faced them directly and smiled. "Sly and Morgaine, step forward."

With hands still linked, they took one step forward and stood in front of the JP.

Lynne said, "As we have created balance and harmony here today, we ask that you, as a couple, always enjoy the same. Are you, Morgaine, prepared to pledge yourself to Sylvestro?"

Morgaine responded, "I am," with no hesitation. She cleared her throat and recited, "I, Morgaine, pledge myself to you, Sly, and our marriage. I will love and cherish you always and never forget the gift of love that you have given me." She slid a white gold ring with a Celtic knot design on his finger and said, "Accept this ring as a symbol of my love and commitment."

Sly had been coached the day before the ceremony and responded appropriately, "I will."

Then Lynne addressed Sly. "Sylvestro, are you prepared to pledge your devotion and love to Morgaine?"

"I am," he said happily. He kissed Morgaine's hand, which wasn't part of the ceremony, but it made everyone smile. "I, Sylvestro, am ready to spend my life with you. I will *always* honor the commitment I make today. I promise to love and care for you forever."

The group sighed as he placed a matching ring of white gold on her finger. He noticed that she still wore the one he had given her on Yule but she'd placed it on her index finger, leaving her ring finger open for her wedding ring.

He continued his vow with, "Wear this ring as a symbol of the love and devotion I will always have for you."

Morgaine responded, "I will."

Lynne smiled. "Through these vows and the exchange of rings, Morgaine and Sylvestro have made their intentions of marriage clear before you, their cherished guests, and their Gods. They have pledged themselves to one another and look forward to a bright future. We join in giving them our blessings."

Gwyneth said, "Blessed be," and the others followed suit.

When it was quiet again, Lynne said, "Sylvestro and Morgaine, by the power invested in me, I now pronounce you partners in life... husband and wife." She extended her hands. "The circle is prepared to be closed. Spirits and guardians are released. I send this circle into the cosmos to do our bidding." She whirled 360 degrees and scooped up the air from the floor to over her head. "The ritual is ended."

Everyone broke the circle to hug and congratulate the newlyweds.

When Sly returned to Morgaine, he saw her crying. "Honey, what's the matter?" He opened his arms and she stepped into his embrace.

"Absolutely nothing, I'm just ridiculously happy."

Then she responded to something he hadn't heard. "Thanks, Chad." She stepped back and smirked, "Chad called me a wimp but gave us his best wishes too."

Sly kissed her nose. "You're no wimp, woman." Curious, he asked, "So, Chad's here. Is that what Lynne meant when she said something about the spirits attending?"

Morgaine smiled. "I doubt she was aware of Chad specifically, but any friendly spirits or elementals that chose to attend were welcome to be part of the ritual."

Sly glanced around. "Are they still here?"

She chuckled. "No, they were released as the circle was opened."

"Whew. I'm just getting used to Chad. I don't think I could handle a whole houseful of spirits."

"Nope. All you have to do is live with a houseful of me. My apartment's not the biggest."

"I'm not worried. It's bigger than mine, and I never felt crowded with you there—just cozy."

"What's going to happen with your apartment now?"

"I listed it in the newspaper as an eclectically furnished one bedroom with a history of happy tenants."

Merry strolled over. "You can say that again."

Roz overheard and joined them. "Does anyone have a single friend they'd like to see move into the love shack?"

Morgaine and Sly glanced around the room. Nathan had his arm around Gwyneth's waist, and she was leaning against his shoulder with a content smile on her face. Jason turned and winked at Merry. Roz blew Konrad a kiss, and he pretended to catch it and put it in his pocket. Then something else passed between them and they chuckled.

Sly shook his head. "I can't think of anyone I know who needs the magical power of apartment 1B, can you, Morgaine?"

She grinned. "No, I can't. Isn't that wonderful?"

"It is indeed."

Merry smiled. "I guess we'll let fate decide who needs it next."

"Might as well." Morgaine stroked Sly's cheek. "After all, fate's been doing a pretty good job so far."

Sly pulled his beloved into his arms and gave her a tender kiss, looking forward to a very long, very happy life together.

Acknowledgments

I'd like to thank my dear friend, next-town neighbor, and fellow writer Stephanie Green for her encouragement and support from the beginning of my writing career. In addition, I'd like to thank her for brainstorming with me when this series was no more than a kooky idea.

I also want to thank Laurie Cabot for her permission to refer to her in this book and for her years of dedication to reeducating the public about the craft. She taught me most of what I know through her poignant book, *Power of the Witch*.

I also want to thank Sherrilyn Alden for teaching me all the rest I know about witches and the craft as well as giving me the details of her own handfasting ceremony contained in these pages. Also thanks to her mother, Lynne, a justice of the peace and high priestess who performs these ceremonies regularly.

About the Author

Ashlyn Chase describes herself as an Almond Joy bar. A little nutty, a little flaky, but basically sweet, wanting only to give her readers a scrumptious, satisfying reading experience.

She holds a degree in behavioral sciences, worked as a psychiatric registered nurse for several years, and spent a few more years working for the American Red Cross, where she still volunteers as an instructor. She credits her sense of humor to her former careers since comedy helped preserve whatever was left of her sanity. She is a multi-published, award-winning author of humorous erotic romances.

Represented by the Nancy Yost Literary Agency in New York City, she lives in beautiful New Hampshire with her true-life hero husband and a spoiled brat cat.

Where there's fire, there's Ash:
Check out my news, contest, videos, and reviews at www.ashlynchase.com.
Find me on Facebook, http://www.facebook.com/ashlynchase, and be my friend.
Chat with me: http://groups.yahoo.com/group/ashlynsnewbestfriends/
I tweet as GoddessAsh.

ESCAPE TO THE WACKY WORLD OF
ASHLYN CHASE
READ ON FOR EXCERPTS FROM

Strange
Neighbors

The
Werewolf
Upstairs

AVAILABLE NOW FROM SOURCEBOOKS CASABLANCA

From *Strange Neighbors*

"When you've haunted a building since the Beatles met Ed Sullivan, you see a lot of changes," Chad said to Harold, who haunted the building across the street.

The two ghosts floated between their buildings, high enough that the air currents from traffic below didn't affect them. Still, they swayed occasionally in the autumn breeze and had to compensate to remain face to face.

Harold contemplated the elegant old brownstone sadly. *"I don't like to complain, mind you, but when your new owner ripped off the roof, did he have to replace it with a God-awful glass and steel penthouse? It's an eyesore here in historic Back Bay!"*

"I miss the old *owner. He was a crotchety, grumpy, eccentric recluse, but he didn't change anything."*

"Change comes hard for most of us, Chad—living or dead—yet change is the nature of the world. You'd think we'd get used to it after all this time. I've been going with the flow… but enough is enough."

"I know what you mean, Harold. Change can kiss my ass."

Chapter 1

*A hand reached out to her. "Would you like to dance?"
She followed the line of a crisp white sleeve and looked
up into the sparkling eyes of her mystery man. He had
to be a GQ model to possess a face and body like that.*

"Merry? What on earth are you doing?"

Poof And just like that, Merry MacKenzie's day-
dream evaporated.

"Dad, I'm exhausted. I have to rest."

Merry collapsed on the worn leather sofa sitting in
the middle of the sidewalk in front of a beautiful antique townhouse. She yanked an inhaler from her denim
jacket, shook it vigorously, and squirted the mist into
her mouth. Inhaling a deep breath, her constricted lungs
eased. *Ah, relief.*

"We're almost done. But while you're resting, let me
say this again—if you ever need or want to move back
to Rhode Island, you can."

She rolled her eyes. "Fine. But right now, I'm still
moving into my apartment. How about letting me un-
pack before you make me feel guilty for leaving you?"
She reclined on the sofa so she could expand her dia-
phragm and rest.

"Come on, Merry," her father said as he loomed over
her. "One last push."

"No. I'm tapped… Gonna die now."

"I know you're tired. We've been moving your stuff

into your new apartment all afternoon. Or, I should say, new to you, old by any other American's standards."

"Well, I happen to love it. Jeez, did you look around? Did you notice that thick, solid mahogany banister? I don't know how you could miss it. It practically blinds you, gleaming in the light of the crystal chandelier," she said. "Everything is in really good shape. Apparently the landlord lives in the building and made sure it was all replastered, but kept the period details like the wide crown moldings. And while you're noticing, check out the marble stairs. The elevator is all mahogany and brass inside."

"Why do you care about the elevator? You live on the first floor—thank God. I can't imagine carrying all this crap up to the second or third floor."

"And moving *in* is only part of the fun! I'll be up half the night unpacking. Who knew I had so much stuff?"

"That's the way it is when you move. You always have more than you thought you had and it always takes longer than you think it will."

"I've never moved before, so how could I know?"

Mr. MacKenzie frowned. "Merry, Matt and I have to get going soon. It's getting dark. Are you okay?"

"Just one more minute, Dad." Merry glanced around at the lengthening shadows, wondering where west might be and if she'd have a sunset view. She looked up at tree limbs silhouetted against the twilight sky. Dry leaves rattled in the autumn breeze, and for a moment she thought she saw… *Great. First night on my own and already I'm seeing ghosts.*

Then she spied a man with long, dark hair leaning against the wrought iron fence that surrounded the brownstone's small lot. Dressed all in black, he almost disappeared into the shadows, and she might not have noticed him at all except for his pale skin and intense eyes. Something about the way he cocked his head and stared at her caught her attention. A shiver rippled up her spine.

"You can rest when you're inside. It's getting darker by the minute and you know my eyesight's no good for night driving."

"Have Matt drive home. Where is he, anyway?"

Her father peered toward the heavy oak and beveled glass front door of the building. They'd left it propped open with a marble pedestal from the foyer. "I don't know. Last I saw, he stopped to talk to someone. Must have been the landlady."

A second later, her younger brother raced down the steps babbling, "Dad, did you know Jason Falco owns this building? Do you believe that? Jeez, I'm going to have to visit Merry every chance I get!"

She groaned. "You'd better not, pickle-head. And who's Jason Falco, anyway?"

"You're kidding!" he shouted. "You don't know who Jason Falco is?"

Mr. MacKenzie folded his arms. "Calm down, Matt. It's a fairly common name. It could be anybody. Come on, Merry. Get up."

"Can't… too tired."

Some kind of secret signal passed between father and son. The next thing Merry knew, the couch tipped and they unceremoniously dumped her onto the sidewalk. *Oomph.*

"Hey!" She scrambled to her feet while her brother continued chattering as if nothing had happened.

"He's the lefty pitcher for the Boston Bullets! I swear. I was just talking to his aunt. Oh—she wants the door closed, by the way. It's getting cold in there." As if to illustrate the point, a chilly October breeze blew crisp, brown leaves around their feet.

"Why didn't you say so in the first place?" Merry admonished. "Do you want my neighbors to immediately hate me? Get on the other side of the couch with dad; I can't lift another thing."

Merry marched into her new apartment building, hoping to find the landlord's aunt so she could apologize. No one seemed to be about, but she heard voices from the second floor. As her father and brother staggered and grunted through the front door under the weight of the leather sofa, a young man appeared at the top of the wide, curving staircase.

Long muscular legs in jeans and sneakers had come into view first. Then Merry saw his flat abdomen and broad shoulders under a navy blue knit jersey, and then finally his face.

"Whoa, let me help you with that." He jogged down the steps and grasped the side of the couch her brother had left teetering.

Oh, my lord! What a handsome face it was. Dark, thick brows stood out against his light skin and clear blue eyes. She couldn't identify his hair color easily, since it barely showed under a blue baseball cap. Maybe milk chocolate brown. Merry thought the style was called a buzz cut. The length nearly matched the brown whiskers of the five o'clock shadow on his strong jaw.

"Thanks, man." Matt did a double take and grinned. "I can't wait to set this couch down so I can shake your hand. Believe it or not, my sister's moving into your building and didn't even know who you were."

The handsome hunk just laughed.

Merry put two and two together and decided this must be the famous Jason Falco. *Not bad. Not bad at all.* On the other hand, if her brother insisted on embarrassing her in front of her hottie landlord by pointing out what a baseball fan she wasn't, she'd have to have a little "chat" with him before he left. A slap upside the head ought to do the trick.

She stepped back in order for the three men to pass her as they carried the heavy piece of used furniture into her tiny living room.

Her father surveyed the polished hardwood floor already covered with boxes. "Where do you want this, honey?"

"Um… I'm not sure yet."

"Well, hurry up and decide before I get a hernia."

"Sorry, Dad. Just put it down where you are. I'll figure it out later."

Her landlord straightened to a full six feet tall. "I can help her move things around once she knows where she wants them." And then he winked at her.

Be still my heart!

So there her couch remained—in the middle of the living room.

Immediately, her brother stuck his hand out to the stranger. "It's really great to meet you, Jason. Can I call you Jason? My dad and I are big fans. I hear you can throw a 97 mile-an-hour fastball. And man, your curveball and changeup? Incredible! Do you think I can get an autograph?"

Jason chuckled. "Thanks... uh, sure." He sounded anything but sure as he regarded the taped boxes around the room. "Do you have a pen and paper handy?"

"Leave him alone, Matt. He's obviously off the clock," Merry muttered, not caring if her fan-boy brother collected his autograph or not.

"Oh, yeah. Sorry, man. Hey, some other time..."

"Absolutely," Jason said. He smiled broadly and to her relief, Merry thought he sounded genuine. Fine, then the pipsqueak wouldn't hound her to obtain Jason's DNA. *The DNA that gave him those cute dimples...*

"Well, I'll leave you to get settled," her father said. "C'mon, Matt, we'd better get going." He thrust his hand toward Jason and said, "Thanks for your help. I'll sleep better knowing my little girl is in good company."

Crap. How many ways can my family embarrass me? Merry rolled her eyes. "I'm twenty-five, dad. Not exactly a little girl anymore."

Her father dropped Jason's hand and strolled over to where she stood. "You'll always be *my* little girl." Then he kissed her on the forehead and said, "Call me tomorrow, okay?"

Could she *be* any more humiliated in front of an awesomely cute guy? So much for establishing her image as a hip, sophisticated city dweller now that she had finally declared her independence. She sighed. "Okay, worrywart."

Her father pointed at her. "I mean it."

"I know, I know."

As soon as they were out of the way, she planned to revel in her freedom, kick up her heels, and have some much needed *fun!* Whether they liked it or not.

From *The Werewolf Upstairs*

"HERE ARE YOUR KEYS, DEAR. THANKS FOR COMING upstairs to get them. Now don't let your neighbor across the hall scare you."

Roz Wells took the key from Dottie, the apartment manager, and froze. "Scare me? Why would he or she scare me?"

"He's Nathan Nourie." She stepped closer to Roz and whispered, "I call him Nasty Nathan, and I assumed he might scare you because he scares *me*. I'm told he's harmless, but…oh, well, I don't want to influence your opinion by relating my own harrowing experiences."

"Harrowing?" *Oh my freakin' God.* "What's wrong with Nathan?"

"That's what I'd like to know. All I can tell you is he works in a morgue and has an odd sense of humor. Downright morbid, if you ask me."

Maybe she's just easily freaked out. "Okay, that doesn't sound so bad."

Dottie folded her arms and humphed. "You haven't met him yet. If I told you everything…but I won't. I wouldn't want to prejudice you."

"No, of course not." Roz rolled her eyes.

"In fact, most of the tenants here may take some getting used to. If I were you, I'd stay away from the women in 3B, too."

"Why? What wrong with them?"

"Well, they seem to have gotten better lately, but they used to scream and holler all the time. Oh, and don't get me started on my neighbor right across the hall here, Konrad Wolfensen, unless you like nudists. But you're on the first floor, so you shouldn't have to see what I've seen. I swear to God, my eyes can never un-see that."

Roz wondered if leaving her comfortable apartment in Allston and moving to Boston proper had been a good idea, but she wanted to keep an eye on her best friend Merry, having learned her new husband's secret.

She'd confided in her last winter. Merry said she was marrying a shapeshifter, and as crazy as it sounded, Merry was the most down-to-earth and stable person Roz had ever known. There had to be something to it, and Roz needed to know that her best friend in the world hadn't made a horrible mistake.

"Well, thanks for the warning." *I think.* "Oh! I almost forgot to tell you… you know that I'm Merry's friend, right?"

"Which is why you were standing next to her at her wedding and why you knew her apartment was available before I advertised it. Yes, I remember."

"Please don't tell her I moved in. I want it to be a surprise."

Dottie shrugged. "Suit yourself. She'll be in Florida with my nephew while he's in spring training. You know her husband, star pitcher for the Boston Bullets, is my nephew, right?"

Roz gave her a sardonic smile. "I may have heard about that." *Like each time I've heard you talking.*

The door across the hall clicked open and a familiar-looking, gorgeous blond hunk stepped out of his apartment. A short-sleeved black T-shirt exposed luscious biceps and stretched across massive, taut pectoral muscles. When he turned around to lock his door, Roz noticed his tight butt and hair so long it almost reached his waist.

Don't drool, don't stare, don't drool…

"Oh, hello, Konrad," Dottie said with syrupy sweetness. "I was just welcoming our new resident."

Some welcome.

"This is Rosalyn Wells. Rosalyn, this is Konrad."

I wish I could shed thirty pounds twenty seconds ago. A hottie like him would never be interested in a lump like me.

"Oh, you're Merry's friend." He nodded at the key in her hand. "Are you moving into 1B, her old apartment?"

"Yes, I am." *Why, oh why did I wear my oldest, rattiest sweatpants today?*

"I remember meeting you at the burger restaurant a few months ago, and then I saw you again when you were Merry's maid of honor. You looked ravishing in that blue dress, by the way."

Roz was taken aback. *Oh, no, he isn't gay, is he? Good-looking, sensitive, notices and remembers details; sheesh. It's always the good looking ones. But I'll take a compliment wherever I can get it.*

Merry was usually the one who attracted male attention. Roz had never considered herself memorable in the least. Her figure was less than svelte, and her dark brown hair was too straight to hold a style. She usually just swept it back into a bun for work. At least she liked her eyes. They were big and blue, but her eyeglasses hid them. Wearing glasses gave her an authoritative appearance, good for the courtroom, but lousy for dating. "You remember me?"

"Of course I remember you. Welcome to our humble abode, Rosalyn."

He extended his hand, and she grasped it. His big warm paw held hers in a surprisingly gentle clasp. Some kind of energy passed between them, something she'd never felt when shaking the hand of a colleague.

"Call me Roz."

"I'd hardly call this building humble," Dottie said. "That chandelier in the foyer must have cost my nephew a fortune."

"That chandelier has been there since my hair was short. Your nephew just bought the building when? Last summer?"

Suddenly the crystals in the chandelier downstairs tinkled and clanged together.

Dottie jammed her hands on her hips. "For God's sake, Chad, haven't you gone into the light yet?"

Konrad elbowed Roz's arm. "Chad is our resident ghost."

Dottie rolled her eyes. "Yes, God forbid I leave him out when telling you about the other residents."

"There's a g-ghost haunting the building?" *What kind of fresh hell did I just get myself into?*

"Yes, but he won't bother you if he likes you," Konrad said. "I didn't even know he was here until the séance." Konrad looked at the chandelier. "You leave the new woman alone, all right, Chad? She's a friend of Merry's."

Nice of him to intervene for me, but...The back of Roz's neck prickled. "You held a séance?"

"Sure, didn't Merry tell you?"

"No. I think I would have remembered that."

Dottie shook her head. "She was the only resident who couldn't make it, besides my husband. She said she had to work. My husband said he had to keep an eye on the building. I don't know where he thought it was going. Well, I have work to do now, but before I leave you, Roz, you should know that I'm not happy with loud parties or tenants who cause trouble. And I live right above you."

Konrad leaned toward Dottie. "Is that some kind of threat? I don't recall her saying she's a party animal."

Wow, is Konrad this protective of all the tenants, or is it just me? Nah, he and Dottie probably have some kind of history. "Oh, you don't have to worry about me," Roz said quickly. "I live a quiet life." *Not by choice...*

"Good. We'll get along swell, then."

Dottie gave Konrad a dirty look, stepped into her apartment, and closed the door.

"Can I help you move in? I'm pretty strong." He flexed his sizeable muscles.

Holy Christmas! I haven't seen muscles like that in... ever! Whoa, didn't Dottie say he was a nudist? What I wouldn't give to see...but no. Even if he showed me his, I'd never show him mine.

"Weren't you headed somewhere else?" Roz asked.

"No. Would you rather I was?"

She chuckled. "Of course not. I just thought...oh, never mind. It'd be nice to have company while I wait for the movers."

—⁓—

"Hi, new kid." Chad followed Roz down the stairs. Most of the residents seemed like kids to him. After all, he'd been haunting the place since the 1960s. Okay, so Konrad was older, but he was a werewolf. Other than Konrad, not even the super, Ralph, or his wife Dottie, or the vampire Sly could claim Chad's age or experience.

"That's right, kid, we have a vampire. The only reason the landlady didn't mention him was because she doesn't know he's living in the basement. Heh, heh.

"I'll bet you thought I was swinging from the chandelier, didn't you, kid? As much fun as that would be, I'm afraid my astral body doesn't work that way. It's not like I have an invisible body. I'm a spirit. That means I have no astral ass to sit on.

"But just like a corporeal person who loses one sense and strengthens the others, I may have lost my body, but I've strengthened my mind to razor sharpness. Yeah, I'm smart as shit.

"Ha, ha. I wish. Actually I've learned to use my mind to affect objects, so even though I wasn't literally swinging from the chandelier, I concentrated really hard on the chandelier swinging until it did. It's called telekinesis. If I were able to ride it, I'd do it every day until the damn thing came crashing down. You have no idea how badly I need entertainment."

Chad followed Roz into her empty apartment, continuing to chat at her, as though she could hear every word. After all, he never knew when he might run into a sensitive soul who could sense, hear, or see his presence.

Roz glanced up at Konrad. "I just want to take a quick look around to figure out where I'm going to put things when the movers come."

"Would you like me to step outside?"

"Only if you want to."

Chad continued, still hopeful. *"The others in the building don't know much about me, except Morgaine and Gwyneth. They're the witches in apartment 3B, and they're noisy because they're phone-sex actresses. Some of their clients like screamers."*

Still no reaction from the new tenant. Damn. I like making Dottie and Ralph's ceiling fan spin around. Dottie thinks I'm riding it, and Ralph, who doesn't believe in ghosts, scratches his head and tries to find a logical explanation. A short in the wiring? Oh, come on. It wouldn't work at all, if that happened.

Roz pulled on her hoodie sweatshirt and fumbled for the zipper. "It's cold out. Don't you want to get a jacket?"

Konrad shook his head. "Nah, I'm good." He opened the apartment door as wide as it would go and said, "Hang onto this a minute." He carried over the marble pedestal table from the foyer and propped the door open, presumably to carry furniture through it.

Roz shivered. "It's freezing in here, too, but I'd better wait to turn the heat on. Otherwise it'll all just rush outside."

Oh, maybe she sensed me! Chad floated in front of her and made a scary face. *"Muu haua huaha. Damn, I hope you're sensitive and just ignoring me because we're not alone. I'm sick of talking to myself all the time."*

Konrad opened the front door for Roz and held it as she stepped right through Chad to the outside. Disappointed, he floated back upstairs, hoping to find one of the witches to talk to.

DEMONS
ARE A
GIRL'S BEST FRIEND

by Linda Wisdom

A BEWITCHING WOMAN ON A MISSION...

Feisty witch Maggie enjoys her work as a paranormal law enforcement officer—that is, until she's assigned to protect a teenager with major attitude and plenty of Mayan enemies. Maggie's never going to survive this assignment without the help of a half-fire demon who makes her smolder...

Praise for Linda Wisdom

"Hot talent Wisdom does a truly wonderful job mixing passion, danger, and outrageous antics into a tasty blend that's sure to satisfy."
—RT Book Reviews

"Entertaining and sexy... Ms. Wisdom's stories have something for everyone." —Night Owl Romance

"Wickedly captivating... wildly entertaining... full of magical zest and unrivaled witty prose."
—Suite 101

978-1-4022-5439-0 • $7.99 U.S./£4.99 UK

50 Ways to Hex Your Lover

by Linda Wisdom

"A magical page-turner...had me bewitched from the start!"

—Yasmine Galenorn,
USA Today bestselling author of *Witchling*

JAZZ CAN'T DECIDE WHETHER TO SCORCH HIM WITH A FIREBALL OR JUMP INTO BED WITH HIM

Jasmine Tremaine is a witch who can't stay out of trouble. Nikolai Gregorivich is a vampire cop on the trail of a serial killer. Their sizzling love affair has been on-again, off-again for about 300 years—mostly off, lately.

But now Nick needs Jazz's help to steer clear of a maniacal killer with supernatural powers, while they try to finally figure out their own hearts.

978-1-4022-1085-3 • $6.99 U.S. / £3.99 UK

Hex Appeal

BY LINDA WISDOM

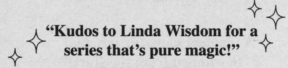

"Kudos to Linda Wisdom for a series that's pure magic!"

—Vicki Lewis Thompson,
New York Times bestselling author of *Wild & Hexy*

**JAZZ AND NICK'S DREAM ROMANCE HAS
TURNED INTO A NIGHTMARE...**

FEISTY WITCH JASMINE TREMAINE AND DROP-DEAD GORGEOUS vampire cop Nikolai Gregorivich have a hot thing going, but it's tough to keep it together when nightmare visions turn their passion into bickering.

With a little help from their friends, Nick and Jazz are in a race against time to uncover whoever it is that's poisoning their dreams, and their relationship...

978-1-4022-1400-4 • $6.99 U.S. / £3.99 UK

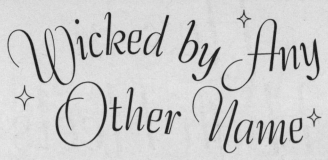

Wicked by Any Other Name

BY LINDA WISDOM

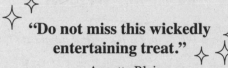

"**Do not miss this wickedly entertaining treat.**"

—Annette Blair,
Sex and the Psychic Witch

STASI ROMANOV USES A LITTLE WITCH MAGIC IN HER LINGERIE shop, running a brisk side business in love charms. A disgruntled customer threatening to sue over a failed spell brings wizard attorney Trevor Barnes to town—and witches and wizards make a volatile combination. The sparks fly, almost everyone's getting singed, and the whole town seems on the verge of a witch hunt.

Can the feisty witch and the gorgeous wizard overcome their objections and settle out of court—and in the bedroom?

978-1-4022-1773-9 • $6.99 U.S. / £3.99 UK

Hex in High Heels

BY LINDA WISDOM

Can a Witch and a Were find happiness?

Feisty witch Blair Fitzpatrick has had a crush on hunky carpenter Jake Harrison forever—he's one hot shapeshifter. But Jake's nasty mother and brother are after him to return to his pack, and Blair is trying hard not to unleash the ultimate revenge spell. When Jake's enemies try to force him away from her, Blair is pushed over the edge. No one messes with her boyfriend-to-be, even if he does shed on the furniture!

Praise for Linda Wisdom's Hex series:

"Fan-fave Wisdom… continues to delight."
—*Romantic Times*

"Highly entertaining, sexy, and imaginative."
—*Star Crossed Romance*

"It's a five star, feel-good ride!" —*Crave More Romance*

"Something fresh and new."
—*Paranormal Romance Review*

978-1-4022-1819-4 • $6.99 U.S. / £3.99 UK